✿✿✿

Run Away Charlotte

Written by H.M. Shander

✿✿✿

Copyright

Published by: H.M. Shander
Cover Design: Brett J. Miller - brett-james-miller.weebly.com
Cover Images: ©yurkaimmortal - Fotolia.com,
                ©lexuss - Fotolia.co
Editing by: Kim Hayashida –
                NovelCreationsHawaii.weebly.com

Shander, H.M., 1975 – *Run Away Charlotte*
ISBN: 978-0-9938834-0-8 (print version)
ISBN: 978-0-9938834-1-5 (e-book version)
First Edition
Printed by Createspace

✿✿✿

Dedicated to everyone who took a chance and read my debut novel. May your time between these pages be well spent, as mine was in writing it.

✿✿✿

Contents

Prologue
✿✿✿

January, 2004

Ding.
Ding.
Ding.

The elevator chimed at each floor as it slowly inched its way to the top.

Why is it when you're in a hurry, this blasted thing seems to move like molasses? Come on 16.

Charlotte tapped her foot uncontrollably with nervous energy. When Joe said he needed her to come over ASAP, she dropped what she was doing and left work immediately. It baffled her why he was so insistent she come today. He was moving. Surely, there were more important matters to take care of?

Ding. Sixteenth floor.

Finally.

She was so anxious that she stumbled out of the elevator as she raced towards the penthouse suite.

The door was already ajar, and she could pick out Joe's voice coming from within as he directed the movers. The voices floated out into the hall, and a little girl with a head full of blond ringlets opened the door further.

"Aunty Char-wette!" She squealed and ran to Charlotte's open arms.

"Hello, Hannah." She planted a kiss on the child's cheek and carried her into the apartment. "Where's your daddy?"

Hannah wriggled out of Charlotte's arms and ran screaming towards the bedroom, yelling, "Daddy! Aunty Char-wette's here!"

Charlotte glanced around the barren apartment. Boxes piled up against a wall. Furniture lovingly wrapped in protective plastic. *Finally, after nearly twenty years of living here, he's moving into something different. More space for his family. A better neighbourhood. How strange and unwelcome it looks now. Back then, it was...*

"Charlotte!" Joe interrupted her thoughts and strode towards her with a megawatt smile on his face.

"Happy birthday, Joe. Sure you couldn't find a better way to spend it?" She beamed as she gave him a big hug. "It looks so... empty."

"You won't hear me complain. Best birthday gift ever is moving away from here. It'll be nice to move into a house on a street where Hannah can learn to ride her bike, and we can play basketball on the driveway. And we'll be closer to you."

"And have yard work – which you've never had to do your whole adult life."

"Won't be so bad." He stepped aside when a couple of movers pushed past, their dolly stacked with boxes.

"You'll miss the view."

"Indeed. Not too many views of the city like this. But it'll be better."

Charlotte watched the men leave. "So, what's the big urgency? I left work as quickly as I could. You sounded funny and highly secretive when you told me to get over here."

His face lit up. "I found something of yours. Something I think you'll want."

"Something of mine? I thought I took everything when I moved out." She wracked her brain trying to remember what she'd left behind.

"Well... not everything. Come with me!" He took her down the hallway and into her former room, turned nursery.

Charlotte saw it before she had even entered the room fully. Her eyes focused immediately on the large, faded white box, wrapped in a velvet red ribbon that called to her from atop a bare mattress. Her breath hitched. Her pulse sped up. It transfixed her. It was her very own Pandora's Box sitting there, holding unfathomable truths within. It had been years… many years, since she last saw that box. "Where…"

"Your closet." Joe looked down at her as a memory crossed his face. "Don't you remember?"

Charlotte did remember; she just chose not to. That one night, years ago, in anger, or sadness, she'd shoved that white box into the far corner of the closet and covered it with a t-shirt. Tucked so far back, it was destined to be left behind when she moved into her own place.

Joe smiled at her. "I figured you would want it, and if not, toss it in the dumpster on your way home."

Her hands started to shake. "I don't know."

"I know you're very curious to read the note that's in there."

"You read it?"

He nodded and smirked at her in a way that made it hard to be angry with him. "Did you want to open it here or at home?"

She stared at the Pandora's Box sitting like a bright light in an otherwise dark room.

Joe understood. He always did. "Take the time you need. But not too long, the movers will be coming for the stuff in this room shortly." He turned and closed the door as he exited.

Charlotte stepped over to the mattress and sat down on the bed like a yogi master, placing the white box on her lap. With shaking hands, she pulled at the red ribbon.

It's been years. Does it really matter anymore what's inside? It's not like it changes anything anyway.

She searched the empty room, as if she was being watched. Her eyes darted everywhere.

Stop it! It's just a box.

She placed the ribbon on the mattress and lifted the lid, inhaling deeply to steady herself.

Maybe this isn't a good idea. Nothing good will come from opening this.

Charlotte glanced at the door, willing it to stay shut, but she continued to raise the lid, and then set it beside her.

The note!

Her hands trembling, her pulse racing, and her thoughts spinning like a tornado, she picked up the plain white envelope from inside the box and held it to her chest.

It can't mean anything now. It's been years.

She checked on the door. Still closed. Letting the envelope fall to her lap, she rooted through Pandora's Box. The next item she extracted was a hoodie, navy blue in colour, size large. She lifted it and smiling in spite of the sadness she felt, gave it a whiff.

Still smells of his cologne. Faintly.

She buried her face in it, trying to wrap her mind in its fragrance as she felt hot tears forming. As if moved by an outside force, Charlotte felt her arms slide into the fleecy fabric, and the neck of the collar stretch over her head as she pulled it on. Keeping the hood up, covering her coppery waves as she continued rifling through the rest of the box.

Picking up a handful of mixed CDs, she read the labels listing the titles. Music they once danced and made love to. The songs with powerful lyrics once highlighted, now faded. How fitting that the opened package of now expired condoms was scattered across the CDs. Underneath the homemade discs was a plethora of pictures.

Charlotte gathered up the pictures and blinked rapidly to help her focus on the two people featured within. A bronze haired male with eyes that sparkled like the Caribbean Sea, his arm draped over her shoulders. The pictures made her smile – they were young, innocent, and happy. Very happy. Some would argue that they were in love. The tears fell fast, and marked up the hoodie with dark, damp marks.

She suddenly felt the presence of a small child and turned towards the door. Her niece stood in the doorway, head cocked, looking all adorable like three-year-olds do when they are someplace they shouldn't be.

"Whatcha do-in?"

"Looking at some old pictures," Charlotte said, wiping away her tears, hoping her mascara hadn't turned her into a raccoon.

"Are you sad?"

"A little."

A voice from the outside of the room called for Hannah.

"You'd better go."

Hannah walked over and put a little kiss on Charlotte's hand. "Wuv you, Aunty Char-wette. Don't be sad."

Joe popped his head into the room. "Hannah Cooper Harrison! I told you to leave your aunt alone."

The three-year-old lowered her head as she paraded out of the room.

"Children," Joe said as he watched his daughter jump down the hall. "Sorry for her intrusion." Joe continued to stand at the entrance to the room. Returning his gaze to his best friend, he leaned against the doorframe. "You okay?"

"I opened Pandora's Box. I knew I shouldn't have, but I couldn't help myself."

Joe crossed the room and sat down. "It's closure." He held her shoulder firmly, but lovingly.

She looked up into his face. "I already had closure."

"So now you have more." He wiped her tears and kissed her forehead. "I really didn't think you'd actually open it." Reaching out, Joe took hold of the pictures she held, and started flipping through them. He pulled one out and commented, "That's a good one of the two of you. Was this in Jasper?"

"Yeah. Look how young we were. The picture of youthfulness. Not like now, with the greys, baby weight, and wrinkles."

"You're still beautiful, Charlotte. Even at the ripe old age of twenty-nine."

She raised an eyebrow. "Anyways…" Her gaze turned back to the white envelope on her lap.

"Have you read it?"

"I don't think I can."

"Want me to read it to you?" He reached for the thin letter, his gentle fingers freeing it from her grip.

Charlotte shook her head as tears fell down her cheeks. "It makes no difference. No matter what it says, I can't change the past."

"But if you could, would you read it?"

Slowly, strength finding a foothold within, she took back the note, and calmly pulled it from its confines. Unfolding the paper, she started reading aloud.

Dear Cat

yes

Chapter One
✿ ✿ ✿

1994

It was the end of summer, the summer of heat. July had proved to be the hottest month on record, and August was a close second. The sweltering hot weather was forcing everyone to some place air-conditioned, and JT's Pizzeria was no exception. For once, Charlotte enjoyed going to work, not only to take a break from the stifling feverish air, but to hang out with her friends. Although her basement suite apartment was relatively cool, it was much more comfortable at the restaurant. JT's Pizzeria kept the restaurant at a refreshing 19°C, much nicer than the 29°C outdoors.

With a busy start to their shifts, Charlotte and her friends didn't get much time to talk before serving the customers, some of which waited over an hour to have a seat in the restaurant. The busy supper rush had finally quieted down by the time Meadow clocked out at 9:30 pm, which afforded Charlotte time to sit down with her in the ripped up corner booth for her break.

Meadow, a plump brunette, slid into the booth across from Charlotte. She fiddled with her hair, redoing her long braid, "So tell me the good news!" Her smile was warm and genuine, and always spread from ear to ear.

"I got the job!"

"At SEARCH?"

Charlotte's smile lit up her deep hazel eyes. "Yep! I can't wait. Science Education and Research Communications Hub, here I come!"

"Oh my gawd, that's so exciting! You get to leave this dump! What'll you be doing?" Meadow secured her unruly hair in a loose braid, and gave Charlotte's hand a squeeze.

Charlotte explained in a rapid-fire succession, "For now, selling tickets to the galleries and movie theatre. I start on Tuesday. They wanted me to get used to the system before the busy weekend crowds. I can't wait to leave here. I'm tired of going home smelling like pizza. Now, maybe I'll be able to study astronomy a little further and get to check out the observatory."

"Awesome. I'm so happy for you! You'll do great." Meadow leaned against the back of the booth, "When are you giving your notice here?"

"As soon as I get my schedule. Need to make sure I'll be getting enough hours to make up for the lack of tips. I can't say I'll miss this place." Charlotte had worked at the Edmonton based family restaurant since she graduated from high school. Her salary and tips helped pay her bills, but she really didn't like the job. She worked into the middle of the night, getting home as late as two in the morning. The only appealing part of her job was that she worked alongside Joe, her best friend and comrade.

Until the staff really got to know Charlotte, they thought she was Joe's kid sister, as they had the same long, lean build and wavy hair. Hers a coppery colour, his a gold blond.

He walked over to their table. "That rush was a doozy. Glad you came back wearing the appropriate length skirt Charlotte and not those nice dress pants. You know that upper management prefers the 'shorter the better' type of skirts."

Charlotte sighed. It was embarrassing to have her boss reprimand her for showing up looking respectable instead of borderline trashy, like the waitresses at the restaurant a few blocks up the street. She hated wearing a skirt that hit mid thigh.

Without a word, Joe tapped his watch.

The girls giggled as he slid in beside Charlotte and pushed her against the wall of the booth. "Now ladies," he smirked, "it's time to finish off the cigarettes. Give it here Charlotte," he said as he released his playful push on her before moving to his side of the bench. Joe took a long drag off her short stub of a cigarette.

"What's the good news, Charlotte? You've been lit up all evening."

Smiling at her best friend, she explained. His smile faded somewhat as she glowed with excitement about moving on to bigger and better things.

"Don't look so sad, Joe." She touched his thin arm.

"It's not like I'm going to miss you or anything." He tilted his golden head towards the brunette across from them. "I just feel bad for Meadow... as now I'll have to bug her relentlessly."

"Only until Brad arrives." Meadow smiled.

Joe's voice was laced with sarcasm as he rolled his eyes. "Yes, only until your Prince Charming arrives."

"And speak of the devil..." Standing at the hostess podium was Brad. Charlotte cocked her head to let Meadow know. "He's early."

Meadow extinguished her cigarette in a hurry, saying goodbye to Joe and Charlotte before leaving with Brad.

Charlotte leaned closer to Joe. "Don't you think it's weird - Meadow's relationship with Brad? I mean, come on, he was a senior in high school when she was born. He lives downtown, and has everything at the touch of his hand, thanks to that stock market gift he has, and Meadow is literally fresh off her parents' farm."

Joe laughed, "Women are so attracted to money and power. Why do you think I don't have a girl? No money or power."

Oh Joe, you could have any girl you want if you only looked beyond this place. None of the girls here are good enough for you.

As he stood up, Joe brushed his hair out of his eyes. "I hope someday you'll do better than Meadow and not be blinded by the almighty dollar."

Charlotte didn't laugh with him. "Joe, she's still our friend."

"Yeah, but she's not my best friend. If you date a guy like that, Charlotte, I'll let you know it's unacceptable. Unless you're in it for love. True love." He gave his hand to her to help her out of the booth. "Now, back to work, Miss Cooper, before the boss comes out of his office and sees you still sitting here."

"Yes, sir." Charlotte saluted him in laughter as she went around the restaurant wiping up a few tables preparing for the incoming late night groups. She loved her best friend Joe. He always looked out for her and had been for the past few years. She often wondered what would have become of her life, had she not had Joe.

The following Tuesday, Charlotte started her shift at SEARCH. She met up with the general manager Norah, - who had interviewed her, and then proceeded to introduce her to a variety of staff members on a tour of the facility. Many university students, scientists, visiting dignitaries, and professors, all who claimed SEARCH as their "home". There was an abundance of space allowing them to conduct their experiments and the like, and gave the general public a glimpse into the exciting world of science. The hands-on public galleries housed different branches of the scientific field, such as physics, chemistry, biology, astronomy, and the like. There was also a giant movie theatre playing mini-documentaries at the top of every hour. This is what Charlotte would be doing, selling admissions to the public part of the building. Since Charlotte hadn't used a computer since high school, she knew mastering the system was going to be a steep learning curve; however, it was a minor issue and nothing she couldn't handle. The other cashiers flew through the customers, while she processed one long, painfully slow transaction with Norah's assistance, to every ten of her co-workers.

By her third SEARCH shift, an evening shift, Charlotte had learned the system and was much quicker at processing the sales. That evening, a young man about college age, came up to the cashier's desk. "I need the key to the projection room please," he asked her as he looked briefly around the desk. He had a hint of an accent that she couldn't place, and his eyes were the most breathtaking shade of blue-green; so vibrant they may have been coloured contacts.

Charlotte also looked around her desk area, underneath binders and piles of visitor guides, unsure of what key she was supposed to give him.

No one explained the keys. Damn, I must look like such an idiot, because I don't know what he's talking about. Third day on the job, and I'm already screwing up.

The young man sensed her panic and confused state. "It's on a yellow tag. Tony usually leaves it here."

Tony? Who is Tony? I don't remember meeting anyone called Tony. Charlotte continued moving papers and pamphlets. The bronze-haired man, with powerful eyes, bent over the counter and aided in the search.

The cashier beside her, Paulette, who had just finished helping a customer, told the accented young man, "He left it in the GM's office for some reason."

"Thanks," he said and walked past the long, grey curvy desk. Halfway to the GM's office, he stopped and spun around. He came behind the cashier's desk and reached out his hand. "I'm Andrew, by the way. I work upstairs in the projection room."

Charlotte blushed and shook his hand. *Soft, not like others that are always rough and callusy.* "Hi, I'm Charlotte. I'm new here."

Andrew laughed. "I know."

Oh my gosh. Hot guy probably thinks I'm a total dork now.

He started to wander away, and then exclaimed, "Nice meeting you, Charlotte."

After he disappeared into the GM's office, Charlotte whispered to Paulette, "Is that where the keys go?"

Paulette looked at the befuddled cashier. "Usually, when a shift change occurs, they just drop the key here, as the next projectionist is typically in within half an hour. At the end of the night, it's locked up in the GM's office. For some reason, Tony left it in there today."

"Got it," she mumbled as she made a mental note.

Andrew walked by with the key in hand and hit the "up" button on the elevator beside the desk. He winked at her as he stepped in.

Charlotte was signing over her float at the end of her shift to Norah when there was a knock on the office door. The general manager opened it. It blocked Charlotte's view, but she had no problem recognizing the accented voice on the other side.

"The projection room is closed and locked up." She saw Andrew's hand as the key transferred to Norah. "Have a good night." He poked his head around the door, "Oh, hi, Charlotte."

"Hello." She felt a tinge of pink race into the apples of her cheeks.

He stepped into the office, and Norah let the door close. "How was your shift?" He waltzed over and leaned casually against the table where her float sat spread out in neat little piles.

"Good. All balanced," she explained as Norah placed the piles of cash into a nondescript grey bag. Charlotte tucked an unruly piece of hair behind her ear, feeling self-conscious. She stood up and grabbed her coat off the back of her chair.

"You leaving?" he asked.

After a moment's hesitation, she nodded yes.

"Me too." He smiled at her, the left side of it reaching higher than the right. "Can I walk you out to your car?"

Charlotte looked expectantly at Norah, who nodded approvingly, sensing her hesitation.

"Sure," Charlotte squeaked out, surprised at the sound of her voice.

"Sweet, let's go."

She put her coat on, and said goodnight to Norah. Andrew also bid Norah a good evening as he walked beside Charlotte through the lobby and out into the dark parking lot.

"So, how's the new job going?" Andrew asked pleasantly, as he zipped up his coat and re-adjusted the backpack on his shoulders. He slowed his pace to match hers.

Charlotte tightened up her coat in response to the fall breeze. Her thin frame hunched inside the polyester fabric lining of her coat. "Really good. Everyone's super friendly."

He winked at her, those eyes sparkling from the streetlights that lined the ordinary concrete path. "Yes, that's the great thing about this place. Everyone likes their jobs so they're happier to be around. I don't think I could find someone here who wasn't happy."

They continued walking out to the parking lot, passing along the right side of the large reflecting pool. In the middle of the water was a small grassy island, accessible by taking steps across a small concrete bridge. After silently walking around the reflecting pool, they reached the edge of the parking lot.

"Which car is yours?" he asked, looking around and counting out the four remaining vehicles.

She pointed to the back row, where a lone red car sat, shining under the glow of the streetlight.

He walked beside her. "You see those signs over there?" He turned and pointed behind him to where two cars remained. "Closer to the building - that's staff parking. First come, first filled." He smiled. "Park there next time, if there's a spot available. You won't have so far to go at the end of an evening shift."

"Okay, thanks." She reached into her pocket and retrieved her car keys. "This is me." She unlocked her car and yanked out the sticking key.

"Put some WD-40 on your key next time, it'll help." Before she had a chance, Andrew opened the door for her. "In you go."

"Thanks for walking me to my car," she said as she climbed in, throwing her purse onto the passenger seat.

"You're very welcome. See you tomorrow?" His voice was melodic and ripe with a thick European accent.

"Yes." She blushed a little more, feeling warm all over. *Okay, he's a little dreamy.*

"Have a good night, Charlotte." He closed the car door, but stood there until she started it. He waved and walked away.

By the middle of September, Norah gave Charlotte a very promising schedule of nearly 35 hours a week. Once she saw it, Charlotte excitedly gave her notice to JT's Pizzeria. She worked a few double shifts between her two jobs, knowing her waitressing career was over. She was tired, but happy to be nearly done with JT Pizzeria.

Of course, coincidentally, each night she was working at SEARCH, Andrew seemed to be working too. He always came to the GM's office to drop off his key at the end of his shift, and if Charlotte wasn't ready, he'd wait, and then walk with her out to her car, always opening her car door for her.

At first, Charlotte thought it was a tad creepy, but after a couple of weeks it started to feel normal and just part of her shift.

One night, after a very busy shift Andrew glanced towards Charlotte. "The observatory's open. Skies are clear. What do you think? You want to go?"

She looked excited, and as always, her face lit up whenever Andrew talked to her. "I'd love to. I've never checked out this observatory."

"Excellent." He smiled at her and sat on the table where she was counting her cash. He glanced down at the piles. "You're almost done?"

"Yeppers." Charlotte finished counting her float and signed it over to Norah. Grabbing her belongings, they walked out the main doors. Instead of walking towards the parking lot, they walked around the building on the left of the reflecting pool. He'd stop occasionally, pointing out an inlaid cement stone in the sidewalk, and explained that each stone they'd walk over represented a planet, and how it was spaced from the sun, which was just outside the observatory.

I know this already, but I'll humour you.

They walked over Mars, Earth, Venus, Mercury, and two steps later the Sun, as they continued towards a small building that looked as if the roof had been pulled sideways off of it.

They walked into the flat, roofless building, which housed several telescopes, each pointing towards a different celestial object. The space was tiny and cramped, lit only by the glow from a red light hanging on the wall behind the telescopes.

Andrew led Charlotte over to a tall, white haired man. "Lloyd, meet Charlotte, our newest cashier."

Lloyd turned to her and in the deepest voice she'd ever heard said, "Welcome to my home." He chuckled. "Just kidding, but I'm here often enough, it should be my home."

Charlotte shook his enormous hand, which covered her diminutive one. "Pleased to meet you." He reminded her of Santa Claus, larger than life, with lots of white hair and towering over her at what she guessed was 6 feet 5 inches. He was definitely taller than Joe and that was saying something.

"If there was anything you ever wanted to know about astronomy, you ask Lloyd," Andrew remarked, "He's incredible."

"Thank you, young man." Lloyd pointed towards the eastern part of the building. "Those two telescopes, the Meade and the Celestron over there, they're looking at Saturn and Jupiter."

"Ooh, I'd love to see those," Charlotte spoke up, her voice full of enthusiasm.

"Right this way, pretty lady," said the white-haired man and guided them past a couple of smaller telescopes.

Charlotte followed with Andrew on her heels. She peered into the first telescope and gasped at the clarity of Jupiter and a couple of its larger moons, amazed at how easy it was to see the red spot. *Oh my gosh. So breathtakingly beautiful.* She felt a lump forming at the back of her throat, and the visible moisture in her eyes. She moved onto to the next telescope.

Andrew looked at her funny. "You okay?"

Shit, damn hormones. "Yeah, Saturn's always been my favourite planet, and it's so incredible to see it like that. She's

tipped slightly, and the rings are reflecting the light. I'm in awe."
She smiled brightly and holding firmly to the eyepiece with her
right hand, took another glimpse at the beautiful ringed planet.
She stepped down off the step stool and felt Andrew's hand on her
back, as support, which caught her off guard.

Not able to tear herself away Charlotte needed to take another
peak through the telescope, and stepped back up, staring into the
eyepiece as long as she could. "Brilliant," she whispered and
repeated over and over. She felt Andrew's hands move to the top
of her arms.

Lloyd arrived unannounced and chuckled beside her. "Isn't it?
I just love staring at the stars."

Charlotte, whose hair glowed almost as red as the light, piped
up, "Did you see Shoemaker-Levy 9?"

The Santa-like man smiled, and in his deep voice said, "Of
course. Nothing like it. Did you?"

She sighed, "I tried to catch a glimpse. I was in Toronto at the
time, but wasn't able to see it. I bet it was incredible." She looked
at Andrew who was looking at the pair of them.

"Shoemaker-Levy 9?" Andrew shook his head.

"Oh. My. Gosh! It was the most spectacular thing," Charlotte
started rambling, picking up speed as she went along. "This
comet, Shoemaker-Levy 9, well it was on course to slam into
Jupiter see, but it turned out the comet was actually a long line of
fragmented pieces instead of one solid piece. It impacted just a
few weeks ago and kicked up some incredible dust, or so the
pictures show. I was really mad that I missed it." Her voice was
full of regret when she slowed down.

Lloyd nodded, "I was in Calgary at a R.A.S.C. meeting, but
was fortunate to have seen it. I heard it was cloudy here."

"What's a R.A.S.C. meeting?" asked Andrew.

"The Royal Astronomical Society of Canada," he explained to
the confused Andrew, and then gazed down at Charlotte. "Do you
know a lot about astronomy, or just that particular event?"

She looked down at her weathered shoes, and then back up into
the soft face of the older man. "I know lots. I have multiple star
charts at home. Used to spend my summer evenings just watching
the stars. I studied the summer before this one at ORO, and loved
it, but my high school marks weren't quite high enough to get into

any of their programs. Missed it by two percent." She again looked down.

His deep voice softened, "Yes, Ontario's Radio Observatory has a great program. One of the guys here studied there." He looked around, searching for him.

"It boggles my mind that we're always looking back in time when we look up. Things that happened many years ago, millions, billions, even."

"Charlotte you're welcome to come out whenever you'd like. It's always great having someone in here with your love for astronomy."

They stayed until well after midnight talking with the other astronomers and looking at anything they could find for Charlotte, since it wasn't busy. She enjoyed looking at the nebulae and galaxies and even a double binary star system. It felt good to be a part of that experience, and to feel joy within her soul.

As the place was getting ready to close up, Andrew and Charlotte started walking, side by side, to their vehicles. "That was *really* fun. Thank you for suggesting it," she said smiling as the gentle breeze brushed her face. She had a small skip to her step.

"I'm glad you enjoyed it so. It was neat seeing you in your element. What were you doing in Toronto a few weeks back?"

She stopped smiling. "It's complicated, and I *really* hate talking about my personal life. Sorry." *Sometimes life puts you on an uncharted path that leads absolutely nowhere. I guess I can add that to the long list of things my mother ruined for me.* Hoping to change the topic, she asked, "You don't come out here very often do you?"

He chuckled. "No. I don't mind looking at some things, but I don't possess the knowledge or interest in all things astronomy that you seem to." He winked, and she noticed his eyes boring into hers, peering into the depths. "I never went to anything like this when I was younger. My parents were too busy." He stopped at his alabaster-white Fiero, parked beside her red Beretta.

"I love your car, but aren't Fieros a bit dangerous?"

"Only if the engine catches fire. But not too worry - I keep her finely tuned."

After throwing her bag inside, Charlotte leaned against her own car. "Where did you grow up? I've tried placing your accent."

"Russia. My parents have dual citizenship and frequent between the two."

"Andrew isn't a Russian name though. What's your last name?"

"Wagner."

She laughed, "Aside from your accent, I wouldn't have thought you were Russian at all."

He joined her in laughing. "My grandmother was a widow with four kids, see, and ended up marrying this nice German fellow named Franz Wagner. So my dad is a Wagner, but my half-uncles are all Medvedkov's. Anyway, my mother's from Canada, and met my father in Russia. One of those fluky meetings, love at first sight, they fell in love and got married within weeks. I happened to be born there, in a little town called Novorossiysk; it's near the Black Sea." Charlotte shook her head. She wasn't very good at geography. "Near Krasnodar?" Again, she shook her head. "My younger brother, Jonathan, was born in Toronto. They wanted us to have proper Canadian names, since it was very likely we'd be traveling between here and there. We used to spend our summers there on a farm outside of Novorossiysk, until the past few years. Then Jon and I had to start saving for university."

"Wow. Are you in university now?" She gazed at his blue-green eyes as they reflected the streetlights they stood beneath. She felt like she was under a spell.

"Second year of business. I took a year off between high school and now."

"I was told if I did that, I'd never go back to school."

"And?" He rocked back and forth on his heels.

"I didn't go." Charlotte looked beyond Andrew towards the building that was lit up in a changing rainbow of colours. "I tried to get into a program at ORO, but my application was rejected. By then, I was completely out on my own and didn't have the resources to make my application sparkle by acquiring what they needed. It's all good now. I live on my own and can manage my bills, so it's not too bad." She rambled on, "For now, working, living my life… this is great."

"It's tough, I know. And expensive," he added as an afterthought. "I managed to get a few scholarships, but still university is pricey. And I still live at home with my mom."

She carelessly spilled, "I've been on my own since I was sixteen." *Dammit, me and my foolish mouth. What is it about him that makes it hard to keep my mouth shut?*

"You moved out when you were sixteen? That's crazy!" Andrew looked at her like she *was* crazy.

"So I found out, but I made it work. Rented this place with my former friend and her boyfriend, and finished up high school."

Andrew interrupted, "Former?"

"Yeah. We stopped being friends when I lived there. Turns out we weren't really that good of friends to survive being roommates. My boyfriend spent a lot of time there and that upset our friendship further."

"Really? Why? Was your boyfriend in love with your friend?"

"Yeah. Something like that." She paused and stopped her tongue from saying anything more by biting it. Speaking cautiously, she finished up, "But whatever. Everything was over before I moved out. I only lived there for a few months, before moving into my current place. It's nice there -- no roommates. I don't think I could do that again - live with someone." She laughed louder than she'd expected.

"How old are you, Charlotte?"

She looked into his eyes, having nothing to hide with her answer, "Eighteen, but I'll be nineteen soon. You?"

His eyes brightened. "The day I first met you, that was my birthday. Turned nineteen." He looked at her, and breathed out, "Really? You're only eighteen?"

"Really. How old did you think I was?"

"Older. You come across as much older."

The cool breeze blew Charlotte's wavy hair onto her face, and it hid the warm creeping colour flooding across her cheeks. She pushed her coppery strands away and responded, "It's cool that we're close in age." She shifted again and tightened her coat. "Most of the people I worked with at my last job were older, not like old older, but a few years older than me. It'll be nice to work with people around my age."

Andrew glanced back towards the SEARCH building, and then rested his gaze on Charlotte. "Most of the people here are university aged. It's a great job that helps pay for school, and the hours are pretty flexible. The managers are pretty relaxed too. As long as I still get my job done, they're okay with me studying."

"That's great." She smiled, wondering what he would be studying specifically. Business seemed like it had a broad range of topics.

He interrupted her thoughts, "You should come up there one day. It's a different view of the theatre. I can give you the code to the elevator so you can come up."

"I'd like that. What time is it?"

He looked at his watch. "Twelve-thirty."

"Really? I need to go. I work at ten tomorrow morning, and I need my beauty sleep." She retrieved her keys from her coat pocket. "Are you working tomorrow?"

"At four."

"Well, I'll see you in passing." She climbed into her car. "Goodnight, Andrew."

As he closed her door, he said, "Goodnight."

The next day near the end of her shift, Charlotte's heart skipped a beat when Andrew came over to her desk, and like a secret spy, slipped a note into her hand.

"It's the elevator code, so you can come upstairs. Come up when you're done."

Her smile faded. "I can't tonight. I'm working at my other job. It's my last Saturday night there." She looked down and focused on a long scratch across the top of the desk.

He still beamed. "That's okay. The code works all the time. Just call me before you come up. It's very dark in the room, and I don't want you falling down the stairs." He continued to stare at her.

"Great. Another time, then?"

"Absolutely." Smiling, he asked, "Where's this other job?"

She sighed. "I work at JT's Pizzeria, a real nasty little place. Three shifts left, and then I'm done. Finally." She kept her head down while telling him this, not because she had anything to be ashamed of, but she was just really looking forward to leaving that place behind. It was as though the bosses at JT's demanded that no one take her final shifts, or trade with her, so she was working the closing shifts. On the plus side, at least Joe would be there to suffer alongside her.

Andrew grabbed his key, turned, and walked away. "Have fun at your other job!" he said as he walked over to the elevator on the other side of the cashier's main desk and pushed the "up" button.

"Oh I will," she whispered sarcastically and waved as he stepped into the elevator.

Chapter Two
✿✿✿

Charlotte walked up to the huge building complex, entering through the double sliding doors. A whiff of disinfectant and the smell she referred to as "old people" greeted her as she stepped through the second set of sliding doors. Wearing sweats and an old high school t-shirt, with her hair pulled back in a braided ponytail, she signed herself in at the main desk and proceeded into the main part of the building.

Charlotte had signed up for the Youth-Elderly Connection Program as part of her grade twelve outreach unit. The program involved matching high school students with a senior's housing complex in the area, for a weekly one-hour visit. It brought joy to the residents in having young energy around, and was great for the students, most of who carried on with the project beyond their high school years.

Caritas Covenant was a little different than most senior homes. This facility had elderly residents who, for whatever reason, no longer had family around. So they matched Charlotte up with Mrs. Kennedy, a short time later. At her urging, Joe had also joined and was connected with Champ. For almost three years she'd been coming by for a game of cards with Champ and conversation with Mrs. Kennedy. They'd become family, in a way. At least to Charlotte.

"Good morning, Charlotte," a familiar greeting rang in her ears as she walked the length of the hallway.

Charlotte turned in the direction of the voice. "Good morning, Sister."

The young nun asked, "Here to see Mrs. Kennedy and Champ?"

"Yes, ma'am."

"They're expecting you. They're in the lounge today."

With a quick step to her pace, she headed down the dusty green corridor, emerging at the brightly lit lounge that smelled strongly of hibiscus flowers and cinnamon. Beaming, she walked over to the old man in the wheelchair and tapped him gently on his good arm, while placing a tender kiss on his cheek.

"Good morning, Champ."

The old man with a full head of snow-white hair smiled. "Goo... goo...good... mor... mor... morning." He never took his blue-grey eyes off her. Many years ago, Champ had a stroke that rendered his left side un-useable, making him permanently confined to a wheelchair. Sadly, it affected his speech as well. It did not, however, weaken his ability to beat Charlotte in their weekly cribbage game. She patted his hand lovingly, and then walked over to where Mrs. Kennedy sat in her chair, pulled up daringly close to the table.

"Good morning, Mrs. Kennedy." She looked warmly at the octogenarian grandmother, with thinning carrot-red hair, and dark skin that had recently been kissed by the sun. Her chocolate-brown eyes held secrets that her mind could no longer share, as her Alzheimer's progressed quickly between visits. For now at least, Charlotte was content that Mrs. Kennedy knew who she was. There was no telling if she would at their next visit. "I brought you both some cookies. Chocolate chip oatmeal." She handed her one.

"Thank you, deary." Her hands trembled slightly as she held the cookie. "How's Elizabeth doing? She never comes to visit me."

Charlotte didn't know who Elizabeth was and figured she was maybe a daughter, or a friend. All Charlotte knew was that it was part of the disease. "She's good, Mrs. Kennedy. Tending to her garden." She hated lying, but was advised by Nurse Agnes to go with it; according to her, it was one of the paths of memories her brain still had.

"Good. Good. She always grew the biggest roses."

She set the container near Mrs. Kennedy, and then placed a still warm cookie in the palm of Champ's good hand. Champ kept his focus on Charlotte, while he slowly gummed the cookie, swallowing quickly. She expertly wiped up the melted remains from his mouth and fingers. "How was the cookie, Champ?"

He nodded his head up and down, to signify it was good. "Wh… wh… where's… J… J… Joe?"

"He couldn't make it today, but he'll be here next week." Charlotte looked lovingly at the man folded in his wheelchair, his left arm limp in the specially designed armrest, his posture sloping to the left, and unable to straighten up. For reasons she didn't understand, Charlotte always felt drawn to the elderly man who stuttered, but who always looked at her like she was a breath of fresh air.

She passed him his half-full cup of coffee and let the semi-warm brew pass between his lips. "So, are you ready to beat me again at crib?"

His half-smile stretched up to his weathered eyes, the wrinkles deep from the eighty odd years he'd been on Earth.

An hour later, Charlotte moved his final peg into home. Once again, Champ proved that he was a strong crib player, winning another game against the fair-skinned teen.

With the game over and the half dozen cookies eaten by the elders, it was time for Charlotte to head home. A couple of tender kisses to their cheeks, some warm pats, and a few reminders that she'd be back next week, Charlotte headed back down the green corridor. She tightened up her running shoes once outside, under the heat of the autumn sun, and began the ten-minute run back to her basement suite, wishing against hope, that she had grandparents like Champ and Mrs. Kennedy.

Chapter Three
✿✿✿

The following Tuesday, Andrew caught up to Charlotte. "Happy belated birthday," he exclaimed as he leaned over the counter to look for the key.

"Thanks." She grabbed the key and passed it to him. "How did you know? I never mentioned the date?" Charlotte's voice piqued with suspicion.

"I have my sources," said Andrew as he winked. "How was your weekend by the way? You weren't working here."

She spat out in rapid explanation, "Busy! Worked the Friday day shift here, and then my final shift that night at JT's Pizzeria. I had my cousin's wedding in Leduc to attend on Saturday, so I got there early in the morning to help finish setting up, then the wedding in the afternoon, dinner in the evening, party all night long. Then the gift opening on Sunday. Finally got some sleep yesterday, and then I celebrated my birthday with Joe last night – he spoiled me and took me out for dinner."

He gave her a once over, stopping at her eyes, "Party all night long, eh?"

She blushed and sniggered a bit. "Yeah, it was great." *And a long time coming. God it felt good to get out and unwind.*

"I'd like to hear all about it," Andrew said with a promise in his voice, "but I need to get upstairs. When are you done?"

"Five."

"Are you going to come up and visit me?"

"Sure."

"Great. Take the elevator up and when you get there, you'll see a phone outside the door. Call 156 and I'll come and unlock the door. Be prepared; it's quite dark." His radiant smile made her heart race.

"Can't wait."

Charlotte finished her shift and cashed out promptly at five. When she didn't grab her things from her locker, a co-worker, Russell, questioned why she was leaving her things behind. "I'm going up to the projection booth," she replied.

"Ooh, are you and Andrew dating?" he asked.

I wish. "No, we're just friends," she answered.

"Sure you are," Russell said, sarcastically.

"No really we're just friends." *Why should I have to explain this to you? It's none of your damn business.*

"Ah-huh."

Therefore, instead of leaving her belongings in her locker, she changed her mind and grabbed her things. She didn't like Russell, and felt he was only there because his granddad was on the board of education for SEARCH. Russell was nosy, smug, and asked too many questions - too many personal questions. So far, she had been able to deflect his intrusiveness, but it was so irritating.

Proceeding up the elevator, punching in the code she had memorized, Charlotte stepped off the elevator and walked through a sizeable room with a star-lit ceiling, where books lined the walls, and astronomy charts filled up the little spaces between the bookshelves. She went through the cosily lit room and used the phone hanging on the wall to call Andrew.

He picked up the receiver on the second ring.

"Hey," she said, "I'm just outside the door."

"Be right over," he exclaimed, and within a minute the door opened. "Come in quick and close the door."

She did as told and was beyond surprised at how dark the immediate area was, and how chilled the air felt, as if the air conditioner was on high.

"Now, it's super dark in here. Wait here 'til your eyes adjust."

She could feel that they were standing on a metal grate, and Andrew guided Charlotte's hand for the metal railing, invisible to her in the darkness. His touch electrified and warmed her hand like a fire; her pulse speeding underneath her skin. Her eyes were still adjusting, but her ears could hear something quite loud. "What's that noise?"

Standing beside her, Andrew leaned in towards her ear, "The movie reels running through the projector. Can you see the stairs in front of you?"

Charlotte looked around, and down, watching the metal stairs come slowly into view. "A little."

"Take my hand, and let's go. There are five steps here."

She felt the soft warmth of Andrew's hand in hers as she counted out the stairs, one by one, until she reached the bottom. Charlotte held on tightly to Andrew's hand as she adjusted to the dark room, following him over to a desk, barely illuminated in a soft blue glow and scattered with papers and textbooks.

"All good?"

"Yeah," she breathed as the connection between them was broken. "This is a pretty neat space." She had no idea what to call any of the equipment, but it occupied a full length of a wall. "It's cold in here too." Putting her bare arms through the sleeves of her coat, she started to warm slightly.

He looked over in the direction she was looking, and as though answering her thoughts explained, "They control audio and visual, making sure the people get what they came for – great picture and sound."

"Cool," she replied, and turned to look at the papers on the desk. "Working on homework?"

"A paper for one of my classes."

She nodded.

"So tell me about your weekend." He leaned against the desk, blocking the small, book-sized desk lamp, and giving the room a spooky glow as it cast faint shadows. The glow from the bulbs projecting the movie were now responsible for being the only immediate source of light.

She sighed, "It was good. But I'm exhausted."

"Fun weekend then, eh?"

"Weddings usually are," she smiled. "I danced all night long. The DJ stopped before I did. Then I went with some people from the wedding to a country bar, met some of my friends there, and we shut that bar down. Then we all went back to Joe's place."

"Who's Joe?" he asked, raising an eyebrow slightly, folding his arms across his chest.

She couldn't help but notice his toned arms pressing against the edge of his sleeves. Charlotte's face lit up. "Joe's my best friend. He works at JT's Pizzeria. He's got a pretty swanky apartment, so we went back there to unwind."

Andrew nodded slowly. "Lots of you?"

"Well, there was Joe, Meadow, myself, Trevor, and Peter." She counted on her fingers. "Five of us. It was enough. Ever played Twister while seriously drunk?"

Andrew shook his head. "Can't say I have." His voice had a bit of an edge to it.

Charlotte smiled at some memory she clearly wasn't about to share. "It's super fun!"

"I'll take your word on that."

She walked towards the front of the room and looked out the huge window. She was looking down into the movie theatre. "That's a pretty wicked view. Can they see us?"

He walked up behind her and pushed a button. She heard a loud whoosh sound that made her jump a bit. "I just blew the lens off, to clear away the dust. It gets magnified 1000 times and shows up as a dark speck on the screen." He pushed the button again, and then answered her question. "But no, they can't see us, unless the main light is on in here."

"Oh, neat." She looked at the movie screen far in front of her, but saw no particles of this amplified dust he talked of.

His voice was quiet beside her ear as he stood behind her, "So then what did you do after the engaging game of Twister?"

She turned quickly, looking up at him. He was much taller than her 5'5" frame, standing at least 6 feet tall, maybe taller. His eyebrow rose again and curiosity rang through his Russian accent. Charlotte studied the face before her, wondering if he ever shaved, because he always seemed to have a hint of a 5 o'clock shadow. She was eye height to his perfect lips, full and currently pouty. Even in the dark, they looked soft. Coming back to her senses, she said, "Well, Joe and Meadow fell asleep on the couch after Peter went home. But Trevor and I, we snuck out trying not to wake anyone, and went for a walk in the river valley."

"Plastered?"

"Partly," she answered, somewhat annoyed, "anyways, we found this great spot and watched the sunrise. It was mesmerizing." She paused recalling the vividness of the morning,

"The colours of the bright morning sunlight, the pale pinks and purples with a hint of tangy orange. They painted the eastern ridge overlooking the river valley golf course far below. It was peaceful, beautiful, and serene. I felt like I got to see a sneak peek at heaven. I love watching the sun rise. It's an extraordinary way to start the day." Her voice sounded as though she were dancing. She shook her head slightly and came back into the room, "So... we waited until the sun was quite a ways up, and since we'd sobered up, we walked back to Joe's place and woke everyone up."

He looked at her, intrigue and curiosity dancing across his face.

"We had to," she answered to his silent question. "We left without keys and needed someone to let us back into the building. I then fell asleep on the couch waking up a few hours later and barely making it to the gift opening. Of course, I had seen everyone the night before, so I had to go home, shower, and change. Couldn't do the walk of shame in front of my family."

"Sounds like you had a really good time."

"I did." She laughed, and Andrew laughed with her.

"That would be something else, eh? To do the walk of shame in front of your parents."

"Oh no. I couldn't even imagine."

"We try so hard to be adults, but we're always someone's child, aiming to please."

"I've never been someone's child, not in years," Charlotte said quietly as she walked back to the little desk and sat down.

He heard her quiet comment and saw a sad expression briefly cross her face and disappear. Clearly he knew there was some sort of a story there, but wasn't going to push for it. She'd volunteer it when she wanted to. Sensing the sadness in her demeanour, he quickly changed the topic, "What did you do for your birthday?"

Charlotte looked him over, and paused shortly before answering. "We went out for a steak dinner, even though I'm not a steak girl, but Joe insisted. I can never say no to him. I was home by nine and in bed by ten. That sums up my weekend."

"Sounds like a fun weekend, without much sleep, but I'm glad you had a good birthday."

"I so did. What about you, what did you do?" She yawned at the mention of a lack of sleep.

"Nothing nearly as exciting as you. Homework, studied a little, and hung out with my mom and brother. Jon and I went to see a movie, but it wasn't great." He scratched his bronze head, carefully placing the hairs back into place when they moved. "One of the downsides of being a broke university student. No parties."

"But I thought that university students like to party?"

"Not all of them." He winked those breathtaking blue-green eyes. "Sometimes, I'll go with my friends to the dance clubs, but it's not very often. It's expensive, with cover charges and drinks, and I'm trying to save for next year's tuition. Once that's done, then I'll be able to go out more."

"At least you know what you're doing, and you're preparing for your future."

"I'm trying."

"I mostly live paycheque to paycheque, but that's okay," she blabbed out indifferently. *I really need to start thinking before speaking.*

"You're not worried about money issues?"

"Not really."

"What if your car breaks down?"

"Then I get it fixed."

"With what money?"

"I use my line of credit."

"And when do you pay that back?"

She didn't know if he was being serious or being a complete jerk, so she answered in a bit of a playful sarcastic tone, "It's okay *Dad*. I have a savings account that I can dip into."

He looked at her cautiously, and then burst out laughing at his own line of questioning. "I'm sorry. Money has always been a big deal to me, so I thought you were being blasé about it. That was rude. I apologize."

"Apology accepted. I'm never blasé about money. It doesn't grow on trees. I keep my savings in a bank that I never use, so it's there if I need it, but I don't have instant access to it. My tips went into one account, and my paycheques are direct deposited into my main account."

"Smart girl."

"Thanks," and she expressed a grin. "My growing up, as it was, I understood the importance of money and planning for your future, not necessarily education, although it helps, but being financially prepared. I don't have thousands upon thousands of dollars, but I'm prepped for any kind of emergency." She shuffled her feet. "At least I hope I'm prepared."

"Good. It never hurts." Andrew walked over to the front of the room and pushed a button to make the whoosh sound again. "Dust," he said to Charlotte. "So, we've established that you like to go to country bars and play drunk Twister. What else do you like to do in your spare time?"

"I just like hanging out with my friends. We used to go to this other restaurant down the street, after we finished our shifts at JT's, and we'd hang out there until the sun came up. Like vampires. Hang out until the sun rises and sleep all day, only to prepare for the next shift."

"And now? Do you still hang out at JT's?"

"Not so much, since I've been here, except when I'm working. But I plan to go back to JT's and hang out there until Joe and Meadow are done, just not as often. It will really irritate the bosses, but I'll be a paying customer, so they can't say much." She laughed a little louder than she expected. "But I miss seeing my Joe all the time."

Andrew looked her over, up and down. "You sound kind of sad about it."

"I am, a little. I'm certainly much happier here. The work environment is way better, but I miss my Joe, and hanging out every day, complaining about customers and co-workers."

He stepped forward a little, looked deep into her eyes, and effectively closed the distance between them. "You have me. You can complain about the customers to me. I used to be a cashier; I know what they can be like."

"Really, you were?" She smiled, and fought back a blush. He was close enough to her that she could smell the mint gum he was chewing. "What made you become a projectionist then?"

"A job opening." He laughed and stepped back a little. "More money, and I get to hang out here and study. Why not change jobs?"

Charlotte was surprised at how easy they could talk with each other. Before she knew it the movie ended, and she stepped aside to let him work. When she said it was time for her to go, Andrew offered to walk her to her car, as he was going to go out and grab a bite to eat anyway. They came down the elevator, Andrew's hand on the small of her back. She didn't look back to confirm, but swore she heard a clucking noise come from Russell at the desk as they were leaving.

They walked in silence to the staff parking spots. Andrew paused in front of her car and took a deep breath, "Hey, do you want to go for supper next Saturday with me?" he asked as she opened her car door.

She stood there beside her car, blankly staring at him. *He's finally asking me on a date, and I have to turn him down!* She frowned slightly. "I can't, Andrew."

He laughed awkwardly, the air between them like a dark grey cloud. "You have a hot date or something?"

I would never consider him hot. She didn't know how to speak for a moment, and then begrudgingly volunteered, "Yeah, a date with Trevor."

"The guy from the sunrise?"

"Yeah."

"Well," he chimed up in what he hoped was a chipper sounding voice. "Have fun."

She stood there motionless, gazing in his direction with the door open to her car. *Did I do something wrong? Should I not have mentioned the date? He did ask though, and I can't lie although maybe I should've. He looked so hurt. Maybe I should cancel on Trevor. It's not like I see a future with him, just a little fun.* She didn't understand why the air between them felt so awkward.

Andrew spoke up. "You should get going. Your interior lights are draining your battery."

She blinked and answered, "Okay," and climbed in, still gazing at him through the side window.

"See you soon," he said as he closed the door.

"Definitely," she whispered through the window and waved as she started up the car.

Feeling sad, she watched him shuffle over to his side of the car with his shoulders slumped. He didn't turn around as she put the car in reverse and drove past.

Chapter Four
✧✧✧

Another long week presented itself. Charlotte was busy working the long one to nine shifts. She wanted to go upstairs to the projection room when she cashed out, but Andrew seemed a little distant towards her. He didn't say much when he came to get the key to the room, and certainly didn't seem as friendly and outgoing as usual. In addition, he never even asked her to come up and join him; therefore, she trudged through cashing out and walked to her car alone. She missed that he wasn't there.

Charlotte spent a lot of time back at her old stomping grounds – JT's Pizzeria, hanging out and bugging her former bosses. The Friday night before her big date with Trevor, she sat with Joe and Meadow telling them both about Andrew, their conversation in the projection room, and his sudden apparent distance.

"You told him what?" Joe said in an overpowering voice. He shook his head. "You told him that you like to drink and walk around outside, pissed out of your mind I might add, but you then refuse to tell him anything personal? Charlotte, sweetheart, *that* alone told him spades about you. Without even trying, you gave off the impression that you are… umm… shall we say… loose?"

"What? I did not!" Her voice held fierce conviction, until realization set in and replaced her tightly drawn lips with the soft expression of defeat.

Trying to change the subject, Meadow asked, "What's he like?" She stood beside the table, holding a coffee pot. Not yet on a break, she had to look like she was serving customers, even if it was a former employee and Joe. She put her hand on Charlotte's shoulder.

"I think he's sweet, very old-school like, but friendly and easy to talk to. It's like I've known him forever." Charlotte sighed as she said it. "He was trying to ask me out, I think, like on a date, but I told him I have a date with Trevor."

"He asked you out?" Meadow piped up.

"Yeah. But now he's ignoring me." She hung her head.

Joe interrupted, "He's keeping his distance *because* you have a date with Trevor. Geez, sometimes you two can be so dense." Joe shook his head. He was rail thin, tall, and lanky, but such a pillar of strength to his friends. He stretched out his legs beneath the table, nearly kicking Charlotte in the shins.

"If you weren't going on this date with Trevor, would you be going out with him?" Meadow asked, as she poured Charlotte another cup of coffee.

She looked across the table at Joe and up to Meadow. "Yes."

"So cancel on Trevor, and go with Andrew," Joe quipped up after taking a drag of his cigarette.

Charlotte just stamped out her cigarette. "You know I can't do that, Joe. I already told Trevor I'd go. I can't bail on him. Besides, what if it didn't work out between Andrew and me? He's so easy to talk to. I'd still want to be his friend, just like I am with you, Joe."

"You and I have a unique friendship, right?" Joe inquired.

Charlotte nodded. *Where are you going with this?* She watched as Meadow walked away.

Seeing that they were alone Joe said, "Our friendship developed out of necessity, wouldn't you say? You needed a safe haven, and I needed you to be safe."

Charlotte cringed. She hated when he brought up that time in her life. She glanced around to see where Meadow was. She never shared any part of her broken past with anyone except Joe and she was careful to make sure no one "accidentally" overheard.

"Why are you so concerned about it not working out with this Andrew, if you've yet to have an actual date with him?" Joe asked her as he passed her the container of creamer cups.

She picked out one creamer cup and played with it before pulling back the lid and dumping the contents into her hot coffee. "Because I like him, Joe, but I don't want to lose anything. What if the relationship didn't work out?"

"So what? You'll never experience it if you don't go for it."

"But I'm afraid to go for it. There is something really neat about him. Something…Ugg, I can't think of the word. He's the only friend I have there."

"You'll lose your heart regardless of whether or not you remain friends; you wear your heart on your sleeve. Being friends on the other side of a break-up just means that you weren't meant to be." He looked at her, letting the words sink in.

Silent for a moment, she then spoke up, "I don't know. I'd love to, you know date him, if he ever asked again. Our friendship is so easy now, I'd hate for it to be a strained relationship, if something were to happen. You know, like how things ended with Don."

"Yeah, cause you and Don had great chemistry." His voice was loaded with sarcasm. "You two were never meant to be friends. It was good when he quit here. The tension between you two was unbearable." He shook his head.

"That's why I think I shouldn't date co-workers."

"Wish you'd decided that before dating Don." Joe never held anything back with Charlotte and was always directly honest with her, something she hated yet adored about him. With Joe, you knew where you stood.

Charlotte grabbed a sugar packet and poured it into her coffee.

Joe smirked. "Since when do you like sugar in your coffee?"

She laughed easily with Joe. "Since now I guess."

"So now what?"

"I don't know."

"Charlotte, let me ask you something." Joe leaned across the table, glanced around and then lowered his voice. "About us?"

Charlotte leaned back against the booth and crossed her arms. "What?"

"Oh, don't be like that." His green eyes closed softly.

"Fine." She uncrossed her arms and leaned on the table. "What?"

"How long were we friends before you were interested in me more than that?"

"I don't know, Joe. I've known you for so long, maybe in my early teens? Maybe living away from you made me realize how truly great and wonderful you are. I missed you when I couldn't see you daily. Then I'd see you, and my hormones kicked in and we gave it a shot." Her pale cheeks filled with a slight pinking at remembering their awkward attempt at being a couple. "Plus, you were older and wiser. You were trustworthy, but then again you've always been trustworthy."

"And why did we break up?"

She thought for a moment. "Many reasons really. It was incredibly weird, because we'd always had a big brother/little sister relationship. My aunt thought it was weird too." She smiled and added, "And kissing you just felt wrong."

"Gee thanks a lot!"

"You know what I mean, Joe."

"Yeah, I do. Just giving you a hard time." Joe patted her hands. "We weren't supposed to be anything more than best friends."

"I know that now. Whatever plan is in store for us, it never included you and I being a couple."

"Precisely. Maybe that couple is you and Andrew." He saw the look on her face. "From what you've told me, he seems solid and trustworthy, and maybe he could handle the truth about your past. And if you're as good of friends as we are, then if something were to happen from a romantic involvement, I think your friendship will be strong enough to endure that fallout. Don't you think?" Joe leaned back. "Every person that comes into your life has a purpose, Charlotte, whether it be as a protector, like me," he beamed with pride, "or a lover, like Don was, or maybe your soul mate. We shall see what becomes of Andrew. When I meet him, I think I'll know. I'm very good at reading people."

Charlotte didn't say anything, but simply drank up her sweetened coffee. "When did you get so wise?"

"I'm the amazing Joe." He patted himself on his skinny chest, hidden beneath an oversized green polo shirt. "I've always been wise." He scooted out of the booth, smoothed out his black server's apron, and adjusted his top, tucking in the too short, yet too big top, into the back of his pants. "Now, if you'll excuse me, my dear Charlotte, I need to get back to serving the fine people that visit this dump of a restaurant. Be thankful you escaped."

"Joe?"

"Yeah?"

"Love you." She blew him a kiss.

"You too. You know that." He caught the blown kiss, walked away and started chatting with Meadow.

Charlotte slithered out of the booth after leaving some change on the table.

"Where are you going?" Meadow asked, as Charlotte walked up to the front.

"I'm going home to rethink things." She laughed a little laugh. "Talk to you later."

Meadow patted her on the shoulder. "I'll call you tomorrow."

Charlotte went home and cuddled on the couch watching one of her favourite movies, *When Harry Met Sally*. The main characters started out as friends, then they were not, and then they fell in love. Why was life not like the movies?

Charlotte was at work on Sunday, discussing with Norah about possibly putting in some extra shifts, when she saw Andrew heading for the cashier's desk. He stopped when he saw her and for the first time in a week, he smiled at her, his blue-green eyes lighting up, along with his smile. She couldn't help herself and smiled back an even bigger smile.

"Happy girl," he said to her cheerful face. "Must've been a good date last night?"

"Actually, no," she spit out her answer, her smile fading.

Andrew's blue-green eyes flashed a brief hint of anger. "Why not?" His smile didn't return.

Charlotte shrugged her shoulders. "He didn't show. I waited at home where he said he'd pick me up at 7 and by 8:30, he still hadn't shown up, so I left and went over to JT's Pizzeria and hung out there."

"Why didn't you call me then?" There was a combination of anger and excitement in both his voice and his eyes.

She smiled as she lowered her eyelids. "I didn't have your number."

He pulled a pen from his backpack and wrote on her arm. "There, now you do." He winked.

Damn. That's hot. Her knees weakened beneath her as she felt his soft hand holding her arm. "Great, I'll call you." She blushed slightly as her heart sped up.

"You're adorable when you blush like that." He searched her face. "It doesn't take much does it?"

She felt the heat stinging her cheeks and looking around wondered if anyone else noticed. "Guess not," she said barely audible.

"You working tonight? Or did you just finish?"

"Just started."

"Excellent. I take my break for supper at 5:45, care to join me?"

Her heart skipped a beat. "Upstairs?"

"No, in the café. I didn't bring a supper."

"Sure. Come find me when you're ready."

He smiled his beautiful smile, one that lit up his entire face and made her all warm and fuzzy on the inside. "I'll find you."

"I'll be looking." They parted for their job locales, as though no awkwardness had happened between them, and her date with Trevor was just something to forget. They were back to the easiness of their fast friendship.

At supper, they sat in a corner, tucked up against the glass wall that separated them from the gift shop. The space was a little more private, shielding them away from the general public. It was typically used by the staff, as the table had a superficial wobble to it, and the laminated top was filled with nicks and scratches, with the odd etching of initials.

"So," Andrew started saying after taking a big bite, "I'm curious about your dating history."

Charlotte nearly choked on her hotdog. "Excuse me? My dating history?"

He smiled. "Yeah. I know it's personal info, but you seem to be able to share random bits with me. I figured, maybe you'd share this too."

"Are you always this direct?"

"No point in beating around the bush."

"Then you go first. Spill the beans about your history." *Haha! Take that!*

He laughed hard as he hadn't seen the redirection coming. "Fine. There has been the odd girl here and there; however, nothing serious. Nothing that lasted over two weeks."

She stared at him in shock. "Nothing over two weeks? But you're a good looking guy." The words flowed from her lips before she could bite them back. *Shut. Up. Charlotte!*

Andrew blushed. "Thank you, but I'm sure that had nothing to do with it. We just weren't compatible." He swallowed another bite.

"How many would you classify as your girlfriend?" Her head rested in the palm of her hands, as her elbows supported her cocked head and widening smile.

Returning her smile with one of his own, he lifted his hand raising up four fingers.

She looked surprised and yet was delighted. "Four's a nice number."

"You go. Your turn."

She thought while she was chewing and finally said, "Similar to you I suppose. There was Don, the one that had an affair with my roommate. He was a co-worker, so that was uber-unpleasant when we broke up. He's the reason why I'm hesitant to date co-workers." Shaking her head she continued, "There have been a few guys since, but nothing close to serious. I think I dated each a few times before ending it."

"Did you always end it?"

"Yeah." It never really dawned on her until that point that she was the breaker not the breakee.

He looked at her thoughtfully. "Was it because you're afraid to let people know you? And it's just easier to let them go than it is to let them in?"

She was aghast and tried to think of an appropriate response. She opened her mouth, but nothing came forth as her eyes flashed with intense realization that maybe he was the one who could see her for who she truly was. Blinking the thought away, she noticed the way he was staring at her.

"It's okay, I get it." He walked his hand closer to hers and rested it on top.

Charlotte stared at his hand, her mind blank. Andrew's hand pulling at hers like a magnet - the field surrounding them, encasing them in their own private world. Suddenly the noise in the background of the cafeteria disappeared. Charlotte's mind screamed. *He can read you like an open book – best to really watch what you say and do. You're not hiding from him like you think you are.* The air between them was electric with confusion and apprehension.

"Well, I can see that I have effectively ruined this fine meal." He looked into her eyes and searched her face, trying to read the new expression across her unblemished façade.

She smiled. "I'm just in shock. No one has been able to read me so well. Except Joe. But that's only because he's known me for so long."

"I promise you that I'll never hurt you."

"You shouldn't make promises you can't keep. Besides you don't know me," she said threateningly.

"I'm willing to learn. There's something interesting about you - the way your brow crinkles when you're thinking about something deep, and the way you look at me, like there's something there, a spark of something promising. Your dimples when you smile. You're worth getting to know better."

"I doubt that very much." She scrunched up her garbage and tossed it on the tray. "And those are all superficial things."

"Hey, don't talk like that." He lifted her chin with his finger, feeling heat spread from that point of contact. "I want to know about you, what you like, what you don't like. What makes you tick?" His finger lingered on her chin, which started to quiver.

"Why don't you come over tomorrow night, to my house? I'll give you a glimpse into my life, and you can see if it's worth it to you." She looked at him, staring into his eyes looking for an affirmative.

"I'd absolutely love to."

She swallowed hard and pulled away from his gentle touch. "This will not help the rumours floating around that you and I are dating!"

"Who's been saying that?" He put his finger down, but continued to look at her.

"Russell."

"Figures." He laughed. "I don't give a rat's ass what he thinks. He's such a jerk." Andrew shook his head. "Besides, you and I, we're really the only people who count as far as that's concerned right?"

She nodded hesitantly.

He added, "You need to learn to turn a deaf ear."

"Easier said than done."

"I know. Or just tell Russell to shove it."

Charlotte laughed easily. "Yeah right. That'll be the day." She stood up. "Let's get back to work."

The next evening a firm knock sounded from the top of the stairs. Excited, Charlotte raced up and unlocked the screen door. "Hey, Andrew."

"Hello."

"Come on in. Leave your shoes here." She turned and headed back down the stairs. "You can hang your coat here." She pointed to a coat hook with three hooks at the base of the stairs.

Andrew descended, stopped at the bottom and hung up his coat. He looked left into the brightly lit kitchen where Charlotte was.

"Can I get you something to drink?"

"Sure, what do you have?"

"Tea, coffee, and some pop – the generic cola kind." She watched him as he glanced around the tiny space. It was just enough space to hold a small fridge, a two-burner stove and a little bistro table with two chairs. Still, it was homey in its decorations of photographic landscapes torn out of a calendar and taped to the eggshell coloured walls. A thick dark blue curtain covered the small basement window.

He stopped and stared when he saw her food shelves stuffed full. "Can I ask why you have so many boxes of the same cereal?"

She looked over at the shelves. "Well, I was never allowed to have the fun cereal when I was growing up, so now when I see it on sale, I stock up."

Standing beside the shelves, he counted, "There's seven boxes of Froot Loops and five boxes of Mini Wheats." He looked at her curiously.

"So?"

"That's weird."

"Not really. It's not like they're all open or anything." She ignored his questioning gaze as she filled a kettle with water and lit the gas stove, placing it on top. "Does tea work?"

"Yeah sure."

Great, now he thinks I'm weird for stockpiling my food. Well, you grow up hungry and see what you'd do. So glad he didn't open the cupboard then and see my stash of canned tuna, nor my fridge with the loaded trays of fresh fruit and veggies. Oh the horror of having food in one's house. Charlotte smiled and gestured into the living room. "Let's go in here. It takes awhile for the water to boil."

They walked into the living room, and Andrew laughed out loud. "Do you really have your Christmas tree up already? It's not even Halloween."

She wanted to be upset because he was laughing at her, but she understood how that might seem weird to him, or most people really. "Well, I never really celebrated Christmas as a child..."

Andrew interrupted, "Are you Jewish?"

"No."

"Sorry... continue."

"Anyways, I never celebrated it so when I moved out on my own, I bought a Christmas tree that I could have up for as long as I wanted."

He studied her. "And how long is that?"

"The first year, it was up for six months. Now, it goes up around my birthday, and I take it down by the middle of January, sometimes later."

He glanced over at the Christmas tree. "You've already got presents under there?"

"Just a couple. For Joe and his brother David, and their mom. Little things that I found for them that I didn't want to forget later." She looked delighted with that. *They're the only true family I've got and I like to spoil them as much as I can.*

"Guess that makes it a more affordable way to celebrate the holidays."

"Precisely!"

He walked around the tiny living room that contained the oversize Christmas tree and looked at the random 4"x6" photos she had taped to the wall. "Who's this guy?" He pointed to a tall blond. "He's in a lot of pictures."

Charlotte grinned. "Oh that's my Joe," she smiled as she said his name. "My best friend Joe."

"Oh, so that's Joe." Andrew stared at the variety of pictures. Half of them contained shots of Charlotte and Joe, and in almost every one of those pictures they were both laughing, Charlotte's face lit right up, her dimples nice and deep.

Charlotte pointed out various shots and explained those taken at Joe's place or in Calgary at his mom's house. She tapped on a picture of an older lady. "That's Joe's mom, Mrs. Harrison. She's better than wonderful. She's a great mom to Joe and David." *And me.* Her voice swelled with affection.

Andrew considered his next question carefully, "Where are pictures of your family?"

Without missing a beat, she explained, "We never had a camera growing up, so no pictures." *Whew, dodged that bullet.*

"That makes sense," he said not truly convinced. His fingers touched a picture on the edge of the others. "I like this one."

"That was taken not too long ago. I was at Joe's for a party."

"You look really happy."

"I was, well still am. My life is pretty decent." The kettle started whistling. "Excuse me." She returned in a moment with two steaming mugs of tea. "Liquorice okay? It's all I have, and it's my favourite."

"Umm… smells good." He placed it on the weathered coffee table and sat down on the loveseat. "You read all of these?"

She looked at the stack of books, read some of the titles, and then said, "Just not the top one. Not yet."

He picked up the top book *A Brief History of Time by Stephen Hawking* and quickly read the back cover. "You're seriously reading this?"

"Yeah, it's not so bad."

He gave her an incredible look.

"What? I love cosmology and astronomy, although I do have to say some of the math is like way out there."

"What did you take for math and science in high school?"

"Math 31 and all the 30 Sciences." She took a drink of her tea. Andrew was still staring at her. "What?"

He shook his head. "I don't know. I… I… just…"

"Never expected someone like me to love the sciences?" she interrupted, indignation ripe on her tongue.

"Sort of. I knew you were into astronomy, I just didn't know it was that much of a passion. It's pretty cool to know that you're a bit of a nerd." He smiled and set the book down.

She leaned back in the loveseat. "Well, that I can live with. I don't mind being called a nerd. I thought you were going to say something worse."

He peered into her hazel-green eyes. "Can I ask you something, sort of personal?"

Charlotte met his gaze full on, "You can ask, but I might not answer."

Chuckling, he said, "Fair enough. If you're so interested in the sciences, why aren't you in a university program where you could eventually make more money than a cashier?"

She pondered the question for a brief moment. "Being a cashier isn't a bad job, I'll have you know. It's better than waitressing. But as to why I'm not in university?" Pausing and reflecting, she continued on, "Well, it's expensive. I don't have that kind of money saved up."

He let that sink in, all the while looking at her. He was having a hard time understanding her motives. "Scholarships are all over the place. And with your marks, which I assume you have..."

"Besides, I tried once. Remember, I told Larry about ORO? I wasn't accepted. So I gave up on the idea." She ran her finger along the top of her mug. "What? You're looking at me funny again."

"You're really incredible, you know that?"

She blushed, "No, but thank you." They drank their tea in silence for a bit, smiling at each other. Charlotte broke the quietness of gentle sipping sounds. "So you haven't left yet."

"No, why would I?"

"Because I'm weird."

"Charlotte, I think you're pretty cool." Blushing as he spoke, Andrew lowered his eyes.

Sensing he was uncomfortable, she asked, "Would you like to watch a movie? I have no cable, but I do have a few movies."

"Let's see what you got." Andrew went over to check out her movie collection. "You have a lot of chick flicks."

She nodded. "Nothing like a good tear jerking romance."

"No thanks." He read more titles. "How about 'Star Wars' then?"

"Great. Are you a fan?"

"They're okay. I wouldn't say I'm a huge fan, but they're good to watch."

"How can you not be a huge fan? 'Star Wars' is like the most epic battle between the forces of good and evil. I always wanted to be Princes Leia, a beautiful princess who's strong and fierce, and finds her Han Solo."

Andrew laughed. "You really need to get out more."

She giggled. "Perhaps." The opening credits started rolling, and she stated, "I'm glad you're my friend."

"I'm glad too."

Chapter Five
✿✿✿

As the weeks rolled on, the friendship between Andrew and Charlotte blossomed. One Saturday afternoon at the start of December, after work was finished, Charlotte hung out behind the cashier's desk, waiting as patiently as possible for Andrew to come and bring the key down. She'd invited Andrew out to her aunt's place, for dinner and a swim, where she was house sitting for the weekend. He showed up just after five, and the pair walked out to their cars.

In his sweet Russian accent, he asked, "Where does your aunt live?"

"On a farm just south of town, about a half hour from here." She gave him brief directions, and then said it would probably be easier to follow her. As they drove away, she looked back in her rear view mirror to make sure the alabaster white Fiero followed closely behind. Feeling nervously excited, she sang along to the radio to calm the butterflies. She was taking a giant leap inviting him out to a place she once lived, and letting him see that side of her.

As they arrived at her aunt's place, Charlotte drove around the enormous circular driveway and parked in front of the house. Andrew pulled right behind her and grabbed a small bag from the back seat.

After dropping his bag in the foyer, they walked down the hall and into the kitchen. Charlotte started preparing supper.

"Nice place your aunt has here." He looked around the expansive kitchen.

"Thanks, it's not bad."

"You don't care for it?"

"It's so far away," she complained, "twenty minutes from the edge of town, plus whatever time you need to get around. I like where I am. A few short minutes to anything, and I can get there by walking. Here, you have to drive if you want to go to the store or get a coffee." She opened the cupboard and pulled out a box of spaghetti and a jar of sauce. "This is as fancy a cook as I get." She laughed.

Andrew peeked as she opened the door. "There's not seven boxes of Froot Loops in there?"

"No," she snickered, "just at my house. Here you'd be hard pressed to even find one box of sugar-coated cereal, let alone seven. She never eats the stuff."

He walked around, through the dining room, into the living room, past the master bedroom and down the hall that connected to the kitchen. "She doesn't have a Christmas Tree?" In a mocking voice, he said, "How can you stand being here?"

"Oh haha. Very funny. Aunt Carol buys the real trees, and those aren't available until a bit closer to Christmas."

Andrew nodded, and then asked, "What's over there?" He pointed to the other side of the eating area.

"Her office, and my old room." It came out before she could stop herself.

He went across the kitchen and peeked down the hall. His voice rose as he said, "Your old room? I didn't know you'd lived with your aunt. It doesn't look like much of a bedroom?"

Silently kicking herself, she said, "No, not any more. I think she's preparing to knock out the wall between my old room and the master bedroom to make it one big master suite."

"Can I ask why you lived with your aunt? Where are your parents?" He looked questioningly at her.

The shock of being asked caused Charlotte to drop the entire box of spaghetti into the boiling water, and it splashed scalding water all over her arm. "Oh damn!" she screamed. She grabbed a pair of tongs and pulled the cardboard box from the water, leaving the spaghetti in there. She threw the box into the garbage, wrapped a cold wet towel around her arm, and went to work at getting the pasta to pull apart so it would not be a clumpy mess. She felt Andrew's burning eyes looking at her. *I'm such a nitwit.*

"Are you okay?" he asked.

She sighed as she now let the cool water run over and numb her blazing arm. "Nothing I can't handle," she said keeping her back to him.

"Can I help with anything?"

"Sure. Grab a couple of plates and the cutlery." She dried off her arm and pointed in the direction of the cupboard door, "And use the placemats on the table. Do you want some wine with supper?"

After grabbing the plates, he turned to her. "Sure." His accented voice was ripe with pleasure.

"Around the corner, in the dining room, is a wine rack. Go and pick a bottle. My aunt's boyfriend makes it."

"Really? Very cool." He disappeared into the dining room and returned with a pinkish looking bottle. "How does a Zasmerano sound?" He read out the label slowly.

"Sounds good to me." She stirred the pasta. "Wine is wine to me. Can't appreciate the difference between a red, white, and blush anyways."

Andrew set the table, and digging through the cupboards found a couple of wine glasses. "Do you have family around, besides your aunt?" He turned around to search her face, and study her expression.

Hearing his question, she stepped away from the boiling pot of water. "My Aunt Carol and my cousin Elaine. That's about it." She looked him straight in the eye. *Stop pestering me about my family. I won't crack, and I'm not sharing.*

"What does your aunt do?"

"She's an air traffic controller. Usually Elaine watches the house when she's gone, but they're on a mother-daughter trip for a weekend getaway."

"That's nice."

Charlotte bit her tongue to stop the words again from flowing out of control. "It is." *Elaine is lucky like that.* She tried to push away the green-eyed monster that surfaced in her answer.

He saw it flash across her eyes, something like jealousy, and then it was gone. Sensing a lot of discomfort he changed the topic slightly, and piped up, "My mom never travels anymore. Dad always traveled back and forth between here and Russia."

"Traveled?"

"Yeah. He used to come here to visit when we were younger. But now that we're older, we're the ones that do the traveling."

"How often do you go?"

"Every second summer since the split. My brother Jon and I spend the summer with dad's family, usually helping out with chores on the farm."

"How long have your parents been split up?"

"Since I was twelve. Dad moved back soon after the split. He always preferred Russia to here, said the winters were better. We only go for the summer. It's too hard to go over Christmas, but we did once."

"I'm sorry. I can't imagine what that would be like." There was a strong sense of empathy rolling off Charlotte's tongue. *Sadly, I know all too well what it's like to be away from family over Christmas. At least you get to see one parent.*

He leaned on the raised counter, watching her swirl the softening pasta in the boiling water. "You get used to it. He writes us letters all the time, and sends us packages. We're even starting to email a bit back and forth. He's never been distant with us, and he still talks with mom, but it's different."

"That's good that you keep in touch. Family's important." *Or so I'm told.* She finished preparing the spaghetti and passed the pot to Andrew. She gave the warmed sauce a stir, and brought the small pot with her. "Wa-la!" she said and put it down on the table.

"Looks delicious." Not a hint of sarcasm in his voice.

"Oh yeah, clumpy spaghetti. What everyone orders when they go out," Charlotte joked as she rolled her eyes. They sat down and she exclaimed, "Dig in!"

They filled their plates, and Andrew poured them each a glass of the blush wine.

"To friendship," he toasted.

"To friendship!" she echoed and took a sip. "Damn, that's good." She licked her lips.

It didn't take long for Charlotte to feel the affects of the wine, and it got stronger as she finished eating. Her cheeks burned, not unlike her blushing episodes. She laughed too easily at the conversation and Andrew noticed too. "Are you tipsy already?"

Charlotte giggled. "Yeppers."

"Wow, you're a cheap drunk." His tone was one of concern and bewilderment, not condescending.

Her hands shook a little as she refilled her empty glass, and Andrew's half-full one. "Yep. Doesn't take much."

"Good thing you're not driving tonight." He looked at her cautiously. "Do you always get like this, or did you start drinking on an empty stomach?"

"Always like this. My friends Joe and Meadow like to give me a hard time about it." She tried to keep a straight face, and then busted into a giggle. "Seriously, it doesn't take much."

Andrew got serious, "Then maybe you should slow down?"

Charlotte smiled as she sipped on the second glass she'd just poured. "Maybe?"

"Good grief, you'll be passed out on the floor before you know it."

"I don't pass out."

"How do you know?"

"Because my friends would've told me. And I don't get sick either, and amazingly enough no hangovers." She smiled at him. "I know my limits."

"Do you?" he asked, taking a sip of the wine, and keeping a watchful eye on her.

She giggled again, the scarlet colour remaining in her cheeks and staining it permanently. "Hard to believe, but yes. This may be my last glass." She stood up and slightly stumbled to the sink and put her empty plate into it.

Andrew was right behind her, ready to catch her if she stumbled any harder. "Thanks for supper."

"Anytime. As long as you like spaghetti, then I can make it. Otherwise, you're screwed."

"Not a cook eh?"

"Not in the faintest sense of the word. I hate cooking," she giggled lightly turning around and leaned away from him against the kitchen counter. "Like really hate cooking. I'd rather never have to cook again ever in my life." She snickered. "Pots and pans scare the bejeesus out of me."

"Then you need to find a man who cooks." His eyebrow lifted and a hint of a smile tugged at his lips.

She looked at him curiously, and after taking a sip of liquid boldness, winked at him and placed her hand upon his chest, feeling the taunt muscles beneath. "Do you cook?"

He laughed and this time his cheeks emblazoned a bit. "Sometimes."

"I see." She took another sip never breaking eye contact, her hand firmly placed on his chest. "Let's go for a swim!"

"Now? Shouldn't we clean up first? Shouldn't you sober up a touch first?" He placed his hands on either side of her and leaned on the counter, closing the distance between them in a breath.

"Nah, I'm breaking my own rules tonight. First play, and then I'll clean before I go to bed. It'll be fine." She waved her hands all around.

"Is swimming a good idea?"

"When is swimming not a good idea?" She ducked underneath his arms, and nearly toppled. Then she walked towards her aunt's bedroom, trailing her hands along the wall. "Go put your shorts on - there's a change room downstairs in the pool room, which you can't miss. You'll see it at the bottom of the stairs. I'll just be a minute." She closed the double doors of her aunt's room. Andrew grabbed his bag by the front door and headed downstairs.

She emerged in a black one-piece bathing suit that suited her lean and trim figure. Her normally loose coppery hair pulled into a quick braid that hung down her back. She went to the kitchen and topped up her liquid courage by drinking down the remainder wine in her glass. She grabbed another bottle of wine from the dining room, and headed down to the pool with their glasses.

She pulled back the door to the pool area, and Andrew was already there, changed. He looked great. Better than great. As he stood there, she admired his toned and smooth chest, a hint of a rippled abdomen, and strong looking arms. His wider, yet not overly broad shoulders accented his narrow waist. He had a great body. She also noticed his total lack of chest hair, something that immediately turned her on.

He broke her ogling by saying, "Let me help you." He grabbed the glasses and smiled while checking her out, his eyes slowly skimming up and down the length of her body. "I thought you knew your limits."

"Sometimes it's good to test them. Besides, it's more for you than me. You don't seem to be affected at all."

He smiled warmly at her. "No, I don't have much of a buzz."

"Well, drink up!" She held up the second bottle and filled their glasses placing them on the poolside table. "Now, help me roll back the pool cover."

Then Charlotte turned on the pool lights and turned off the overhead florescent glare. The room was suddenly basked in a faint blue glow. "That's better," she commented. She grabbed her glass, sat down beside the pool and dipped her legs in. She savoured the taste of the pale pink liquid.

Andrew sat beside her. "This is nice." He dipped his legs in as well and took another sip of wine. "The water is nice and warm." Then he pushed himself in completely, splashing her.

"Drew," she exclaimed, "you got me all wet!"

"Are you a good swimmer?"

"I may not have won many trophies in high school, but I assure you, I can swim. I was on the dive team until I was a senior," she said, not sure why he was asking until she felt herself being pulled off the edge and into the pool. She broke the surface of the water laughing. "Thanks. Now I look like a drowned rat," she said, referring to her bangs, wet and hanging in her eyes.

"Nah, you're still beautiful."

Although her cheeks were already blazing from the wine, she felt them increase in heat.

"You blush so easily. Even with the wine you've had tonight, I can still see the change in tone." He ran a fingertip down the length of her inflamed cheek.

Her heart sped up; her breathing hitched slightly. "Guilty," she exclaimed, after trying to dunk him in the pool.

He was stronger and more prepared for that, so he managed to be the dunker instead of the dunkee. He laughed in earnest when she came up for air. "You can try, but you won't win."

They wrestled in the water, and stopped for a moment when they both noticed that Andrew was carrying Charlotte, her legs wrapped around his waist. Their faces mere inches from each other. They stood there, locked together, gazing into each other's eyes as though under a spell.

"I want to kiss you," he said softly looking at her lips and slowly raising his gaze back up into her eyes.

"Don't ask, just do it," she whispered through her smile, her arms wrapped tightly around his neck.

"One should always ask." He searched her hazel-green eyes, seeking out permission. "You're more than a little tipsy, and I don't want to take advantage of you."

"You're not, I promise." She leaned a bit in response to his forward tilt.

Their lips sealed together, and their hearts seemed to beat in time. The taste of his lips was magical and Charlotte never wanted the moment to end. She parted her mouth slightly to his advancing, deepening kiss. Feeling her head spinning, and her pulse racing at a rapid pace, she fought with her breath, trying fervently to catch up.

Andrew tasted a hint of coconut on his lips as he slowly kissed off the kiss. They stayed in the enchanted embrace for a while. Charlotte put her head on his shoulder and rested, while he rocked them back and forth in the chest deep water.

Eventually, he walked them back to the edge of the pool. He reached for his wine glass and took a big gulp. "Well, that changes things," he tried to whisper to himself but Charlotte overheard.

"For the better," she whispered into his ear, and then drank another half glass of the wine, before she went over to the diving board and did a perfect dive into the deep end of the pool.

Not to be outdone, Andrew got out and did a half-assed flip off the diving board, creating a huge splash.

"Four point five," Charlotte yelled with delight when he emerged in the shallow end.

"Yeah, that sucked. I knew half way into it, it wasn't going to work. That diving board needs to be higher." He pushed back the water off his face, up and over his head. His eyes even bluer as they reflected the soft cerulean glow from the pool lights. He gave her another kiss.

"Sure it does!" Charlotte giggled and tried swimming away, when Andrew caught up to her and pulled her under again. She grabbed on to him with fear in her grip as he pulled her up.

"Scared you?"

"A little."

"Sorry," he said, as he slowly brushed her lips with his.

Breaking away from the touch of their wine-laced kiss, she inquired, "Things are going to be different between us now, aren't they?"

"Just better, not different."

"But I think we're no longer friends now." For a moment, her voice sounded sad.

"We'll always be friends."

"You know what I mean." Charlotte crookedly swam to the edge of the pool and quickly drained her wine glass. "Hot tub time?"

Andrew finished his off too. "Sure, but it looks cold out there."

"That's the best part of the hot tub being outside. Racing through the snow, freezing off your feet and then hopping into the hot tub." She opened the patio door and precariously stumbled the few steps out on to the deck, stood on the ledge, and pulled open the hot tub cover. The chlorine-scented steam rose up like an explosion against the starry sky.

The hot water felt mesmerizing against her quickly chilled skin. Andrew ran from the pool, after closing the door. He slid into the hot tub and sighed as Charlotte turned on the jets. They each sat in their seat gazing up at the clear, starry sky for long while.

Then Charlotte started to giggle wildly, breaking the serene silence that surrounded them.

Andrew whispered, "What's so funny?"

"I just thought of a bad joke," she whispered loudly while continuing to giggle. Then she hiccupped.

"Do tell..." He smiled at her while watching her become more intoxicated by the minute. Her eyes seemed far away, and her body moved slowly. Clearly, she did not know her limits.

"When do astronauts eat their lunch?" she paused and then burst out giggling, likely scaring the wildlife that he felt were just feet away from them before he could answer. "At launch time!" She was so loud and laughed so hard that she had a hard time catching her breath.

Andrew laughed briefly at her joke, but instead noticed her super flushed face and not just her cheeks, even her ears seemed to glow a bright shade of crimson under the cover of the starry sky. He turned serious. "I think it's time to get out now, Charlotte."

"Nah, I'm good!" she said, laughing as her face fell forwards into the hot tub.

Andrew, fuelled by terror, pulled her head out of the water. "Yes," he said firmly, "it's time to get out!"

She was still laughing a weird maniacal laugh that he'd never heard before as he shut off the jets and climbed out first. When he turned around, her head was bobbing face down in the water. "Charlotte!" he screamed and pulled her face back out of the water. Hoping to make the situation tolerable, to himself more than Charlotte, he explained, "The hot tub seems to have accelerated your intoxication. You can't even hold your head up out of the water." He pulled her up on to her feet where she tottered on the seat, and with a huge effort she managed to step over the edge of the hot tub, onto the ledge, pressing hard against him as she tried to balance herself. He clutched her tightly as he replaced the cover on the hot tub, and stepping off the ledge onto the cold deck, wrapped his arms around her waist. Holding her up as he dragged her into the pool area since she could barely move her feet, he closed the patio door behind them. Feeling relief that they were back inside and out of the hot tub of drowning death, he lowered her into the plastic deck chair. "Where are the towels?"

"Inside the house, in the bathroom." She hiccupped again and melted her body into the moulded form of the chair, her expression going serious as a heart attack.

He debated; should he take her dripping wet into the house or did he think he could leave her for a few seconds to grab a towel.

When she started laughing at nothing, and her face turned the most brilliant shade of red, he thought it best to take her with him. Supporting her dead weight, and two weak feet, he got her over to the bathroom. He wrapped a towel around her, and then grabbed one for himself.

Charlotte's giggling stopped suddenly, and she went pale, sliding down the nearby wall until she was on the floor. He watched her cautiously and curiously, unsure of what was happening. He had never seen anyone react so strongly to alcohol before. It was like a bad episode of the Twilight Zone. Incredibly, Charlotte must be super sensitive to it, and the hot tub intensified her reaction,

"Andrew," she called out blindly, her eyes closed, "I think I'm going to be sick." She turned to the toilet beside her.

"Okay, that's probably a good idea." He continued to stand there dumbstruck to the sudden turn of events.

She scooted a little closer to the toilet, lifted the lid and immediately threw up into the bowl.

Andrew took a horrifying step back as a whiff of foul smelling vileness filled the air. "I'll go find something for your tummy," he exclaimed as she threw up again.

"Upstairs, in the bathroom," she blabbered incoherently between hurls.

He ran upstairs and searching the bathroom in her aunt's bedroom, Andrew could find nothing. Even an exhaustive search of the main bathroom, he still came up empty handed. "No luck," he said flipping on the bathroom fan, his own stomach threatening to toss from the smell.

Her head leaned against the cool edge of the toilet. "Sorry," she whimpered sounding half a note away from crying.

He grabbed a nearby washcloth, soaked it in cool water, and placed it on the back of her neck.

"Thanks." She flushed the toilet and lay down beside it, the towel now around her waist.

Andrew grabbed another towel to cover her up, and then sat against the opposite wall. It wasn't long before he could hear her softly snoring. He'd never seen anything like that and realized she wasn't kidding when she said she reacts quickly to alcohol. Whispering to himself, he said, "Holy smokes, it's barely nine o'clock, and she's passed out. Cold. Her friends have been lying to her if they tell her she never passes out."

With his head against the wall and his eyes shut tight against the surprise of the evening, he deliberated for a few minutes about whether or not he should leave her alone. Deciding she was safe in the rescue position, he decided to go and tidy up.

He went to the poolroom, and grabbed the pair of wine glasses and the half-empty bottle of Zasmerano. Between the two of them, they only drank a bottle and a half. He knew of people who could drink that all by themselves and not react so violently. Maybe the hot water of the tub just shot her intoxication levels through the roof. He changed back into his regular clothes, checked on Charlotte, who was still softly snoring on the floor, and went upstairs to tidy the kitchen up.

Returning quickly, he went into the TV area beside the bathroom and made up one of the couches. Grabbing a blanket, he laid it across the cushions and added a throw pillow. Then he went and picked up Charlotte, grunting slightly as he carried her dead weight into the TV area, and placed her gently on the couch. He covered her up. Then he found a bucket under the bathroom sink, and placed it beside her head, on the floor. Sighing, he stretched out on the other couch and turned on the TV.

His thoughts strayed from the bad sitcoms to the beautiful lady who'd captured his heart. He was worried about her, and the obvious alcohol intolerance she had. He thought about everything she'd said, that she once lived with her aunt, but deflected quickly any inquiry of her parents. What was the story there? Eventually, after wrestling with his thoughts, he fell asleep.

Sometime in the morning, Charlotte grunted and woke wiping the drool off her mouth. Her head spinning, she clamped both her hands over her closed eyes. Even through tightly sealed lids, the TV seemed so bright. She carefully sat up, eyes slowly opening, wondering why she was sleeping on the couch. She looked over when she heard a snore coming from the other couch, and was shocked to see Andrew sleeping on it. She went to stand up, but feeling dizzy, sat back down noting she was still wearing her bathing suit. Immediately, she grabbed the blanket and covered up. Staring at the clock on the VCR, she focused hard on the tiny numbers – it blinked 10:22. She assumed it was morning, but it was always hard to tell in the faintly lit room. She attempted to stand again, and successful this time, walked to the bathroom.

Man does my head ache. What in fresh hell happened last night? As she walked up the stairs, each rise rattled her head. She popped a couple of Tylenol and quickly changed into real clothes, then went into the kitchen. She was surprised to see it all tidy and clean, hardly any evidence of the dinner she'd prepared the night before, aside from the gleaming pots on the countertop. She remembered making spaghetti, but didn't remember cleaning up.

She grabbed the coffee pot and started making coffee. She didn't hear the approaching footsteps over the pounding of her head, until Andrew whispered, "Good morning," in her ear. Completely surprised by his voice, she jumped and spun around rapidly, causing her to lose her balance.

Andrew reached out to steady her with his hands firmly holding onto her waist.

"Morning," she replied, wondering if he was going to let go. "Some night last night eh?"

I remember eating dinner and going for a swim. I think I remember laughing, a lot, but was there more to it than that? She managed to speak the only answer she thought of, "I guess so." Feeling her head beat firmly against the front of her brain, she placed her hand across her forehead.

"Hung over?" He reluctantly released his hold.

"I guess."

"You were pretty drunk!"

"I must've been. I don't remember much of anything." She held on to the counter as she turned back towards it.

Andrew's expression changed. "Really? It was a great night, right up until the end."

She stared blankly at him as her head took another beating. "What am I missing?"

"What do you remember?" He pulled a couple of cups down from over the sink and poured them both a mug of coffee.

She grabbed hers, inhaling the rich aroma and walked to the kitchen table. "I remember eating supper with you." She smiled. "That was nice." Thinking a little harder, she looked at the pained expression Andrew wore. "I know I changed into my bathing suit, and I vaguely remember swimming."

He sat across from her at the table. "Vaguely?" His tired eyes blinked with a hint of disappointment. His five o'clock shadow only marginally more shadowed.

Searching her fuzzy and unfocused memories she replied, "Yeah, but I remember lots of laughing."

"Yes, there was lots of laughing. Mostly from you." He concentrated on her eyes as if willing them to remember the incredible fun.

"I couldn't have been that drunk." She shook her head and instantly regretted that.

"You were."

"Oh my gosh. Did I do something stupid?" Her voice turned panicky.

"Nothing stupid." He smiled at his own memories of their enchanting first kiss.

"What did I do?"

"Well… you kept putting your face into the hot tub. I had to keep pulling your head out of the water."

She smacked her head and then groaned. That didn't help her headache. "Geez, good thing you were there, then."

His smile saddened and his voice dropped, "Yes, you could've drowned."

She shuddered. "I'm sorry."

"It's all good. I got it handled."

"I wasn't a very good hostess."

"Don't beat yourself up. You were great." He was smiling again. "What else do you remember?"

She thought long and hard, drinking her black coffee. "That's about it. Dinner, and some swimming, mostly me being under the water."

"Nothing else?"

She looked at him sternly. "You keep asking me that, like there's something important I'm missing."

He looked solemnly at her. His heart sunk, but he lied through a smile when he told her, "Yeah, we saw a couple of shooting stars. It was incredible."

She stared at him and nodded slowly. "Oh yeah," she whispered, "I think I remember seeing that."

Andrew's heart ached a little. She clearly did not remember kissing him. She had to have been drunker than he realized. He felt very sad that she didn't have that wonderful memory to think about all day long.

They finished drinking their coffee. He reached across the table and affectionately gave her hand a gentle squeeze. "What time do you work today?"

She thought for a second, "One, I think. You?"

"Four."

They looked away from each other, the air between them suddenly awkward with a tangible tension. Finally, Andrew got up and put his mug into the dishwasher. "Thanks for last night."

"Yeah, it was fun. I think," she laughed a little, giving him a quick hug. "Sorry I wasn't a better hostess."

"You were fantastic, but I'm going to go. I wasn't intending to stay the night and need to get home and change. Imagine the gossip if I showed up at work wearing the same thing as yesterday." He winked at her, instantly putting her at ease. "Feel better, and I'll see you in a few hours."

"Thanks, Andrew." Charlotte smiled and stared into the blue-green eyes before her, holding back an urge to wrap her arms around him. "Thanks for taking care of me last night."

"Maybe we can do this again, soon, without the alcohol?" his accented voice suggested with a plea.

"Maybe."

There was no promise in her response and he accepted that at face value.

She stood at the front door, waving until he drove away, then went to lie down to rest for a few minutes.

Chapter Six
✿✿✿

Charlotte stood behind the desk, methodically pulling the tiny ornaments off of the two-foot tall tree that adorned the cashiers' desk. She placed them in the box and was removing the red sparkly garland, when she saw Andrew walk over, carrying a cash float. Excited, she giggled inside as he slid it into the drawer.

"You're working here tonight?" Charlotte asked, pleasantly surprised. "I thought Russell was working?"

"Called in sick, or something." He smirked. "I'm picking up extra shifts to make up for the ones I had to give up for Toronto."

"Well, this will be fun."

The bronze-haired Russian smiled. His hair a little shorter and spikier than normal, the result of too much mousse. The blue-green of his eyes winked at her. "So how was your Christmas and New Year's?"

"It was good. Really good."

"What did you do?"

Visited with Champ and Mrs. Kennedy and got my ass handed to me, again, by Champ in crib. Mrs. Kennedy isn't doing so well though, and is starting to not remember me, but I'm sure you don't want to hear that. She twirled her seat, hair flying as she spun. Giggling, she stopped and answered. "Well, madre, I mean Mrs. Harrison, Joe's mom, came up for the holidays. I spent Christmas Day with the Harrisons, and it was so nice to catch up with her and David. We just hung out at Joe's place, sang carols, baked up a storm and laughed. On New Year's Eve, she went and visited with her friends so we could celebrate like we usually do." She spun her chair the other direction. "How was Toronto?"

"Cold, but it was great to see dad."

"Yeah, that was nice that he met you and Jon there. Then you didn't need to go all the way to Russia."

"Yes. It was much easier, but it's nice to be back."

"Right on. Did you do the touristy thing and visit the CN Tower?"

"No time really, but I've seen it before."

She spun her chair again and then processed a movie ticket for a customer. The majority of their sales were prior to three, but they usually picked up again after supper for the evening shows. However the city was under a nasty cold snap, and ticket sales were slower than usual. This gave the pair lots of time to chat.

Charlotte looked at Andrew, carefully and cautiously. *I want to talk to you, but I'm afraid of how to say it. Something tells me that you're not going to be happy to hear it though.* Ever since that night at her aunt's, he'd been acting different towards her. Not distant, but the reverse, as if he was trying to find a way around her "just friends" stronghold. She tapped a pencil on the desk.

"Something on your mind?"

"Actually yeah." *Oh man, so much.*

"So tell me."

"I don't want you to read too much into it. It's just a date."

Perplexed, he looked at her, noticing the way her gaze cast downwards. Taking a quiet breath, he urged her to spill the beans.

"His name's Chad. I met him at my cousin's wedding."

"Oh yeah?" His voice was detached and even.

She carried on, "We're going out for dinner and then out for line dance lessons. Joe and a few friends are going to meet up with us around eleven. Maybe you could bring some friends and join us?"

"At a country bar? No thanks." He shuddered. "So *not* into that hillbilly music."

"Oh."

"When is this magical date?"

"Saturday." *I can see by that look in your eye that you're not thrilled. I knew I shouldn't have said anything. Geez, I can be so stupid sometimes.*

Andrew was silent for a while, typing something into the computer. "I'm sure you'll have a good time." He tried to hide the jealousy in his voice, but did a terrible job of disguising it.

"You're sure you won't come to the bar? It'll be fun."

"I promise you, I'll have more fun sitting at home watching movies than I will hanging out in a country bar." He avoided meeting her gaze head on.

"Okay."

Charlotte changed for the third time into a pair of dark jeans and a nice button up pink top. She stared into the full-length mirror firmly attached to her bedroom wall. *I should be able to dance well enough in this, and yet still look okay. I don't want to dress like a floozy. It's just line dancing.* She heard a knock at the top of the stairwell from the locked screen door.

She hurried up the stairs. *Geez, Chad, way to dress up. A little casual for a country bar, don't you think?* He looked like a rapper, not someone who claimed to be into country music. Dressed in a pair of baggy track pants, a ribbed white tank underneath an unzipped letterman jacket that bore the name "Rebel" across the sleeve, and the year "1991", which she assumed was his graduation year. He wore sunglasses, although it was dark outside. His cap slightly twisted to the side, covered the shaggy dark brown hair. He was taller than she remembered, standing at what she guessed was over six feet tall. He looked a lot stronger too. Maybe the suit he wore at the wedding hid his muscles.

"Hi, Chad," she said. "Good to see you again." She let him into the little landing at the top of the stairs.

"Thanks," he said in a deep gruff sounding voice. For some reason his voice made the hair stand up on the back of her neck. *When we'd talked on the phone last week, he hadn't sounded so throaty. Maybe he has a cold?* "Come on down," she said hesitantly, "I'm just finishing up." She started moving down the stairs and walked into the tiny living room at the bottom of the stairwell, listening to the heavy footprints behind her.

He followed her in and looked around. "Nice place you got here." He walked over to look at the CDs she had on top of her stereo. "Good selection."

"Thanks," she said. "It's a nice little basement suite that I rent from the people upstairs. It's tiny, but it's my home." Her voice swelled with pride.

"Cool." He turned around, and in taking off his sunglasses, revealed eyes as black as coal. They looked her over, slowly, up and down, to the point where she started to feel very nervous about going out with him.

So thankful that I'm meeting Joe and Meadow later. She stifled an internal shudder. "I'll just grab my purse from the kitchen, and we can go for dinner. I'm starving." Moving quickly she exited the living room, walked into her little kitchen, and reached for her purse sitting atop the little fridge.

"I'm starving too!" he spoke from behind her.

Frightened that she hadn't heard his footsteps behind her, she turned around and looked right into the top of his shoulders as he glowered over her. Her breathing quickened to match the sudden increase of her pulse. *Damn, I'm suddenly very nervous.*

He stepped closer to her, and in his gravely voice breathed into her ear, "Are you scared of me, Charlotte?" He subjected her to a full body look, a smirk tugging at his mouth.

She couldn't answer as she was paralyzed with fear. Her heart beat as fast and as loud as a thousand race cars in the Daytona 500. It drowned out the sound of anything but what spoke into her ear.

"Don't you think I'm hot?" he asked, his face close to hers as he wrapped a strong arm around her, pinning her firmly against him. His hot, moist breath reeked of booze and garlic, and the way he eyed her made her sick.

Again, she couldn't answer.

"You're a fine piece of ass," Chad said, as he licked his lips. His arm around her waist slid lower, and he grabbed at her backside, harshly.

It happened so fast that she didn't really see it coming, or believe what was about to happen. She was flung to the floor with enough speed and force that she smacked her head hard on the linoleum covered concrete floor and temporarily blacked out. Occasionally, she regained semi-consciousness, but felt out of control as she felt the weight of the panting man on top of her, holding her still. Trying not to feel anything, she tried to separate her mind from her body, but knew in her mind, from the forcefulness of his hands, where exactly on her body they were. She felt her arms pinned down. Her back felt raw from moving across the floor, the top of her head sore from slamming into the cupboards. The garlic-booze breath was horrible as his drunken sloppy kisses covered her mouth preventing any sound from escaping. His rough tongue licked her neck, and she felt it trail down across her chest. She felt fear beyond anything she ever had before in her life as the strong hands on either side of her head squeezed it and slammed it repeatedly back into the floor. Blackness constantly took over, and whether it was minutes or hours, the passage of time lost all meaning. Fear had an incredible way of altering time and space.

When he finally left, she didn't immediately know. Charlotte came to with the most astounding headache she'd ever experienced in her life. Trying to sift beyond the sounds she could hear - the tick-tock of the clock hanging on the kitchen wall, the quiet hum of the refrigerator, the pilot light coming from the tiny stove, the pounding of her heart. She listened. For him. Laying there as still as a statue, not moving a muscle or even blinking her eyes until she was sure, absolutely sure, she was alone. Then she sat up slowly, feeling dizzy, and immediately threw up. Looking down, she was nearly naked, which although she suspected, because she felt so cold and detached, still surprised her. Her shirt buttons ripped off her shirt, slid down her arms as she sat. Her bra hitched up above her breasts, her pants and underwear not within view. Grabbing what was left of her shirt she tried to cover herself up. She threw up again, and crawled out of the little kitchen to the stairs. Glancing up the stairwell, she saw the back door partially closed and assumed he was gone. She threw up some more and crawled into the raised living room. She grabbed the cordless phone off her coffee table. Scared, she dialled the only number she could think of, the only one she'd been thinking of during her ordeal.

"Hello?" said the Russian accented voice, laughing as the phone call interrupted some revelry.

Breathlessly she whispered, "Andrew?" She threw up again, covering the lower shelf of the second-hand coffee table as she grabbed her lower stomach. Pain radiated everywhere. She could barely focus, except on his voice, which she hung onto like a lifeline.

"Charlotte?" His laugh halted.

She could barely move her lips let alone hold the phone. "Help me, please." She collapsed on the commercial grade carpet of her basement apartment.

Panic completely overtook Andrew's voice. "Where are you?"

"Home." She threw up again. She was now covered and sitting in puddles of her own vomit.

"I'm on my way."

Charlotte barely heard the clicking before she passed out.

She woke after a couple of minutes and tenderly reached for the blanket off the couch, having no energy to move onto something more comfortable. She lay there silent and still, pain covering her more than the fleece throw, when she heard a knock at the top of the stairs. *Andrew.* She thought she'd yelled "down here," but it came out as a quiet whisper. Ears like a hawk, she listened as he opened the screen door. He kept calling out her name. *Down here.* She yelled louder, her screaming voice no louder than the faintest whisper.

He descended the stairs and gasped when he saw the blood and vomit on the floor of the kitchen to his left and the puddles of puke before him trailing into the living room. Running to the dishevelled Charlotte on the floor, and seeing more vomit around her, he knelt and picked her up into his protective arms.

"Charlotte! Charlotte!" he screamed at her until her hazel-greens connected briefly with his eyes. Her mascara caked around her swollen eyes, her soft copper waves stuck together in an unnatural state. Her body felt dead and limp. To Andrew, she barely looked like the Charlotte he knew.

She blinked at him, fear registering on her face.

"What did he do?" he looked horror-struck.

"You need to ask?" she breathed out and passed out again, this time safely in Andrew's arms.

She woke when she felt cold hands pressing on her wrists, and felt herself hoisted onto something solid yet soft. She blinked and looked around slowly, trying to focus on someone. "Drew?" she cried out softly.

He stood before her, looking deeply into her still focusing eyes. "I called the police and EMS. You wouldn't stop passing out."

She cried as she tried to look at him, noticing his blue-green eyes lined in red. He looked like hell. Shuddering, not from the cold, but from the way he looked and the way she felt. She appreciated the sudden weight of a blanket placed on top of her. She could hear other voices, in trying to locate their owners, she cried out in a pained whimper, "My head hurts." Feeling for his hand, she grasped it tightly. "I'm scared." Closing her eyes to everything around her, she let hot tears escape. She listened to the paramedics work on inserting an IV into her arm, retreated to her dark place, and she blanked out again.

In a shaking, accented voice, she heard Andrew whisper into her ear, "Stay with me. I'm here with you." He repeated it over and over. Charlotte focused on the words, on the sounds, on each little inflection his voice made. Then he announced, "The cops are here." Her slowly beating heart suddenly jumped and started racing once more.

A soft voice, a women's voice, came over to Charlotte's other side. "I'm Constable Ryan. Can I have your name please?"

She turned her head carefully towards the sound of the soothing female voice, keeping her eyes closed. "Charlotte Cooper," she breathed out in a murmured sigh.

"Miss Cooper, can you tell me what happened here tonight?" Her voice was warm and comforting, but still, just thinking about what happened was hard enough, actually vocalizing it was stomach wrenching.

Charlotte turned her head to the other side and threw up, narrowly missing Andrew's shoes. Her eyes closed tight. "I was raped." She barely breathed out, righting her head. Another round of sickness trying to escape stopped any further explanations. She turned her head as her mouth released the poison.

Andrew observed as Charlotte's covered body started shaking. He grabbed another blanket and threw it over top of her, horrified as her whole body convulsed and went still. "Charlotte?" he cried out.

He stepped to the side as the paramedics went to work on restoring the normal beating pattern of her heart. He heard them shout, "Let's go!" as they lowered the gurney and began transporting her up the stairs. He followed them up and out to the waiting ambulance, parked there with its lights flashing, oblivious to the curious neighbours staring out their windows, or Charlotte's befuddled landlords standing out in the snow, wondering what happened to their tenant in the basement of their home. He hopped into his sports car and chased the ambulance to the nearby hospital.

He parked quickly in the emergency parking lot, barely having thrown the car into park before hopping out and racing to the parked ambulance. He caught up with the paramedics as they wheeled her into the ER.

Charlotte looked motionless and grey on the gurney. Her normally beautiful, shiny, coppery hair was now all matted and caked with blood and vomit. Her usually bright and lit up face was stiff and sad looking.

The paramedics wheeled her into a private exam room, and gently lifted the lifeless looking Charlotte onto the exam bed. They stayed with her until the nurses took over, and a doctor came in. They gave what information they had to the staff, and took off, taking the gurney with them.

Charlotte moaned and cried as the nurses and doctors worked over her, falling in and out of consciousness. She listened as the doctors described her lacerations and the need for stitches. It was too much to hear, and she wilfully allowed the darkness to encase her.

It was in the middle of the night when Charlotte blinked awake, feeling a warm arm wrapped around her. Blinking rapidly, she turned and saw a sleeping Andrew snuggled into her. She shook his arm gently. "Drew?" she whispered.

He grunted and quickly woke up. "Charlotte?"

"Where am I, Drew?" The room smelled terrible, antiseptic like. She heard muffled voices that sounded female. With her eyes fully opened, she glanced around. The light above her bed was soft, lighting up the immediate area, and she noticed the salmon coloured blanket covering her. On her left, the side rail was up, as if preventing her from falling out of bed. She scanned the room further as Andrew moved. It looked like she had a private bathroom and closet.

He sat up, nearly rolling off the hospital bed in the process. He rubbed his eyes and slipped into the chair beside Charlotte as she rolled over. "You're in a private room at the hospital." He blinked and searched her face, watching as the reality of her injuries hit her like a freight train. "I'll give you the Coles Notes version of the night." He shook his head and rapidly listed out, "You were raped. You called me. I called the police. You were brought here and given a rape kit, x-rays, a multitude of blood tests, a pregnancy test, and a CT scan."

Charlotte interrupted, "A pregnancy test?" She paled further. "Is that a possibility?"

Andrew held her hand. "No. Maybe it wasn't a pregnancy test. Maybe it was something to prevent it. I don't know. So much happened so quickly." He saw her visibly relax, and then continued, "You have multiple bruises on your body, some stitches in your head, and a major concussion. I gave a statement to the cops. I haven't called anyone, except my mom, but only to explain you were in an accident. You seemed very upset when I asked if we could call any family members, and demanded I not tell anyone about what happened." He sighed and he carried on. "Your nurse is nice. She took you for a shower, and got you into a clean gown and underwear. You fell asleep and only stopped screaming when I climbed into bed with you."

Charlotte remained pale but watched Andrew as he spoke. "What was I screaming?"

"A combination of things. You were either crying out my name, Joe's, 'NO', or yelling out 'Mom, stop'. I have no idea about the last one." He saw Charlotte cringe as he mentioned the yelling of her mom. "Care to explain that?"

She closed her eyes and muttered, "No."

"Okay then." He stretched out. "How are you feeling?"

She rolled slowly onto her back, grimacing the whole time. She cast her gaze towards the ceiling. "Terrible."

"Do you want something for pain? There's a standing order for Tylenol-Threes if you want."

"I'd rather not." She put her bruised arm over her head, shielding the soft light above her and casting shadows over her bruised face. "Now what?"

"Now we wait. Make sure you're okay and not still passing out. Once that happens, you'll likely be released sometime tomorrow, er, today." The date on his watch reminded him that it was Sunday.

"I'm supposed to work at ten."

"You're not going in, Charlotte."

"But I have to."

"You'll need to take some time off. A couple of days at least. I can call in sick for you."

She turned and stared him hard in the face. "Fine. But don't say anything about what happened. Please."

Andrew groaned. She had nothing to be ashamed of. This wasn't her fault. He sensed that wouldn't help, so instead he said, "I promise to only mention that you were in an accident."

She whispered, "Thank you." Turning gingerly onto her other side and pushing against the rails, she motioned for Andrew to climb back in to bed.

He was so exhausted he didn't argue. He climbed under the covers and felt Charlotte's arm fall gently onto him, and he listened as her breathing became very rhythmic and slow. Holding her hand tenderly, he too fell asleep.

A fter supper on Sunday night, and giving another statement to Constable Ryan, Charlotte got permission to be released from the hospital. The attending doctor gave her some handouts on rape counselling, and encouraged them both to visit a counsellor. After gently patting Andrew's shoulder, she left.

"Will you drive me home?" She sat on the edge of the hospital bed, putting on a pair of oversized sweat pants that the nurse brought her. Charlotte looked carefully at Andrew as she gathered her hair into a low ponytail.

"You want to go home?" The thought upset him more than it seemed to upset her.

"Yes."

"I don't know that your place will be ready for you. I think they still have to clean it up, gather evidence, and all that."

She sighed, folded her arms across her chest, and started to cry softly. "Where do I go then?"

"I don't know." And he really didn't. "What about your parents' place?" He watched her shudder violently with that idea. "Your aunt's?"

"She's rented it out for the month to someone while she's gone."

"Humph. That won't work then."

Charlotte stood up slowly from the bed, her body aching with every movement, as she tenderly lowered herself into the wheelchair the nurse had left with them. While Charlotte wheeled around in the warm entrance to the hospital, Andrew ran around to the emergency room side of the hospital, started his car, and hid the parking ticket he'd acquired. He drove it over to the main entrance to get Charlotte and wrapped his coat around her shoulders. Once securely fastened, he blasted the heat and they drove off.

"Where are we going?" she asked when he didn't make a left out of the parking lot towards her house.

"Someplace safe for now. It's hard to figure out where to go when I can't tell anyone what happened." There was a note of resentment in his voice.

Charlotte looked at him softly. "But you can understand why, can't you?"

"Not really. You did nothing wrong!" He hit the steering wheel as he peeled out of the intersection. "He did."

"You just don't understand." She turned to look out the window and watched the snow-filled trees zoom by.

Andrew drove around aimlessly for a while. Finally, he drove into the parking lot of JT's Pizzeria.

"What are you doing here?" she asked, her eyes wide.

He put the car into park. "I don't know. Maybe your friends are working and can help? I can't think of anything." Andrew shrugged his shoulders.

She glanced at the clock on the dash. It was nearly 8pm so it was highly likely they would still be here. She arched her head and looked in the parking lot. *Yep, there's Joe's car.*

"I don't want to do this, Andrew. I want to go someplace else. Take me to a hotel even." Her voice was a fake version of strong.

He opened his door and came around to help her onto her feet. "I'll follow your lead. Whatever you tell them. They're your best friends, Charlotte. Surely, we'll be able to come up with something for the immediate future." He stood there and extended a hand to her.

She stayed in her seat, but after realizing that he wasn't going to cave and take her away, she begrudgingly took his offered hand. Slowly and cautiously, she pulled herself to a standing position, wincing slightly, and then placed her arms into the sleeves of the leather jacket he'd wrapped over her shoulders. She leaned heavily on him as they shuffled into the restaurant. She was barely at the hostess podium when she heard the familiar voice of her friend Meadow.

"Charlotte? What the hell happened?" the brunette exclaimed as she approached the couple, the panic in her voice matched only by the pace of her steps. "Your face!" She turned into the kitchen and yelled towards the back, "Joe, get out here now!"

Andrew followed Charlotte's lead over to the staff booth across the restaurant. "Can I sit down first, please?" She continued to lean hard on Andrew as she walked towards the table.

Meadow watched in horror when Charlotte sat down, as it looked as though Charlotte was sitting on pins. Joe wasted no time responding to Meadow's urgent plea, and quickly approached the trio.

Charlotte managed to slide into the booth, keeping her face towards the window, as Andrew slid in beside her. Meadow slid in across from them, with Joe sitting on the edge.

"What's going on, Charlotte?" Joe asked, his voice soothing, but sounding very big brother like. He reached out for her hand on the table and she pulled away.

"I'm Andrew, by the way," he said, introducing himself to everyone.

"We know," Meadow retorted, not moving her eyes from her friend. "Charlotte?" They all focused on the one tucked into the corner, shaking.

The copper-haired victim took a long slow breath, and then another, not looking at anyone directly in the eye, preferring to stare out the window. "I need your promise," she said to the window and no one in particular.

"For what?" Joe asked, leaning into the center of the table, trying hard to hear Charlotte's whispers.

She shook her head, and spoke quietly, "Not to repeat what I'm about to say."

"Okay," they both agreed, nodding to each other, then to Andrew and back to watching Charlotte's face as Andrew wrapped his arm around her shoulders.

"It's okay. You're safe here," Andrew noticed that Joe and Meadow again looked at each other briefly before they resumed studying their friend, who was now pale and distraught looking.

She turned her head into Andrew's shoulder, "I can't. I can't say it." She fought to say the words, but couldn't fight the tears.

Andrew looked across the table at her best friends, who were staring at them with looks of concern and horror. "You are strong, Charlotte. Let us help you stay that way."

Her already lowered voice, dropped even further. It was barely audible when she breathed out, "I was raped last night." Her body started to shake violently. "I need to throw up."

"Breathe, Charlotte. Nice and slow. Come on." Andrew coached her, hoping that by encouraging her to focus on her breathing, it would take away from the stomach churning. "Charlotte, it's okay. You're safe here." Andrew whispered once again into her ear.

Meadow and Joe just sat there stupefied, neither moving nor speaking, having heard what she said more by her actions than the spoken words. Meadow broke the thick silence first, whispering, in words that were clearly not thought before spoken, "Oh my gawd, are you okay? That's why you didn't show last night. We figured you were having such a good time that you decided to ditch." Seeing the repulsive look on Charlotte's face, Meadow back peddled, "I'm so sorry."

Joe went to slide out of the booth. "Who is he?"

Andrew took hold of the conversation. He was quiet and yet firm, trying not to draw any further unwanted attention from the other patrons in the restaurant who were starting to stare in their direction. "Sit back down, Joe, and I'll tell you what I know." He explained in as few words as he could, giving the barest of information, not wanting to relive the details himself. "She hasn't decided whether or not to press charges, but all evidence has been collected just in case. Her house is under police care, so I'm trying to figure out where she could hang out for a few days. I'd have her stay at my house, but I still live with my mom, and I'm not sure how that would go over. Charlotte doesn't want anyone to know what happened, either."

After the briefest of moments, Joe started, "Well, that's easily remedied. Come and stay with me, Charlotte," Joe said. "You know I have the space, and it's a very secure apartment building."

Meadow nodded in agreement. "It's really the safest place."

Andrew looked over at Charlotte. "Do you have any other options? You can't stay at my place, and yours is a write-off.

Where else are you going to go? I can grab your clothes from your place, and meet you over at Joe's."

Charlotte remained quiet and unfocused, turned her head away from the group and looked back out the window at the fast food restaurant beside her.

"Come on, Charlotte, say something." Meadow prodded. She reached across to hold onto Charlotte's hands.

She sighed and answered, "Fine. But *I* want to stop at my place and pack." She had no feeling in her voice.

"I don't think that's a good idea, Charlotte." Andrew was shaking his head.

"It's the only way. I know where my stuff is." She continued to stare out the window.

Andrew looked across the table at Joe and Meadow and shrugged his shoulders in a mixture of bewilderment and total confusion.

Joe leaned back in the booth. "Normally Charlotte, I'm on your side, but in this case, I'm going to agree with Andrew."

"No. I want to go. I need to get my stuff," Charlotte said more to Andrew than to Joe.

"Absolutely not, Charlotte!"

"You can't stop me."

"If I'm driving you, I certainly don't have to take you to your place. I can just drive you straight to Joe's."

"Andrew. I need my stuff. Please. I'll be all of five minutes."

Joe shrugged his shoulders. "Good luck arguing with her. Her stubborn streak's a mile long."

Andrew slumped back in his seat, exhausted. He didn't have the energy for arguments. "Fine, Charlotte, but you get five minutes."

"That's all I'll need," she replied.

Joe spoke up, "Okay, I'll leave work now. It's not like it's super busy in here, and I can't go, right Meadow?"

Meadow looked around the half-empty restaurant. "Yeah, it's dead. It's a Sunday night. I'll close for you." She pushed him out of the booth. "Go!"

Joe returned to the booth within a couple of minutes, having donned his coat. "Let's go. I'll follow you to her house," he said to Andrew, "and then you can follow me to my apartment."

Andrew slid out of the booth, and waited as Charlotte lifted herself out gingerly. She walked very slowly and Andrew overheard Joe whisper, "I'm going to kill the son-of-a-bitch that did this."

"Not if I get to him first," Andrew whispered back.

Chapter Seven
✿✿✿

They eventually got into Andrew's sports car, and Joe followed close by in his Mercedes. Andrew thought it unusual that a teenager would have that fancy of a car. Together, they arrived at Charlotte's basement suite a few minutes later. Joe met them at Andrew's car, before his engine had stopped.

Charlotte got out slowly, and stood looking at the house before her. She had lived there for over two years and had always felt safe. Now, everything was different. For a moment she did not move. She simply couldn't; her feet cemented to the cold, snowy ground, holding her firmly in place.

"You don't have to do this, Charlotte," Joe started, standing protectively beside her. "I can go and pack a quick bag for you." He extended his hand. "In fact, give me the keys, and I'll be right back."

Just wait. I need a minute. Charlotte shook her head, and steadied herself. "Give me a sec." She started putting one foot in front of the other, as she inched down the driveway to the backdoor, flanked by her two male friends. *I can do this.* She ascended the two stairs up to the covered back porch. The screen door had crime scene tape across it. She pulled it down slowly, methodically watching it float to the floor. The stainless steel handle turned when she tried to open it. She glanced up at the landlord entrance. A sign indicated all inquiries would be dealt with at the front. *She's nothing if not practical. I'm sure she got a few knocks.*

With hesitation and Andrew right behind, she closed her eyes and slowly descended each stair, one step at a time, until she reached the bottom. *It smells funny in here.* She felt her stomach doing flips, unsure of what to expect. Looking up at the ceiling, she silently turned left and walked into her kitchen. She lowered her gaze slightly and stared above the fridge. *Just look at the purse. It's there on top of the fridge. Don't look around. Focus.* Like a horse with blinders on, she reached out in a painfully slow movement, and lifted her purse up and down, feeling it get lighter as Andrew took hold of it. She turned quickly, shaking violently, and closed her eyes falling against Andrew's chest, silent tears escaping. *What was I thinking? I shouldn't be here. I can't do this.* She pulled herself deep into his jacket, and as close to Andrew as she could.

"Okay, we're done. You go stand over there by the bathroom and we'll finish up." He wrapped his arms around her and escorted her over to the bathroom on the other side of the stairwell.

Charlotte heard Joe announce, "I'm on it!" as he disappeared into the living room, making a sharp turn to the right into her bedroom. She concentrated hard on hearing the drawers open, and the sound of clothes being punched violently into a bag. He emerged a minute later with two duffle bags, and a few hangers draped over his arm. "Grabbing her toiletries," he said as he pushed past them into the bathroom. Things were dropping into the sink as he tossed moisturizers, brushes, and some makeup into the duffel bag. Charlotte continued to bury her face into Andrew's chest. She heard Joe stomp out of the bathroom. "Done. Let's get the hell out of here."

Joe grabbed her a winter coat and exchanged it for the one she wore, passing Andrew's back to him. They watched as Charlotte, with her eyes firmly closed, tapped along the wall until she felt the stairwell and walked up the stairs, leaving her home behind her.

They quietly sealed the door and made their way to their vehicles. Joe put everything into the backseat of his Mercedes, and met Andrew and Charlotte at the car. He helped Charlotte lower into the sports car and closed the door behind her. He walked over to Andrew before he could get into his side. "I didn't expect that."

"What?"

"For everything to be cleaned already. Aside from her furniture re-arranged a bit, it looked, well, normal."

Andrew shuddered. "Well, you didn't see it a couple of days ago."

"You mean last night, amico?"

"Geez, it's only Sunday?"

Joe patted Andrew's shoulder. "Come on, let's go. You need some sleep." Andrew didn't argue. "Okay, follow me to my place. I'll drive reasonable. It's not even five minutes from here. Just park in visitor beside the main doors."

"Thank you," Andrew said.

"Anything for her. She's worth it." Joe's eyes shone with pride and deep love.

"I agree," Andrew whispered to himself.

They both hopped into their vehicles and drove silently to Joe's apartment. The huge cream-coloured tower was called "The Breckenridge" and stood tall amongst the smaller apartments flanking it. Joe pulled in ahead of them, and Andrew watched as the underground parkade door opened and the black Mercedes disappeared. He pulled into a visitor parking stall and was assisting Charlotte out when Joe arrived, carrying all her stuff.

As they followed him through the building's main entrance, Joe unlocked the doors, and headed to the elevator where Andrew watched Joe press "16". Arriving on the top floor, they accompanied Joe as he exited to the left. Andrew looked around noticing that there were only three suites, one at their end of the hall, and two opposite each other at the other end.

Joe unlocked the door and deactivated the alarm. "Home sweet home," Joe pronounced. "Follow me. You've been in here before, Charlotte, but to help Andrew out I'll give a quick tour." He smiled warmly, looking at the pair.

Both were overwhelmed and exhausted looking. Charlotte remained pale, and stood robotically, her hands pulled into the sleeves of her baggy winter coat. Her eyes distant and glassy, reflecting the entrance lights. Andrew kept his hands in his jacket pocket, looking around nervously.

They took a left turn off the foyer and walked down a hallway. Joe flipped on the hall light as they went. "My room's there at the end of the hall," he pointed to the end of the non-descript corridor. "My guest room, which will now be Charlotte's," he said to Andrew as he entered, and placed Charlotte's bags on the massive king sized bed. He took a quick right, opening the bi-folds that hid the huge walk-in closet and hung up the mishmash of clothes he'd grabbed from Charlotte's basement suite. "There's your own private bathroom, with shower." Joe pointed as Charlotte just stood there transfixed. "This is your home now Charlotte, for as long as you need. It's safe here." Continuing on when no one spoke. "I'll get you your own key and give you the alarm code in the morning." He stood there for a minute, and calmly spoke to Charlotte, "I'll be in the kitchen making some tea." After giving her a hug, he bent down and planted a gentle kiss on her cheek.

Andrew nodded, as Joe left. He moved the bags onto the dresser for Charlotte, watching her just stand there in the middle of the considerable sized guest room. He noticed she had yet to move. She stood motionless, arms crossed over her chest, eyes unfocused and ears not hearing or taking anything in; her face was a blank canvas. Sensing she was overwhelmed, he suggested, "Let's go get some tea." Leading her by the hand, they slowly walked out into the hallway, and back towards the foyer.

Andrew was impressed at the size of the place. He whistled as he stepped into the spacious living room, with thick beige carpeting and what he guessed were twelve-foot high ceilings. The living area had an oversized sectional couch that looked super comfortable, with another oversized matching sofa beside it. Both sofas were leather and the colour of a dark sky. A huge white table sat in the middle of the u-shape of couches. A big screen TV sat against the wall surrounded by bookshelves full of movies.

As he turned to his right, he found an amazing kitchen. The counter tops were marble, in a gorgeous dark navy, which upon further inspection also contained several flecks of jewel tone colours. There was an expanse of countertops, along the two walls of the kitchen, ending in a peninsula at the far end. No shortage of space and storage in this kitchen. The cupboards were a dark mahogany, and contained an ample sized pantry. All the appliances were black, and looked fantastic in the spacious kitchen. It appeared like the entire place was lifted from a feature apartment out of *House and Home* magazine. In addition, there was a sit down island, which Joe was standing at, pouring water into a teakettle. He placed the kettle onto the gas stove and turned it on.

"Nice place, Joe!" Andrew whistled again, clearly impressed. "A nice hangout indeed. My mom'd love a kitchen like this"

The tall, lanky friend looked around comically. "Not bad, eh? It was my dad's," he said answering a question written with invisible ink on Andrew's face. "He left it to me in his will. The car was his too. No way I could afford a place this size on my wages."

"Oh," Andrew swallowed, "sorry about your dad." He sat at the island on a tall, bar-height stool, and pulled out one for Charlotte.

"Thanks. I can't say I am. It's been several years, and I really didn't know him very well. Left my mom when I was nine. Hit it big on some stocks, and bought this pretty place. He died a rich man, leaving everything to David and me. I got this suite, and David got the one in Calgary. His way of apologizing maybe? I've lived here ever since. It's a great place and the view's incredible. Lots of walking trails nearby. It's great." Joe looked over at Charlotte. "When was the last time you ate?"

She mumbled inaudibly.

"What was that?" asked Joe, eyebrow raised high, leaning over the island counter to hear her better.

"Hospital." Charlotte locked her gaze on Joe.

He straightened up and went to the fridge. "You need to eat." He dug through and pulled out some food. "Nothing fabulous, but it'll fill your belly." Scooping out some yogurt into a bowl, and grabbing some granola to pour on top, he pushed it towards her after topping it with some fresh berries.

Looking at both men she picked up the spoon, and forced some into her mouth.

"That's it." Joe encouraged as she ate another, and another. "When did you eat last, Andrew?"

"I don't honestly remember." He suddenly felt hungry, possibly hungrier than he was tired, and he was exceedingly tired.

Joe made another yogurt-granola-berry concoction and slid it towards Andrew. "Eat up."

"Thanks," he said, tasted a few bites. "I have class in the morning, and I work tomorrow evening," Andrew stated to Joe, but kept looking at Charlotte, "but I don't want to leave her alone."

"Not a problem, my friend. Mondays and Tuesdays are my days off, and I'll stay with her."

Andrew sighed with relief. "That's great. Thanks. Can I come by after work? It will be later, around ten-ish?"

"Absolutely. Mi casa et tu casa, so feel free to come and go as you choose." Joe took the screaming kettle off the stove and poured the tea. "Want some?" he asked Andrew.

"Sure."

"It's liquorice. Charlotte's favourite," Joe said, winking at Charlotte.

Andrew looked up warmly at Joe. "It's good. She's made it before." He watched as Charlotte finished her bowl of yogurt and started sipping her tea.

After a few minutes, she yawned. "I think I'm going to go to bed." She lowered herself off the stool, slowly, methodically. "Thanks for the food, Joe." She grabbed the empty bowls and went for the dishwasher.

"I got it, Charlotte." Joe removed the dishes from her hands. "Wait until breakfast!" He winked again.

She started walking out of the kitchen. "Are you coming?" she asked in Andrew's direction. "Will you stay with me?" She had a look of trepidation in her eyes, as if asking him to stay would mean she knew she couldn't do it on her own. *I hate feeling so weak, but I don't want to be alone. Bad things happen when I'm alone.*

He glanced at the clock on the stove. Although his mom allowed freedom, he tried to respect that she worried about him when he was gone all the time. "I'll stay until you fall asleep, but then I need to go. I don't want to, but I have class tomorrow."

She looked between Andrew and Joe, trying to remove the panic she felt.

Joe walked over and placed his long arms on her shoulders. "My room's down the hall, Charlotte, and the alarm will be set for any doors or windows opening. All the lights will stay on as well." He squeezed her gently. "I promise you'll be safe here. No one will hurt you here. Ever."

She nodded, slowly and unsure. "Okay. Thank you."

Joe bent down and kissed the top of her forehead. "Goodnight, Charlotte. Credetemi, il mio amore."

"Goodnight, Joe." She reached out her hand to Andrew. They walked down the hall, and into the enormous guest suite. "I'm going to take a shower." She rummaged through the bags on the dresser until she found a blue nightshirt.

"I'll wait here, and put away your clothes." He opened the top dresser drawer and started placing clothes inside. Stopping briefly he asked, "Charlotte, what did Joe say to you, the amour part?"

The sparkle in her eyes was transient.

Sensing that it was perhaps too personal to ask he added, "You don't have to tell me, if you don't want to."

"No, it's okay. It's Italian for 'trust me my love'. Joe's always told me that, ever since..." She shook her head. "Anyways, it's a big brother thing he says."

"Cool, I didn't recognize the language, but it sounded nice."

She tucked her nightshirt under one arm, grabbed the smaller toiletries bag, and went into the ample sized ensuite. She closed and locked the door, and stripped down. Standing in front of the mirror, she couldn't believe the way her face looked. It was the first time she saw herself since the incident. *Oh my gosh! I went out in public looking like this?* A small stitched cut on her forehead. A deep bruise forming on the apple of her cheek. Bruises along her collarbone. Charlotte did a head to toe count of the bruises that were covering her body and lost interest when the number passed thirty. Some bruises, the smallest ones along the length of her forearms, were fading to a nasty yellow colour, but the larger ones on her back and upper arms were turning a deeper shade of purple. Her normally clear, unblemished skin looked like someone had made a poor connect the dots game on it. Her back was a road map of scratches and more bruises. She sighed, opened the shower door and turned the water on. The steam opened her pores, but did nothing to rinse away the molecular filth she felt everywhere. She soaped everything up, noticing that she was very swollen "down there", which surprised her. Shampoo spilled down her face and stung her eyes. She rinsed and started feeling a deep rage boiling within her.

Her thoughts raced through her mind. *I should've just met him at the restaurant. I should've met him at the bar. Why did I have to let him into my house? How could I have been so stupid.* She started throwing her head against the shower stall wall.

Andrew, who was folding up some shirts and placing them into a drawer, heard the noise in the guest suite. He knocked on the door. "Charlotte?" He twisted the door handle rapidly. Locked. "You okay?"

The distressing sound continued.

Suddenly there was a knock on the guest bedroom door. "Everything okay in here? I can hear banging from the kitchen."

"Charlotte," he called out, alarm rising in his voice as he turned to Joe.

Joe knocked a little firmer than Andrew did, and it seemed to stop the banging instantly. "Charlotte!"

"What?" she questioned, a whimper in her voice.

"What are you doing?"

"I don't know," and her voice broke.

The men stood there looking at each other. Both knew that opening the door and entering the bathroom while she was there naked and deeply exposed was a bad idea, and yet they both knew she needed someone. The banging resumed.

"Charlotte!" Joe's firm voice echoed in the guest suite, "We're coming in."

The banging stopped. "NO!" she yelled. "Please, just give me a minute."

"You have one minute starting now. If I hear it again, I'm just coming in."

Charlotte blasted the cold water, cooling down the internal rage she was trying desperately to contain, and rinsed away the remaining soap. Shaking and freezing cold, she grabbed a towel off the shower door's towel bar and started to dry off.

"Thirty seconds."

She wrapped the oversized plush towel around her, unlocked the door and sat on the toilet. She heard it open, and felt the rush of cool air. As the steam cleared, she saw Joe and started to cry again. He knelt on the floor before her as she sobbed, "I'm so dirty still, and full of bruises. Why did I let this happen?"

Joe wrapped his arm around her, letting her cry as he told her, "You didn't let him, Charlotte. He's the bad guy." He picked her up and trying not to put too much pressure on her bruises, carried her out of the bathroom and sat her down on the bed. Andrew grabbed her nightshirt off the bathroom counter, and gave it to Joe. He pulled the purple pajamas over Charlotte's head, and childlike, she tucked her arms into the sleeves, and robotically stood up, letting it fall over her towel wrapped body. Once it hit her knees, she reached under the shirt and released the towel, letting it fall to the floor.

Still sobbing, she climbed into the middle of the bed, pulled the covers up over her, and rolled into the fetal position.

Andrew turned off the bedroom lights.

"NO! Leave the lights on!"

Scared at the way she freaked out, Andrew quickly flicked the switch in the bathroom, providing some glow to the guest suite, as Joe began to lie next to Charlotte. He watched as Joe tenderly wrapped a long thin arm around Charlotte and held her tight.

Joe motioned with his eyes, for Andrew to lie down. The bed was generous enough.

Andrew, still dressed in the same clothes as yesterday, lifted the comforter and climbed underneath. He faced Charlotte, and gently pushed the wet, sticky tendrils of hair off her face, while she was spooned into Joe. He wondered briefly, what an outsider would think, if they were to peek in and see two grown males, snuggling a sobbing female. Dismissing the thought as quickly as it came, because at the moment, he knew Charlotte was safe, encased in love and strength.

His plan was to stay awake and then head home, but Mr. Sandman had alternate plans and before he could resist, Andrew fell asleep.

When he woke up it was morning, as the sunlight streamed in from the east facing windows. Andrew blinked rapidly, taking in his surroundings for an instant. He looked over at Joe, who was already sitting up on the bed, and glanced around. Andrew rubbed his eyes, got out of bed, and looked at the time on his watch. "Shit, it's after nine. I'm late for class."

Joe stood up and stretched.

"That was a rough night. I've never heard someone scream and yell so much in their sleep." Andrew ran his fingers through his bronze hair, trying to fluff out the matted down side of his head. "I didn't think it would ever stop. And then, that high pitched scream of 'Mom, no!' over and over again. What in hell is that all about?" He shook his head. "She did that in the hospital too."

Joe shrugged. "Rough night." He stretched again, touching the nine-foot ceiling as he did so.

Andrew gestured that he needed to make a call. He was going to have to do some explaining to his mom. He tiptoed out of the bedroom.

Charlotte stirred, and prying open her eyes, swollen from crying, looked up at Joe. "Where's Andrew?"

"Making a phone call." He sat down beside her, took a stray piece of her clean but kinky coppery hair, and moved it out of the way of her eyesight. "How are you feeling?"

"Sleepy."

"I'm going to stay here all day, so feel free to sleep. There's no pressure to go anywhere, do anything, or even talk, if you don't want to. I'll call and reschedule our appointments with Mrs. Kennedy and Champ as well."

"Thanks, I don't want to see them when I look like this." For the first time in days, she attempted a smile. She rolled and turned into Joe, falling back asleep.

Andrew tiptoed back in, as Joe got off the bed again. "Everything okay?" he whispered to Joe, noticing that Charlotte had moved and rolled over.

"For now." Joe looked back to the peaceful looking Charlotte. "Everything okay with you?"

"Yeah. I just needed to call and chat with my mom. She was worried when I didn't come home again, but I explained, again, that Charlotte was in an accident and was terrified to be alone. She seemed to accept that, however, I do need to go home, shower, and change. I'll miss class today, but I do need to be at work for four."

"First let me get a breakfast into you."

Andrew shook his head.

"Amico, you need refuelling. You aren't going to be good for anyone if you yourself are not taken care of. Now, come on. I'll make you an omelette."

Andrew nodded and Joe left the guest room. Andrew went into Charlotte's bathroom to freshen up by splashing some cool water on his face. It was only Monday. He just lived through the longest two days of his life. It felt like a month had passed. Drying off, he peeked on the sleeping Charlotte, and left the bedroom, leaving the door ajar.

Andrew heartily ate up his breakfast with Joe. "How long have you two known each other?" he asked between bites.

"Years. Seven or eight maybe? She was in the same class as my younger brother David. He always harboured a crazy crush on her, and was a little pissed when we started dating."

Andrew nearly choked. "You dated her?"

Joe smiled as he leaned on the island. "Yeah, but not for very long, and she was older than when I first met her. She was twelve, going on thirty! We dated a couple of months maybe. It didn't work out for us."

"You dated a twelve-year-old?" Andrew's tone implied deep disgust.

Joe stood up straighter. "NO! God no! That's just wrong." He stated firmly, "Let me clarify. She was twelve when we first met, but we didn't date until she was older." He put the word date in air quotes. "When she was like fifteen, but then I was even older and it was just plain weird."

"How much older are you than Charlotte?" Andrew was suddenly very critical of the man before him.

"Five years."

"When you dated, did you, ah, well, you know?"

"Have sex with her? No. She was fifteen! Besides, kissing her always felt weird. She was too much like a little sister to me, and I know she thought of me like a big brother. I was her protector."

Andrew stared at his now empty plate. "I should've known there was something there between the both of you; she seems very relaxed around you."

Joe laughed a little. "And for that, I'm glad. She's never hidden herself from me. But I've seen her do it with others and you. She's an intensely private person and doesn't tell anyone anything more than they need to know, and even that's pushing it."

Andrew nodded and agreed, "She doesn't share information at all."

Joe looked Andrew square in the eyes, "No, she doesn't!"

"So now what? How can I help her through this if she won't tell me what's going on in her head?" Andrew pushed his empty plate forward towards Joe.

"Wish I knew, amico." Joe put the dishes into the dishwasher. "Wish I knew what she needed. I think the main thing, right now, is for her to know and feel that she's safe."

Andrew looked quizzically at Joe. "Do you know what that 'mom thing' is all about?"

"Not my story to tell." Joe stood up straight and crossed his arms, a look of complete knowledge flashed wordlessly across his face. "For now, with this, we'll take it moment by moment, day by day. Let her call the shots, I guess. She's already expressed a desire for help – her asking you to stay last night had to be monumental for her." Joe wiped down the counter. "I'm going to clean myself up. Help yourself to anything."

"Thanks, Joe."

Joe waved as he walked away.

Charlotte slept all morning, although Andrew could tell it was not a sleep of the peaceful, restful variety. Whenever he checked in on her, she was muttering nonsense words, and had clearly tossed and turned in the bed, as she was now lying diagonally in it, pillows tucked around her like fences.

A ndrew headed home after Joe insisted he get a full lunch. He'd missed a day of work yesterday, and wasn't looking forward to going back in, he wanted to be with Charlotte. When Andrew arrived, Norah was working at the desk. She motioned him towards the office and asked what was going on. Repeating the script he told his mom, all he told her was that Charlotte had a terrible accident, and was still recovering. He hoped she'd be up and ready to return to work soon, but he didn't know when. It wasn't a lie, just a twisting of the truth, and he didn't provide any more details. He laughed at the irony that Charlotte was rubbing off on him.

Feeling melancholy, Andrew went up to the projection room and while the movies were playing, he kept wondering about Charlotte. He replayed the last couple of days over in his mind, shuddering violently at the recall. How his heart was inflating, wanting- no - yearning to protect this fragile lady in his life. Someone who, as of yet, failed to return his unrequited love. He was happy when the phone interrupted his desolate thoughts.

"Projection," Andrew answered.

"Drew. Hi."

He sighed and smiled. "My lady, how are you? It feels like it's been days since I've talked to you. I miss you."

"I miss you too."

"When did you wake up?"

Exhaling, she answered, "According to Joe, about an hour after you left."

"How did you sleep?"

"Horribly. Bad nightmares. I'll spare you the details." Her voice sounded flat.

"Have you eaten?"

"Of course, Joe made sure of that." He could hear a hint of a smile as she said that.

"How are you feeling?"

She sighed, "Achy, and sore."

"Mentally? Emotionally?"

She laughed a weird sounding laugh. "Completely unstable, yet safe for now, and loved."

"I'm happy to hear that."

"Are you coming by after work?"

He wanted to, really. "I can't. I should spend a couple of nights at home. Plus I have class tomorrow. Maybe on the weekend?"

"I'm not going to see you until the weekend?" She sounded as if she were nearly crying suddenly.

"I'll figure something out. I'm working tomorrow night, and Thursday and Friday night." He was working out his schedule. "How about I'll come by on Wednesday, okay?"

He heard her sniffle, "Okay."

"You can call me anytime you want, day or night, okay?"

"Okay," she paused and after a silent minute said, "I'm going to go. Joe's made me some supper."

"Call me before you go to bed?"

"I'll try."

"Talk to you soon," he said as he hung up.

Chapter Eight
✿✿✿

The next few days were baby steps for Charlotte. Joe was home all day Tuesday and into the evening. They spent Wednesday together until Joe needed to head to work at four. He reminded the-still-terrified-to-be-alone Charlotte that Andrew was on his way over from the university, so she'd only be alone for an hour at most. There was supper in the fridge that they could re-heat in the oven when they got hungry.

Andrew and Charlotte made small talk that evening discussing oddball things he'd overheard at work, and some upcoming university events. They also discussed her return to work on Friday. It was going to be her first day leaving Joe's place since she'd gotten there. Andrew was picking her up after university and taking her to work.

The days were manageable with someone around, but night-time was worse, as it played on her fears. She was unable to sleep alone. As hard as tried, she continuously awoke after screaming herself awake from a repeatedly real nightmare, which she would then barefoot it down the hall, sweating. Climbing into bed beside Joe, she managed to keep him awake with her constant tossing and turning from her bad dreams.

By Thursday night, and on Joe's insistence that she would be okay as he was just down the hall, only a few short steps away, with his bedroom door open, and her bedroom door open, with the hall light on, and the apartment armed, she was able to sleep alone in her own bed. She made it through that night, without a peep, but only because she had snuck into Joe's bathroom and taken a huge swig of the Nyquil he stored under his sink. It afforded them both a solid sleep, hers free from nightmares of Chad's return, his free from the screaming.

F riday arrived, and Charlotte prepared for her first day back at work. Andrew picked her up at three thirty, and held her twitching hand on their way down to his car. They drove in silence, listening to a dance mix CD with a strumming beat that matched the way the nervous blood pulsed through her veins. They parked his alabaster-white Fiero in the staff parking lot, and Charlotte tried to calm her racing heart. *I don't know that I should be here yet. I'm too jumpy and scared. My bruises are only just healing.* Her facial and neck bruises had already faded, and those that hadn't, were hidden well with some makeup. Her long sleeve sweater over a t-shirt covered the larger bruises on her arm. She didn't have a huge selection of clothes to choose from, being that most of them were still at her house, but she made do.

"Ready?" Andrew asked as he watched her breathing rapidly. "It'll be okay! Remember, they think you've been in an accident. I wasn't more specific than that, but they'll likely think it's a car accident." He got out of the car, and went over to open her door. He extended his hand and held tightly to hers as they walked down the sidewalk to the front entrance of SEARCH.

Huddled together against the elements, they made it safely into the building quickly, Charlotte's eyes darting around everywhere. She was glad that she wasn't walking so stiff anymore, but couldn't help feeling as if all eyes were on her. *Am I walking normally, like someone who's actually been in a car accident? Not like someone who was violated. What if they can tell by the way I walk, that something happened? Oh geez, I really should've stayed home. I can't do this and possibly have to answer questions. What if I get some detail wrong and they know I'm lying?*

Andrew piped up quietly beside her, "They're just making sure you're okay."

"I hate being the focus of their stares though."

They walked to the GM's office and knocked. Paulette, a former cashier, now a manager, opened the door. "Hi, Charlotte. Welcome back. How are you feeling?"

"Better. Thanks." Carefully, she tucked her purse into a locker while removing her coat. She felt Andrew's gentle hands pull the collar of her t-shirt back up, as it had slid down, revealing a large healing bruise on the bottom of her neck. Charlotte glanced at Paulette who quickly turned around, and in doing so, let on that she'd seen the bruise.

"All good," Andrew whispered, and to Paulette's turned back he asked, "Can I get the key please?"

She grabbed it off the desk and passed it to Andrew. She looked over at Charlotte and back to Andrew. "Is everything okay?"

He looked at Charlotte, and then to Paulette. "Yeah. She's got some nasty bruises from the accident, but she's okay."

Charlotte nodded her approval. "Healing each day." Her voice was unconvincing.

Paulette then launched into a story about how she was in an accident a few years back and the bruises she got, especially the one across her chest where her body slammed into the locked seatbelt. She went on and on about how long it took the bruises to heal, and afterwards heard from a friend that if she had applied vinegar compresses, that the bruises would've disappeared quicker.

"Good to know, I'll try that," Charlotte commented.

Andrew simply said, "Well, thanks." He walked her over to her desk and whispered, "I'm just upstairs if you need me. I'll be down on my break okay?"

"Okay," she whimpered briefly and tenderly gave him a hug.

Charlotte worked her shift without incident, and upon cashing out, hastily made her way up to the projection room. She called Andrew and started to panic when he took more than a minute to come and open the door for her. Constantly searching the depths of the shadowy hallways and the emergency stairwell lurking around the corner, she felt like invisible eyes were watching her.

When Andrew did manage to open the door, Charlotte looked like she was losing control. "Hey, you okay?"

Charlotte took a deep breath, pushed the bad feelings into the pit of her stomach, and said, "Of course, why do you ask?"

He searched her over and replied, "You look as though you've seen a ghost."

"Nah," she said. "All good." Glancing around as she stepped onto the metal grate.

He closed the door behind her and headed down into the projection room. "Sure?"

"Really. Just nerves, is all."

He walked towards her and stopped. "You're safe here."

"Geez, I know that. Why do you keep telling me that?"

Stepping back he replied, "Because I want you to believe it. You don't need to put on a brave face for me, Charlotte. I saw the aftermath and spent the first couple of nights with you." He stood there, a concerned look of confusion on his face. "You know, sometimes I can't figure you out. One minute you are scared to be alone, and the next minute you act all brave."

Charlotte felt bad for the concerned look she saw on Andrew's face. "I'm sorry." She took another deep breath. "I'm just trying to deal with this all. I'm nineteen, an adult. Aren't I supposed to be able to take care of myself?"

"No one's saying you can't, Charlotte." He gathered up some papers and shoved them into his backpack. "So that's it. That's why you're acting this way. But I want you know something. I'm here to help you. That's all. I'd never hurt you. You don't need to put on a brave face for me."

Her voice softened. "Thank you." She reached out her hand to him.

"Don't hide from me. If nothing else, tell me what you're thinking. Promise me you'll try."

"I'll try."

"Okay," he said as he squeezed her hand. He continued to hold it, rumours be damned, after his shift finished as they walked out the main doors into the biting January air. "I could get used to this." He stared down at the bond between them. "Holding your hand all the time."

Charlotte's cheeks warmed. "I could too, but we're just friends, okay? You understand why, right?"

"No, but I'm willing to play along." He smiled at her as they walked the snow covered, curving path to his car, the cold air nipping at their exposed skin.

"My walls aren't ready to come down yet. It's a scary world behind them and I don't want you to see me like that."

"Whatever you're protecting, I can handle."

She blushed, but in seriousness said, "It's my heart I'm protecting, and I can't let you into that yet."

"I do understand. Joe told me it was a dark place." Her eyes popped. Andrew raced to cover, "But he told me nothing, I swear! Ask him. He just told me that it was a dark place, and said it wasn't his story to tell."

"Well, that does sound like something Joe would say." She looked at him, her eyes returning to a normal size as her suspicion faded.

They got into the cold car, and after cranking the engine, he questioned, "Can I ask you something, Charlotte?"

"Sure," she turned to face him. His cheeks were rosy from the walk in the bitter cold, and he had a five o'clock shadow. But he looked serious and adorable, and seriously adorable.

"That night… Why did you call me first? Why not 9-1-1? Why not Joe?"

"You'll think I'm silly," Charlotte turned away as she spoke, her breath visible in the cold air. It left a frosty oval on the passenger window.

Andrew twisted in his seat, "Try me."

She stared at him hard, gazing into his blue-green eyes. Holding a deep breath and fighting back the fearful tears that always surfaced when she remembered any small part of that horrible night, she spoke, "Your face was the one thing I was focusing on. I kept trying to remember every detail of your face, when I was conscious, and then I kept repeating your phone number. You have a rhythmic number, and I just kept the numbers going. In a way, I was able to focus so hard on that, I don't remember much else. Except the pain, and my head banging into floor." She saw him wince a bit. "Sorry." She reached out and grabbed his gloved hand. "But I'm forever glad you came. You were my angel that night. You kept me alive. It sounds crazy, I'm sure." She lowered her head. "As for Joe, well, I knew he was out so I had no way of getting a hold of him." *Plus, he's been through enough with me. I figured he could have this one off.* She wasn't sure, but she thought she maybe saw a tear in his eye.

Charlotte watched his face and saw the dance of emotions flick in and out of his eyes. Calmly he stated, "I've never been so frightened before. That phone call. Your voice was so quiet, and yet I could hear you screaming with panic. It's so hard to describe. And when I got there…" He shuddered uncontrollably. "Well, it's a good thing he wasn't there anymore. I'm totally against corporal punishment, but I would've made an exception for him."

What did I do to him? Will he ever forgive me for dragging him into that? "I'm sorry you had to see the mess, but I couldn't think straight." She gave his hand a gentle squeeze. "For the rest of my life, I'll be forever thankful for you, for being there in my head, saving me from what was really going on, and for the tender care afterwards. I couldn't ask for a better friend." Overcome with the violent memories, she started sobbing, burying her face into the palms of her hands. "I'm sorry. I'm depending on you so much."

"I don't mind you depending on me."

She felt her hands being pulled away from her face and onto her lap. She looked through her blurred vision into his glassy eyes.

"I just wish there was something I could do to help you."

"You are, by just being you." She rested her head against the headrest. "I love you."

"I love you too." He smiled at her.

"You're one of my best friends, Andrew," she offered, "I'll cherish you always."

"Best friends," he said with a hint of rejection in his voice.

Despite the windows fogging up, the car's engine had warmed up and he drove her to Joe's place.

Charlotte let them into the quiet apartment and turned off the alarm. She spotted the note on the side table beside the door that reminded her that Joe was working until three in the morning. She hung up her coat, kicked off her shoes, and padded barefoot into the living room.

She turned around and undid the ponytail she wore, letting her copper locks cascade over her shoulders. "Take your coat off and stay awhile."

Andrew continued to stand in the foyer, his coat and shoes still on. He looked forlornly at her, casting his gaze downwards.

She commented as she walked back to the foyer, "You're not coming in, are you?" She sighed. *Looks like I'm going to be*

*sleeping alone tonight. And by alone, like really totally alone. Just
me, in this huge apartment.*

"I think it's best that I go home."

"If I said I needed you, would you change your mind? At least
stay for a couple of hours?" She stepped towards him.

"I know that you don't really need me," he said, "so perhaps
another night. But thank you for being honest with me." Andrew
gave her an enduring hug goodbye, promising to return in the
morning. He waited until the door closed and locked. Then he
listened with his ear to the door until he heard her punch in the
code that armed the doors and windows. Secure that she was safe
in her fortress, he went home.

Charlotte changed into her pajamas and after another swig of
cough syrup, curled up on the couch. She channel surfed until she
found a movie she recognized. Against her will, sleep beat into
her, and she vaguely recalled Joe picking her up and carrying her
into her bed. She remembered feeling like a little girl as he tucked
her in, feeling a kiss planted on her forehead and hearing the
words, "Good night, sweet Charlotte."

A few days later, Andrew and Joe were in the kitchen.
Andrew was over for dinner and they were laughing and
trading video game tips, when Charlotte paraded into the kitchen.

Joe looked up after slicing a cucumber. "You look chipper."

"Who knew I'd be so happy to get my period."

Joe's colour drained from his face, as he wasn't comfortable
discussing those types of things. Those conversations, he thought,
should only happen between girls.

"What? It's a normal thing to happen." She smiled.

"If you say so."

"Hey, I'm not pregnant with that bastard's baby."

"But we knew that," Andrew added to the conversation, clearly
not as uncomfortable with the topic as Joe was. "Your pregnancy
test came back negative."

Charlotte remembered sitting in her doctor's exam room, ten
days after the incident, waiting nervously for the results of the
blood test. "Yes, but this is just more proof. I'm very relieved.
Can you imagine what a pregnancy conceived by..." she couldn't
say the word, "... well, let's just say I'm glad I'm not pregnant."

The remainder of January steadily improved. Charlotte felt more secure, day-by-day, in being alone, both during the day and especially at night. She was no longer being shuttled around, having picked up her car from her house. Refusing to enter her suite, she instead sat in the warm sports car with Andrew. It took awhile to get the car started as it had been sitting in the cold weather, unplugged, but with a little love, it warmed up. Joe got her a parking pass, so she got to park in the heated underground parking conveniently parked beside Joe's Mercedes, which had the stall nearest to the elevator.

One particularly bad Saturday, Charlotte was working the one to nine shift. Andrew had called down to inquire how things were going, and uncharacteristically, she suddenly snapped at him. He came down just before five and told her to grab her coat; they were going out for a bit. She shook her head no, and Andrew stomped over to the GM's office and knocked on the door.

Paulette answered.

Andrew demanded to Paulette, "I'm taking Charlotte out for her break. I'll have her back when she's calmed down."

"It's been a rough day for everyone, Andrew," Paulette told him. "Charlotte isn't the only one who's been screamed at today."

He looked over to the cashier's desk and cocking his bronzed head asked, "Does everyone else look like they're on the edge of a breakdown? She needs a break."

Paulette looked over and couldn't help but agree. Charlotte did look like someone who was one angry customer away from snapping, or worse, crying in front of the customers. "Fine, but have her back soon."

Andrew laughed sardonically. "I'll have her back when she's calmed down, and not a minute before." He yelled across the small distance, "Charlotte get your things and let's go."

She stared long and hard at him and shook her head no.

Andrew advanced towards the desk. "I'm not asking you. I'm telling you!"

Charlotte put up her hand in a stop position, and answered, "Fine! I'm coming." She scowled as she stomped past him into the office, and grabbed her bag and coat. "See you soon," she marched past Paulette.

Andrew held her hand firmly as they raced out to the parking lot and passed a bus full of chattering customers who were just leaving. Charlotte shivered, and Andrew knew it wasn't from the cold. They needed to move faster. He unlocked the car door, and she slid in, sinking into the moulded vinyl seat as he closed the door and went to his side, dusting off the fresh layer of snow on the car. He didn't even have to look at her, once he got back in, to tell she'd been crying.

"Rough day eh?" he asked putting the car into reverse.

She wiped her tears, looking out the window at the dark roads. "Where are we going?"

"Food court at the mall."

"That works."

"What's bugging you? You've never snapped at me before."

"Customers. Irritated customers."

He looked at her, at her watery eyes, and just knew that that wasn't the problem. "What's really bugging you? You've had days before where the customer's never happy, and you've handled it way better than this."

She looked at him thoughtfully, and then stared ahead. Remaining resolute in her quietude, she said nothing until he had pulled into a parking spot a few minutes later.

"What?"

"It's nothing."

"It's something. You're a wreck." They exited the car and made a mad dash for the door.

She stomped her feet at the entrance of the mall, kicking off the freshly fallen snow. "I think I saw him."

Andrew didn't need her to elaborate further on who the "him" was. "Charlotte, you need to call the police. You should've called me."

"And what would you've done? By time you came down, he would've been gone. Even more so with the police."

"Are you going to press charges?"

"Not likely."

Andrew's mouth dropped. "Really? Charlotte, he'll just keep doing it to others. It'll get worse each time."

Charlotte shook her head. "I can't do it. I can't relive it over and over again. I don't remember that much and that which I do," she shuddered violently from head to toe, "I wish I didn't."

Andrew didn't argue with that. "I don't need to remind you that you're still physically healing from ... from ... that creep."

He placed his hand against the small of her back and led her into the darkened food court, a neat little place where only the lights from the dozen or so food vendors lit up the small, round area. Decorated with cars cut in half, hanging from the ceiling with their hood/tail lights blinking, it added a weird sort of ambience to the place.

"When did he come in?" Andrew asked as he led them to a table near the corner. It was darker there, and fewer people.

She shrugged her shoulders. "Sometime this afternoon, just before you called down."

A thought popped into Andrew's head. "Did he use a credit card?"

"No, cash."

"Well, there goes getting a full name," he said, and then questioned, "Was he alone?"

"He could've been, I guess. I didn't serve him, Colin did. I didn't pay attention to what he bought." She shivered again. "I was frozen, so to speak."

"Charlotte, you have to throw me a bone here. Give me something to work with."

"Am I on trial and don't know it?" she said rather loudly.

"No, I'm sorry! I just want that asshole behind bars. He needs to pay for what he did."

She stared blankly at him. "I'm not that strong. I can't face him and put him behind bars."

"You underestimate your strengths, Charlotte."

"No, I don't!" She smacked the table in protest and shook her hand from the stinging slap. Glancing around, she noticed a few patrons staring at them. Lowering her voice, and stretching across the table she said, "You don't understand how humiliating it'll be for me. I'll be the one on the stand reliving every awful second. I'll be the one they're judging, wondering if I gave off the wrong message, and they'll question everything I did, or didn't do. They'll ask why I let him come over, instead of meeting him somewhere. They'll make it look like it was my fault it happened." Her voice quivered as she glanced around nervously.

"You don't know that for sure."

She glared at him, and even in the darkened space, he could see the colour of her eyes changing from hazel green to dark brown, like they did when she was upset. "You're right. I don't know that for sure; however, I do know for sure that I suddenly need a cigarette."

Andrew gave her a puzzled look. "You don't smoke."

She glanced around the other food court patrons. "I do when I'm stressed."

He continued to stare at her. "I've never seen you smoke before, you know when...," he trailed off.

"I'll be right back," she said getting up and walking over to another patron. She came back and sat down, smoking the bummed cigarette.

Andrew blew the smoke away. "Yuck."

"Sorry." She cleared the air between them with a wave.

"Where have you been smoking?" he asked trying to understand how she'd managed to keep this hidden from him.

"Joe's balcony."

"Does he know?"

"He offered them to me, so I assume he knows," she said sarcastically.

"Hmmph," he replied. "How long have you been smoking?"

"A few years."

"Oh," was all he could get out. After watching her take a few disgusting drags off her cigarette, he asked, "So, what do you want to eat?"

She glanced around at her options, nothing really catching her interest. "I'm not super hungry. I don't know."

He stood up. "You need to eat."

She took another drag and blew it behind her. "Surprise me then." She finished it off before he came back and then popped a mint from her pocket into her mouth, hoping to mask the smell.

Andrew returned and placed before her a tray with two burgers, two fries, and two chocolate milk shakes. "Dig in," he said, unable to take his eyes off her. "Feeling better?" he asked after a silent dinner.

"The smoke definitely helped."

"I had no idea."

"Hey, we can't all be perfect."

He muttered something unintelligible. "Anyways, about that guy..."

"Drop it please."

"No, I want you to be safe. And once that loser is behind bars, you'll be safer."

"Yeah, until he gets out, and then I'm his number one target."

"It wouldn't be like that."

"Can you guarantee that?"

"No," he replied solemnly, "I can't."

"So, let it go please." Eventually, she started to relax a little as the conversation lightened up. Knowing she was a huge Star Wars fan, he mentioned that he had rented the trilogy and re-watched it. When they started debating the moment that Han and Leia fell in love, she started to smile.

Andrew checked his watch and showed Charlotte. It was nearly six thirty. "Are you ready to go back?"

"Yeah, we kind of have to. There won't be a seven o'clock show if you're not there to run it."

She grabbed the tray of wrappers and empty cups, and tossed them into the nearby trash can. "Thanks for rescuing me."

He winked at Charlotte. "You are most welcome." He reached for her hand and he kissed it lightly. "I'll always be here for you."

They walked out of the food court, and back out into the cold air. The temperature felt like they dropped a few more degrees, as the wind howled, blowing the light snowflakes all around them. Yet neither of them felt the chill when they huddled into each other as they walked back to the car.

The day after Valentine's Day, Charlotte, with her posse of friends, Andrew, Joe, and Meadow, ventured over to her basement suite to help her get moved out. They spent that one brief afternoon in February packing up what Charlotte wanted to keep. Whatever they didn't take out that day, she was getting rid of. The moving crew, scheduled to come early next week, would pick up and haul the junk over to Goodwill. They'd take anything remaining - the loveseat, her stereo, her bed, and the bistro table and chairs. She paid them a lot of money to do it, and she was not interested in taking the time to try to sell it, or to keep it in storage for who knows how long.

She found that aside from a few photo albums, a box of books, a garbage bag of clothes and a box of her personal things, there wasn't much she wanted. Even her Christmas tree still sat in the corner of her apartment. She'd had plans to take it down, but that plan quickly derailed because of the "accident". Charlotte picked off the few ornaments that were on it, but left the tree as it was.

Meadow seemed to have the strongest stomach of the four of them, and she tasked herself the duty of cleaning out the fridge and cupboards. Charlotte, understandably, couldn't even look towards the kitchen. She heard items hitting the garbage bag, and could only guess what the inside of the fridge would look like, and smell like, six weeks without having moved any of it. Charlotte's few cooking supplies were boxed up and marked GOODWILL.

They packed up the back of Meadow's truck with the few boxes of Charlotte's stuff, and aside from that day, Charlotte returned to her basement suite to let in the moving team, and then the maids to do a moving out clean. She never ventured down into her basement suite again. The moving company packed up her remaining items and took out her belongings, while she sat beside Andrew in his locked car. When the maids signalled that all was done and her place was super clean, she knocked on the landlord's door.

With Andrew at her side, she got her damage deposit back and signed her move out forms. She cried with relief as they drove away that final time, and to her new home - the Fortress – the nickname Andrew had given Joe's apartment.

Andrew surprised Charlotte with a gift - a long rectangular box. "Here, a housewarming present for you."

"You got me a gift? Andrew, you shouldn't have." She sat slumped in the Fiero, parked in visitor parking at the apartment, the car still running, as Andrew was off to work. Eagerly and smiling, she tore off the cherry blossom wrap and asked, "A lava lamp?"

"Yes, a lava lamp." He watched her face, seeing confusion tug at the corners of her lips. "It's orange see, as I know you love that colour when it's in the sky. It's rare and beautiful." He pointed to the picture on the box. "The globs rise and lower when it's turned on so it's very calming to watch. Plus, it's a great nightlight. You can leave it on all night and it won't disturb your sleep, because it's not too bright." He smiled.

She looked at the box and back to Andrew. With a genuinely grateful voice she exclaimed, "Thank you Andrew. It's the most perfect and thoughtful gift I've ever received." She held it close to her chest.

"Don't shake it though, it causes the blobs to mix with the other fluid and then it doesn't work as well."

"Thank you. I promise to take good care of it." She got out of the white car. "See you later?"

"Yeah, I'll come over after work."

"Bye." She stepped back and watched him drive away.

Chapter Nine
✿✿✿

Charlotte sat out on the balcony the first week of April. She had just returned from a long run. It was cool, but not cold, the first sign that spring was finally coming. She didn't even bother to turn on the tower heater. Instead, she sat bundled up in a blanket from the couch, and sprawled out in the lounger, wearing a hooded sweatshirt with the words "Golden Bears" across it. The sun was setting, casting swatches of faded yellows and golden oranges across the western sky.

She was smoking a cigarette when Joe slid open the patio door and came to join her. He wore a matching green sweatshirt over his tee. David, Joe's younger brother, had bought them each sweatshirts from the university as a Christmas present a few years back, after the one semester he spent there, before he transferred to U of C. The forest colour complimented the muted green colour of Joe's eyes, and the setting sun highlighted his golden hair, making him look ethereal, a real catch, just not for her.

"Hey, what's up?" he asked, gazing at her with a curious glance. He grabbed at the pack of smokes on the table and pulled one out.

"Watching the sun set." She laughed. "What are you doing?"

"Sitting here with you."

"Haha," she chuckled.

"Can I ask why there are so many fruits and vegetables in the fridge?"

She smiled shyly. "Sure you can ask."

"I thought I just did." He lit up the smoke and stretched out his long legs. The deck was wide enough that even his legs didn't touch the white metal banister enclosing them.

"Fine," she started saying before she took a long drag. Exhaling she continued, "Jason helped me."

"Really? Did he now?"

"Yes."

"You've been spending an awful lot of time at the grocery store, Charlotte, and I'm going to blame Jason for that."

Her eyes twinkled. "It gives me something to do. Andrew's been so busy lately with school and studying. He writes his finals in a couple of weeks, and I don't want to distract him." She stared out into the distance. "He's been applying for a variety of scholarships too, so he spends whatever free time he can find looking through the books to see what he can qualify for."

"So you've been hanging out at the grocery store?"

"Yeah. It's been nice."

"I'll bet."

"He asked me out."

"Jason?" Joe blew out a grey coloured breath, trying his best to make a smoke ring.

"Yeah, we're going to go out on Monday night."

Joe took another puff from the cigarette. "I thought you and Andrew were an item though?"

"I wish." She shook her head. "I mean..." she tried to cover, "I mean that we're not. We're not an item. "

"But the hand holding and stuff?"

"Just friends." She took a drag and blew it away, stamping out her smoke in the ashtray. "He's never asked me out since the first time."

"You're not leading him on are you?"

"Oh gosh, I hope not. I told him I wanted to just be friends."

"I've seen the way he looks at you, Charlotte, and more importantly, I've seen the way you look at him."

"And how's that?" She adjusted the blanket on her lap. With the sun deeply set, the air felt much cooler. *Is it that obvious how I look at him? But I can't date him. Because then it ends badly, and we lose that something special we had before we started dating. And then it's ugly. I need Andrew to be around and by not dating him, I think that's a good thing. Can't I be just friends with him, like I am with Joe?*

"You look at him like he's a gift that you desperately want to open before Christmas morning." Joe re-crossed his sweatpants covered legs and tugged on his sweatshirt. "But I'm curious about this thing you have going with Jason, so why don't we double date on Monday? Then I'll know if it's something I should continue to be curious about." Joe looked at her, the corners of his smile turning up.

Charlotte looked expectantly at him, a smile crossing her face. "With who?"

"Chelsea?"

"You like her?"

He nodded.

"Well, she's very cute, the couple of times I've seen her. You'll make an adorable couple." She playfully punched him in the arm. "When are you going to ask her out?"

Joe smiled and put out his smoke. "Tomorrow. She's in for the evening."

"I hope she'll say yes."

"My powers of charm have yet to be used. She'll say yes," Joe said jubilantly. "Aren't you cold?"

She shook her head. "Not at all."

"I'm going in. Brr…" He stood up and opened the patio door. "Do you want me to turn on the patio heater?"

Looking behind her towards the tower heater and then back to Joe, she shook her head. "I'll come in when I see the first star to wish upon."

Joe walked over to the edge of the balcony and gazed up staring hard. "There's one." He pointed towards the southeastern sky.

Charlotte moved to stand beside him and looked in the general direction he'd pointed. "Where?"

"There, that orange-ish one."

"Joe, that's Mars, not a star."

He turned around and leaned on the banister. "Well, then I'm glad I didn't make a wish on it."

"Me too!"

They laughed together as Joe walked inside, hanging his head out he reminded, "Don't stay out too long, it's cold."

"I'm good." She smiled inside as he closed the patio door.

The next day, Charlotte and Joe walked over to Cariatas Covenant. The seniors' complex was much closer to the Fortress than it had been to the basement suite Charlotte used to occupy. They entered the double doors, signed in, and made their way down the green-carpeted hallway to the open lounge area. No matter how many times they visited, the pungent smell of ammonia and old people always hit Charlotte like a freight train. She liked the open lounge area as the fresh flowers hung in baskets from the ceiling, giving the space a fragrant break from the antiseptic smell.

Grey-blue eyes greeted her before she sat down. "Good morning, Champ." She smiled and placed a kiss on his cheek.

"Mmm…mmm…more… more.. ning… ning…," he stuttered out. His speech had had another set back with a mini stroke a few weeks earlier, making his words harder to form. Still, he always tried his best when she was around.

As they usually did when they arrived, Charlotte and Joe produced a small container filled with fresh baked goods. This week, Joe, with Charlotte's assistance, had made what he called 'Bountifuls' – a sweet treat made from super healthy ingredients but tasted like a decadent peanut butter cookie. Tenderly, she uncurled Champ's gnarled fingers and tucked one into his palm. Bringing the cookie up, he happily gummed up what he could get in, and she helped him chase it with a sip of luke-warm coffee.

"How's that Champ?" Joe asked.

He nodded his head, looking down towards the container.

"Would you like another?"

After seeing another bob, Charlotte tucked in a second cookie into his palm. "You ready to kick my ass at crib?" She pushed the deck of cards and crib board closer to him.

The elderly gentleman, with a full head of snow white hair, shook his head.

"Maybe next time?" she asked, and then grabbed a cookie for herself. "Mrs. Kennedy in her room?"

Mrs. Kennedy's Alzheimer's condition got worse over the last couple months. Joe and Charlotte were strangers to her on her "bad" days, and when that happened, she preferred to stay in her room rather than come visit. It upset her when she couldn't remember who Joe and Charlotte were, as she figured she should know them. She was easily frustrated, and her caregivers suggested that she visit, but she refused.

Joe and Charlotte had been weekly visitors for over two years, and even though Mrs. Kennedy and Champ were not family to either of them, she thought of them as so. It pained Charlotte to not visit with Mrs. Kennedy, who she thought could resemble her grandmother.

She wiped away a tear as she finished her cookie and looked over at Joe. He smiled at her, as though he could read her mind. He gave her a nod, and Charlotte launched into telling Champ about the newest movie playing at work.

Champ looked at her, and stuttered out, "You... you... spp... eak... of love."

Charlotte looked over at Joe, who nodded in agreement. "I did no such thing."

"You can hear it in her voice, can't you, Champ? They way she speaks about Andrew."

The white-haired man gave her his best lop-sided smile. His good hand curled towards his chest, and stabbed against him. "The... the... heart... kn... kn...knows what... it... it... wants." His aged blue-greys stared hard at her.

Charlotte's mouth dropped.

Joe laughed.

Champ's eyes lit up. He nodded.

Joe tapped Champ's good hand, and leaned closer to the octogenarian. "I've been telling her that for some time. Thanks for the confirmation." He winked.

She sat there indignantly, eating another cookie and finishing up her Styrofoam cup of terrible tasting coffee. It was horribly bitter, and no amount of milk and sugar were having an effect on it.

After they finished treats and conversation, Charlotte tightened up her sneakers, and raced Joe home on foot, taking the longest route home. She thought long and hard about what Champ said about the heart knowing what it wants.

Chapter Ten
✿✿✿

After Andrew's finals, he was over at The Fortress dining with Joe, his new girlfriend Chelsea and Charlotte. Joe had put together a fancy little meal for the four of them to celebrate his promotion to manager at JT's Pizzeria.

In the middle of the meal, the phone rang. Joe grabbed it.

"Hello? ... sure, can I tell her who's calling?... okay, just a sec..." He passed the phone to Charlotte. "It's Jason."

Andrew mouthed, "Jason?"

Charlotte jumped up and grabbed the phone. "Hey... good, just eating... sure, where? ... that sounds good... meet you there at seven?... Great, see you Friday." She hung up and walked back to the table to rejoin the silent group.

Andrew stared at her. "Who's Jason?"

"Uh oh," Joe chortled and looked back and forth between Andrew and Charlotte.

Charlotte shifted in her seat. "He's someone I'm sort of seeing."

"Like a boyfriend?"

"Ah, I don't know if we are officially dating." She took a bite of her pork roast.

Andrew put down his fork. "When did this start, and why didn't you tell me?" His voice pitched higher.

She turned to face him. "When would there have been a chance, Andrew? You've been so busy studying for your finals, and researching and applying for scholarships. I think since spring break I've seen you for a total of ten hours, and that's only when we pass by each other at work." She peered at him. "I wasn't going to drop it on you. It's no biggie, really. We're not serious about each other." *He doesn't mean to me what you think he means, Andrew. I want to be with you, but I can't be with you. To let you in would be to give you my heart, and I'm afraid of what you'll do when you have it. At least with Jason, it's meaningless. Just a guy. Someone to go out with.*

He rubbed his stubble covered chin, placing his thumb over his lips for a moment. "I know I had a lot on my plate, and I'm sorry if you thought I was ignoring you, but I didn't think you'd start dating someone."

"Because I can't? Last time I checked, I wasn't with anyone else." *Because we're not a couple, you fool, so stop acting like we are.*

Andrew started, "No, I guess you're allowed to date. I just wish..." he stopped himself as he wiped his hands on his napkin.

Joe answered for him, "He just wished it was him that you were dating. Am I right?" Joe's eyes sparkled with that comment. He enjoyed trying to push the two of them together, in less than subtle ways.

Andrew's cheeks flushed a deep crimson. "It's not like that, Joe."

"Sure, sure," he commented and finished his food, and then refilled his and Chelsea's glass with wine.

Charlotte continued to look between Joe and Andrew, multiple thoughts racing through her head. *What the hell, Joe! You know I can't date co-workers. It never ends well, remember? And Andrew... what would you do if you knew me. Like really knew me. I'm a walking disaster. A magnet for bad luck. Surely you can do better?* Her face slumped as she thought.

"What are you thinking, Charlotte?" Andrew asked in direct response to the change in her facial expressions.

She shook off the thought. "Nothing."

Looking at her peculiarly, he rested his elbow on the table and asked, "How did you and Jason meet?"

Shifting her gaze from her thoughts to Andrew, she responded, "At the grocery store. He works there part time in produce, and since Joe and I are working different shifts, we don't shop together anymore, so I've been going in the evenings."

"Frequently," Joe added, leaning back with a mischievous grin on his face. He was enjoying himself.

Charlotte shot him a look and continued, "He was helping me select the better fruits and vegetables, and then he started flirting with me…"

"And she reciprocated," Joe interrupted. "Have you seen the inside of our fridge? We have a lot of produce in there! No chance of getting scurvy in this place."

Charlotte tucked a stray copper strand behind her ear. "Anyways, he asked me out for coffee. I met him at the coffee shop. Harmless right?" She looked up into Andrew's waiting blue-green eyes. "And then coffee led to a dinner out, sometimes a movie. Always someplace public."

Andrew couldn't believe his ears. "How long has this been going on?" He ran a hand through his hair and took a quick sip from his wine glass, looking briefly between Joe and Chelsea. She was clearly uncomfortable and not wanting to get involved in the conversation.

Charlotte thought it over and vocalized, "A month?"

"A month? I see." Andrew was silently discouraged, as it started right after spring break, in the middle of an intense round of studying where he wasn't purposely ignoring her, but not spending time with her either. Dammit. He needed to learn that she needed quality time with him, especially if he ever wanted her to be his girlfriend.

The atmosphere around Charlotte had changed. Andrew's shoulders were tense and his relaxed nature was long gone. Joe was done with his embarrassing comments as he seemed indifferent suddenly and picked at the remainder of his food. Chelsea was drinking back the wine at an astonishingly impressive speed. Joe winked at Chelsea and then suggested to both Andrew and Charlotte, "Why don't you double date?" He raised a golden eyebrow while looking at Andrew. "You could meet him and see what he's like. He seems pretty nice."

"You've met him?"

"Of course. I do shop for groceries too." Joe laughed.

Charlotte unexpectedly perked up. "No, that wouldn't be good."

Andrew peered at her. "Jealous? That I couldn't find someone to join me, us?"

No, I know you could. You're so attractive. Even though I can't date you, I just don't want to see you with someone else. So yeah, I am jealous. Besides, who would you bring? She shifted uncomfortably in her seat and conceded briefly, "Sure, a double date sounds fun!" She snorted very un-ladylike. *There's no way you'd give up a work shift... Hmm..* "Why don't you join us on Friday night?"

His brows furrowed as he mulled it over. "Sure. Friday. Just tell me where."

Seriously? She looked astonished. "Earls, 7pm."

"Great." He dug back into his food, and helped himself to a second piece of pork roast.

The tension in the room was thick enough to slice through, but Chelsea managed to diffuse it by knocking over the refilled wine glass in front of her. Eventually, happiness re-joined the meal as talk turned to summer plans. The ladies cleaned up the dishes, while the men went into the living room and decided on a movie from Joe's expansive collection to watch.

O n Friday night, they met at Earls. Charlotte jumped out of her vehicle and ran under the overhang of the main doors to take shelter from the wicked lightning storm raging in the heavens. Wearing high heels, she nearly tripped on a lip of the doormat and stumbled into Andrew's back.

"Hey, Charlotte," he said turning around. In front of him was Erin, a co-worker from the gift shop.

"Hi, Andrew, Erin," she uttered checking out the knee length skirt Erin wore, just visible beneath the long jacket. Her brown hair twirled into a cute ballerina style bun, and her fringe brushed nicely above her eyes. Charlotte had to admit that Erin was beautiful, and seeing Erin before her made her feel less than average. She'd always believed in being a no fuss type of girl - no makeup, hair left as God intended, which was usually wavy, and wiry. Her aunt once described her look as lazy, but to Charlotte it was natural. She never wanted to be more than who she really was.

Tonight though, was different. Charlotte had tried to apply makeup, but thought it made her look clownish, so she washed it off, opting instead for a dusting of translucent powder to hide the shine of her pale skin. Swapping her standard issue black jeans and sweatshirt for a long black skirt and a sapphire coloured top made her feel uncomfortable. The fact that she was also in the only pair of heels that she owned, didn't help with her comfort. She wondered how women walked in those shoes every day.

Charlotte looked out into the parking lot, cringing almost violently when she heard the crack of thunder overhead, as she waited for Jason. He arrived shortly and joined the trio under the overhang. Charlotte introduced Jason to her friend Andrew, and his date, Erin. Jason extended his hand, and firmly shook Andrew's and then Erin's hand.

Jason was shorter than Andrew expected, with a small Buddha belly, and a receding hairline. Dressed in plain black pants, with what looked like a yellow polo shirt covered by a brown fleece jacket. Andrew pegged him at about forty years old, and as he thought it, questioned what a man that age was doing with a nineteen year-old. Then he wondered what exactly Charlotte found attractive about this man.

Charlotte stood under the overhang feeling awkward and uncomfortable. Jason led the group into the restaurant with Charlotte at his heels, and Andrew directly behind.

He commented close to her ear, in a whispering tone, "Couldn't find anybody younger? What is he, forty or something?"

She pivoted and under her breath said, "He's twenty-five." She saw Andrew flinch.

They sat and ordered drinks, before ordering their entrees.

Charlotte constantly looked self-conscious and uneasy, tugging and readjusting her blouse, which was lower cut than he'd ever seen her wear before. He thought she looked magnificent, if not a little distressed. He was happy to see her wearing something other than dark clothes. The sapphire colour was breathtaking against her pale skin, perking it up slightly.

Charlotte downed her first drink rather quickly and felt the immediate changing affects as her body reacted to it. Her cheeks started to flush, and her eyes were not so focused either. *What, Andrew? Why are you looking at me like that?* She'd hardly eaten anything, so by the time she had her third drink, she was a goner.

The bad jokes soon followed, and when it came time to go to the bathroom, Andrew insisted Erin help her.

When the ladies were out of earshot, Andrew stated, "I think Erin and I'll drive Charlotte home tonight."

Jason scoffed. "I don't think so. She'll be coming home with me. She's usually like this."

"Drunk?"

"Yeah." He leaned a little closer to Andrew. "Between you and me, since you're her friend and all, I think she needs help."

"How so?"

"I think she has a drinking problem. She orders drinks every time we go out. Even when I don't. And not just one either. She once snuck in a coffee mug with vodka and coke into the afternoon showing of that Johnny Depp movie."

Andrew scratched his chin. "Really?" This puzzled him. It was so out of character for Charlotte. "How's she getting home each time then?"

Jason fiddled with a spoon. "I drive her home. She never lets me up to her apartment though. I think that roommate of hers doesn't allow her company."

"Who, Joe?"

"Yeah. I guess he takes her to get her car the next morning. But don't worry, I'd never let her drive drunk. If she was that insistent, I'd call the cops."

"I think you just earned a bit of my respect."

Jason smiled awkwardly. "Thanks."

Andrew cocked his head. "They're coming back."

Charlotte stumbled to the table, with Erin tightly holding her arm for support. Erin glared at Andrew, but neither Charlotte nor Jason noticed. She staggered in her torturous heels and unintentionally fell into her seat beside Jason. Then she started getting louder. The staff told her to settle down or they'd force the party to leave. The copper-haired beauty sat quietly giggling at the table, her date completely oblivious to this out of character behaviour.

Finally, the awkward evening came to an end when the bill arrived. Andrew shook hands with Jason and gave a hug to Charlotte, whispering for her to call him in the morning. Snuggling into Jason, she giggled a goodbye and waved.

As they got into Jason's truck and drove away, Erin glared at Andrew. "She wouldn't freaking shut up in the bathroom."

"Oh yeah, about what?"

"You. Must've said your name a hundred times."

The next morning came and went, and by the early afternoon, Andrew finally got the call he'd been waiting for.

He picked up the phone after answering "projection", and was pleased to hear Charlotte's voice on the other end of the line. "Good afternoon, Charlotte."

"Ssshh, Drew, you don't need to be so loud."

"Hung over, are you?" he roared as he sat smiling on the little desk in the projection room.

She sighed, "You have no idea. My head's pounding."

"What are you up to today?"

"Don't know, day off," she paused, and then asked, "what did you think of Jason?"

The line was quiet for a moment. "Not much."

"Really?"

"Yeah. He's not bad. Old looking for sure, but... you can do better. You certainly didn't seem yourself last night though, and that bothered me. A lot."

"Wow."

"I guess the better question is, what do you think of him?"

"He's okay. He's fun, and he makes me laugh."

"Nothing wrong with laughter, unless it's alcohol fuelled."

He sounds mad. "What do you mean by that?"

"Do you get drunk every time you're together?" It was not so much a question as much as it was a statement. "He thinks you might have a drinking problem!"

She thought about it a minute, "Really? He thinks I have a drinking problem? How odd." Charlotte laughed then. "Well, I don't drink when I'm grocery shopping, so clearly I'm not a raging alcoholic." Sarcasm floated off her tongue.

"But when you go out on a date with him?"

"I have a couple of drinks, yes."

"Do you know how many drinks you had last night?"

"One, two?" *I wasn't keeping track.*

"Try four!"

"Four? Wow. Guess that explains the hangover this morning."

Andrew's side of the line sounded like he snorted. "Yes it should. How sick did you get?"

"Not as sick as I should be. Maybe it's just wine that makes me sick, after mass consumption."

Andrew's heart jumped when he thought of that wonderful night, many months ago where she had kissed him, but sadly didn't remember.

Her sharp voice brought him out of his reverie. "And what was the big deal with bringing Erin? Why her?" Charlotte sounded angry.

Andrew's voice cracked with laughter, "Jealous?"

"Yes," she said before she could stop herself. *Shut up! Why did I not think before I said that! I'm such an idiot!*

The line between them was silent for many heartbeats and breaths. He truly didn't expect her to say yes, but he'd hoped. He jumped off the little table and paced the floor with the receiver pressed firmly into his ear, hearing her breathe, and waiting for further conversation.

Charlotte was mad at herself for not having control over her mouth, and she abruptly ended the silence by speaking up first, "I gotta go."

"Charlotte?"

She sniffed. "I'll talk to you later, okay? I gotta go."

No goodbyes, just the line going dead.

Charlotte went back to work on Sunday, a day shift, passing Andrew at the end of her shift when he started his.

"Look, Charlotte, about Friday." He gently reached for her arm, as she turned away. Instead, he caught the edge of her sleeve.

"It's okay, Andrew." She pulled it free, trying in earnest to smile at him. "I need to cash out, and you need to get upstairs. You'll be late." Not looking back in his direction, she pushed past him and headed for the GM's office.

"Honeymoon over?" Russell joked after seeing the brief exchange.

"Bite me!" Andrew said to Russell as he walked to the elevator and pressed his finger on the "up" button.

The tension between Andrew and Charlotte wasn't hard to miss, by anyone. Whenever Andrew came near the desk to pick up his key, Charlotte suddenly needed to be somewhere else, or got so involved talking to a customer that she couldn't do more than glance in Andrew's direction. If she happened to be in the office when he arrived, she remembered that she forgot something at the desk or needed to go to the bathroom, urgently. If he happened to phone down, she'd have someone else answer the call. She was taking the cold shoulder move to new levels.

He didn't understand what the big deal was. So she was jealous, because he brought Erin. Big deal, Erin meant nothing to him, and he knew Erin felt the same about him. It was a business deal, really. If Erin joined him, he'd buy her dinner. Erin was aware of who they were meeting. However, there wasn't an ounce of chemistry between them; in fact Erin was a little pissed off with Andrew as she felt largely ignored all night. Charlotte and Jason had more chemistry than they did, even though that seemed off. Whatever Charlotte's bizarre reasons were for being jealous, it was putting a wedge between them. She definitely seemed to be distancing herself from him and he didn't like that, it felt like his heart was bleeding.

After a couple of weeks of being given the cold shoulder, for reasons Andrew couldn't understand, he grabbed Charlotte by the hand as she was leaving and pulled her into the open elevator with him. He put his hand over her mouth, silencing the words she wanted to say. "You're going to talk to me, Cat, and you're not leaving until you do." The elevator doors closed and he dropped his hand immediately when he felt her tense up and saw true fear shoot through her eyes. "Sorry, I didn't mean to scare you."

Andrew gently pushed her out of the elevator and dragged her down the short hall to the projection room, and then entered the normally dark room as he held open the door for her. With the room lit up and on her own accord, she walked down the metal grates, over to the desk and leaned against the wall.

"So, what's going on with you, Cat? Why are you avoiding my calls and being so conveniently away from the desk or office when I get to work? You're either hiding out in the office, or you're downstairs getting something, or you're in the bathroom. I know when you're here, I see your car. You can't keep hiding from me." He stared into her green eyes, ringed in brown, the most beautiful shade of hazel green he'd ever seen. Something flitted across them, an emotion he couldn't put his finger on.

She just stood there, and refused to talk, looking away from his face. She pulled her hands into her navy-coloured long sleeve shirt. *I want to tell you, Andrew, but I know you'll be on the first flight out of here.* Nevertheless, she resisted. She felt vulnerable around him and her walls were fighting to stay stable, although she was on terribly shaky ground. As her arms crossed to further barricade herself, she kept a seriously stern look on her face.

Andrew stood before her, trying to keep out of her personal space, and asked in the calmest voice he could muster, "Is this about the comment I made about your drinking?" No response. "Is it something I said about Jason?" Still no answer. She didn't even flinch. "Cat, please, talk to me," he begged of her, his voice cracking. "Tell me what I did. Tell me something."

"Why are you calling me Cat?"

He laughed. "Because you're just like a cat, playing these cat and mouse games with me. It just seemed to fit." He resumed his serious face and said, "So, now that that's clear, what did I do wrong?"

She sat down in the chair, pulled her legs up and wrapped her arms around them, further barricading her heart, and spoke in a quiet voice, "It was nothing that you did."

"Was it something I said then?"

"No." She shook her head and made to stand up. She barely made it to her feet when he was directly in front of her.

"Then what?" Andrew stopped her from running away as he blocked her movements, with his hands on either side of her, effectively caging her against the wall. "You said you were jealous of Erin." He saw the fire of recognition light up in her eyes. "You should know there's nothing between us. We didn't even hold hands. She's actually quite pissed with me for ignoring her."

She looked up and searched the depths of his turquoise coloured eyes. They softened as he spoke, and she knew at once that he spoke the truth. She knew he had no reason to lie to her, but still she kept her guard up.

He was so close to her, he could smell her sweet coconut smell in her hair. "So, now that you know that, why are you avoiding me?" He tried to make eye contact with her again, but she averted her eyes. Instead, she looked past him, towards the bank of large windows. The theatre was lit up with the pre-show slides promoting SEARCH, and their sponsors, flashing across on the screen.

In a voice caught somewhere between a whisper and a cry, she stated slowly, "We broke up."

Andrew continued to stand there, searching her eyes, waiting until she made eye contact with him. "Okay. So what does that have to do with ignoring me?" He tilted his head to one side.

"Because I love you." The voice strong with conviction mirrored the flash in her eyes.

He was dumbstruck still, as this was information he already knew. They'd been telling each other that for awhile. "I love you too, but you know that."

"No, I mean I have real deep feelings for you," she paused, and then rambled on, "seeing you with her just un-caged the jealousy I didn't truly understand, because I'm not a jealous person. I didn't understand why I was feeling the way I was feeling, until I talked with Joe and he said it was jealousy. Once I truly realized that that's what I was experiencing, I kept having all these dreams about kissing you in my aunt's pool, and I'm not sure where they keep coming from, but it's vivid and it feels so real. The smell of the chlorine, the sound of the water, and this blue-green colour I see everywhere in my dreams."

Music to his ears, Andrew smiled, and took a step forward, their bodies together, almost close enough to feel each other's pulse. "Those aren't dreams, Cat. That happened." He placed his hands on her face and bent his head enough to brush his lips along hers. He'd been waiting for this day, ever since that night in the pool. This kiss was warm and real, filled with wanton emotion, he felt her surrender beneath him until suddenly she broke it off.

"Stop!" she exclaimed, pushing away his hands from her face and catching her breath. "You can't do that."

He took a step back, licking his lips that tasted like sweet coconut. "Okay." He looked very puzzled.

"You can't kiss me like that." Moisture started to fill her eyes. "Why not?"

She stood there, tears welling up in her eyes, changing her eye colour to a more brilliant shade of green. A salty drop escaped and stained a trail down her cheek. "Because you can't," she sighed and hammered on, "my timing sucks, to realize that these deep feelings are there. It's not fair to you."

"Do you hear me complaining? I've been waiting for you to admit to yourself that you have these emotions, these wonderful feelings." He smiled, in spite of the clearly tormented love of his life standing in front of him. He wiped away her tear with the gentlest of touch.

"I'm pregnant," she blurted it out so fast it caught her off guard, and she immediately cast her gaze downwards when the words finished flying out of her mouth. *So deal with that and tell me it's not fair to you.*

Andrew stopped smiling, looking at the top of her head as she stared at her feet. He stood there motionless, unable to tame his wild thoughts, until the timer went off, reminding him to start up the movie. "Hold that thought." He worked quickly, feeding the reels into the projector, cleaning the screen with a couple bursts of air, and getting the audio lined up and dimming the lights in the projection room. Then he came back and stood in front of her, leaning against the desk. "You're pregnant?" He looked her over, noticing her slumped stature and crestfallen expression on her face. Uncontrollably, he stared at her tummy. "For real?"

She fought to hold onto her self-composure. "Yes, for real." Her voice laced with ugliness.

"How far along?" He wiped a sudden bead of sweat from his forehead.

"About five weeks?" She looked into his eyes, expecting to see anger and disgust, and found neither. "I found out the day after our double date. I was late, and I'm never late. I snuck over to the drugstore and bought a test. I knew when I called you."

"But how?"

"What do you mean, how?" She screwed up her face, as a parent would do when preparing to give the facts of life talk to a child.

"I don't know how to ask without sounding like an idiot...," he paused, "but how? I thought you'd be afraid to do that, you know, after what you went through. Before." Watching her carefully as she looked like she might collapse, he instinctively reached out to her. Instead of taking his outstretched hand, she slowly lowered herself back into the chair at the desk.

She tipped her head down as she spoke, "Well, I knew that if I was going to be a proper girlfriend, I'd have to put out. I didn't know if I could handle that or not, so whenever we'd go out, I'd start drinking. I needed to find a way to make THAT job easier. If I was drunk, it likely wouldn't hurt, and with any luck, if I was drunk enough I'd likely not remember. Him. "

"Ouch. That would make any man swoon, to know that the girl he's dating hoped to drink enough that she wouldn't remember their lovemaking. Do you remember me mentioning that Jason remarked that he thought you maybe had a drinking problem?" Andrew grabbed a nearby chair and sat beside the quivering Charlotte. "Oh, Charlotte!" he wiped away her tears with his finger, "any man worth his salt wouldn't expect you to put out to be a proper girlfriend." He had an overwhelming urge to smack whoever told her that was what made a decent girlfriend. He cleared his throat. "Why didn't you use protection?"

"I thought we did." *He says he did, but like an idiot I was too drunk to know if he actually did or not.* Charlotte buried her head in her arms.

He couldn't see the tears, but could tell that she was crying as her body was shaking.

"I'm such an idiot."

"You're not an idiot. A little confused on what a real man would want from you, but definitely not an idiot." He rubbed her back, and slowly Charlotte lifted her head. "What did Jason say when you told him?" He looked at the face she was making; boiling emotions were starting to surface. "You told him, didn't you?"

"Why do you think we broke up?"

"Oh. My. God! Really?" He jumped up, wanting to kick something. "What a bastard!" he shouted over the noise in the projection room. He checked on the screen, and then walked back to Charlotte, who had turned her head to watch him. "Is that a proper thing to do? Is that a man who really wants the best for you? To abandon you in a time of need. Fuck!" Andrew was mad.

She heard him curse as he paced along the back wall, constantly checking on the screen and then the audio, before pacing back across the room. Even though the projector was very loud when it was running, she could hear every word he said, he wasn't trying to be quiet.

"So, what do you do now?"

"I don't know, Drew. I'm scared!" she shouted back across the room to where he stood. "This isn't the life I'd imagined having, being a mother at nineteen. Well, I'll be twenty when the baby's here. I don't want to be MY mother." She watched him pace. "Everything's going to change. EVERYTHING!" She shouted more, "Where am I going to live? I'm sure Joe won't want a baby in the apartment. What am I going to do with the baby when I'm working, because I'll still have to work full time because I'M ONLY NINETEEN!" Her voice fell. "I'm nineteen and my life's going to be forever different from this day forward." Then she whispered, "And I'll be all alone, and I'll blame the baby and my metamorphosis will be complete - I'll have turned into her."

Andrew stopped pacing and walked over to her, arms shaking from a controlled urge to scream. "What do you mean you'll be all alone and you'll turn into her? Who? Your mother?"

"Think about it, Drew. Do you think you'll really hang around as much when my demands are directed at a baby? Will I be able to socialize here for hours on end? I think you'd get very tired of my boring way of life." She carried on, "What about Joe? I'll likely be out on my own soon, and he's so wrapped up in Chelsea, that I doubt I'll see him much more than I do now, and I'm living with him! Meadow will be consumed with schoolwork. So where does that leave me, Drew. ALONE!" She threw her hands up in the air. "ALONE!" she yelled again, wiping burning angry tears away.

He stared at her and calmly questioned, "What about your mom? Why are you afraid of turning into her? You mention her vaguely, and I want to know more about this part of your life you keep such a tight lid on."

The copper-haired teenager collapsed into a sitting position on the cold, hard floor. Every barrier she'd put up around her crumbled down like the Berlin Wall. A rage from deep inside of her was surfacing, and she felt her heart race and the adrenaline pound through her. She wanted to run, needed to run, before everything was raw, bare, and exposed. She started to shake, violently, and clenched her fists into tight little balls, digging her nails deep into her palms. She was confused, and hurt, and angry and sad. *I feel like dying, because dying would be easier than having to say anything. Anything I say can make him turn and run faster than the speed of light.*

A voice came from her that countered the quasar of activity beneath. It was calm, concise and clear. "Are you sure you really want to know?"

Andrew nodded and said, "Yes, please tell me."

"You've been warned. It's not pretty."

He sat beside her and grasped her shaky hand. "Something tells me I shouldn't expect it to be."

Chapter Eleven
✿✿✿

Charlotte didn't remember much about her childhood. Most of the memories were blurry at best. There were no pictures for her to look back on fondly and reminisce. That which she remembered was dark and scary, and to protect her, her mind covered it, leaving that part of her life a dismal grey.

Her earliest memory of her mother, Lucy, was when she was about six. Lucy had just celebrated her 23rd birthday, with a crowd of people Charlotte didn't know. She clearly recalled seeing her mother swinging on the playground swings, her beautiful long coppery hair blowing off her tanned face as she soared her swing higher into the air. She was happy, laughing, and having a good time. For years after, Charlotte tried to focus on that face, the one of her mother's true smile. Lucy rarely smiled and sadly that was the way Charlotte remembered her.

Charlotte recalled once asking her mother if she could get some new clothes. She was eight, and very thin. She wore things that would fit a four year-old, and the ones she was wearing, she'd had for years. Bought from Goodwill, they were too big for her when she got them, and now, years later, they were starting to fit tight. In addition, the knees of her pants had stains and were worn through; her sleeves had a hole in one of the elbows.

"Charlie, how many times have I told you that money doesn't grow on trees? I can't afford to get you new clothes all the time."

"But mom, I've had these since I was little," she pleaded.

Whack! Smacked right across the left cheek. "You'll never talk to me like that again, Charlie!" The rail thin female towered over her daughter, making her cower.

Charlotte stood there in silence, trying not to cry. Crying always made things worse and you *never* wanted things to get worse. Lucy would lose her temper, and Charlotte would suffer the consequences. She looked down upon her weather-beaten shoes. She wouldn't walk away, not until her mother said it was okay. You only made *that* mistake once.

Finally, with her head lowered and her urge to cry still bubbling inside, and the overwhelming need to soothe her stinging cheek, she heard Lucy utter the words. "Go, and get out of my face. I don't want to see you for the rest of the day."

Charlotte turned and went to play in the corner of the only closet they had. It was the only place she could go and stay out of sight from Lucy.

They lived in a bachelor suite, on the ground floor of a four-story walk up, in a rougher part of the west end. The building was original and had useless owners, who kept the maintenance to a bare minimum. Things were rarely repaired or replaced.

Their sparse kitchen had six cupboards that contained a few cans of beans or tuna, maybe a box of pasta and some soup. That was usually it. The mismatched dishes usually sat in the sink, and only got washed when needed again. The stove had one workable burner and their fridge was a 1950's relic. It rarely contained more than a carton of milk and some fruit. If Charlotte were a good girl, Lucy would "splurge" on some fresh fruit. Sometimes there would be red, juicy apples, but only when Charlotte brought them home. A house a block away with a magnificent sized apple tree, always dropped apples on the public side of the fence. Charlotte would bring those damaged, thrown away apples home on her way back from school.

A kitchen table and chair, that were discovered beside the dumpster and dragged back into their home, finally gave them a place to dine at. A rich-looking mahogany high-backed chair with armrests, was also found beside the dumpster and added to the mismatched set.

The living room wasn't much better. A hand-me-down hide-a-bed became Charlotte's bed. A faded and scratched brown wood coffee table, with a missing foot, added to the ambiance of the decrepit suite. They had one lamp, a nice cream-coloured base with a gold shade. It was one of a small handful of electrical appliances Lucy allowed. Power was expensive and not included with the rental of the place so the lamp was rarely turned on.

Lucy's bed lay tucked along the opposite wall of the couch. Her double-sized bed was a small step better than the couch, even with the sag in the middle. No doubt it was a hand-me-down as well. The sheets were a splurge from Goodwill. The few clothes Lucy owned piled up on the floor. Beside the bed was the closet, where at the bottom, in the corner, were the few toys that Charlotte was "lucky" to have.

The bathroom lay beyond that, with a bathtub, a toilet, and a rusty, dirty sink.

They were poor, and even by age eight, Charlotte understood that they had no money. However, there was always somewhere dry and warm to go, and there was usually some sort of food to eat, and threadbare clothes to wear. Lucy always reminded her that things could be worse.

Charlotte curled her tiny body into the closet and shut the accordion door, playing with an armless Barbie and a truck. She was out of sight from her mother, and she kept quiet, hoping Lucy either would go to work, doing whatever it was she did until the wee hours of the morning, or until she passed out. Charlotte did not prefer either. She was often left home alone.

Charlotte came home from school the next day and was surprised to see a bag for her on the coffee table. Eagerly she opened it and found some new-to-her clothes and shoes, and even a puzzle and a book at the bottom. Charlotte beamed. "Thanks!"

"Momma's sorry, baby girl. I should've got you some new clothes before. I hope you like these and that they fit." Lucy's face was a hard one to read. She looked like she was frowning, and yet it was as if she was crying, her eyes glazed over.

Charlotte didn't care though and excitedly tried on the new clothes. Sure, they were too big, but if she rolled up the sleeves and made a little knot on the bottom of the shirts, they'd fit perfectly. The brown pants were too long, but a quick flip and they fit too. The waist was huge though, and had a hard time staying up, until she thought to roll down the top, and then it fit better.

The puzzle was 500 pieces, and the outside picture was of a castle high up on a hill. The book was an astronomy book, detailing constellations and information about the planets.

Charlotte was over the moon excited. She ran up to Lucy and gave her a big hug. "Thanks. I love them all."

"Momma made some money last night." Lucy smiled sadly. "Now we need to get you a winter coat and boots. They didn't have any at the store, but I'm sure there are some in the lost and found at school. Do you think you could borrow one for the season?"

Every year at Lucy's insistence, Charlotte dug through the lost and found bins; preferably near the bottom as that stuff had been there the longest. Lucy had Charlotte "borrow" a coat for the winter and return it when the warm weather appeared. This way, in Lucy's mind, it was never stealing. However, Charlotte knew it was the only way she would be able to stay warm, as the winters could be unbearably hostile. Therefore, she borrowed winter clothes, always returning them. She always returned them clean.

Lucy and Charlotte would walk a few blocks with their bag of clothes and hang out at the laundromat, playing cards and drinking the free coffee the shop always offered, usually loaded with powdered cream and cubes of sugar to cut down on the bitterness. It was surprisingly fun hanging out with her mother there. They would read trashy magazines and strut around the place in a nightdress, as everything else would be in the wash. Sometimes, the music played, and the two of them danced and twirled. Charlotte loved laundry day, as rare as it happened, maybe every month. Charlotte learned to hand-wash her underwear at home so she always had a clean pair to wear. The walk home from the laundromat was hard; the clothes were wet, adding several pounds to drag home, and they still needed to be hung up around the apartment, or if it was a nice day, hung up outside. Charlotte loved the way her clothes smelled when they hung up outside – fresh and with a hint of blossoms.

Things stayed pretty even for a couple of years. If Charlotte did anything to warrant a slap across the cheek, Lucy was always buying her something the next day. As the incidents increased, however, the amount of "gifts" decreased.

Charlotte had always been the odd kid in class, with no real friends, going by the nickname of Gnarly Charlie. In grade six, a week after school started, a new student joined their class, with a mop of shaggy brown hair and deep brown eyes to match. He was built like a quarterback. His name was David, and he was stuck at the back of the class next to Charlotte.

The other kids took no notice of the new kid. Most of them too righteous to play with anyone who wasn't a part of their clique. For a couple of weeks, Charlotte watched David wander aimlessly at recesses, having no one to play with. Finally, she went up to him.

He walked near the bike racks, admiring the few bikes some kids were brave enough to still ride with the approaching winter. The weather was getting colder, and Charlotte had just borrowed a pair of mitts from the lost and found.

"Hi, David. Want to play with me?"

He studied her, then a curious look overtook his baby face. "Don't you have someone else to play with?" He cocked his head over to the herd of girls playing with the large red rubber ball over by their grade six door.

"Nah, they don't play with me." She sat on top of the metal bike racks.

A boy from the fifth grade came up and stood by Charlotte. "Don't touch my bike," he yelled at her.

Charlotte was used to this type of treatment and just rolled her eyes. "I won't. Wouldn't want it anyways."

He glared at her. "If anything goes missing, I'm coming after you Gnarly Charlie. You're always stealing things."

"I borrow, never steal!" she yelled and growled until the boy ran away.

David remained rooted to the spot. "Are they always like that to you?"

"What, them? Yeah." She hung her head as her dirty, stringy, coppery hair fell limply beside her cheeks. She swung her bruised, uncovered legs. She wore a faded dress with yellowed lace.

"Yikes."

She looked back up at David. "It's okay, I'm used to it. It's the way it is."

"Have you always come to this school?"

"Yeppers. Makes it even sadder, doesn't it?"

"Yeah."

"So, do you prefer to be called David? Or Dave?" She looked at him earnestly.

He smiled. "David is fine."

"Cool." She smiled an ugly smile when she said, "Everyone calls me Charlie, but I hate it."

"So what do you like to be called?"

"Charlotte."

"Okay, I promise to always call you Charlotte."

"Thanks." She giggled. "Where did you move from?"

"Calgary." He kicked at a rock and flinched as it struck a nearby bike.

Charlotte looked around nervously, hoping no one saw.

"My parents just got divorced."

"Oh."

"When dad moved here for work, mom thought it best that we follow to make visitation better. Besides it's cheaper to live here than there, at least that's what I hear her and Joe talk about."

"Who's Joe?"

"My big brother. He's sixteen, and he's been saying how much cheaper things are here."

"Oh. I don't know about those things. Only lived here all my life."

"Where do you live?"

"See those apartments down there?" She pointed down the winding street. "Those white and brown buildings, past the other school? That's where I live."

"We live just back there too. There are some houses behind that; that's where we live."

"Wow. You're close. Do you walk to school?" Charlotte watched as he kicked again at the rocks and dirt with his sneakers. She noticed that his were all in one piece and had a check mark on the side of them.

"Sometimes. But sometimes Joe will drop me off."

The buzzer sounded. The boy with the shaggy brown hair, and the girl with the limp coppery hair walked back towards the school together.

"Let's be friends," Charlotte stated.

"Okay," David agreed.

Their friendship was that simple. Every recess they played together, whether it was playing ball or just walking and talking in the field. Whenever they had class assignments, they paired up. Finally, Charlotte had a friend, someone who didn't call her Gnarly Charlie, and more importantly, accepted her the way she was.

They had a particularly intensive assignment that required extra time after school to devote to it.

"Want to come over to my house and work on it? Mom usually has cookies for us."

"Like real homemade ones?"

David looked at her weirdly. "Yeah," he answered.

"I'll have to ask Lucy first." They went to the office, and she called home.

Her mother answered on the third ring, slurring a "Hello."

"Can I go over to David's after school? We need to work on our Egypt assignment."

"Be home before supper!"

"Okay." She could hear another voice in the apartment besides Lucy's, possibly belonging to a man.

"I'll leave you a can of soup to eat."

"You won't be there for supper?"

"No, going to go to work early today."

Charlotte slumped and David whispered, "You can stay for dinner at our place. Mom won't mind."

"David says I can stay for supper."

"Fine!" she yelled forcing Charlotte to pull the phone away from her ear. "Go have supper with your new friend and see if I care." The phone slammed down unexpectedly. Somehow, she knew she was going to pay for that later.

Shaking, she hung up the phone and turned back to David. "I can stay for supper."

David and Charlotte walked to his place after school. His home was only five minutes past Charlotte's apartment, but it was far nicer and bigger. To Charlotte it was like walking into a mansion. A front door that you didn't have to walk through a hallway to access. The carpets were clean, so Charlotte immediately removed her shoes. The house smelled fresh and everywhere she looked, things seemed in good shape and condition.

"Come in." David gestured when Charlotte just stood in the foyer.

"Wow. My whole place could fit into your living room and kitchen."

"Really?" He led her into the kitchen. "Would you like something to eat? Mom usually lets us have a couple of cookies and a glass of milk before she gets home."

"That sounds great, thanks." She reached out and touched a brown sofa chair before she followed David into the kitchen. That chair looked as exquisite as it felt. The soft fibers felt like velvet beneath her fingertips as she rubbed it quickly, thinking it must be super comfortable to sit in too. Instead she sat at the table, on a black vinyl chair.

"Hello?" bellowed a voice suddenly from the front door.

Charlotte froze. David noticed and stepped out of the kitchen looking towards the front door. "Oh hey, Joe."

"Hey, dork," said the tall boy, who stepped forward and ruffled David's hair. "Hi, I'm Joe," he said as he walked towards Charlotte.

She pulled her legs up and wrapped her arms securely around them. "Charlotte," she said meekly.

"Ah, you're the Charlotte David speaks of. Nice to meet you." Joe opened the fridge.

She heard some whispers from the two boys standing at the fridge, but couldn't figure out what they were saying. Finally, David came back and placed a plate of cookies and a glass of milk in front of Charlotte.

She reached for a cookie and took a bite. A moan of delight escaped her lips. "This is really good," she said between bites.

Joe stared at her. "You don't get out much do you?" He sat across from her.

He didn't mean it as an insult, but that's exactly how Charlotte took it. She pushed the plate away from her.

Joe laughed. "It's okay. Eat your cookies. There's more where they came from." He pushed the plate back towards her. "You look like you could stand to eat a few cookies." He looked at her still curled up in the chair.

"Thanks." She didn't meet Joe's look and weakly grabbed another cookie.

David sat down beside her and started pulling out his assignment. Charlotte pulled out her papers from her plastic bag and scattered them on the table. While they were working on their Egypt assignment, Joe added a couple more cookies to her plate and refilled her milk glass. Twice.

After an hour, the front door opened, and a lovely looking woman with chestnut-coloured hair came in. She walked right by the table and dropped her bags on the counter, and then turned back and gave each of her two children kisses on the cheek. "Hello, darlings. Sorry I'm late."

"Mom, this is Charlotte, from school," David introduced.

"Well, hello, Miss Charlotte. It's nice to finally meet you. David talks a lot about you." Charlotte felt her cheeks warm. "You've been such a nice friend to him."

"Thanks. It's nice to have a friend at school."

She looked warmly at Charlotte. "Don't you have friends at school, dear?"

David chimed up. "Nah, the other kids are mean to her."

She placed a hand on her hip. "That's not very nice."

"It's okay," Charlotte stated, "it's because we're poor. I'm not like the other kids."

"That's not an acceptable reason to not like someone. Oh my, that's just sad." She turned back to her bags on the counter. "Can you stay for supper, Charlotte?"

"Yes, ma'am."

"Great. We'll have chicken, rice, and peas." She started fussing in the kitchen.

Charlotte noticed how Joe helped his mom, without her asking, putting away the groceries and getting clean dishes from the cupboard. David and Charlotte cleared their papers away, and Charlotte helped set the table. It was the best dinner Charlotte ever had the pleasure of enjoying in her life. She had two huge servings, eating up every morsel of chicken, every grain of rice, and every plump pea. After supper, Charlotte helped the boys clear the table and load up the dishwasher.

"Thanks so much for dinner, Mrs. Harrison."

"Oh please, dear, call me Claire." She gave Charlotte a quick hug. "It was nice to have you for supper."

"I'll walk her home okay, mom?" David asked.

"I'll join you," Joe added. "Then we can stop at Rick's and get my tape back that he borrowed."

The three of them walked, in the dark, quietly to Charlotte's place. "I'm good here, guys," she said at the roadway nearest her apartment.

"I said I'd walk you home Charlotte, and I mean it," David stated.

Sighing, she walked up the grass to the darkened apartment. After sliding open the unlocked glass doors, she reached inside and flicked on the nearest light. The tiny suite filled with yellowness. Charlotte was mortified. Their clothes from yesterday's laundry day were hanging up all over the apartment on a homemade clothesline. Newspapers and flyers were scattered all over, and the place looked very messy. A total opposite of the neat and tidy home she just came from.

Neither of the boys said anything except, "Now you're home. See you tomorrow."

She closed the glass door behind them and started pulling the clothes off the line. Little did she know that David and Joe stood in the shadows, cautiously watching their friend fret around her tiny apartment.

"Did you see the size of that place Joe? I thought she was kidding when she said it was small."

"I know. Did you see how much she ate at supper? I couldn't believe it. What does she bring for lunch?"

"I've never seen her eat lunch."

"Really?"

David shook her head.

"Aw man, that's really sad." Joe looked through the patio doors, watching Charlotte throw the clothes into a pile. "We need to have her over more often."

"I agree."

Charlotte enjoyed her after-school time with David. It was nice for her to get away from her reality for a while. She wondered how long she could stretch out working on this project. She turned off the light, crawled onto the couch and covered herself up with a thin blanket. She stared out into the dark street, until she fell asleep. She woke up several hours later when her mother started violently shaking her.

"Wake up, Charlie!" her mother screamed.

"What? What is it?" she said, suddenly alarmed.

"Did you have a nice time at your friend's house?"

Charlotte tried collecting her thoughts. It was still dark outside. What time was it? After being shaken again, she finally mumbled, not yet awake, "Yes, it was nice." Charlotte didn't know her answer was the wrong one, until it was too late. She felt the sting before she heard it, and her mother threw her against the couch. Slapped awake with fear, Charlotte's eyes opened wide and saw the second blow coming. She tried to move, but Lucy was quicker and adjusted her smack. Lucy pinned Charlotte's arms down on the couch with her knees and slapped her hard across both cheeks.

"Had a lovely time, did you?" Smack. "I work hard and this is how you repay me." Another smack.

Charlotte could smell something funny on her mother's breath, but it wasn't alcohol. She was acting drunk though. Lunatic, crazy drunk. Finally, after a few more smacks, Lucy stumbled to her bed and fell on it. Charlotte was now too scared to fall asleep and stayed up for the remainder of the night, watching the sun crest the horizon. Without making a sound, she got dressed, cleaned up for school and opened the patio door. She shut it quietly, and ran to school as fast as her tired legs could move.

She'd always felt safe at school. Until that day. Around noon, a loud knock came on the classroom door, and Charlotte's teacher went quickly to answer it.

"I want to see my daughter now!" bellowed a voice that made Charlotte's stomach curdle.

"Mrs. Cooper, please! We're still in class," said Mrs. Amandes very sternly.

Charlotte paled when her mother pushed passed her teacher and sauntered into the classroom. She was barely dressed, in a halter-top that didn't fit her properly and skin tight pants. Her hair was straggly and in desperate need of a wash.

"Oh, Charlie, there you are!" She walked over to her and said in a wickedly sweet voice. "You scared mama when I woke up and you weren't there."

Charlotte looked around the classroom, begging with her eyes to have someone intervene.

"Let's go home." Charlotte didn't move. "NOW!" Lucy yelled as several students jumped. Charlotte grabbed her things. Lucy pushed her daughter out of the classroom telling Mrs. Amandes, "Charlie will be gone for the afternoon."

Charlotte walked as slow as she possibly could, while her mother shoved at her from behind. Lucy acted very strange, and it scared Charlotte to the core. She was terrified for what waited at home, sealed away from the rest of the world. Unfortunately, even as slow as she was moving, it wasn't a long walk.

Charlotte's heart stopped when the patio door opened and a strange man was there sitting on Charlotte's bed. Lucy kicked her through the door, and Charlotte tripped over the coffee table landing in the man's lap.

"Well hello, Charlie," said the strange man.

She didn't like that he knew her name. Beads of sweat formed at the back of her neck, as she quickly pushed herself up and away from this man. She stepped backwards towards the kitchen but froze as she felt trapped and had nowhere to go. She heard the patio door slam shut and the click of it being locked.

"Charlotte, this is Barry. He's my… friend…" Lucy said in a sugary sweet voice, pulling the sheet of curtain across the patio door.

Charlotte started to panic, looking between the short, dark skinned man in a cheap green suit, and her mother who was dressed as if it were a spring day. She stared at Lucy, whose eyes were wild and wide. She noticed that her stance was unstable as Lucy braced herself against the wall. Charlotte started to figure out just how high her mother was. "Mom, whatever you're thinking, please don't do it." Charlotte pleaded.

"Oh child, you worry too much."

Charlotte looked from her mother to the man named Barry who was still sitting on the couch. He had produced a lighter and was melting something on a spoon, the flames flickering around the concave shape of the spoon. She watched in horror as he produced a syringe and pulled the watery looking fluid into the needle, and then pressed the plunger to release some. The beads of sweat turned into rivers on Charlotte as it raced down her back.

"Charlie, come here." Her mother called sweetly, her thin arms opened wide, as if waiting for a hug.

Charlotte was frozen. Her feet were made of lead, her heart pumping wildly, and her brain yelling at her to run.

"It's easier if you co-operate."

She remained rooted to the spot, watching in wide-eyed horror as Barry passed the syringe over to Lucy. She watched her mother stab herself with the needle and push the fluid into her arm.

"Not all of it, Lucy," said Barry calmly, in a deep gravely sounding voice that did nothing to soothe Charlotte's frayed nerves.

She watched as Lucy got a wild smile stuck on her face and suddenly looked very peaceful, leaning against the wall, her head tipped back slightly, stringy strands of hair falling behind her. Then Barry stood up and pounced over to Charlotte, reaching her in as few as four paces. Charlotte started screaming as he picked her up, carried her over to Lucy's bed and laid her there. He straddled the tiny twelve-year-old, pinning her down effectively with his knees on her small hands. Charlotte's gaze was filled with hatred, terror, and pure, unadulterated fear. Her mother, in her relaxed persona, sauntered over, and holding the needle with the remainder of the clear fluid, injected it into Charlotte's arm. Charlotte screamed as the needle pierced her arm, feeling the hot liquid pooling underneath her skin. She closed her eyes tightly, trying to shut out the pain visually. Within moments, Charlotte felt very relaxed, her fear fading, and she stopped screaming. She remembered hearing Barry laugh and say, "Well, that worked better than I thought, hey, Luce?"

Charlotte no longer knew where she was. She was in a whole other time and place. She felt euphoric and happy, completely different. A voice belonging to her mother seemed to be crying, but was looking at her upside down, when Charlotte opened her eyes. Was she at her head? Was Lucy stopping her from floating away? She could feel hands on her arms holding her firmly to the bed, and yet she felt very light, and breezy, floating up and away. She was warm and glad for the cooling breeze she felt while flying, as she felt very hot. Suddenly lightning struck her, and she hollered in pain. The lightning had caught her on fire, and she was burning. Oh the intensity of the burn; it felt like it was ripping her apart. "Make it stop," she yelled to the clouds. Another sharp bolt of lightning, and swiftly Charlotte was again flying above the clouds, rising higher and higher, and falling fast. Time took on a different meaning in the clouds, and she didn't know if it was hours, minutes, or days that she floated around, lost in space. Eventually, she floated down into a peaceful sleep.

She awoke later, rolled off Lucy's bed and headed to the bathroom. Looking in the mirror, she saw a ghost staring back; her skin was paper white and stretched tightly over her bones; her coppery hair, nearly brown with dried sweat, plastered to her face. She sat on the toilet and winced in pain as she wiped. She noticed the blood and figured she was getting her first period. Without panicking, she folded up some tissue and placed it in her underwear. Then she looked at her arm and saw a pair of bruises forming near her wrist. She stood up and then quickly turned around, throwing up as she turned. At least she made it to the toilet.

Slowly, images of fear emerged. Barry. Her mother. Hot spoon liquid. Needles. Did her mother really inject her with some kind of drug? What kind of mother did that? Was that what being high was like? As far as punishments went, the floating part was okay, but she remembered the lightning pain and decided that maybe it wasn't a great punishment. She had so many questions, and no one she dared to ask.

She exited the bathroom and saw that she was home alone. She was fearful of leaving, but even more terrified to be there alone. She walked over to her bed, aka the couch, and curled up, pulling the sheet up over her, trying to mentally escape the horror of the past hour, or was it two?

A soft knock sounded against the patio door that brought Charlotte out of her head. She got up and pulled back the sheet. David stood there with an envelope.

She opened the patio door a crack. "Hey, David."

"Hey, are you okay? I missed you at school today." He looked at her with a weird glint in his eye.

"I've only been gone since lunch." Charlotte rolled her eyes.

David shook his brown head of hair and stared at her. "That was yesterday, Charlotte. You missed school today."

"All day?" she said quietly, trying to piece together the actual length of time. She thought it was only an hour or two. "Wow, I must've been really tired then. I just woke up."

"Are you okay?"

She leaned against the glass, suddenly exhausted. "Yeah, flu or something." She didn't match his gaze. "Why did you pop by?"

"Homework. I told Mrs. Amandes I'd drop it by." He pushed the envelope through the little opening of the door.

"Thanks, David."

"You're welcome, Charlotte." David looked past her into the apartment and looked back at Charlotte. "Well, see ya." He stood there reluctantly, not wanting to leave.

Charlotte started closing the patio door, saying, "Bye," as she sealed it shut.

Lucy didn't come home for another two days, and so Charlotte missed more school. She was absolutely terrified to sneak off, have her mother show up unannounced at school, and have drugs injected into her as punishment.

When Lucy did come home, she was a normal version of herself. Distant, but at least she didn't smell funny and could walk straight. She also looked better than she had in a while, like she'd gone shopping and had a trip to the haircutters. Lucy kept looking at Charlotte with a strange expression on her pale, thin face.

"What happened that day?" Charlotte asked.

"Nothing."

"Do you know what day I'm asking about?"

"No."

"Then why did you say nothing?" Charlotte cursed in her head. "That day, you dragged me home from school. What happened?"

Lucy sat down on her bed. Her mother was maybe twenty-eight but she looked like she was much older. The bags under her eyes were full and dark, her skin a sallow shade, and her eyes were dull and lifeless. She weighed a hundred pounds if that, but at least in this moment, she was looking better than she had last time Charlotte saw her.

"I drugged you."

"Why?" She kept her voice in check, not wanting it to crack with sadness and show any emotion.

"I owed Barry money. I gave you to him to pay off my debt."

Charlotte wasn't old enough to understand what Lucy was implying. "I don't get it."

Lucy murmured in a rambling trance, "But you had to be drugged first, and then it wouldn't be painful. That's what I told him, and that's what he agreed to, and it was awful to watch and see, and I had to hold you and pay off my debts because I'm not working enough."

"What are you talking about, mother?"

"Do you remember?"

"Remember what?"

"That's good." Lucy slumped back on the bed and fell asleep.

Charlotte took a long look at her mother, and noticed the line of bruises inside her arms. Her twig like arms were marked with different shades of yellows and purples.

With permission from Lucy, who woke up hours later, Charlotte returned to school. She had so much work to catch up on, having missed nearly a week by the time Lucy came out of her haze. She spent her free time, with Lucy's blessing, at David's house after school, trying to get caught up. They did homework, and when David finished, he assisted Charlotte in getting hers completed. Within a week, she was back on track, but by then it was nearly Christmas break.

Lucy dropped a bombshell when she told Charlotte that she'd be going away for a while.

"How long will you be gone for?" Charlotte asked, thinking it would be a couple of days, maybe three or four.

"I don't know. A week, maybe two."

"A week? So what am I supposed to do?"

"Stay here and stay out of trouble."

"What about school tomorrow?"

"Well, go, and come here right after."

"And that's it? What about food and stuff?"

"Charlie, I've raised you well enough that you should be able to take care of that while I'm gone."

Charlotte looked at her mom. "You're seriously leaving me here, alone, at the age of twelve, for two weeks?"

"Yes." Lucy glared at Charlotte. "Now behave while I'm gone. Otherwise, I'll have to punish you again."

Charlotte blanched as she stepped back and said nothing. She watched as her mother packed up a small plastic bag, and then walked out the patio door, wearing flip-flops, and shorts with a tank top. The outside temperature had to be -15C if it was even that warm.

The next day, Charlotte sat alone at her desk after school, not wanting to leave. Christmas vacation was about to start, but Charlotte didn't want to leave school.

"Charlie, it's time to go home now," Mrs. Amandes stated, looking at Charlotte with warm and tender eyes.

"There's nothing I can help you with?" Charlotte stood up and walked to the blackboard, gathered up the chalk and placed it in a neat pile at the one end.

Mrs. Amandes placed an aged hand on her shoulder and gently steered her to the classroom door, "No, honey, it's time to go."

Slowly, under Mrs. Amandes's watchful gaze, Charlotte got on her borrowed winter jacket, donned her borrowed mitts and hat, and started trudging through the snow towards her apartment.

Joe pulled up beside her on the road. "Hey, Charlotte, want a ride?"

"No thanks," she said to the road.

"Charlotte, it's freezing out there. Get in here at least and warm up."

"I'll be home soon. Thanks, Joe."

"Charlotte, please," David called out.

Charlotte stopped dragging her feet. They were freezing, being that she had no socks on and her canvas shoes were wet from the snow that morning. She slowly walked over, and got in the front seat that David vacated to sit in the back.

"Why so glum?"

"Because mother's gone."

Joe snickered. "I thought that would be a good thing?"

"Not when she'll be gone for two weeks." She had no feeling, no hint of sadness, and no hint of joy in her statement.

"Charlotte, that's not right."

"Maybe not to you, but that's how things are for me. I'm not sure if it's good I'll be home all alone for Christmas or a bad thing."

Joe looked at David in his rear-view mirror.

Charlotte stuck her feet under the heater, allowing the warmth to permeate into her skin. She zoned out, and didn't notice that Joe had passed her apartment and was parking outside his house.

"You're staying here, Charlotte. Mom and I will work out the details, but for now, you'll stay here. End of story. I have half a mind to call the police and report her."

Joe parked the car and ran into the house. He was on the phone when Charlotte and David came in. David escorted Charlotte to the basement. "Our spare room's down there, so is Joe's room, so you won't be down there by yourself. Mom will be home soon, and we'll figure something out, Charlotte."

They sat around the kitchen table, eating another wonderful dinner made by Mrs. Harrison. She spoke up first about Charlotte's situation. "So Charlotte, tell me, do you have any family in town?"

"No, ma'am."

"What about your father? Grandparents?"

"Apparently my father left my mom when she was pregnant with me. Lucy has no family. She was raised in a foster home."

"Oh dear."

"Told you, mom," Joe said as Mrs. Harrison placed her hand on Joe.

"I know." She looked warmly at Charlotte, a benign sparkle in her eyes. "I want you to stay here, of your own volition, until Christmas okay?"

"What does that mean?"

"I want you to stay here, because you want to, not because I'm asking you."

"Okay."

"Okay, you'll stay?" David asked.

Charlotte looked first at David, then at Joe before settling on Mrs. Harrison. "I don't know. What if my mom comes back, and I'm not there?" She thought her shudder was internal, but the look of consternation from Mrs. Harrison and Joe told her they saw her fear.

Joe answered first, "We could leave her a note with our phone number on it. She can call us, if she gets back." He shrugged his shoulders.

Charlotte slowly nodded, apprehensively. "Okay, I'll stay."

"That settles it then." Mrs. Harrison stood up. "Boys, can you clean up? I'm going to make sure Charlotte's well set up." The lovely mom took off, taking Charlotte's hand with her, and led her downstairs. "Okay, here's a spare bedroom, which David showed you. There's the bathroom. It's primarily used by Joe, so it's very teenage boy smelling." She laughed soothingly. "There are extra towels in here," she pointed to a small closet. "Please make yourself at home. Help yourself to anything you need." Mrs. Harrison wrapped her arms around Charlotte.

Charlotte folded into Mrs. Harrison, feeling her arms wrap tightly around her. She felt secure.

"Thank you, Mrs. Harrison."

"You are most welcome." She only broke free of the embrace when Charlotte pushed back.

Charlotte looked up and saw Joe leaning against the doorframe.

"All cleaned up, Joe?" Mrs. Harrison asked her oldest son, having only just noticed him when Charlotte looked in that direction.

"Yes."

"Thank you." She gently patted Charlotte on the shoulder, and walked away. "A minute, Joe?"

"Sure, mom." Joe followed his mom up the stairs as Charlotte went into the bathroom to wash her hands.

Charlotte waited a moment, then followed and only stopped when she could hear voices talking, about her.

"Joe, she can't stay here for long, only until Christmas. The authorities need to be informed." Her voice hushed.

"I know, mom."

"Something isn't right in that house. Did you see the look of fear when she mentioned her mother coming back, and her not being there? What kind of a mother leaves a twelve-year-old for two weeks, without any means to get food, and over Christmas?"

"Her mom's weird, Mom, like off the wall weird," David added to the whispered conversation.

"I know. You told me about that incident where she showed up high out of her mind and dragged Charlotte home."

"I think her mom drugs Charlotte too."

"What?" Mrs. Harrison's voice rose a faint octave.

"Well, she missed school the next day, and when I went to see her, Charlotte's eyes were all weird like."

Charlotte instinctively reached up and touched her eyes. *Had they really looked like that?*

"Oh, dear." Then she whispered something inaudible and finally, clearly stated, "I'm going to head out and pick up some clothes for her. She can't be in threads."

"You're the best, mom." Joe said.

"I'll be back."

Charlotte waited a few minutes and then opened the door to the basement. Joe and David were on the couch watching TV. "Can I join you?"

"Of course." Joe scooted over and Charlotte sat between them.

She sunk into the cozy couch and relished the softness of the blanket he spread over her.

A while later, Mrs. Harrison returned from shopping and presented Charlotte with a couple of bags of clothes.

"For me? Really?" Charlotte peeked into the bags. "All brand new? Really?"

Mrs. Harrison nodded.

"Thank you so much! I've never had brand new clothes." She jumped up and gave Mrs. Harrison a big hug, tears welling up in her hazel eyes.

"You're welcome," she said in reply, continuing the hug, as she looked at her two sons. Then without thinking, she kissed the top of Charlotte's head, as a loving mother would do. Charlotte melted in her arms, sobs racking her tiny body. Mrs. Harrison, shocked, held on a little tighter. "Oh, Charlotte." She kissed the top of her head again. Minutes later, exhausted, Charlotte pulled away.

"Thank you."

"You are most welcome."

"Is it okay if I go to bed now?"

They all glanced at the clock. It wasn't even eight. Mrs. Harrison nodded, "Sure. Your room is all set up."

"Can I sleep up here on the couch? I don't like falling asleep alone."

"I can sit with you," Joe offered. "I need to finish reading that book before going back to school."

Mrs. Harrison raised her eyebrows and then conceded. "Okay."

Joe and Charlotte went downstairs, and after asking permission, Charlotte took one of the hottest and longest showers of her life. She stepped out of the shower smelling like a clean teenage boy, thanks to the male scented bar soap in the shower. She rummaged through the bag, found a pair of brand new pajamas and a small bag of pink panties, and quickly got into them, feeling the softness of the fleecy material against her body. Using Joe's comb, she combed through her squeaky clean, shoulder-length coppery waves and gave her teeth a solid scrubbing with the new toothbrush. It felt good to be thoroughly fresh and in clean, new clothes.

She walked into the guest bedroom, and climbed into the soft bed, allowing the fresh smelling sheets to hug her senses.

Joe stood at the doorway in a pair of grey striped pajamas pants and a navy top. He held a thick book in his long fingers as he leaned against the doorframe. "All ready for bed?"

"Ah-huh," she said.

Joe came over and turned on the lamp. "Where shall I sit?"

"Beside me on the bed's okay."

"You're sure?" Joe asked as he sat next to her and leaned against the headboard. She turned her back to him as he started to read.

Eventually, she fell asleep, although not soundlessly. She started screaming and bolted up in bed, staring blankly at Joe, who had stumbled back into her room. Seeing through him, she continued to scream, until Joe came over and put his hands on her shoulders. "Hey," he whispered, "it's okay. It was just a dream. A bad dream."

"No, she's coming back, and that'll be the death of me." Charlotte shook with fear, but still had not yet focused on Joe, who stood before her.

He sat down n front of her and placed his hands tenderly on her face. He said gently, yet firmly, "Charlotte, look at me please, look into my eyes."

Blinking slowly, her eyes became clear and focused. "Joe!" she exclaimed. She reached for him and buried her face in his shoulder.

Her sobs were heartbreaking, but Joe just let her cry them out, not saying a word, just held her close. Whatever it was that kept her strong in front of her mother, crumbled around her, as she felt safe in this place. He vowed immediately to never break that, and to protect her always. He wrapped his rail thin arms around her, and held her tightly. By morning, she had cried herself out, and Joe tucked her into bed, himself exhausted, and fell asleep beside her.

Charlotte woke up, feeling more alive than she had in years. She sat up in the bed, and in doing so, woke up Joe who had been soundly sleeping seconds before. "Joe."

"Hey," he said sleepily. "Rough night, eh?"

Charlotte nodded in agreement. She went to the bathroom and upon exiting, followed Joe upstairs where Mrs. Harrison sat around the kitchen table, reading the Saturday paper and drinking coffee.

"Good morning, Mrs. Harrison."

"Good morning, Charlotte, Joe." She raised an eyebrow at Joe. "Sleep well?"

Joe and Charlotte exchanged looks, but Charlotte answered, "No, Mrs. Harrison. I had constant nightmares and kept Joe up most of the night. Sorry."

Sighing quietly and looking at her son for confirmation, she then said, "Are you okay?"

"Yes, ma'am. I'm feeling much better today. Thank you again for your hospitality and for the new clothes. They feel nice."

Mrs. Harrison stood up. "You're welcome. Now can I get you breakfast?"

"Where's David?" Joe asked, as he pulled out pancake mix.

"Still sleeping."

Mrs. Harrison whipped up pancakes, and Charlotte set the table, marvelling at the matching dishes and noticing the air of happiness between the two adults. They laughed with each other, and encouraged Charlotte to join in, but she wasn't sure how. She'd never been a part of such things. Eventually, Mrs. Harrison placed breakfast on the table, and they championed Charlotte to continue eating until she was full.

After breakfast, David, Joe, and Charlotte bundled up and walked through the sunshine and cold, fresh air to her apartment where they left the Harrison's number beside the phone. The kitchen had a small pile of dirty dishes in the sink, a cup of something stuck to the countertop, and an overflowing garbage that gave the area an immediate stinky smell. The remainder of the apartment was dingy as well, a stark contrast to the clean, nice smelling and tidy home at the Harrisons.

For the next three days, including Christmas, Charlotte felt joy and happiness, as she celebrated with the Harrison family. She woke up on Christmas morning and saw that there were a couple of gifts for her under the tree. She never celebrated Christmas before, and the Harrisons treated her like family. She was constantly in awe of the love shared between the boys and their mother. They had a family dinner with Mrs. Harrison's parents, where there was another gift for Charlotte. She couldn't believe that she was getting gifts, and she had nothing to give them. As her gift to the Harrisons, she assisted wherever she could, whether it was cleaning up, or washing dishes, or taking out the trash. She was grateful to be a part of this magical day.

The next day, they were sitting around the table eating a nice brunch, which Charlotte ate heartily and consumed two glasses of milk, discussing plans to visit SEARCH later that afternoon, when the phone rang.

"Hello," Joe said, and then, with hesitation, passed the phone to Charlotte.

Charlotte instantly paled as he handed her the phone. Only one person would call her. "Hello," she said timidly.

Everyone at the table heard Lucy shout through the receiver, "Get your ass home immediately!"

"Yes, mother." She got up and hung the phone back in its cradle. She turned around somberly and told everyone, "I need to go."

"We'll come with you, Charlotte," David said, who looked at Joe and his mom, who went white as a ghost.

"No, it's best I face this alone." Her whole demeanour changed with that call. Gone was the laughing, funny twelve-year-old girl, and in its place a frightened child, terrified of what lay waiting for her at home.

"I'll help you pack."

"It's okay, Joe. I'll just go like this. I'll come back and get the other stuff later." She shuffled to the front door and grabbed her borrowed coat.

"Promise?"

"Yeah." She looked at Joe and then to Mrs. Harrison. "Thank you for everything."

"Be safe, Charlotte," she said blowing her a kiss.

The door closed, and the three of them watched Charlotte walk down the road.

"I'm scared for her, mom." Joe hugged his mom.

"Let's bake a pie and take it over. It'll give us an excuse to check up on her." Mrs. Harrison wrapped her arms around Joe. "If things are bad, we'll call the cops."

Charlotte made the walk in less than five minutes, taking a short cut across the snow-covered field. Although the air was frigid, and there was newly fallen snow, she wasn't cold. Her blood pumped like a racehorse, and the escalating adrenaline pushed her forward, keeping her warm. She arrived at the patio door and took a quick breath bracing herself for what lay inside. She had barely paused when the door flew open and her mother grabbed her harshly, pulling her into the bachelor suite. Lucy slammed the patio door shut, making it jump on the track and just narrowly missing Charlotte's fingers as she crashed it closed.

"Where have you been?" Lucy yelled, inches from Charlotte's face, her wretched breath nearly knocked her daughter over, as Lucy's super-human strength shook her violently.

Charlotte stared at her mother. Something was clearly wrong, more wrong than normal. Her hair, although usually dishevelled, looked like it had ignored a brush for months and was a tangle of mats and knots. Her typically unfocused eyes were looking in different directions, one pupil more dilated than the other. She appeared thinner too, as if her bones would poke through the stretched-out skin. Charlotte quickly noticed when Lucy grabbed her that the purple marks on her mom's arm were much bigger and very distinctive. "I was... I was... over at the Harrison's." Charlotte tripped over her words, the sight of her mother distracting to her thoughts. "They invited me over for Christmas."

"Did they now?" Lucy stammered out, ripping off Charlotte's borrowed winter jacket. "Did they get you these nice things?" She yelled and tugged on the hem of her new shirt.

Charlotte nodded her head.

"Do you love them more than me?" Lucy asked, fear in her voice for the briefest of moments.

Charlotte knew better than to hesitate, and answered promptly, "Of course not, mother."

"Good!" She yelled again and added, "Then we must remove traces of them from this house."

Without warning, Lucy dragged Charlotte to the pair of mismatched kitchen chairs, and threw her into the one with armrests, the mahogany chair with the crack along the back. With Lucy's sudden strength, she slammed Charlotte onto the hard wood chair, knocking the wind out of Charlotte, leaving her breathless and gasping for air as she heard the crack stretch. Charlotte's heart pounded, racing loudly as her mother produced a roll of grey tape from out of thin air. She watched in total fear as Lucy pulled and ripped off a small piece, holding it in front of Charlotte's face.

Sweat started pouring out of Charlotte's forehead, and her eyes got huge. "What are you going to do, mother?"

Her mother laughed a maniacal, ear-piercing laugh that made the hairs stand up on the back of Charlotte's neck, and pimpled her skin with gooseflesh. She continued to laugh as she applied the tape across Charlotte's perfectly pink lips, pressing firmly. "Now, they'll never hear you scream!" She wailed in malevolent laughter.

Charlotte's hazel eyes stretched wide in horror, staring at the demon standing before her. Whatever her mother was on, it was different and had changed her completely. Lucy had become demonic, and her scary laughter was proof to Charlotte that her mother was no longer present.

Lucy continued to shriek in song as she secured Charlotte's terror-frozen hands to the armrest of the kitchen chair with the grey tape, the cuffs of her shirt pushed up mid forearm. Lucy danced around singing in a tongue unknown to man. She twisted and turned, and twirled into the kitchen, producing a pair of rusty silver scissors, and spun her way back over to where her daughter sat unprotected from the force of evil consuming her.

She giggled inhumanly, and then sang in the sweetest voice that made Charlotte's heart skip a beat. "Time to rid you of these Christmas presents." Wielding the rusty silver blades in front of the hazel eyes pleading for her to stop, she started cutting the cuff of Charlotte's sleeve, shaking as she went. Sometimes the tip of the pointy scissors dug into Charlotte's arm, as the scissors sliced up the fabric, leaving behind nip marks until the blades stopped at the shoulders. Then they started at the other cuff, slashing her skin as they cut through the long sleeve t-shirt. "You'll never have nice things as long as you live under this roof," Lucy said calmly, although the look in her eyes was anything but.

She sliced the blades across Charlotte's chest, effectively separating the shirt from Charlotte's body, leaving more bloody little nips in her pale skin along its path.

Then Lucy quickly did the same to Charlotte's pants, starting from the ankle and ripping the fabric all the way up to the hips, laughing maniacally as she went.

Charlotte closed her eyes, hoping to shut out the visual of her demonic mother smiling as she chopped up Charlotte's brand-new clothes.

"Oh, you don't want to watch," she said snidely, as she threw down the scissors and grabbed the grey tape once again. Cackling, she ripped a piece of tape and then placed it viciously over Charlotte's eye, followed by a piece of tape on the other eye.

Charlotte's world went dark, but her ears sharpened in contrast.

"Look at you, so ugly now." Lucy laughed. "No one will ever love you, Charlie. You're a horrible, worthless person, and I hate you." She spit on Charlotte with the last word.

Charlotte's heart sank, deep into the pit of her stomach. She wanted to cry, but was afraid her eyes might drown. As much as her heart was breaking, it continued to race at a breakneck speed. She listened hard as she heard her mother fall over, and then as Lucy grunted and rebalanced herself. She padded away and returned quickly, the sounds of metal slicing through the air in a snip-snip fashion. She felt her head yank backwards and the scissors chop freely through her coppery waves. Her head started to feel lighter, and much cooler as she imagined her hair falling softly to the floor.

Lucy continued to chant repeatedly, "I hate you and you messed up my life," with each slice of the silver blades.

She winced when the tip of the pointy blade dug into her scalp, causing another round of maniacal laughter to erupt from Lucy. She could feel something hot and wet spread over the pain.

Suddenly, Lucy stopped laughing and Charlotte braced herself for something worse. She heard a loud crash and braced herself even further, as not being able to see made the sound even more frightening. Nothing further came, and she stretched out her hearing, listening for the coming assault, but it was quiet. Eerily quiet. She couldn't move, couldn't see, and couldn't scream. The nightmare she was a part of was as real as it got, although she hoped it was just a bad dream.

She waited and waited, listening for her mom. Did she leave? She didn't remember hearing the patio door open, or feeling the cold air rushing in when it did, nor the main door. Was Lucy sitting somewhere staring at her, waiting for Charlotte to make a move and would then continue to torment her and kill her? She wondered, briefly, if her mother had fallen asleep, but she listened for the sound of rhythmic breathing to back up her theory, but heard nothing. It was beyond strange.

She wiggled a little, having sat motionless for so long and the sudden movement stimulated her bladder, telling her it was nearly full and time to empty it. She wiggled a little further, since no one yelled at her, wondering where her mother had disappeared to. She started counting her breaths to pass the time, waiting for Lucy to return and free her from her prison.

After counting to a thousand, the urge to relieve her bladder was incredible and increasingly painful as she held it in. She tried calling out, but the sound coming from her mouth was incoherent. She wanted to cry, the agony of not being able to pee, and thinking of the pain, her bladder released itself. Charlotte hung her head in shame and in relief, as the warm fluid pooled around her seat and ran down her legs, a strong ammonia whiff floating around. No one said anything about her peeing herself, and it caused her to think again, about where her mother went. Surely, she hadn't taped Charlotte to the chair and then took off to finish up her two-week "holiday" or wherever or whatever it was that caused her to be gone over Christmas. She wasn't that cruel, was she?

Then she heard a knock on the patio door that made her blood turn cold.

"Ms. Cooper?" the recognizable female voice called out again, muffled through the glass door. "Merry Christmas. We brought you a homemade pie."

Charlotte started screaming as loud as she could, hearing her own gagged voice, rocking her chair, kicking, and hoping to make contact with something, anything that would make noise. She kicked hard and knocked her toes against the coffee table, screaming in pain as one of them broke, and then with all her might tried to push over the table with her foot. Success.

The voices called out, much clearer, this time as the patio door slid open a notch. "Everyone okay?"

Charlotte made as much noise as humanly possible, and heard an audible gasp as the velvet sounding voice called out, "Charlotte!" It sounded like pity, but quickly she felt warm hands on her bare shoulders. "Get that sheet and pass it here," the voice, belonging to Mrs. Harrison, cried. She wrapped something around Charlotte's body. Charlotte heard more gasps and the padding of feet across the carpet to the kitchen.

Mrs. Harrison covered up one of Charlotte's ears with her warm hand, and whispered, quite loudly, into the other ear, obviously trying to block out the outgoing phone call from reaching Charlotte, "Everything will be okay."

Charlotte tried listening beyond Mrs. Harrison's voice. She heard a male voice, which could have been Joe's, saying, "Dead... abuse... drugs..." but couldn't make sense of any of it.

She tensed up when she felt the edge of the scissors against her wrist, but then felt relief when she heard them slicing through the tape that bound her against the hard wood arm. Something warm and wet dripped on her arm as the blades freed her. She felt more drips as the scissors freed her other arm and gentle hands slowly peeled the duct tape off her wrists, allowing for a rush of blood into her extremities. She felt tender hands on the side of her cheeks, gently pulling the sticky tape off her lips, accidentally removing the first layer of skin with it. Charlotte was now able to talk and moved her mouth to form a word of gratitude, but no sound came forth.

Mrs. Harrison's voice cracked, "Charlotte, I'm so sorry we didn't come sooner."

Was she crying? Charlotte wanted to see and after she rubbed her wrists, she reached up for the tape covering her eyes.

"No, honey, let the professionals take it off your eyes. I don't know how to do that without... without hurting you further."

Charlotte slid her hand up to the top of her head, gasping audibly as she felt what was left of her hair, and the huge chunky scab on her scalp the scissors carved out. Large sections of her soft, coppery waves were gone. Her hair had once reached beyond her shoulder blades and now, most of it was less than an inch long. She started shaking uncontrollably, and in the far off distance, heard the wailing of sirens.

"Come, Charlotte, let's get you changed into some clean clothes." Mrs. Harrison lifted her up out of the chair that held her prisoner, keeping the sheet firmly around her. Charlotte was glad for the sheet as when she stood up, the cut top flopped down. Parts of her pants and panties were still soaking wet, and the other parts had dried and were stuck to her skin. Walking blindly, and guided cautiously, she entered the bathroom and heard the door close shut behind her.

Mrs. Harrison was very discreet and kept Charlotte as covered up as she could while removing the remnants of clothing. She stepped out to grab a fresh set of clothes, while Charlotte gave herself a quick wash with a wet washcloth. Mrs. Harrison said nothing except, "I'm so sorry," over and over again as she helped Charlotte into some tattered clothes. Charlotte wondered how bad she looked.

When they emerged slightly fresher from the bathroom, two police officers were there, and an ambulance team.

Mrs. Harrison tightened her hold on Charlotte and whispered into her ears, "Charlotte, there are some police here and some EMTs."

The male officers introduced themselves as Constables Hawthorn and Larocque. The second officer asked, "Miss Cooper, can you tell us what went on here this afternoon?"

Charlotte shook her head no.

"Were you hurt?"

Charlotte didn't answer and shrugged her shoulders.

The first officer asked, "Would you like us to help take the tape off your eyes?"

She nodded as he escorted her to the kitchen chair. Once she felt where she was sitting, feeling the tape and the armrests, knowing this chair was her nightmare, she jumped up and started screaming, "NO NO NO NO!" and started to run away. Not being able to see where she was going, she tripped over the body on the floor, and before anyone could break her fall, slammed her head into the corner of the wall.

When Charlotte regained consciousness, she was in a much different room. Thankful that she could open her eyes, she blinked and looked around. She was on a bed with green sheets and pictures of monkeys. An overhead light above bathed her in a yellow glow. There was an empty chair beside her, and a tall table on wheels. The area was enclosed with salmon-coloured curtains.

She reached up and felt a giant goose egg on her forehead. Exploring further up, she touched the top of her head. She hoped it was all a bad dream, but couldn't pull on her hair, as it was too short. It confirmed she survived the nightmare. She tenderly palpated for the wound on top where she'd felt the scissors dig in and then touched her arms, searching out and finding, the nips along her arm and across her chest. She started crying, at first quietly, the tears flowing down the apples of her cheeks. As the tears spilled out, her crying increased in volume.

"She's up," someone said from behind the curtain, and pulled it back. A shuffle of feet, and the first person to step inside the pink wall was Joe.

"Hey, Charlotte," he whispered, as he stepped over to her. He sat at the foot of her bed, and she crawled over to him and into his lap. She curled up into a tight little sobbing ball of arms, legs and broken heart. Joe encased Charlotte in his long arms as she melted against him.

Mrs. Harrison walked in, and having witnessed Charlotte's childlike movements, said nothing, but she did raise her eyebrows.

Joe rocked her, not knowing what else to do or say.

Charlotte continued to sob, her childlike body wracking with each wave.

Mrs. Harrison piped up, "Charlotte, the police are here. They need to talk to you."

Charlotte looked over her knees and above Joe's arm into Mrs. Harrison's warm eyes. She nodded.

"In here," Mrs. Harrison said to someone beyond the curtain.

Charlotte stopped crying, and Joe wiped her tears with his shirt. The constable got very little information out of Charlotte. Joe figured *he* got more knowledge as she stayed curled in his arms, either tensing with a question or relaxing.

Was she ever hurt by her mother? Winced.

Was she afraid of her? More wincing.

Were the marks on her body caused by her mother? She pressed into Joe.

Who taped her eyes shut? A shudder.

Who cut her hair? A soft movement, likely a reaction to touch her head again.

Was anybody else involved? She cowered and pulled herself into a tighter ball when she thought of Barry.

Did she have other family? No answer.

Where is her father? Charlotte looked at the police officer with a blank stare.

Did she know what happened to her mother? Charlotte had no physical reaction when he explained that Lucy had died from a drug overdose in their apartment.

The constable explained to Charlotte, to the other people in the pink-curtained area, how Charlotte was now under the custody of Child and Family Services, and how she'd be placed into a foster home ASAP, until next of kin could be located, and they accepted guardianship of Charlotte.

Mrs. Harrison surprised the unsuspecting Charlotte when she asked if she could be her guardian.

"Yes, you could be. You'd have to apply for it through the courts, and depending on whether or not family is located. They would have access to Charlotte first."

"If I did that now, could she avoid foster care? We know her, and would take care of her, and keep her routines as much as possible, to make this whole situation easier on her. Look how she sits with my Joe."

"That I can't answer, Mrs. Harrison, but I could put you in touch with someone higher up, and they would help you with that."

"Then let's get it done." Mrs. Harrison turned to Charlotte. "That is, if you'd like to stay with us, Charlotte. We'd love to have you."

Charlotte looked up, and a hint of new possibilities flashed across her hazel-green eyes. She nodded.

The doctor cleared Charlotte later that day, having only spent a night in the hospital. The Harrisons became Charlotte's guardians upon her release and pending a short hearing, for temporary guardianship until the courts located next of kin.

Chapter Twelve
✿✿✿

"Mrs. Harrison took care of me from that moment on, until the end of that school year. She asked that I call her mom, instead of Mrs. Harrison, as it was too formal. Eventually we settled on madre, which is Italian for mom. She took me to the hairdressers, although there wasn't a whole lot they could do, but even it out. I got used to wearing ball caps until it grew out, which made me even more of a tomboy." Charlotte spoke softly to Andrew.

Horrified by what Charlotte had just unloaded on him, he held Charlotte tightly.

"She bought me lots of new clothes, which I got to choose." She carried on in a hypnotic-like fashion, "It was a week after the hospital before I spoke to anyone. I told Joe what Lucy had repeated to me that night." She shook her head. "For a little while, I slept with Joe, every night. It seemed to stop the nightmares, and it was too scary to be alone in the dark. I went back to school in the new year with David and remained the social outcast, but oddly enough, I was relieved. At least that hadn't changed. Everything else in my world had."

Andrew wiped a tear from his face. "And then?"

"A mysterious aunt showed up. Somehow the courts located her thanks to my father's name on my birth certificate. She showed up in February, but on madre's insistence, I continued to live with them until the end of the school year. My aunt, who lived on the other side of town, didn't have the means to drive me over there for school, and madre thought it in my best interest to keep everything as it was until the end of June. I got to meet Carol, and she talked about my dad, James MacDougall, who left for the army when he was eighteen. He didn't even know my mother was pregnant with me, or he would've stayed, at least that's what Carol thought. James died when I was ten." Charlotte shrugged her shoulders. "So I moved in with Carol and stayed for three years, until I moved out on my own, back to this part of town."

Andrew couldn't believe his ears. For the past half hour, Charlotte had poured forth a huge chapter of her life, bared the deepest part of her soul, and trusted him with that information. He knew she was expecting him to run, but he stood firmly beside her, still listening in disbelief. His respect for Joe and his family was at an all time high. What a thing to have witnessed and helped her through.

"All my life, I told myself I'd never bring a child into the world unless I had planned and prepared. I never wanted my child to be blamed for my mistakes, as I was reminded daily by Lucy. And yet, here I am, repeating my mother's mistakes." Her shaking returned, and she attempted to lean her head forward, ready to launch it back and knock the sense from her.

In an instant, Andrew foresaw what was about to happen, and he placed his hand there just in time, absorbing the brunt of the blow in the palm of his hand. He pulled her into the tightest embrace he could give her. No intelligent words formed in his head. He just felt the love of his life explode in his tight grasp. Shaking and twisting, he held on harder. "Charlotte," he tried to keep her next to him.

She struggled out of his arms and pushed herself off the floor. "No! I need to go!" Charlotte wept as she pushed past him.

"No, Charlotte, wait." He went to grab her, but she was too quick so he stopped. No point in chasing someone who refused to be caught. He saw the lights from the main door flood into the projection room, and quickly fade.

Charlotte ran to the elevator, and rode it down. Trying to make a quick getaway, she bolted for the door, thankful her car keys were in her pockets. She made all the lights home, and raced for the security of the Fortress. She was surprised that when she opened the door, the alarm chimed, but didn't beep, signalling that the alarm wasn't set.

"Hello?" she called from the front door.

"Hey, Charlotte," called Joe's voice from the living room.

"Hello, Charlotte," came the voice belonging to Chelsea.

Charlotte set her keys in the bowl by the door. "Hey, guys." She looked in the mirror at the door. Her eyes were bright red, a little swollen and they were starting to sting. She looked a little worse for wear. She sighed, and already feeling deflated, thought it best to get this over with now. She slumped into the living room.

Joe shifted his gaze from the TV to Charlotte and jumped off the couch. "What happened? Are you okay?" He practically ran over to her.

Charlotte sat down on the edge of the large couch, facing Chelsea. "You should sit down, Joe." She waited until he cautiously took a seat beside his girlfriend, on the part of the couch closest to Charlotte, never taking his eyes off her. She took a deep breath. "I'm pregnant."

Joe smiled sheepishly. "With Andrew's baby?"

Chelsea smacked him, her face full of concern.

"No," she quietly answered.

Joe's facial expression changed, matching Chelsea's. "Not Jason's I hope?"

"Yes, but it doesn't matter. He's out of the picture."

Joe stood up, anger scarring his face. "The hell he is!"

"Joseph, he's gone, okay? He wants nothing to do with me or the baby, EVER!" Charlotte stood up facing him, the strength of her yell surprising even her.

Joe reached out to Charlotte, placing both arms on her shoulders and gave her a gentle, yet firm squeeze. "What the fuck, Charlotte! You have an incredible knack for picking men." He dropped his arms and started walking towards the kitchen.

Charlotte turned to follow him, anger rising in her chest. "What the hell does that mean, Joe?" She noticed out of the corner of her eye that Chelsea retreated deeper into the couch.

"You have a knack for picking winners for the boyfriend of the year award. You had that date with that major asshole, at the start of the year, which," Joe looked around, "well, you know."

Charlotte's face paled.

"And then you fall in love with Andrew, but do nothing about it, and instead, date another loser, who knocks you up and dumps you!" He poured himself a glass of coke. "Do you know what your problem is? You're afraid to let yourself be happy."

She stood there, fighting the urge to cry, swallowing back her tears, feeling deep within that this was a battle she wouldn't win. *I'm not afraid to be happy. I'm afraid to let people in.*

"You date these losers, and the one guy who'll do anything for you, and has proved that over and over - you push him to the side. Why do you pick the losers? You deserve so much better than that!" He grabbed his drink, walked back over to the couch, and fell in beside Chelsea. He took a sip and set it down. "Have you told Andrew?"

"Yeah."

"Poor guy's going to be nursing a broken heart now, if he wasn't before." He took another long drink. After swallowing a few gulps asked, "So what did he say?"

"Nothing." She paused and played with her slender fingers. Looking up, she added, "I didn't give him much chance to talk as I told him about Lucy." *Why am I even mentioning this in front of Chelsea. Did telling Andrew lessen my need to keep it so secret? Surely, Chelsea doesn't know.* Charlotte took a deep concentrated breath, looked at Chelsea and filled in the blanks. "My mother beat me, sold me to her drug-pushing, raping pimp to pay for her debts, and then nearly killed me." She looked over at Joe, who confirmed with a slight nod of his head.

Chelsea looked as though she'd be ill.

Joe looked at Charlotte. "Seriously, you told him?"

"Yeah, and then I left him there. At work."

Joe whistled a low tune, and then after a bit said, "Well... that's going to impact him further. So what's your big plan now, as far as the pregnancy goes?"

"I don't know." She deflated further.

"Well that's good planning. How far along are you?"

She looked at Chelsea, who absorbed every word and then at Joe. "About five weeks or so."

"I'm assuming that abortion is out of the question?" He searched her eyes for the answer he already knew. "Adoption?"

"Maybe." She shrugged her shoulders.

The tone in his voice rose again. "Seriously? You're thinking of keeping it?"

"I'm confused and frightened about being alone and doing this. I'm scared as hell." She looked hard at Joe. "I'm worried about the whole situation. And I can't run from it. I can't drink to forget about it. The problem is only getting bigger day after day. No matter what I do, it's getting bigger."

Joe breathed out a long sigh. "I don't know what to tell you, Charlotte."

"Please tell me that no matter what happens, which decision I choose, that you won't give up on me, please. Don't tell me I'm making a mistake. Guide me. Support me. Be my friend. Don't let me become her." The tears ran forth from her eyes like a burst water dam, strong and unstoppable.

"That I can do, Charlotte. And you should know that I am ALWAYS here for you. Forever. I'll never give up on you." He stood up and walked over to her, giving her a hug. "I'll always be your friend, and I'll never let you become her. Never ever. Credetemi, il mio amore."

Charlotte, overcome with emotion, sobbed in his arms like a scared twelve-year-old girl.

"We'll get through this, Charlotte. We always manage to find a way, don't we?" He felt her nod. "Now, sit here and watch the *Wizard of Oz* with us. I'll get you something to drink." He walked back into the kitchen and poured her a glass of coke. "Can you drink coke? I think it's loaded with caffeine?"

"Just bring me the damn drink." She laughed through her tears as she accepted the glass.

Charlotte thought a lot about what Joe had said about having fallen in love with Andrew and doing nothing about it. Even Champ had mentioned that the heart knows what it wants. She didn't know Andrew truly felt the same way until just recently. How could she have been so blind? What a mess her life was! She worried now that Andrew would no longer feel the same and that the baby would be the straw that broke the camel's back. And now that he knew about her mother, she couldn't help but wonder how fast he would leave her. Over the next couple of weeks, Charlotte's thoughts seemed to turn into reality.

Andrew was vacant and unfeeling towards her when they passed at work. He talked to her, never truly ignoring her, but it was different. Like he was trying hard to be remote and unfeeling, and it hurt her, deeply. She wanted to be welcoming and friendly, but wasn't feeling up to it. It was getting to be too hard. As it was, the pregnancy changed her already. Her breasts ached all day long, and if she wasn't ravenous with her appetite, then she was throwing up in the bathroom. Her co-workers were starting to get suspicious, but she wanted to wait until the first trimester was over before making any big announcement.

Schedules became routine. Charlotte was now the full time daytime cashier, picking up extra shifts on the weekends. Andrew was now full time evenings, starting at two, so there was always some crossover time between them. He never worked weekends, except on the rare occasions when he filled in for someone. Yet, as often as they worked together, they were hardly together.

The distance between them was noticeable to their co-workers as well. A few commented behind her back when they thought she wasn't listening, that it was a sad thing, and that Andrew was always mopey now. Rumours abounded that he was dating a gallery interpreter.

She was jealous, green with envy, but she couldn't find an acceptable reason for why he shouldn't be able to date anyone. Any life with her would be the death of him. The fun would end. She was a walking disaster, and unworthy of someone like him.

He showed up on a Saturday, covering for a new projectionist, and came up to the desk. "Where's Charlotte?" he asked Russell, as he knew she was working. He saw her car in staff parking. He just wondered where she was avoiding him today.

"Down in the cafeteria, likely," Russell casually answered, "or in the bathroom. I think she's bulimic. I hear the girls saying they overhear her throwing up."

Andrew's colour faded slightly as he walked passed the desk and down the long hallway to the cafeteria, hoping she'd be there. It took him awhile to locate her. She'd tucked herself into the corner and was reading a book, *What to Expect When You're Expecting.*

"Good book?" he asked sliding into a chair beside her, making her jump.

"It's not scary." She continued to read, never looking up at him.

"Thank goodness. What are you reading about?" He looked at her, silently urging her to look at him.

"The Third Month. I'm reading ahead." She looked up at him finally. "I'm almost eight weeks now."

There was a long, pregnant pause between them, and then Andrew spoke up, "I'm sorry for my distance lately."

She put the book down, dog earring a corner to mark her place. "It's okay, I expected it. Once you knew it was only a matter of time."

Andrew shook his head. "It's not like that."

"Sure it is. I let you in, you ran away." She took a drink of whatever clear fluid was in the disposable cup.

"Actually, YOU ran away," he pointed out.

"Regardless, you haven't exactly been around."

He shook his head. "Am I not allowed time to process? You dump two major things on me," he glanced around to see if anyone was listening, "the baby and your mother. I needed time to get through that. And you left me." He looked at her, sadness etched on his stubbly face.

"You would've left. It's too scary to hang out in my life."

He contemplated and chose his next words carefully. "Look, I didn't come here to fight, I came to see you." He gave the book that captivated her attention, a quick glance. "How's the little bean doing?"

"Growing, causing massive morning sickness, and the most intense dreams ever." She attempted a weak smile, but it faltered, never reaching her eyes as her smile usually did.

"I'm sorry that it hasn't been easy."

Pointedly, she straightened herself up. "I never expected it to be easy, Drew. I expected it to be hard. Everything in my life has been hard. It's just the way it is," she growled.

Breaking the direction he foresaw the conversation going, he blurted out, "I've missed you." His voice was honest and sincere.

"Really? I heard you were seeing a researcher. Couldn't have missed me that much." The jealous sound in her tone rang loud and clear. She didn't need to hide it; he knew now how she felt about him.

"I've missed you more than you know." He looked at her, and watched her play with her fingers. "Besides, she's only a distraction."

"I'm sure she'd love to hear that."

"I think she knows. Anyways, look, I came here to make amends, to apologize."

"You have nothing to apologize for. You are not the problem, it's me, and that's okay, it's always been me."

"You're not a problem, Cat. Don't ever talk about yourself that way. Dammit woman. I love you! Can't you get that through your thick head?"

She went to speak, and he covered her mouth with his fingers. He leaned forward, tipping his head slightly as he moved in for a kiss. He dropped his fingers from her mouth and stroked her cheek, feeling the warmth flood beneath them. Their lips touched, and a small spark ignited between them. Charlotte wrapped her arms around his neck, and he lowered his hands and wrapped them around her back. They barely came up for air; finally connecting instead of pushing each other away. They broke their embrace and suddenly felt very much in the spotlight, even tucked away at the back of the cafeteria.

Norah, the General Manager, came looking for Charlotte as her break had ended, and she hadn't shown back up to finish her shift. She was all smiles when she stumbled upon the two.

Andrew looked at Charlotte, who was as red as a lobster, "Guess you're due back at the desk?" He tried to cover up the pregnancy manual before Norah took notice.

"Guess so," Charlotte smirked while standing up. *And there goes my whole I don't date co-workers plan. But really, I don't work* with *him. He's in a completely different department. So does that really break my rule?*

Norah smiled warmly, like she was watching her little sister. "Guess the rumours are true!"

Andrew stood beside her, linked his fingers into Charlotte's and turned her head to kiss her softly. "Rumour confirmed."

Norah left quickly, after her searching eyes spotted the pregnancy book. Charlotte threw the book into her bag. Andrew walked her to her desk and then headed upstairs after another quick kiss. Charlotte had a permanent grin on her face for the remainder of her shift and only vaguely remembered dealing with any customers.

Chapter Thirteen
✿✿✿

Charlotte and Andrew were officially a couple now, and the rumours laid to rest at work. Everyone seemed genuinely happy for them and finally stopped talking behind their backs. Charlotte was much happier, as was Andrew, and it reflected in everything Charlotte did. When she finished work, she would hang out with him for a bit and then head home. Every day was the same, work, see Andrew, finish work, head up to visit with him, and then head home. She tried to sneak in a nap after reheating the supper Joe always left for her, so that she had a little energy when and if Andrew came over after work.

One Sunday night in June, Andrew came over for dinner. They had the place to themselves as Joe was spending a lot of time at Chelsea's place. After eating a pizza, they snuggled together watching a movie. Charlotte getting a little tired, laid her head down on Andrew's lap, and he stroked her hair, rhythmically. After a few minutes, she playfully said, "Andrew?"

"What?" he said innocently, still stroking her hair.

"I feel that." She moved her head from side to side, eventually turning on to her back, gazing up at him.

"Oh, well, it couldn't be helped." He started stroking her cheek, and bent down to kiss her lightly.

She wrapped an arm around him, pulling him down lower, returning his kiss. She loved kissing him.

He moved her slightly, cradling her tiny form gently. Their kisses turned passionate quickly. He extended his hand, gliding it down her arm, across her supple hand, and onto her belly where it rested.

She groaned unexpectedly, as it bubbled from deep within. She stroked his face, feeling the stubble beneath her fingers, a couple days of growth that she found highly sexy. He moved beneath her slightly, and she could feel the bulge below.

"I want to do this, but I'm scared," she said honestly between kisses.

His face hovered above hers, his eyes wide with pleasure, and with the reassuring words, "We don't have to."

She kissed him back, hard, responding to his concern. "But I want to."

"We can stop anytime you feel scared. I promise I won't hurt you." He looked her squarely in the eyes.

She nodded and he picked her up in one smooth motion, carrying her across the living room and into her bedroom. Like a delicate flower, he laid her on her bed, and went to turn on her bedside lava lamp. It bathed the room in a warm orange glow. Slowly and without a sound he moved onto the bed beside her, and started kissing her, softly, gently, without any rush. He whispered in her ear how much he loved her, and reminded her that she could say no at any time. He did not want their first time to be marred with fear and trepidation. He was able to control himself. "Wait," he said, "Condoms."

I'm already pregnant, why would he want to use condoms? Her face fell when reality dawned on her. *Right, they're protection. And he needs to protect himself. From me. In case.* "I don't have any," she said, and then a smile crossed her face. "But I know Joe does. Give me a sec." She dashed out of the room and returned holding some in her fingers. "Three enough? It's all he had."

"Then that will do."

"Now, where were we?"

"Here." He swept her off her tiny feet, and laid her back on her bed. Gingerly, he placed his smooth hand on her tummy, and slipped it under her peacock-blue shirt, moving slowly and carefully, watching her face for any signs that he needed to stop. He kissed her with a little more urgency.

She felt his hand move up slowly, over her soft tummy, and stop just beneath her bra. She kept her eyes closed, sighing peacefully. She wasn't scared of this wonderful man who swelled her heart; he truly loved her, and made her feel safe. She willingly gave herself up to him, without needing any form of liquid courage. She took control of his hand, which she momentarily thought felt as if it had a slight tremble to it, and moved it across the cup of her breast, and stopping, held it there. She kissed him back harder, letting him know he was okay to carry on. She took her free hand and slipped it under his t-shirt, hearing him moan with pleasure.

The hands caressed, and the kisses ignited the fires burning within. Before long, Charlotte sat up and unbuttoned her shirt, and unclamped her paisley printed bra. When her breasts released in the orange glow, the look she saw on Andrew's face was enough to make her heart explode with wanton longing.

"You are so beautiful," he exclaimed faintly as she again grabbed his hand and placed it back on her naked breast. He looked deep into her eyes as she did this.

She gazed at him, and very peacefully declared, "It's okay. I feel safe with you."

In one quick movement, he removed his t-shirt, and she unzipped his pants. She pulled him up on his knees and slowly lowered his pants, displaying his tent of affection for her. He returned the favour, pulling her onto her knees and delicately lowering her pants and panties. She gasped in pleasure, as his hands gingerly glided over her hips. With her fingertips dancing on his skin, they slipped beneath the waistband on his boxers, sliding them down and revealing the beast below. She stared at it, curiously, as she'd never really seen one, just felt the power within it.

Andrew froze, and asked, "You okay?"

She nodded slowly, placing her arms around his neck, feeling the excitement of the moment. They leaned in for a kiss, as her pulse responded to his tenderness.

He then gently lifted her, ever so, and lowered her back onto the bed. He fiddled with a condom wrapper, rolling it down his length. Unhurried, he maneuvered between her long legs, and prepared to come to a full halt, should he see any sign of fear. With a slight quiver in her legs, she opened for him, closing her eyes tightly in the process. He felt her shaking and paused, searching her face. He whispered softly in her ear, "We can stop."

She breathed out deeply, and held him harder, pulling him closer. "I don't want to," and she opened her eyes to face him. Her face spelled desire, and in being with him, in her nakedness her body responded, releasing the tension, and melted against him. She wrapped her arms around him, under his, and pulled him up, closing the distance between them.

He felt the briefest moment of hesitancy when he made contact but the smile on her face told him he was not in danger, that he was being gentle, and tender and loving.

She gasped when he entered, not from pain, but incredible pleasure. She never felt safer in all her life, never felt the all-consuming connection of true love. They rocked together, moaning with delight, breathing the most gentle, yet intimate form of love. Minutes later, when he exploded deep inside her, she sighed and held him tighter.

When he opened his eyes, he saw her crying. "You okay?"

"That was the single best moment of my life," she cried, kissing him hard. "I love you so much."

"I love you too, Cat." He rolled off her, slowly stroking her breasts and belly.

She guided his hand lower, and he was pleasurably astonished when she stopped below the small growth of her expanding uterus.

He looked at her peaceful face, and inched his fingers lower, checking out the curves and valleys, and finding the hidden spot. He found a little nub that she reacted favourably to, smiling largely, as his wet fingers rolled and stroked it. It didn't take long for her to be gasping for breath, and grabbing at him, pulling him closer, gently sucking on his bottom lip. When she herself released, the most serene look crossed her face. He kissed her attentively, as he retracted his hand, and wrapped his arm underneath her. She nuzzled into his neck, whispering thank you, repeatedly. He responded with thanks of his own, and held her tightly, breathing in her sweet sweaty smell.

Their lovemaking finished, Charlotte cradled into Andrew's chest, covered herself up and quickly fell asleep.

"Thanks for the best day of my life," Andrew sighed into Charlotte's ear. He wrapped his arms tightly around her naked body, holding her securely and felt her head find the perfect spot on his shoulder to drift away on. He could feel her heart beating against his chest. He laid there for a long time inhaling the peace, and the love. He was finally so happy, never knowing until that night what true love was, and how it could change you forever.

He tried not to picture their future, together, but couldn't stop himself. He was in too deep now to turn back. They'd make this work, she didn't have to give up the baby. Would they have a son? A daughter? He wondered if the baby would have her coppery hair, her peaches-and-cream skin, and her soft lips. When he thought about the future, he couldn't help smiling. They could get married first, so then the baby would be his, and Charlotte wouldn't have to worry anymore. He loved her like no one else on earth could, and knew the moment he first laid eyes on her that she'd change his life. Now, here he was, perfectly happy, truly in love, and thinking about becoming a husband and a father. He was at peace with where his life was, and loved how the beautiful sleeping Charlotte made him feel. Feeling that emotion, he fell soundly asleep.

He awoke the next morning, and Charlotte wasn't in bed. The sunlight filtered in through the east facing windows, blanketing the room in a soft glow. He stretched out his ear and heard the shower turn off, and minutes later she emerged in a towel, smiling.

"Good morning, Drew." She kissed him, her kiss even sweeter today. "How'd you sleep?"

He propped himself up on one arm. "Best night's sleep of my life. You?"

"Yeah, awesome." She smiled further, lighting up her hazel-green eyes.

His eyes swept over her, her damp coppery hair in long waves over her pale shoulders, sitting on top of the towel. He wanted to remove the towel and swallow in the complete beauty of her in her rawest form. She smelled like heaven too. It was intoxicating. "I was thinking last night," he began, "that this situation you're in with the baby and all, doesn't have to be so one-sided."

She dropped her gaze to her tummy, staring at the unseen baby within. Without thinking, she placed her hand above it. "What do you mean?" her voice changed from sweet to worried.

"No, no, its all good." He reached for the baby-protecting hand, and lifted it to his mouth, brushing it with kisses. "I was thinking," he painted more kisses up her arm, watching her skin produce little bumps of gooseflesh. "Maybe we should get married. Then I can be it's father, you can be my wife, and we can live happily ever after." He was so unprepared for the sound that came out of Charlotte's mouth.

She started laughing, and looked at his saddening face. "You can't be serious?"

"I am." He sat up straighter, still holding her hand.

She retracted her hand, and stood on her feet. "No then," she said abruptly.

"We'll make it work, and it'll be fine. We can do this, our love is extraordinary."

She searched his blue-green eyes, seeing the truth behind them. "Yes, our love is extraordinary, like extraordinarily new! Let's not rush into this. We've only been officially dating for a couple of weeks." Sitting down quickly on the bed, her expression changed.

"You okay?" Andrew asked, concerned at how her expression went from light-hearted to deeply troubled.

"Morning sickness."

"You're sweating." He brushed a hand over her face, pushing the suddenly damp hair off. He felt a ping of concern deep in the pit of his stomach.

"It passes. It's been getting better the last few days. The waves of nausea… " She forced a smile and started feeling better.

After her shower and getting dressed, she asked, "Are you in at four today?"

"Yeah." He looked at his watch. "You've got to get going! You need to be at work soon," he stated.

"I know. I have ten minutes to be out the door."

Andrew grabbed his clothes and threw them on, thinking how fast the time was flying by. He raced out into the living room to tidy up while Charlotte finished getting ready for work.

She came into the living room looking simply stunning, in a knee length pencil skirt, with a white top tucked perfectly into it. She looked much older than her true age, but as he reflected on that, she'd always looked and acted much older, wise to the world.

"You really are breath-taking, Charlotte."

They kissed. "Thanks, Drew."

Throwing the dishes into the dishwasher, and the pizza box in the garbage, they left, securing the Fortress.

Charlotte had an enjoyable day, daydreaming more than she expected. The day passed quickly and soon she saw the love of her life enter the building. They kissed quickly at the desk, as he came behind her to grab the key off the desk.

"You coming up after?"

"No, I'm going to go home, and get some sleep. Feeling a little off, tired I think." She winked and leaned in for another soft kiss.

The tall man with bronze hair, and caring blue-green eyes, whispered in his accented voice, "No more nausea?" He felt her shake her head side to side. "Good." He broke their public embrace.

"I'll see you tomorrow then?"

"You're in at four again?"

"I might come in early." He smirked.

"I'll be here." She blew him a kiss.

Andrew spent his time writing Charlotte a beautiful love letter, professing the feelings he felt for her and outlined how easy their future could be. He went home, happy, and was ecstatic to hear her voice on his personal answering machine. She talked until the machine cut off, and then left another message, in a breathy voice, that bid him a good night.

Before heading into work the next day, Andrew stopped off at a flower shop, picked out a bouquet of beautiful flowers and put the love letter inside. Then he headed into work. He expected to see her seraphic face, the one that lit up from within whenever she saw him, as he approached the desk. He was quite early for his shift, but she wasn't there. The parking lot was full, but he couldn't remember if he saw her car or not. Silently carrying the bouquet of flowers, he knocked on the office door.

Paulette answered, glancing at the fresh cut stems. "Hey, Andrew." She turned to look at the board that held the keys. "The key isn't here yet."

"I know, I'm early. Where's Charlotte?"

"She went home early, around noon, complaining of stomach cramps. She looked a little green so I sent her home."

"Thanks, Paulette." He walked slowly over to the desk, and dropped the bouquet off, and as a horrible thought of a miscarriage popped into his head, he bolted for the door. The Fiero's engine redlined as he sped towards Charlotte's apartment.

He zoomed into the visitor-parking stall nearest the building's main doors, nearly hitting the wall as he slammed on the brakes, and ran for the buzzer. He pushed it repeatedly.

A weak sounding voice answered, "Hello?"

"Cat?"

"Yeah."

"It's Andrew... Can I come up?"

Long pause. "It's not a good day today, Drew. I'm very sick."

He started to get very worried. "Cat. Please let me in." Waiting for the sound of the door to buzz open, he tapped his foot. Nothing. He stood waiting for another minute, and then watched as a couple exited the building. Just before the door clicked locked, he grabbed and pulled it open. Within a short minute, he knocked on the Fortress door. "Cat, it's Andrew." He knocked again.

The door opened slightly, the chain securing it to the door. "Andrew," she said sighing.

"Please let me come in. I can take care of you," he pleaded.

"Not today." She lowered her eyes, rimmed in red, and stained with a heavy tired look.

Andrew bartered with her. "You can let me in, or I can stand out here and knock every five minutes until Joe gets home or I get arrested."

She closed the door, and he heard the chain slide off. She let him in.

Closing it behind him, he followed her into the living room. Under his watchful eye, he scrutinized the way she slowly laid down and curled up on the couch. He went to the other end of the couch, lifted up her legs, and slid behind them.

"Paulette said you left early today, because of stomach cramps?"

She wrapped her arms around her tummy. "They've been getting worse."

"Are you throwing up?"

"Just once, but I'm very nauseous."

He felt her forehead. "You don't feel warm."

"I know."

Andrew guessed by the thermometer on the coffee table that she'd already checked.

She continued to lie there, moaning a bit. She sat up after a bit, claiming she needed the bathroom. After a good ten minutes, Charlotte still hadn't returned. He started to worry again, and got up to go and check on her. He walked into her bedroom's ensuite. Charlotte was rocking on the toilet, pale as a ghost. Andrew met her gaze and followed it downward. He saw the drips of blood.

"I'm bleeding. A lot," she blurted out unapologetic for the lack of discretion.

Andrew had been worried that this was happening, ever since he heard stomach cramps. He had hoped he was wrong. "Let's go." He dug around under her sink, looking for some feminine hygiene products. "Pads?" he asked.

"At the far back," she whispered as she moaned.

He reached to the back, grabbed the bag and passed it to her. "Put these on, and let's go. I'll give you a moment of privacy, but I'll just be outside of the door." He could hear her deep moans.

She emerged, looking paler than ever and shifted slowly. "I should pack a bag, just in case."

With an overnight case, Andrew led the way, and encouragingly pushed her, with his hand on her lower back.

Charlotte's far off moans and the sounds of the engine screaming, weren't enough to cover Andrew's thoughts on the ten-minute worrying drive. Without thinking, he carried her into the emergency department, and up to the triage desk. In a voice that wasn't his own, he told the nurse that his girlfriend was likely miscarrying as she was bleeding heavily.

The nurse had Andrew place her into a chair, and she took Charlotte's pulse, her blood pressure and her temperature. All were normal. "How far along are you?"

"About ten weeks."

"Have you had any cramping?"

"All day."

"When did you start bleeding?"

"I'm not sure, but just before we came here, I felt something like a pop and when I went to the bathroom there was blood all over my underwear."

"Any tissue that you noticed?"

"Like Kleenex?" Charlotte asked dumbfounded.

"No, did you notice anything that may have looked like the remnants of bodily tissue?"

Charlotte burst into tears. "Eww… am I going to have to see that?" She reached for Andrew's hands on her shoulders, and then bent over in pain. "I felt another pop." She moaned loudly.

The nurse turned her back to them and looked up at the large board with numbers, names and conditions scrawled across it. "We'll put you in room five." She unhooked the blood pressure cuff. "Follow me."

Charlotte stood up, and was horrified when she looked down. Her nightgown looked like a war zone; there was blood all over the lower part.

The nurse looked over and calmly said, "We'll take care of it, don't worry." She acted as if this was something that happened all the time.

"How could she not worry," Andrew thought, "all that blood came from inside her." He shuddered.

They got into room five, which he was glad to see was an actual room with a door and not one of those non-private curtained off rooms. He recognized the room, however, from when he was here with Charlotte, after "the incident". He shuddered, again, as that memory came flooding back. Andrew was starting to detest hospitals.

"Change into this gown, and put on this maxi pad. Here's a pair of stretchy panties to put on." The nurse opened drawers and pulled out the pads and panties. "I'll give you a minute, and I'll be back with someone from OB."

Andrew looked around the room. "I'll just step outside."

Charlotte, growing paler by the minute, pleaded, "Stay please."

"I'll turn around then."

Charlotte took off her nightshirt and threw it towards the garbage. She pulled on the thin, fabric hospital gown, snapping up the sleeves and tying the back. She went to pull down her panties, when a sharp pain racked her body. She moaned loudly, and fell against the exam bed. Andrew turned around to help her. The pain passed, along with another popping feeling. Her colour drained further.

She started to pull off her bloodied panties and stopped. There on top of the pads she wore to the hospital, no bigger than an inch, was what looked unmistakably like a little alien baby. Charlotte let out a bloodcurdling scream and immediately two nurses burst into the room.

One person went right up to Charlotte and the other bent down, explaining that she was going to remove the underwear.

Andrew fell back into a chair; shaking and turning the colour of sea foam as he realized what that was, on top of the pads. He felt very weak and nauseous. His mind suddenly blank as he closed his eyes.

Charlotte sobbed uncontrollably, as the one woman who removed the panties tried to put on the stretchy pair.

Once the change happened, she stepped out of the room quickly returning with a binder passing it to the other woman who stood there. "Hello, Miss Cooper. I'm Doctor Jones. I see you just experienced a complete miscarriage." Her voice was detached, and not at all soothing.

Charlotte sobbed unable to put words together, "Is that... was that ..."

Dr. Jones calmly said, "Yes," as if it was no big deal to have witnessed that. She just stood there while Charlotte cried and cried. "You've done the hardest part. Now we need to watch your bleeding." She turned around to the pads that sat in the stainless steel bowl on the counter, out of view for both Charlotte and Andrew. She gloved up. "When did you put these pads on?" She turned and leaned back against the counter, waiting on their answer.

Finally, in a moment of surprising clarity, Andrew spoke up, "Just before coming here."

"Do you live far away?"

"Ten minutes."

"Okay, that's a lot of blood to pass so quickly. We'll monitor you to make sure it starts slowing down. The bleeding clots and pain will usually settle now that most of the pregnancy tissue has passed. Sometimes, however, the bleeding continues to be heavy, and you may need further treatment. But let's just wait it out for a bit and see." She looked from Charlotte, who looked traumatized, to Andrew and back again. "I'll be back in a bit to check up on you." She held the stainless steel bowl. "I'll be right back, Sharon." Just like that, she was gone.

The nurse named Sharon asked gently, "Now, Miss Cooper, what can I do for you? Is there anything I can get for you? Can I call anyone for you?" She placed her arm lovingly around Charlotte.

Charlotte just shook her head. She thought about calling Joe or madre, the closest thing to a mother she had, but stopped herself from saying anything. Madre, who had been less than thrilled to hear that Charlotte was going to have a baby, still supported her, just like Joe had done. For a moment, the tears falling were a reflection on the disappointment she thought madre would feel over losing a grandbaby.

The nurse looked between the two of them and before leaving said, "I'll give you both some time to process. If you need anything, please just push the call button."

Charlotte stood there, stiff and unmoving, against the exam table. *I refuse to get on it, or to sit down. I don't want to sit though, what I really want is to lie down. Although, what I truly want is to go home.*

Andrew continued his shocked silence and sat in the chair, fighting the urge to throw up. His eyes unfocused, not seeing anything clearly, and his thoughts were so random, that he started to think he was losing it.

They didn't talk to each other, they didn't touch each other, and they weren't even looking at each other. Like two lost ships in a fog-covered ocean, not knowing how to find the other. Neither had moved in the thirty minutes since the nurse left the room.

When Nurse Sharon returned, she glanced quickly between the estranged couple, and to Charlotte said, "Have your contractions stopped?"

Charlotte nodded an affirmative.

"I need to just check your pads, to see what the bleeding is like." She patted the black padded exam table.

Charlotte shook her head.

The nurse put her hand between Charlotte's shoulder blades. "It'll just be a quick peek."

Charlotte shook her head again.

"She won't get up on the exam table," Andrew piped up coming out of the fog for a brief moment. "She had a rape kit done on her in this very room, and I know she won't get back on that table."

The nurse nodded in understanding. "Okay. I'll see what other arrangements I can make. Clearly this isn't a pleasant room for you both to be in." She walked out of the room.

Andrew slumped back into his chair, tiny beads of sweat forming at the base of his neck. He listened as his stomach churned, which was louder than Charlotte's quiet sobs.

Dr. Jones returned a moment later, and leaned against the counter, observing the two people who were very close to going into shock. She spoke with an air of indifference, and said, "Okay, we took a quick look at the tissue you passed, and it indeed was complete. Your bleeding should've slowed down, and the pains should not be much worse than what you would experience with your menstrual period." She looked at the binder she held. "I've spoken to Sharon, your nurse, and she's explained the room situation. Unfortunately, we're too full to change rooms, so what we are going to do is to have you change your pads and put them into this bag," she pulled out from her pocket, "and we'll check every hour for the next few hours. If the bleeding slows like we expect, we'll be able to release you very soon."

She looked at the statue-like couple. Silent tears falling from both. "Okay. I understand that what happened today has been a shock to you both. It's quite common for it to happen. The reasons for it happening are unknown, but are commonly hormonal problems or genetic abnormalities. Is this your first miscarriage?" When there was no answer, she opened up the binder she carried, flipping through her chart. "Okay. It's hard to say with any degree of accuracy, whether you will miscarry again. Some do, and some do not. You are young, so you have an age advantage that will work in your favour. We recommend you wait until you've had two complete menstrual cycles before attempting another pregnancy." The room was quiet enough to hear the pen scratch across the paper. "I'll leave you some information on miscarriages, right here. There are also some resources in there to help you process what's gone on, and how to move forward. If you have any questions, please feel free to call my office, my number is listed on the back." She glanced between the two, and then talked to Charlotte, "I'll need your pads please. I can show you to the bathroom." She tapped Charlotte on the shoulder, who robotically followed the doctor out of the room.

When she left the room, Andrew grabbed a little bag he found after rifling through a couple of drawers and threw up into it. He cleaned himself up and tossed the bag in the garbage, rinsing his mouth at the little sink, before Charlotte came back in.

She entered, and he instantly threw his arms around her, holding her tightly. Her arms folded up between them, her head rested against the soft spot in his shoulder.

Sometime later, Sharon quickly escorted Charlotte to the bathroom and back. Passing the wrapped pads to the nurse, Sharon remarked that they felt considerably lighter, and she'd see about getting her released.

Returning as promised, she announced, "I have your release forms. If you can sign here, Miss Cooper," she indicated, passing a pen to Charlotte, who scribbled a signature. "You're free to go home. You can leave your gown on the bed."

"Thank you," Andrew said, passing Charlotte a change of fresh clothes from the overnight bag.

"Leave the door open when you leave. If you have any questions, or if the pain returns, or the bleeding increases, please come back and see us." She bid them well and left.

Andrew held Charlotte's hand out of the emergency room. He got her safely tucked into his car, and drove her home.

Charlotte fell into a depressive state afterwards. She was even worse than after the incident. She didn't talk to anyone at work, except for the customers, and even then, only spoke the bare minimum required. She picked at her food and only drank her favourite tea, liquorice, as her source of energy, and it didn't give her much.

Three days after the miscarriage, Andrew had to explain the situation to Norah, as much as it pained him to do so. Charlotte took her float, and he followed her over to her desk. Logging in robotically, she started to process the customers before her. He couldn't watch his beloved Cat moving so stiffly, without emotion. He gave her a quick kiss on her cheek and walked back to the GM's office. He knocked on the door, and Norah let him in. "Can I talk to you?" he asked solemnly.

"Of course," she replied, pushing a chair towards him.

"It's about Charlotte." He rubbed the top of his legs. "She's having a bad week. A really bad week."

"We've noticed. She's not perky like she usually is. What's up? Is she okay?"

"No, not really." He rubbed harder and heard Norah pull her chair up closer to him. She was much older than he was, maybe in her late thirties. She was well liked by the staff and very compassionate, which he needed right now. He knew she'd seen the book that day in the cafeteria. Breathing hard and fast, Andrew blurted out, "Charlotte miscarried on Tuesday." He felt a lump reform in his throat that always bulged when he thought about that day.

"Oh, Andrew," Norah began, "I am so sorry. For the both of you." She placed a warm hand on his knee. "What can I do for you?"

"I don't know. I don't know how to help her, but I needed you to know why she's so withdrawn."

"Indeed she is, but she's still doing her job. Does she want some time off?"

"I don't think so," he quietly cried, "I don't know what to do." He whispered, "We were so happy for a brief moment."

"I'm very sorry, Andrew." Norah said again, as the young adult hunched in the chair. "I'm sorry for your loss."

He didn't want to correct her and inform her of who the true father was. He was sure, like Norah, everyone at work would suspect that the baby was his. In a way, it was. He was ready to take on that huge commitment and raise the child as his own. His eyes overflowed again at the thought of the way his future dramatically, instantly changed course. "If I'm this devastated, I can only imagine how she is, but she won't tell me. She's keeping her walls up. Maybe she doesn't need me."

Norah patted Andrew's shaking shoulders. "Tell you what, I'll cover the rest of her shift, and you take her home to rest. Talk to her okay?"

His voice weak, barely answered, "Okay."

"I'll call Tony upstairs and explain. I'm sure he can cover you or find a sub."

"No it's okay, I'll take her home and be back for four."

"You sure?"

Andrew nodded. His bronze hair lay flat on his head, he hadn't bothered to make it deliberately messy, so he ran his hands through it.

"Okay," she said standing, "I'll go relieve Charlotte, and I'll see you later."

Andrew wiped his eyes as she left.

A couple of minutes later, Charlotte entered the room with Norah, carrying her cash tray. Charlotte looked between Andrew and Norah, asking neither one in particular, "Why am I cashing out? I just got here."

"I think it's best if you took the day off and rested. Come back tomorrow if you're feeling better," Norah answered.

Fire lit up in Charlotte's hazel-green eyes. "You told her?"

Finally, Andrew was pleased to see some emotion, even an angry one, and he nodded as Norah put an arm around Charlotte.

She looked at Andrew and pushed off Norah's arm. "That was our secret, Drew!"

"But it doesn't need to be, Cat. I'm trying to help!"

"By telling everyone I'm defective?" She stared at him coldly. "Thanks a lot, Drew."

"I'm only trying to help. I never said you were defective. I love you so much."

She threw her float on the cash table and grabbed her coat and purse from her locker.

"Charlotte, wait!" He wiped his eyes on his sleeve.

"Don't follow me, Drew!" The door slammed shut as she stormed through it.

Andrew opened the door, but Norah intervened. "Give her a moment."

He shook his head, glancing at the large clock in the room. "Can I have a moment of privacy then?" He watched as Norah exited the office and picked up the phone. A sleepy voice answered on the third ring. "Hey, Joe, it's Andrew."

"Andrew buddy," Joe's voice sounded as though he awoke with the phone ringing, "what's up?"

"Charlotte's on her way home."

"Okay. It's kinda early. Is she okay?"

"No, currently she's pissed off."

"Umm... okay."

Andrew sighed. "When was the last time you saw or chatted with her?"

The line was quiet for a few seconds. "I don't know, our schedules are opposite. Monday maybe. Why?"

Andrew shifted in the chair, and switched the phone to the other ear, sighing. "Well…," he breathed out, trying to hold back his own tears, "she miscarried on Tuesday night."

"Dio non e!" Joe spat out in Italian and then whispered, "Why didn't she tell me?"

Andrew twirled the phone cord. "I have no answer to that. Norah just sent her home though, to rest. She's been very distant, very robotic." He could hear Joe rustling around.

"Thanks for the heads up, amico."

"Joe," Andrew started, again fighting back the tears, "could you do me a favour?"

"Yeah buddy, what?"

The lump started forming again in his throat. "Can you tell her that I love her, and that I'm sorry. I had to tell Norah. She just hasn't been herself."

"Are you okay, Andrew?" he asked sweetly, concern in his voice.

"No, but I will be eventually. I'm really worried about Charlotte though."

Joe sighed, "I know you are. That's why you called me. Come for lunch okay?" pausing and then adding, "Give me some time with Charlotte, and then come over. Please?"

"I don't think she wants to see me."

"Maybe, maybe not. But *I* want to see you. Twelve-thirty okay?"

Andrew could barely whisper out an affirmative.

"No, thank you. She's home. I hear the alarm panel beeping."

The phone call ended swiftly. Joe grabbed a pair of pajama pants and jumped into them. "Charlotte?" he called, pretending to be surprised.

"Hey," she dropped her purse on the shelf by the door, and hung up her coat.

Joe closed the distance between them. He towered over her, and she looked directly into his chest. He kissed her lightly on the forehead. "How come you're home already? I thought you worked until five today."

"I thought so too, but I got sent home."

"Did you get fired?"

She looked up into his green eyes. "You look wide awake. You weren't sleeping were you?"

"No, just talking to a friend, making lunch plans."

"Oh," she acknowledged, not pressing further. "I'm going to my room."

"You okay, Charlotte? Anything you want to tell me?" He followed her down the hall, watching as she grabbed a change of clothes and went into her bathroom. He said nothing as she stepped past him and crawled into bed. "Not feeling well?"

"No, Joe, I'm not," she snapped.

He climbed into bed beside her, wrapping an arm around her. "Did you and Andrew have a fight?"

"No," she sighed, "but he needs to learn to keep his big mouth shut."

"It's only because he loves you, Charlotte," Joe muttered.

She looked into his wise, all knowing eyes. "You know, don't you?"

He held her tightly, pulling her into his chest, stroking her head. "I'm so sorry it happened. I wish I knew."

"What was I supposed to do? Leave a note on the kitchen counter?"

He kissed her forehead again. "I don't know, but we just want to help you."

She didn't mean to, but she yelled, "How can you help me? I'm defective."

Joe sat up. "CHARLOTTE MARJORIE COOPER – I NEVER WANT TO HEAR THAT STATEMENT COME OUT OF YOUR MOUTH EVER AGAIN!"

His strong willed voice shocked Charlotte. In all her life, he had never yelled at her.

"Do you understand me? Never again!"

She looked up into his eyes. They held many emotions, sadness, stress, friendship, love, and anger.

"You are amazing, and wonderful, and better than that!" He looked at her and softened his voice. "Yes, you got dealt a shitty hand of cards, but that doesn't mean there's something wrong with you. For whatever reason, it happened. We'll deal with it. Together. But you are not to blame. Not ever!"

Charlotte snuggled under her blanket, wiping her eyes with the edge. "What if I am? Andrew and I... well, we did it... on Sunday night and right after, well... that's when it started."

For some reason, hearing Charlotte talk like that, trying to explain it, it brought out something in Joe. In a smiling voice, he said, "So, you guys finally did the deed?"

Embarrassed, she exclaimed, "Joe!"

"I'm just happy that *that* finally happened." Changing his expression to a more serious one, he asked, "Did you ask the doctor about it?"

"No."

"Would it make you feel better if you did?"

"I don't know, maybe."

"Well, call and ask. Might put your mind at ease, but I'm sure it has nothing to do with it." He gave her a hug. "Love you, Charlotte."

"You too, Joe."

"Now, are you hurting anywhere? Can I get you anything?"

"No. Just tell me that I'll be okay."

"Will you believe me?"

"Eventually."

"Then I'll tell you when you're ready to believe me. For now, rest, then I'll make you some lunch." He stretched out beside her, crossing his legs at the ankle as she snuggled into him.

She laid her head against his bare chest, listening to the sounds of his strong beating heart. Like a gentle rhythm, it lulled her to sleep.

Joe fell asleep too, and woke up sweating under Charlotte only when he heard the phone sing out it's unique someone's-at-the-door ring. He glanced at the clock on Charlotte's night stand – 12:30 – and pulled himself free from under her dead sleeping weight. Unable to check the TV for visual confirmation of who was at the door, he answered the phone with, "Andrew?"

"Hey, Joe."

"Come on up," he whispered, and then stretched and sauntered to the front door to open it. He brushed the mop of golden curls off his forehead and out of his sleepy eyes. He heard a soft knock on the door a moment later. "It's open." Joe was shocked when Andrew walked in looking so… distraught.

His eyes were puffy and the normal sparkle replaced with dullness. He walked like Atlas, the weight of the world upon his shoulders.

"Sorry about … everything."

"Thanks," he mumbled looking Joe over. There were sleep lines across his chest, and his expression was lacking. Plus he stood there only wearing pajama bottoms.

"Would it be weird if I wanted to give you a hug?"

Andrew stared up at Joe. "Yeah. Is she here?"

"Still sleeping I think." He cocked his head towards her room. "Go. I'll get lunch ready shortly."

Andrew removed his shoes and lightly padded down the hallway, turning left into Charlotte's bedroom. He stood at the entrance to her room, and after taking a quiet breath, entered. Standing silently beside her bed, he watched her breathe, noticing how peaceful she looked while sleeping. He sat down on the bed.

Feeling the bed shift, Charlotte blinked open her eyes. "Drew?"

"Hey, Cat," he reached for her exposed hand, "you still mad at me?"

"No. I understand why you did it."

A smile spread across Andrew's face. "Thanks."

"I'm sorry for snapping at you. Before."

"I know."

"What are you doing here?"

"I was invited for lunch."

She sat up slowly and put her long, lean legs over the edge of the bed. She gazed at him, noticing how the last few days seemed to have aged him. His bright eyes, dull; his smile warm, but cautious; his skin not as smooth and healthy coloured. "I'm sorry, Drew."

"You have nothing to apologize for."

"I'm sorry you're hurting so much. I didn't think this would affect you so much, especially since it wasn't your baby."

"Cat, I care for you deeply, and what hurts you, hurts me. I love you too much to watch you go through this alone. Please drag me down with you. Or let me lift you up."

Charlotte grabbed the sides of his stubbly face, and with eyes overrun with salty tears, she kissed him hard on the lips. When they came up for air, Andrew was crying as well.

He put his head on her shoulder, and she did the same. For a moment all was quiet, and there was peace.

Chapter Fourteen
✿✿✿

Within a couple of weeks, Charlotte came around to her normal, bubbly and cheerful self. She was back to her jogging, and her weekly visits to Caritas Covenant to visit with Champ and Mrs. Kennedy.

Andrew was pleased about her return from the dark and told her he had a surprise for her. He let Joe in on the surprise as well as some of the staff.

One Friday morning, Andrew arrived at the Fortress before Charlotte left for work.

"Happy birthday, Drew!" She gave him a once over. "What are you doing here?" she asked.

"Good morning, m'lady. Your white horse awaits you." He bowed towards her, and pointed towards the floor.

"Drew," she said mockingly and placed a hand on her hip while rolling her eyes, "I can drive myself to work."

"Not today you can't. It's my birthday weekend, and I want to drive you to work."

"You feeling okay?" She smiled at him as she saw something wickedly fun flash across his face.

He extended an arm, and she hooked hers through his. She closed the door and walked beside him, down to his white car.

She was surprised when they arrived at work, but enjoyed walking hand in hand around the reflection pool. Calm waters mirrored the building in both land and sky. They breathed in the fresh morning air, and listened as the birds gave them a private concert. Charlotte buzzed the locked door.

Paulette pushed it open. "Good morning, you two. Didn't expect to see you in until four, Andrew."

Charlotte wasn't sure, but she thought she saw Paulette wink at Andrew.

"Just bringing my pretty lady to work." He smirked as he escorted her to the GM's office. "Now, I bid you adieu, my beautiful lady. See you at four for shift change." He bent down lightly and planted a sweet kiss on her lips, before bowing once again. Smiling at the puzzled look on Charlotte's face, he turned and strolled away. He went home and had lunch, before packing an overnight bag and heading to the Fortress. Joe had packed a bag of Charlotte's stuff, after she left for work, for Andrew's surprise. He placed the bag into his trunk and went to surprise Charlotte.

She beamed when he sauntered in just before four and readily passed him the key.

"Won't be needing it." He winked, unable to control the smile that spread across his face. "Gregory's covering for me." He nodded at Paulette, who stood behind Charlotte. "Now, let's get you cashed out."

She cashed out quickly, thanks to Paulette's help, all while watching the playful smile on Andrew's face. *Something's up. Something is definitely up.*

When she finished, he gave her a quick, loving kiss. "Ready?"

"Where are we going?"

"You'll see." He led her by the hand, pacing himself while stopping every few feet to plant a kiss on the top of her hand, then her wrist, the hollow of her neck. Finally, standing beside his white car, he lifted her up, and she wrapped her legs around him, and planted the most intense, passion-fuelled kiss on her soft, sweet, eager lips.

Feeling weak in the knees, she looked up at him. Breathless she whispered, "What was that for?"

"Cuz I love you." After opening the door for her, he got into the vehicle and started it up. "I like a drink when I travel, want one?"

She nodded, thoroughly confused, but delighted at the same time. "Sure, a coffee would be great."

He drove to the nearest drive-thru and ordered a couple of coffees before heading towards the western sky. Charlotte had no idea how far west they were going until she began to see the Rocky Mountains rising against the setting sun. Andrew refused to answer questions about the destination, despite Charlotte's pleas. It was dark by time they drove into the town of Jasper. Slowly, relying on some map in his head, he drove directly to a little inn nestled in the back of town.

He parked the car, took her hand and helped her out into his waiting arms. "Breathe in that fresh air." He gulped large inhales of mountain air.

Charlotte did the same, and stretched out.

Andrew checked in and escorted Charlotte to their little retreat - a quaint little room at the back of the inn. It was surprisingly decent, despite the 1970's style décor of orange shag carpet and a brown, weathered pull-out sofa. Tucked into the corner of the main room, by the patio door, was an old-fashioned fireplace, a bundle of logs already cut and waiting. A small kitchenette and a tiny bathroom outfitted the main floor.

The bedroom, with a queen-sized bed covered in an orange and brown floral motif bedspread, was up a small set of stairs to the loft area that overlooked the tiny, yet cozy living space. It was there that Andrew dropped off their bags.

He stood out on the balcony, while Charlotte finished freshening up. "Too bad it's dark out, otherwise we'd have a great view of the mountains."

"Maybe tomorrow?" She searched through the darkness, hoping to see an obscure outline in the moonlight, and leaned against the solid plywood deck enclosure. He wrapped his arms around her tiny waist, nuzzling his chin into the hollow of her shoulder. She turned and smiled up at him, snickering lightly, "What are we going to do with our time here?"

He leaned in closer to her. "I was thinking that we grab a bite to eat, then go for a little soak in the hot tub. There's one downstairs by the pool. After that, we relax."

Charlotte's eyes teased. "So? We could've done that at home."

"Yeah, but we don't have a fire place to keep us warm all night, nor a hot tub to sit in."

"No, you're right."

"We need the weekend to relax and be ourselves again. Just enjoy each other, and no other worries."

She reached for his hand and entwined her fingers in his. "I can do that."

"And you will. We'll go back so relaxed and rejuvenated. It'll be good for our souls."

Charlotte couldn't help but match grins with Andrew.

They ate and changed into their swimsuits. The pool felt a little cool to them both, so they sat beside each other in the hot tub and watched the little kids play and splash in the pool.

"Are you getting hot?" Andrew asked as he lifted himself up onto the edge of the hot tub. His face flushed. He wrapped one of her tight curls around his finger.

The heat and humidity caused her hair to curl from waves to ringlets, and pulled the damp strands off her neck. Charlotte wiped a trail of sweat off her cheek. "Very!"

"I dare you to jump in." He stood beside the hot tub, sweat emanating off his perfect body.

"You first."

"Nuh uh. Together."

Charlotte shook her head. "I'll go in slowly." She lifted herself to sit on the edge of the hot tub. Before she could say anything, he swooped her into his arms and started running. "Put me down, Drew!" she yelled, but he ignored her. Suddenly, she felt the cold water surround her.

They broke through the surface of the water, laughing and gasping. She put her arms around him, pressing into his chest to try to stay warm. He wrapped his arms around her slender waist, noting how thin she suddenly felt to him, the stress of the past few weeks having taken its toll on her body. They looked longingly into each other's eyes, before sealing the moment with a kiss.

Time stood still, and for a while, every pain they had both experienced vanished. It was just them, falling, and no one trying to stop them.

Finally, when Charlotte started shivering, they decided to hop back into the hot tub.

"Hey, where did everyone go?" Andrew asked, looking around the vacated pool.

"Don't know. Maybe they were afraid their kids would get the wrong idea from a couple of love-starved teenagers?"

"I'll have you know, I'm no longer a teenager."

"Right you are. You're a decade older than me now." Charlotte giggled. "You're in your twenties, I'm still in my teens." She hopped into the steaming tub. "Whatever, you're still older."

Andrew beamed. "I love you, Cat!"

Charlotte cradled against his chest, and warmed back up. The only sound in the pool area was the hot tub jets, and the beating of their hearts.

Feeling light headed from the warmth, Andrew and Charlotte decided to climb out and towel off, then walk back to their room. While she was in the shower, he got a roaring fire going. Without a word, he opened up the fold-out bed in the room, and the young pair of star-crossed lovers lay upon it. Andrew tenderly held Charlotte against his chest, combing her wet strands with his fingers. She inched closer to him, laying her body against the length of his, watching the flames flicker and dance, until they were consumed by sleep.

Having not closed the floor length, room-darkening curtains before watching the fireplace, the bright light from the morning sun woke up Charlotte as the beams danced across her cheeks. She quickly looked towards the fireplace. The once roaring logs had exhausted themselves and left piles of ash in their place. Charlotte's stomach rumbled as she greeted the morning with a smile. Inching out of the pull-out, Andrew awoke.

"Good morning," she smiled, placing her hand upon his toned chest.

"Morning, Cat," he yawned.

She stood up and stretched. "I'm going to go clean up, and then we'll get some breakfast?"

"Yeah, that sounds good." He rolled over and fell back asleep.

"Drew," the soft voice called out to him. "Drew." Charlotte's sweet voice spoke to him again. He peeled opened his lids, and stared into the eyes of the most beautiful woman he knew. Her wavy, copper hair pulled into a loose knot, with her bangs falling ever so slightly into her hazel-greens. They had the tiniest hint of makeup, and her perfect lips tinted with a pinch of gloss. He reached up to her and pulled her across him. Her sweet giggle was music to his ears. He'd been waiting patiently for his girl to come back, and here she was, in her angelic glory. He kissed her softly, and then tickled her, kissing her more when she squealed with laughter.

"Drew!" she said pushing him away tenderly, "I'm hungry."

"Okay, okay." He rolled out of bed and went to the bathroom. A few minutes later, he emerged dressed with a clean face, fresh breath, and perfectly manicured hair. "Shall we?"

She grabbed her sweater, and together they walked up and down Main Street until they found a nice little place to eat.

"I love Jasper – there are no major retailers here. Just these mom and pop shops." She pointed to a block of little stores, with unique names befitting the wares of merchandise inside.

"I love it here too." Andrew pulled her against the brick wall of a building for an impromptu kiss.

She didn't resist, for a few moments anyway. "What will people think?" she asked breaking away.

"That we're in love?"

"Well that's obvious."

"Who cares? They don't know us from Fred and Ginger." He kissed her again, and added, "You really need to stop worrying what people think," as he pulled her into a whimsically named place called "Hole in the Wall" where they dined on the best eggs Benedict with French roast coffee.

All day long, they enjoyed each other's company, checking out the neat offerings of each specialty shop. They walked around the Rocky Mountain town, hands glued together, and ignored the bystanders with each profession of love.

That evening, after a brief catnap, they checked out the pub that was just off the main floor of the inn. Decorated in the same 1970's style décor as their hotel room, they selected a deep green, curved vinyl booth off to the side of the stage. A live band, the Rocky Mountain Moonlighters, played some very upbeat jazzy music.

Charlotte and Andrew ordered their drinks and food, and listened to the music. After they finished sharing a plate of nachos, the band started playing an old Ray Charles song, *You Don't Know Me*. Andrew slid out of his side of the booth and offered his hand to Charlotte.

"Here?" she whispered and looked around, feeling a little self-conscious.

He nodded in the affirmative.

With trepidation, she slid out, and stood up.

He placed her lean arms around his neck, and in turn, wrapped his arms around her waist. Instinctively, she laid her head against his shoulder, and he nuzzled into her neck. Together they swayed in perfect time to the music, listening to the words the band sang. Andrew gave Charlotte a little squeeze.

The song finished, and the band played a cover of Tony Bennett's *The Way You Look Tonight*. The young couple stayed locked together, dancing entranced by the jazz music that beat in time with their young hearts.

Whatever songs the band continued to play, it kept the couple moving slowly. Their eyes closed, breathing harmoniously and swaying in time to the strums of the bass guitar. For once, they weren't hurting anyone, and nothing was hurting them. Their hearts were full of love and whatever happened in the outside world was in another time and place.

They moved to the melodies for a few more songs, until the band announced that they were going to take a twenty-minute break.

Andrew and Charlotte sat down in their booth, their enchantment broken, as the lead singer walked over and said, "Thanks for that. We've never had a couple dance to our music. You've made our night."

"Thanks," Andrew started, "for the wonderful melodies. We needed that." He looked at Charlotte, a picture of perfection. Her face was serene, and anyone could tell she was lit up from the inside out. She was radiating love.

"Yes, thank you." Charlotte blushed. "It was beautiful."

"My utmost pleasure," he said in his deep baritone voice. "You two, have a beautiful night." He walked away after shaking their hands, and strolled up to the bar.

They finished off their drinks, and headed back to their room. They got a fire going, and pulled open the couch making it into a bed. The firelight bathed the room in warm flickers of yellow and orange. They snuggled up together, Charlotte lying on Andrew's chest, his arm holding her close. Entranced by the flickering glow, they snuggled tighter, content to connect together, no sounds aside from the crackling wood, and the occasional pop.

Charlotte broke the silence when she whispered, "Wish it could stay like this forever."

Andrew kissed her delicately, covering her sweet tasting lips with his. "Me too!" he uttered. Their kisses progressed from delicate kisses on a rose petal, to intense and deep, and passion fired. Andrew slowly moved his hands up the length of her leg, over her hips and stopped at the small of her back. "I want you," he whispered softly into her ears.

The sound of his accented whisper sent tingles through her body. She turned to him and in a voice only the two of them could hear, said, "I want you to want me, as much as I want you."

Their kisses turned into a passionate rage. "You're safe in my arms, Cat. I'll never hurt you," he said in response to a shudder he felt.

"I've never felt safer," she breathed between kisses she felt on her neck. She relaxed into his hold, and welcomed him deep into her soul.

Charlotte awoke in the early morning hours and rolled over to face him. The fire was still going, illuminating the room with it's glowing embers. She stared at the handsome man lying beside her. The light was very dim in the room, and yet, she saw Andrew more clearly than ever before. Despite the constant dealing of bad cards, here was a man that loved her deeply, without conditions, and was always there for her when she needed him the most. He knew her better than she knew herself. His heart was more perfect than anything ever created.

She looked at his face, his eyes were relaxed and tucked into a peaceful sleep. He was her version of perfect; his expertly designed nose; the pale pink lips and three days of stubble growth making him even sexier than before. She smiled at him in the soft ember glow, and whispered, "I only breathe for you, because of you. I couldn't imagine anyone else that fills me up with the love and tenderness you have for me. You make me want to be a better person." She closed her eyes as she stroked his cheek.

Unbeknownst to her, Andrew had awakened when she moved but continued to lie still, thinking she'd gone back to sleep. At her comment, and the gentle way her fingers felt across his face, he sighed, "I love you too, Charlotte."

Her lips found his in the growing darkness, and again, for a moment, time seemed to stand still.

S adly, for the young couple, morning soon approached. It was time to pack up and head back to reality. Both were scheduled to work the next day, and they still had a four-hour drive ahead of them.

They grabbed a quick breakfast before they headed east. The trip home was a quiet one. Charlotte watched the mountains retreat in her side-view mirror, while she held onto Andrew's hand. She relived the magic of the weekend. Sure, it had been a great weekend, truly full of love and wonder, but it had also been a relatively quiet one. Neither had really talked, as they would at work, or in the projection booth, nor even when out for dinner. The conversation was missing. It wasn't an awkward or uncomfortable silence, but she noticed it. They'd spent the weekend, one on one, with lots of intimate connections, so why did it feel so different now? *Is this what love is? The quiet that comes with being in love? That there's no need for constant conversation?*

Andrew drove the road home. He kept it over the speed limit, not racing, but feeling an urgency to get back home. Oh, how he loved the weekend he'd just spent with Charlotte, so deep and personal. He felt he brought out the woman in Charlotte, the one he'd been waiting to see, many times over. A happy, love conquers all type. She smiled lots, and he'd missed that smile. Yet, every time he glanced over at her now, she seemed distant, a little sad. Was she upset that the weekend was over? That they needed to go back to work and live in the real world? He hoped things were back to where they were, just before she lost the baby. He didn't know what she was feeling, but felt asking would be out of the question. Therefore, he held her hand, and kissed it when he thought about it.

Andrew pulled up in front of Charlotte's apartment. They both sat there, looking at each other, lost for words.

Finally, she broke the silence, "Thanks for the most amazing weekend." She smiled a big smile. "I had a really good time."

Andrew looked delighted. "So did I. Maybe things got back on track?" He hoped that it wasn't pushing it to ask.

"I think so," she answered as she leaned over the console for a kiss.

They both got out of the car. Andrew grabbed her bag from the trunk. "See you tomorrow!" he said passing the bag to her.

"Indeed." She winked and waved goodbye.

"Charlotte, wait!" he called out, chasing after her. She turned around, and he grabbed her head in his hands and placed a soft tender kiss on her lips. He felt her weaken slightly. "Until tomorrow," he said, stepping back and letting his hands fall. She just looked at him in awe. He waved and drove away.

She almost skipped down the hall and into the Fortress. The alarm was off. Joe was home.

"Hey, pretty lady, how was your weekend?" Joe called out from the living room as she dropped her bag at the doorway.

She blushed slightly and smiled. "It was good." She stood at the entrance to the living room and propped back against the wall.

"No need for details," he exclaimed, looking up at her face, "but it's nice to see you smile again. You had me worried."

She walked over to where Joe sat on the couch, and she slumped down beside him. Then she turned slightly and leaned against his chest.

"I'm sorry I was mopey. You know, before."

"Hey, you've nothing to be sorry for. I'm sorry it happened, especially when you were starting to warm up to the idea of having a baby." He kissed the top of her head. "But now it's happened, and it's time to move on." He heard her sigh.

"I'm trying. I'm trying to start anew, and I think this weekend was what I needed."

"Good! Whatever happened, it helped. You look radiant!" Joe shifted slightly.

"You know, I had a great weekend. We totally relaxed, we swam, we walked around town, we danced, and we enjoyed just being with each other. So why do I feel like something was missing?" She looked up at Joe's face.

He shook his head. "I don't know, Charlotte. Sounds like you had the perfect weekend. I can't imagine what was missing."

"Hmm," she sighed. "It was quiet like."

"Well, you were busy."

She playfully smacked him. "No, not because of that. Just in general. Like we didn't have much to talk about."

"Okay."

"No, it was weird, now that I think about it. How can a couple not have anything to say to each other?"

"You mean you didn't talk the whole weekend?"

"No, we did, but it was just random stuff. You and I, right now, are having a deeper conversation than Drew and I had."

"Okay, that is weird."

"We shared so much of ourselves physically, but the mental part seemed missing."

"Well, if I may, Charlotte," he began looking down at her, his deep-green eyes full of reason and logic. "You two just went through something traumatic, and he shared that with you. Tried to help ease your burden where he could. Maybe you just needed to share personal space, without talking about it or anything. Maybe, just maybe, he was afraid of going down that road. That if he said anything, you would spiral down a bit, and he didn't want that to happen. Do you think?"

Charlotte reflected on what he said. "Maybe. I've been an emotional anchor tying him to something relatively unstable. He's never been much of a talker, that's always been me. Perhaps he just needed to connect physically with me."

"And, maybe," Joe started laughing, "maybe you overanalyze stuff and see things that aren't there."

"Oh hah hah!" She laughed.

"Guys are different. We don't need the blah blah blah part of the relationship. We're just happy to have sex, and lots of it, and share that with someone special. Don't need no psychoanalytic bullshit. Just let us be us."

"Thanks, Joe. You really know how to change it all around, don't you?"

"You know it, girl." He slid out from under her. "As much as this is enjoyable, Charlotte, you leaning on me and all, I need to get to work."

"Fine. Go," she said, playfully pushing him away. "Maybe I'll come in tonight, and hang out."

"If you want, it likely won't be busy, being a Sunday on a long weekend."

"Well, then maybe I will. Would be nice to hang out and be a pain for you." She laughed.

Joe walked down the hall to his bedroom. "If that's what you want to do, Charlotte."

That was exactly what Charlotte did. After she grabbed a shower and some supper, she drove over to JT's Pizzeria and hung out. She went outside with Joe for a quick smoke, her first cigarette in nearly a week. Then she sat with her former co-workers, each taking a few minutes to sit with her.

Meadow was starting her dental assistant schooling on Tuesday and she was quite excited about leaving JT's Pizzeria and breaking that dependence on her dead-end job. She was living at home, in her parent's basement and would be in school full time. If her course load was bearable, she'd work a couple of shifts a week, otherwise, she'd be devoting her time to school. She wanted to move on and feel more like a grown up. She was turning twenty-one soon, and felt it was time. On more than one occasion, she'd kicked herself for starting college so old, and if she'd gone when she graduated high school, she'd already be making real money, in a real job, with a real future.

Charlotte told her though, that if that happened, then it was unlikely that they would be friends, since they'd met each other while they were both at JT's Pizzeria, and these things happen for a reason. She couldn't help but to agree with that.

Charlotte left to go home sometime before midnight. She sat on the balcony of her apartment, watched the stars twinkle and smoked another cigarette. *Maybe I should move on too? Meadow's going to school. Joe talks about leaving JT's Pizzeria. Andrew's going into his third year. Maybe I should grow up and find something too.*

She exhaled and wondered what she could take. Something that wasn't a long school commitment, because she really didn't want to spend all her free time studying and hanging out with people who were just starting university. She wanted to do something, but was unsure of what. She went inside after extinguishing her smoke and flipped on the TV.

"Late night infomercials..." she sighed, flipping the channels. One commercial caught her eye. They talked about a long distance teaching assistant program that would match you with a school to train at when you were near completion of their twenty-four month long program. You worked on the program in your spare time, as long as you finished within three years of receiving the first course load.

"This, I could handle," Charlotte said, grabbing a notepad and jotting down the information. *I'm really going to get info from a TV ad? I've crossed some kind of line here.* There were other jobs listed on the commercial, but the teaching assistant one sounded interesting. Charlotte went to bed afterwards, thinking about this new possibility.

The next day, Charlotte headed into work ahead of schedule. She started at four, but got there just before 3:30. As she pulled into her spot, she saw a white sports car pull in on her left side. She smiled.

They exited their vehicles together. "Hello, Cat."

"Hello, Drew."

They kissed quickly, and headed down the path towards SEARCH, hand in hand.

"How was your evening yesterday?" he asked, squeezing her hand.

She giggled a little bit, "Good. Really good. I hung out at JT's Pizzeria with Joe and Meadow, and then when I got home, I saw an infomercial for a correspondence school, to take a course in being a teacher's assistant. I thought about it all last night, and all day today, and I think I'm going to phone them tomorrow and request more information."

Andrew let her ramble on. "It's nice to hear you excited about school. Or at least the possibility of it." He kissed her again. "I'm happy for you."

"Thanks," she said, "I'm excited. Can you imagine me working with kids?"

"Yeah, I can, and I think you'll be great at it! If you really like it, maybe ask Paul for a job during the Christmas and spring breaks teaching the junior high camp programs. That could maybe help you out too."

"You're a genius!" she said, smiling at him.

After grabbing his key, he headed upstairs, and she grabbed her float from the office and sat at her desk. Charlotte had a great shift, and her GM noticed it too. When she cashed out at the end of the shift, Norah remarked how nice it was having her back, not just in a physical way, but emotionally too. It was great seeing her having a fun time at work, and enjoying being there. She mentioned that whatever caused the shift in her mood, it was great. She gave her a hug.

Charlotte was really starting to wonder how low she'd really sunk. *I thought I was functioning, but it seemed like that was all I was doing, just getting by. Everyone keeps commenting on how much happier I am.* However, she felt better about herself, and was finally excited about a future, at least a possible future.

After her little talk with Norah, Charlotte went upstairs to see Andrew. She called when she was outside the door, and he raced over to let her in.

They kissed quite a bit in the projection room, until the movie ended and Andrew resumed his job, shutting down the audio system and putting the reels away.

They left the building together and sat between their cars on the curb. The moonlight from the full moon was brighter than the streetlights, making it hard to discern any stars or constellations. Charlotte stared off into space.

"Back to school tomorrow." It wasn't a question, merely a statement that she made.

"Yeah, back to early mornings, loads of studying."

Charlotte leaned against the front bumper of Andrew's car, putting her long legs on the curb. "You excited?"

"A little. Third year, kind of exciting, lots to do to keep me busy." He leaned against her car.

"Yeah." She maintained, "You'll be busy."

He rubbed her outstretched leg. "But not too busy for you, Cat." He winked. "Promise. I won't ignore you."

"Good!" She leaned forward for a kiss. "Because I just wished on a star."

Chapter Fifteen
✿✿✿

Charlotte put her car into park, and stared at the building. It was Friday night of the Thanksgiving long weekend, and it also happened to be her birthday, although she could do without celebrating that; she was twenty today. Her teens were officially behind her, although she didn't feel any older.

At Joe's insistence, she'd switched out her regular daytime shift for an evening shift, since he was working that and he wanted to make her day special. In typical Joe fashion, he made her a wonderful breakfast and took her out shopping. For nothing in particular, just to take her out. They ended up walking the length of West Edmonton Mall, but instead of shopping, spent part of the day riding the rides in Fantasyland – the giant indoor amusement park. She couldn't remember the last time she'd been on a roller coaster, nor screaming so much from pure joy and exhilaration that her throat hurt. Joe won her a little stuffed bear, so she named it Joey. Then they dined at a New Orleans style bistro down Bourbon Street, before parting company.

She continued to sit in her car, until she decided to have a quick smoke before heading in to start her shift. She stepped out of her car and pulled out a pack of cigarettes from her purse. Charlotte was surprised to see, upon opening the pack, that there were only three left. *What the hell? Where'd they all go? I just bought the pack this week. Should've lasted a lot longer than that.*

Shrugging, she pulled one out, gave it a light, and while exhaling, she leaned against her car.

An approaching voice called her name and startled her out of her reverie. Glancing around, she saw Andrew walking up to her from the building. She checked her watch to make sure she wasn't late.

"Hey, stranger," she sucked back another long drag.

He walked up to her, and kissed her on the cheek before saying, "Happy birthday, beautiful."

"Thanks. It's just another day." She moved downwind of him.

"Aren't you going to give up that awful habit?"

"Eventually, but I rarely smoke around you, stranger."

"Would you stop calling me that?" Andrew pulled the cigarette out of Charlotte's hand and stomped it out on the ground

"Would you stop being one?" She crossed her arms in sudden anger.

He went to open his mouth and then stopped. "I'm tired of making apologies to you, Cat. You know that I have to study hard. It takes up a lot of my spare time. If I'm going to keep up my 4.0 GPA, then I really need to focus. I need the scholarships." He sighed. "I'm sorry if our work schedules are out of sync, and we only see each other like ships passing in the night. Blame Russell for that, since he puts the schedule together."

"I will blame Russell for the work schedule, but Drew, we're boyfriend and girlfriend, and lately all I've felt like is a, is a..."

"What?"

She stammered out, "I don't know. But I'm not feeling the connection anymore. It's hard to say I'm with someone when I'm not really with someone. I've seen you twice outside of work since school started... five weeks ago. I'm tired of hanging out here when I'm done work only to watch you study. I want to do something, go somewhere, and be your girlfriend away from here! And I don't think I'm asking for too much, am I?"

"No, you're not." The sunlight reflected off the tips of his hanging head, making them glow a brilliant bronze.

Even when she was making him sad, he was still so handsome. She hated to see him like this, but she was learning to stand up for herself, like he'd taught her. *I want to be a priority to you, at least in your top five things to do, if not in the top ten. Between school, work, your mom, and anything else that seems important, I feel like I'm losing the battle.* "Not that there's anyone else I'd rather be with than you, Drew, but maybe we should…"

He placed a finger over her soft lips. "Don't! Don't even say it. It's not going to happen, Cat. I promise, I'll try harder."

"And then I'll be the reason your marks are slacking, or your mom doesn't see you, or you miss out on a scholarship by that much," she pressed her finger and thumb within a millimeter of each other, "because your demanding girlfriend needs some time alone with you."

He stared at her, looking deep into her eyes. "What do you want from me, Cat?"

"I. Don't. Know." She shrugged and locked up her car. "A guilt free relationship. Where everything is perfect and no one gets hurt."

"You want a fantasy."

"Maybe. But I don't need to feel guilty for wanting to see you, away from here, and away from your books!" Turning, she walked away from Andrew. She marched towards the building, past the reflecting pool where the most colourful flowers still bloomed on the mini island. She stomped through the main doors, and headed through the lobby to the cashier's desk.

She was more than stunned to see an embarrassing display of helium balloons, a dozen of them at least, reading "HAPPY BIRTHDAY" in various colours, all tied to an orange weight. On the desk, in the space designated for binders and manuals, there was a gorgeous bouquet of flowers with the colours of sunsets – pinks, yellows and a sea of orange. Sensing his presence, she turned around and spotted Andrew, a few steps behind her.

"Happy Birthday," he growled as he punched the "up" button on the elevator and stepped in.

The copper-headed adult watched as the elevator rose up to the top floor. She tried to call up to him whenever she had a chance, but he never answered. Feeling even worse, she cashed out alone and took the bouquet with her. She left the balloons behind.

He caught up to her, just before she reached the car. "Cat!" he yelled out.

She wheeled around. "Oh, you're talking to me now?"

"Yeah, I am. Please, don't leave mad."

She opened the door to the backseat and placed the vase on the floor, hoping it would remain standing on her way home. "Drew, it's late. And I'm tired. Thank you for the flowers, by the way, they're beautiful. "

"They're merely a weak reflection of you, Cat."

"Stop it," she blushed.

"Listen, I've thought about what you said." His chest heaved. "And you're right. You are absolutely right." He stepped forward, closing the gap between them. "I decided that you are too important to me right now to lose. So, from now, I promise to try and be a better boyfriend. Okay? I'll give you a few hours a week, away from here, to be with you. It's important to me that you know you're loved. You never ask for anything so I know you bringing it up means it's bugging you." He searched her face, watching emotions flick like someone was channel surfing. He stepped closer, and holding her face between his two hands, kissed her as if his life depended on it.

He felt her surrender to his hold, and that intensified his feelings. Her lips parted, welcoming him home. He enjoyed the sensation of her hands wrapping around his neck, and tangling in his hair.

"Come home with me," she whispered in his ear, as she placed soft little kisses along his neck.

With the strength of a dozen men, he tore himself away from her, and nodded. He kissed her again before saying, "I'll follow you."

The alarm was barely turned off before they were tearing the clothes off each other. A leather jacket dropped on the floor of the kitchen. A black sweater hit the floor down the hall. A polo shirt turned inside out fell to the floor, and Andrew stood there naked from the waist up, kissing with unyielding passion and pushing Charlotte up against the wall. He tugged her blouse out of her black pants, not being able to unbutton the top fast enough. Between his fingers and hers, she was shirtless in seconds, her shirt hanging around her wrists. He pulled open her pants, and let them drop to the floor, letting her step out of them as they continued their passionate dance down the hall. Stopping at her doorway, she unzipped his jeans, and heard the seam rip on her blouse, as she pulled too hard to free her arms from her sleeves. Throwing her shirt to the ground, the underwear clad lovers, pushed into her bedroom.

She felt his strong hands slide under the straps of her polka dot bra, slipping them over her smooth shoulder, feeling a trail of kisses behind his soft touch. She moaned as he tickled his way with his fingertips to the latch of her bra, and in one smooth move, unhooked and freed her breasts. With more force than she expected, he pushed her backwards until she fell onto the top of her bed. He pounced like a lion to straddle her.

A voice that was not hers screamed out, "NO!" She cowered and covered her eyes with an arm, and pulled herself into the fetal position, shouting "NO!" over and over again.

In a nanosecond, Andrew realized his push was mistaken for something aggressive, instead of passionate and he stopped, jumping off her. "Cat? Cat!" he cried out, and flicked on the bathroom light, flooding the room with diffused brightness. "Cat, I'm sorry!" he pleaded. Moving with caution, he sat beside her and rubbed her exposed back. He grabbed the bottom of her comforter and pulled it up over her, making her feel less exposed. "I'm so sorry."

She shed bitter tears. *I know he'd never hurt me, not in that way. So what the hell happened? Where did that intense fear come from?* Trembling, she tried hard not to pull away from him as she felt her arm lift off her face.

"Cat, look at me please!" It wasn't a question, but a soft demand.

She opened her eyes, and looked into his. He looked terrified, scared of what just occurred. He blinked his blue-greens, trying to comprehend what transpired.

"See, it's just me." He touched her cheek as though she would break. "I'm not going to hurt you, Cat."

In a feeble whisper, she said, "I know." She searched for her inner strength to return, and guide her. She clutched the comforter, covering her vulnerability. "I don't know why it happened, but suddenly I was freaked out."

"I'm so sorry. It was not my intention to frighten you." He kissed her hand across the top. "You know I'd never hurt you."

She nodded. "I know." She sat up, keeping the comforter snug. She took a couple of deep breaths. "If we go slow, I'll be fine."

He moved and sat beside her, wrapping his arm around her and pulling her across his chest. He kissed her head. "I'm okay to wait a bit. That took the wind out of my sails."

During the Christmas break Charlotte and Andrew didn't get the chance to see each other very often. They had a handful of shifts together, and the other shifts they only saw each other in passing. Charlotte came down with a cold just before Christmas, and it gave her a rough time. She worked still, wearing an extra layer for warmth, and always had a warm cup of her favourite tea beside her desk to fend off the occasional coughing fit. She looked less than the epitome of health, but she needed to work. Her next payment was coming due for her course, and she didn't want to have to pay interest on her credit card. She even passed on going to the Harrison's in Calgary for Christmas, since she was ill and needed to work the stat holiday shifts that paid her double time.

The day before New Year's Eve, she took a shorter shift, working a four to nine. Andrew was also working that same shift, training a new projectionist.

Andrew came down after the start of the four o'clock show, leaving the booth in the hands of the trainee. He sat behind the desk where Charlotte worked, across the grand foyer of the SEARCH lobby from her usual spot. Andrew gave her a hard time about being at work when she should have been home having chicken soup and resting. She laughed at him, which caused her to have another coughing fit. She stood up and walked further from the desk. After catching her breath, she was able to get a drink of warm tea, which ceased her coughing spell for a moment. She blew her nose, and went to the bathroom to wash her hands. Andrew was sitting in her chair when she returned.

"All better?"

"Yeah." She leaned against her desk.

"See what I mean? You should be at home."

"Well, I'm not dealing directly with the customers, just over the phone, so it's good. And besides, everyone is keeping their distance." She nodded across the great hall, to the other main desk, where two other cashiers dealt with the incoming customers.

Andrew looked across the foyer and waved at the cashiers, both of whom were staring in the direction of the young couple. Andrew laughed. "Children."

He gave Charlotte a kiss, and headed back upstairs. "I'll be back after five."

After getting the new guy to set up the 5pm show, he hopped in the elevator to hang out with his favourite cashier.

Andrew could see that Charlotte was all red in the face as the elevator descended. He dashed over to her desk. "What's up with you?"

"Another coughing fit." She barked, while she stood up, holding her arms around her chest.

"You're not sounding good, Cat. Why don't you go home?"

She started coughing again. Andrew just watched, shaking his head. He passed her the mug of lukewarm tea from her desk. She took a quick sip, but it didn't stop the coughing. She kept on coughing, unable to catch her breath. He watched as she pulled out her purse from under the desk, and dumped the contents on top. She searched for something between coughs.

"What are you looking for?" he asked, panicked at the speed of which her belongings flung across the desk.

She barked out, between coughs and breaths, "My inhaler. It's white."

Andrew helped in the search, while the coughing and gasping sounds continued. "I see nothing." He looked at her.

"Coffee..." she whispered.

Andrew hopped off the chair and ran to the cafeteria down the hall. He poured a cup, and then added a few ice cubes before dashing off. The cafeteria worker called after him. "Follow me then!" he yelled back. He could easily hear Charlotte's coughing as he approached, and noticed how different it now sounded from a regular cough. He passed her the coffee.

She waited until she had a moment and then took a sip of the black coffee, checking more for the temperature than anything else. Satisfied that it wouldn't burn her throat, she gulped the rest down. She started coughing again. She shook her head. The cashiers from across the hall came over to investigate, one by one. Charlotte had a hard time catching her breath.

Andrew stood beside her, watching her and wanting to help. "What do you want me to do?"

Charlotte stood there, wheezing and gasping. She pointed to the phone.

He picked up the phone, and he watched her punch in 9-1-1, before she sat down in the chair, hacking up her lungs. One cashier, Cara, came around the other side of the desk and held her hand.

"9-1-1, what's your emergency?" said the calm voice on the other end of the phone line.

"Medical."

"One moment please, we're transferring you." Andrew waited, watching and listening to Charlotte.

"9-1-1 emergency. How can we help you?"

"I have a medical emergency. She's having an asthma attack and can't catch her breath." Andrew said in the calmest voice he could muster, which wasn't very calm at all.

All the commotion around the desk encouraged other staffers to come over. Paulette, who was the GM on shift, walked over asking, "What's going on?"

"Charlotte's having an asthma attack," repeated Cara in a whisper to Paulette.

Paulette told the other cashier, J.J., standing at the desk, to run to the office and grab the blanket. She threw him the keys, and he took off, as other staff arrived.

The emergency call worker replied to Andrew, "Has she taken her inhaler?"

"She can't find it."

"What's your location?"

Andrew gave out the address and added, "We're just inside the main doors. You can't miss the crowd." He glared at the bystanders.

"Stay on the line until EMS arrives, please. They've been dispatched and should be there within minutes. Now tell me, what does her breathing sound like?"

"Raspy. Very raspy." Andrew placed the phone near Charlotte's mouth and after a few breaths, put the phone against his ear. "See."

"Yes, I heard that, sir." He could hear the clicking of a keyboard. "How long as this been going on?"

"Well, she was having coughing fits all day, but I would say that it's changed drastically over the last ten to fifteen minutes." He glanced at his watch. It was already five fifteen.

Andrew looked over at Charlotte. J.J. arrived. Paulette draped the blanket around Charlotte and rubbed her shoulders.

"When did she start gasping and wheezing?"

"Five minutes ago?"

"Check her fingernails for me. What colour are they? Pinkish or blueish?"

Andrew lifted up Charlotte's hand and stared at the fingernails. "They're not blue-blue, but they're not pink either." More typing.

The emergency call worker continued, "Make sure she loosens any tight clothing around her chest." Andrew looked at Charlotte. She wore a loose t-shirt under a sweater, nothing that looked constrictive. "Make sure she sits up comfortably, and don't mistake drowsiness as a sign of improvement, it could mean things are getting worse."

"Okay." He looked around and noticed quite a crowd had formed. Paulette, the two cashiers from across the hall, the cafeteria worker who had followed him, a couple of researchers, and some of the general public. He looked back at Charlotte. She pushed her purse contents out of the way, put her arm down on the desk, and laid her head on top of it. Andrew turned his back to Charlotte and whispered into the phone, "She just laid her head down on the desk. How close are they?"

"Sir, they are very close. I see that they have pulled into the parking lot."

Andrew turned back around and rubbed Charlotte's back. "Good." To Paulette, he said, "They're outside."

She jumped out from behind the desk and ran to the front doors, and when the paramedics got to the door, she pointed them towards the crowd of people.

"They're here," Andrew said into the phone.

"Alright. I'll let you go. Thanks for calling." The line went dead.

Pulling the gurney, with some black cases on top, the paramedics pushed through the crowd and got to Charlotte. One EMS worker, whose nametag read Colin, grabbed a tank of oxygen and went over to Charlotte. He kneeled beside her, placed a mask over her face and turned on the tank.

"What's your name, miss?" he asked.

She tried to answer, but no sound aside from wheezing escaped.

Andrew answered for her, "Charlotte Cooper."

"Miss Cooper, we're going to take good care of you, okay?"

The other EMS worker, named Seth, passed a hand held machine over, and Colin, the first EMS guy, a tall blonde-haired young man, slipped something onto the end of Charlotte's index finger and strapped it to her wrist. Then he grabbed an inhaler from inside his bag that Seth had passed over and started to shake it.

Charlotte grabbed his wrist with her unobstructed hand and looked at the inhaler. Her eyes were big.

"Salbutamol," he said, showing her the inhaler.

She shook her head. "Allergic," she breathed out and released her grip.

The blonde EMS worker turned to his co-worker. "Need something different." He threw the inhaler to Seth. He turned to Charlotte. "Do you know what you use?"

"White," she breathed. "B..."

"Bricanyl?"

Charlotte nodded while still wheezing.

Seth threw another inhaler towards Colin. He also tossed him a medication spacer. Colin pumped the inhaler into the spacer, lowered the oxygen mask that Charlotte wore, and placed the breathing spacer overtop. She breathed the medication. He placed the oxygen mask back on her face, and took her pulse, her blood pressure, and finally her temperature. The crowd got a little bigger.

Seth stood beside the desk and said out loud, "Can we thin the crowd a bit?"

Andrew looked at Paulette. As General Manager, that responsibility fell to her. She responded as such. "Okay, everyone except Andrew, back to your jobs please." Against the natural curiosity to watch, the crowd broke away from Charlotte's desk. Instead, they gathered around the main desk across the hall.

The EMS worker beside Charlotte removed the oxygen mask and gave her another dose of the Bricanyl. He then did another pulse check, and blood pressure check.

Charlotte's wheezing decreased.

Colin stood up and told Seth. "She's stable, but we'll need to transport. BP is 90/65, pulse is in the 140s, and pulse ox is 82%."

Andrew had no idea what most of that meant, but looked over at Charlotte, concern etched across his face. She was pale, and he could see that she was breathing rapidly, as her chest was heaving. She looked up into his eyes.

The blond EMS worker squatted in front of Charlotte. "We're going to take you to the hospital. Can you walk over to the stretcher?" He stood up.

Charlotte rose up as the EMT held the oxygen tank beside her. She took a few, careful steps to the waiting stretcher. They lowered it a bit so she could get on it without a struggle. Seth now stood behind her and helped scoot her back, and Charlotte lifted her legs on. He propped up the head of the stretcher and Charlotte leaned back against it, as the EMT put the oxygen tank onto a clip behind the head. The EMTs strapped Charlotte in, and Colin covered her up in a blanket.

"Okay, we're good to go," said Seth as he put the cases near Charlotte's feet.

Andrew grabbed the open purse on the desk, wiped the contents of the desk back into Charlotte's purse, and took off in hot pursuit of the two EMTs and Charlotte.

"Can I come with her?" Andrew pleaded as they approached the ambulance.

Seth opened the door. "Sure, ride there," he indicated the right side of the ambulance.

Once Charlotte's gurney clicked into place, Andrew hopped in. Colin got in behind him and Seth closed the doors and started driving to the hospital.

Andrew leaned closer to Charlotte. "Are you feeling a little better?"

Charlotte breathed into her facemask, "Much." With a weary smile, she coughed a little.

The EMT adjusted the mask and produced a stethoscope. He had a quick listen to Charlotte's breathing. He grabbed the areochamber, and the Bricanyl, and proceeded to pump in another couple of pumps. He removed the mask and placed the spacer over her face. She breathed in, taking in as much air as she could, feeling a little more capable of deeper breaths. After a few breaths, the oxygen mask came back on.

Charlotte glanced at the watch like thing on her wrist, as the EMT raised it to look at the reading.

The EMT looked at both Charlotte and Andrew. "Getting better, she's up to 88%, and her pulse is decreasing to the mid teens."

They both nodded, pretending they understood.

It wasn't long before they were pulling into the ER bay and wheeling Charlotte into the ER. Bypassing the triage desk, the EMT pushed Charlotte down a long hallway, and placed her inside a room marked with the letter "A". They assisted her off the stretcher and onto the ER bed, since she still wore the oxygen mask and wrist pulse-oximeter. Before long, a nurse and doctor came into the room.

"Hi, Miss Cooper. I'm Dr. Staley and this is Nurse Savannah." He looked towards the EMTs.

"She presented with acute asthmatic symptoms. Wheezing breaths, a paradoxical pulse, O2 sats at 79%, rising to 82% before transport and 88% during. BP was 90/65 on transport, elevating marginally to 95/65 on transport."

"Pulse?" Dr. Staley inquired.

"High 140s, lowering with treatment, still in the low hundreds."

"Treatment?"

"O2 and Bricanyl. Allergic to Salbutamol," the EMT answered.

"Excellent. It's much easier when you respond to the treatments, Miss Cooper." He looked at her wrists. "Okay, we can put her on ours now." Nurse Savannah removed the wrist pulse-oximeter and passed it to the dark haired Seth, replacing it with the hospital one. All watched as it beeped in silence, and started flashing up numbers. "Good, good!" Dr. Staley said when the numbers were flashing – 92 and 102. "Your oxygen levels are increasing, up to 92%, and your pulse is starting to come down." Dr. Staley removed the oxygen mask and placed a new one on her face, hooked up from behind her bed. "We'll add some medication to this, and get you feeling much better."

The EMTs grabbed their oxygen tank, and placed it onto the stretcher. "Good luck, Miss Cooper. Feel better," they said, and then left the curtained room.

Dr. Staley listened to her heart and lungs for a few breaths. "Yes, I still hear some wheezing on the intake. Savannah, lets add 2 doses of Xopenex to a nebulizer for Miss Cooper." He strapped on a blood pressure cuff and took a listen. "BP is rising, 100 over 70."

Savannah left the room and returned minutes later with a green facemask. She hooked it up to another pump on the wall, and placed the mask over Charlotte's face. "It's a wet medicine, but works well. You should start feeling better soon." She smiled at Charlotte and patted her arm.

Charlotte looked at Andrew. "Sorry," she breathed.

"It's all good." He reached for her hand that had the blood pressure cuff on it.

Dr. Staley had another listen to Charlotte's chest. "Do you have attacks like this frequently?"

"Hardly ever. This one just hit hard and fast." Her voice sounded different with the facemask covering her mouth.

"Do you have a regular inhaler?"

"Yes, but I couldn't find it." Charlotte lowered her gaze and focused on the arm cuff.

"Do you carry it with you at all times?"

"Normally."

"Good." He had another listen. "You're allergic to Salbutamol?"

"Yes."

"You should be wearing a medic alert bracelet. You could've been given the wrong medicine." Charlotte didn't say anything. "Okay, we'll let the medicine work for awhile and then I'll be back."

They took off, leaving Charlotte and Andrew alone.

"Well, I'm glad you didn't go home after all." He found a chair to sit in and pulled it beside the bed. "You're feeling better?"

She smiled a bit. "Yes. It's not painful to breath. And maybe I should've gone home, I would've had my inhaler, and things wouldn't have spun out of control."

"Maybe, but you're in good hands here." He held her hand, as she leaned back against the bed. She closed her eyes, and he could tell she had fallen asleep. Her chest was rising and falling in rhythmic movements. She woke up when Dr. Staley and Savannah came in.

He gave her a check up, checking all her vitals, and announced that she was much better. "Now, I'm giving you these inhalers. Here's your Bricanyl. Use it when you need it. Please carry it with you. This is Advair, a corticosteroid. Take two pumps of this twice a day for a week. If you have no repeat attacks, you can start scaling it back, one pump a day at a time. Each week, you can drop a daily pump. Within a month, baring no more attacks, you'll have weaned yourself off it. Here's a prescription for another. This will cover you for now. Check in with your family doctor in a couple of weeks."

Charlotte lowered her head. If she'd just packed her inhaler, she wouldn't have been there in the first place. She took the inhalers, expressing gratitude for their assistance, and headed out to the waiting area. They both paused at the doorway.

"We have no jackets," Charlotte said, stopping them both dead in their tracks.

Andrew stood there looking at her. "You're right. Umm... how about we take a taxi to drop you off, and then I'll take it to SEARCH." He looked at his watch. "They're closed, but I have my car keys. I just won't have my jacket."

Charlotte nodded, and Andrew walked over to the far wall in the waiting room. He lifted the receiver and had a taxi paged to come to the ER side of the hospital. They both went over and stood in the warm ambulance bay.

"Thanks for being with me."

"Where else would I have been, Charlotte?" He wrapped his warm arms around her.

"Working?" she giggled. She turned around and folded her arms in to her chest, and snuggled into his chest. "I'm glad you were here, and I wasn't alone. Although I could've done without the crowds at SEARCH, I'm still glad you were there."

"I just may have panicked a lot more if I'd come down and heard you'd left by ambulance, rather than having been a witness to it." His lips brushed across her forehead in a moment of tenderness.

"What a thing to watch."

"It wasn't the worst thing I could've witnessed, Cat." He felt her shudder. "Now, c'mon, the cab's here."

They both raced out jacketless into the cold, and jumped into the warm cab. It drove Charlotte to her place, and she paid the cab fare to the Fortress, insisting on paying ahead, since she was the reason he was without his ride. He wouldn't accept payment. She gave him a kiss, a lingering one, and bid him a goodnight. Then she raced into the building, and headed up to her home.

The next day was New Year's Eve. Charlotte had a quick sleep, being that it was after 2am when she got home. It felt like a long time before she actually warmed up. It took a hot bath at 2:30 in the morning, with a thirty-minute soak to warm her back up. Then she crawled into bed and slept like the dead until her alarm went off at 9am. She took her Advair inhaler, twice as per the instructions, and before she could forget, packed the rescue inhaler into her purse. She had a quick breakfast with Joe, who proclaimed a long nap was in his future. She didn't bother to fill him in on the previous night's ER visit, because she thought it was senseless to cause him additional stress. She figured she'd tell him later. Much later. Joe was already asleep on the couch before Charlotte left at 10:30.

Charlotte worked all day, but only because SEARCH was open from eleven to five. Andrew worked the same shift, so they both could bring in the new year at her apartment. Andrew looked as wide-awake as she felt, so she grabbed him a coffee from the cafeteria before they started.

"Did you manage to get home okay?"

"It was very cold getting into my car at 2am. It took a while to warm up."

"I can only imagine. When did you go to sleep?" She sniffled a little.

"After three, I think."

"Yeah, me too. We won't need to party much past midnight tonight."

"Can't anyways. I have the early shift tomorrow!" His voice laced with regret.

"Really? Bummer. I'm in at 1."

"Nice! At least you'll be able to sleep in."

"And clean up." She coughed a little.

"Feeling better?"

"I can breathe, yes, but I still have this cold."

He gave her a kiss at the desk and headed over to the elevator. "See you later, Cat."

"Not if I see you first."

"You never see me first." He smiled as he stepped on the elevator, waving bye.

The day cruised on by, and before she knew it, they were leaving SEARCH at 5:30pm. He was going to follow her home, and help get the party ready for the New Year's Blast.

They got to the Fortress and helped Joe tidy up. Chelsea arrived after six, and started preparing the light snacks and pulling out all the various alcohols she could dig out. She chilled the pop in the freezer, while Charlotte put out a small stack of dishes.

"How many are we tonight?" she asked Chelsea.

"Um, you two, us, Elizabeth and Monty, and Meadow and Brad."

Charlotte counted along, and set out eight of everything.

Joe leaned on the counter and moved things around. "I found it."

"Found what?" Charlotte inquired, looking nervous.

Joe held up a box.

"Not for me, thanks!"

Andrew chimed up. "Ah, Twister... I've heard about this." He smiled.

"It's a New Year's tradition."

Charlotte looked at both men. "No, count me out."

"You're playing, Charlotte. You'll have fun." His tone suggested it wasn't wise to disagree. "Hey, Andrew, can you help me move some of the furniture out of the way?"

They pushed the long table into the corner, and placed the large mat with the coloured circles on the floor. Joe was as giddy as a child.

The phone rang its notification, and Joe flipped it to the correct TV channel to get visual on the main door. "It's Meadow." He picked up the phone and pushed a button, letting Meadow and Brad through the main door. A few minutes later, it rang again. This time, it was Chelsea's friends.

The four couples noshed on the hors d'oeuvres that Joe had prepped all day. Joe made sure that their empty drink glasses were always full. Under Andrew's careful eye, Charlotte kept her drinks to one every couple of hours.

Joe, having consumed a few hard drinks, declared that it was time to play Twister. Charlotte was eager to sit out, but Joe insisted that she join him, Brad, and Elizabeth.

Andrew was in charge of the spinner for the first game, and within a few minutes, hilarity ensued. It didn't take long for Brad to stumble and fall, nearly taking out Elizabeth in the process. However, a couple of more spins found Joe, as long as he was, unable to manoeuver properly, and he eliminated himself. It didn't take long to get another game underway, with the other four couple halves. Monty was the first out, followed quite some time later by Meadow.

A round of drinks for the semi-finalists, and once the shots were swallowed, the final round began. It consisted of Andrew, Elizabeth, Charlotte, and Chelsea. The last one standing would be declared the winner. Joe spun and called out the colour, and then the body part. With sixteen body parts scattered across the mat, it was very tough moving, but everyone was getting to know their competitors up close and personal. It took a few spins and placements, but the first contestant out was Elizabeth. Following her departure, the three remaining players each consumed an ounce of hard liquor.

Andrew noticed that Joe only poured a ½ shot for Charlotte, who was very tipsy already, and very loud. A few spins later, Chelsea lost her balance and landed on a precariously balanced Andrew, causing Andrew's hands to lift first, making Chelsea one of the finalists, alongside Charlotte.

"Woohoo!" yelled Charlotte, who was very red in the face, and laughing loud enough for the neighbours to hear.

Joe poured a couple of shots and passed the less full one to Andrew. They each poured the drinks into their girlfriend's mouths.

"Final round. Good luck to the winner!" shouted Meadow, who was also very red in the cheeks.

Chelsea and Charlotte took their spots on the vinyl mat, and the game began. The alcohol took a firm hold on Charlotte, Andrew noticed. She giggled lots, and told some bad jokes. Chelsea kept on smiling.

"Right foot, red," was the move that brought down Charlotte, and try as she may, she just couldn't do it. She fell over in a fit of giggles and splayed across the mat, as Chelsea lay beside her. "Good job," she said shaking Chelsea's hand, while continuing to lay on the vinyl.

"Another round of drinks. For everyone!" proclaimed Joe as he lined up the shot glasses.

Andrew extended his hand to pull up Charlotte from the mat, but her dead weight caused him to only succeed in moving her sideways.

"Nah, I'm good here." She laughed as Andrew fell beside her. "See that was fun wasn't it?"

Andrew smiled. "More than I thought it could be."

Joe stood over them. "Want another drink, Andrew?" He held a glass with an amber coloured fluid in it.

"No thanks, I'm good. I still have to drive home later."

"Fair enough." Joe went and passed the drink to Meadow, who opened up her throat and seemed to swallow it with ease.

The mood in the large apartment was very joyous and very loud. Joe turned on the music, cranking up the tunes. His 10-disc changer played music from all varieties, including to Andrew's horror, country music. The group of eight continued their festivities, munching, drinking and dancing, with what could only technically be called interpretive dancing. Charlotte's arms and legs seemed independent of her body and moved on their own in separate, weird spastic motions.

Then, just before midnight, Joe held up his wine glass and clinked on it to get everyone's attention. "Thank you everyone for coming! The clock is counting down. Less than ten minutes until the start of the New Year. It's an annual tradition for everyone at my New Year's party to say something that they are thankful for, and something that they are wishing for in the New Year." The small crowd gathered closer. "I'll start." He cleared his breath, "I'm thankful for having such wonderful friends in my life, who make me feel complete. My wish for 1996 is that you will all continue to hang out here."

Cheers erupted all around.

Chelsea smiled, and announced in a near whisper, "I'll go next." She took a deep breath. "I'm thankful for Joe, and his unending generosity. For having met all of you. My wish for 1996 is to get a full time job."

Monty went next. He said he was thankful for Elizabeth and all she has done in his life, and his wish for 1996 was that she'd move in with him. Cheers erupted again, and Elizabeth said "yes". Then followed by saying that she was thankful for surviving the layoffs within her company, and was hoping that her mom would go into remission.

Meadow's turn followed. "I'd like to give thanks to Joe, a great friend, who always puts up with my crap at work."

Joe interrupted, "You make working there tolerable!" He laughed.

"And I give thanks to all of you for being patient with me while I finished up this semester of school. On that note, I'll be happy in 1996 if I could get honours." She raised her glass to the "here, here" and clinked against Brad's. "You're up, honey," she said to him.

He cleared his throat. "I'm thankful for this party. You sure make an old guy feel young again. My wish for the new year is to travel a little more."

Andrew was next. All eyes were on him, as he took a big breath, and started, "I'm thankful for all of you, and for Joe, and for Charlotte. 1995 was a helluva year, but we managed to make it through, a little worn out on the edges, but we survived. Together. So I am very thankful for that. I hope 1996 brings peace and prosperity and good luck to replace the unending bad luck we seem to have."

Everyone rose his or her glasses to that, and Joe gave a little nod to Andrew, that almost went unnoticed. Charlotte saw the exchange.

"Well, I guess that leaves me," she said looking between the two men who flanked her sides. "What I am thankful for? Better yet, what am I *not* thankful for?" she giggled, the alcohol making her voice louder than necessary. "I am very thankful that I have such amazing friends, who are constantly there to support me and help me, and give me a place to live," she said looking at Joe, "and who reminds me that life is worth living." She glanced at Andrew. "I am thankful that they willingly drop what they're doing to help me out, and that they forgive my mistakes so easily. I am beyond blessed to have you all in my life." She took a deep breath, fighting the tears that threatened to punch through. "Now, as for 1996, well, it just better not be a damn repeat of 1995!" She laughed loud and raised her glass. Everyone drank up the remaining fluid in their glasses and topped them up. They looked over to the countdown showing on the TV.

"Less than a minute everyone!"

The group gathered into the living room, and watched the final seconds of 1995 go away.

"Ten, nine, eight, seven, six, five, four, three, two, one... HAPPY NEW YEAR!" They all shouted together.

Couples were kissing and dipping, and hugs all around. More champagne toasts, and then a few of the group departed. They bid farewell to Monty and Elizabeth first, with Brad and Meadow minutes behind. Then Joe and Chelsea retired to the big white sofa in the living room while Andrew said goodnight to Charlotte.

"Are you sure you have to go? It's not even 12:30," she pleaded. "You won't spend the night?"

Andrew held her hands, kissing them gently. "I have to work in the morning, and I don't have a change of clothes." He winked.

"You should keep a set here."

"Yeah, right." His blue-greens twinkled. "That would be too tempting, Cat."

"Please stay. I need you to stay. With me. Please."

"Cat, I need to go. Okay?" His accented voice was firm.

"Drew, you're twenty years old! It's New Year's Eve. I think your mom can handle being by herself tonight. Christmas is for families, New Year's Eve is for friends."

"No, Cat, I need to go."

Charlotte pouted like a little child begging for more chocolate when the answer was no. "Fine, go then."

Andrew smirked at the pouty expression she was giving him. "Oh, Cat, you're so irresistible." He embraced her and gave her another kiss. "I love you, but I'll see you sometime tomorrow." He stepped back as he grabbed his coat and put it on. He looked at her, as she stood there watching him. "Be good. Goodnight." He opened the door and walked out, closing it behind him.

Charlotte grabbed her jacket, and headed out onto the balcony. The balcony had the tower heater on, warming up the immediate space surrounding it to a toasty 2C, so it was not as cool as the rest of the deck that hovered around -15C. She sat on the deck chair and reached into her pocket to pull out a pack of cigarettes. She had just lit one and taken a puff, when Joe came out.

"You doing alright?" He opened his hand, and she dropped the pack of smokes into it.

She took a long drag and blew it away from him. *Yep, my love has run home, because his momma is lonely.*

He sat there beside her on the patio furniture. "It was a great night."

It was fabulous indeed. Still stings that he wouldn't spend the night.

"I know you're upset that he had to go home, but there's still plenty of party time left. We're going to make nachos and watch a movie on my new laserdisc player."

She asked him a question that came out of nowhere, "Do you think we'll ever get married?"

"You and me?" He raised an eyebrow. "How much did you drink tonight?"

"Yes, well, no, not you and me married, but do you think we'll marry other people?" She turned and looked at Joe, with his long thin legs stretched before him, smoking a cigarette.

He took a puff. "I don't know. Maybe. I think you'll marry before I do."

"Really?" She took a long drag of hers.

"Charlotte, you're twenty years old. Are you truly thinking about marriage?"

"Yeah, for some reason I am."

"To Andrew?"

"Maybe, I need to find a way to tie myself to him, so he stops running from me and stays. Makes me more of a priority than school."

"The school thing is only temporary. You know that. Three more semesters." Joe finished off his smoke. "But, you're too young, if you ask me, to be worrying about such things like marriage. It's 1996 now. Make this a great year. Be young, be wild, and have fun." He sighed. "Marriage is reality. Tied down. Commitments. Responsibilities. You have someone to answer to. I don't think you're ready for that, not yet."

"Are you?"

"Hell no, but don't tell Chelsea that! And apparently, once I turn twenty-five, it'll be downhill from there. She's already dropping little subtle hints about forever."

"Better get busy living then. Time's running out. You've got two weeks until your birthday." She laughed. "You better get inside and live a little with Chelsea." She pushed him towards the door.

"Don't stay out too long," he said in his best big brother type voice.

"You know me."

"Yeah, I do. Don't pout and stay out too long!" He walked through the patio door.

Charlotte had another cigarette before heading inside. She figured it wasn't a good idea to smoke anymore that night. She went in and took her breathing medications. She certainly didn't want to have another asthma episode. Then she bid goodnight to Joe and Chelsea, and went into her room to read for a bit before going to sleep.

Chapter Sixteen
✿✿✿

Bang, bang, bang. "Come on Charlotte, we're going to be late!"

"Coming!" she yelled from her ensuite. "Give me two more minutes." She emerged in her black tracksuit, and joined Joe in the kitchen. He was wearing his best sweatpants and university hoodie.

He grabbed the bouquet of fresh cut flowers, and locked the door behind them. "Do you think she'll like them?"

"Yeah, she'll love them. Probably thinks they're from the garden."

"You mean Elizabeth's garden?"

Charlotte laughed. They walked out of the building and breathed in the crisp January afternoon air. It was an odd month, weather wise. The air was cool, but not cold. For the first time in many years, the January temperature was above freezing, and several Edmontonians made good use of the conditions. Sidewalks were full of strolling couples and families, and Charlotte and Joe were part of that.

Today was Mrs. Kennedy's 89th birthday, and they headed over to visit her. Since it was nice, they took advantage and walked the ten-minute pace. They had plans to run the long way home afterwards.

"So, how's the brand new year treating you?"

"Oh Joe. Same old, same old."

"That bad eh?" He snickered and asked, "How's your course coming along?"

She laughed. "At the pace I'm going, I think I'll be done by July at the latest. With Andrew working and studying, it's given me a lot of time to complete module after module."

"Well, good for you."

"I suppose. But since I'm going through the course so fast, I'm quickly draining my account."

Joe took a quick breath. "Do you need money?"

"No!"

"Because I can give you some. Think of it as the Joe Harrison Scholarship Fund."

"Ha ha, very funny!"

"Are you getting good grades at least?"

Charlotte looked ahead to the corner they were crossing, without answering Joe.

"Charlotte?"

She looked up at him, her cheeks flushed pink not from the cool air, but slight embarrassment. "I have a ninety-seven percent average."

"Holy shit, Charlotte, that's awesome. Something to be proud of."

She had a small skip to her steps. *Joe's proud of me.* "Thanks."

"Always knew you were smart."

"You overestimate me. It's not rocket science."

"Maybe not, but it's still impressive. Let me be proud of you, okay?"

Smiling, Charlotte continued to jaunt along the sidewalk.

"So when are you applying for the practicum part?"

She put her hands into the pockets of her tracksuit. "The instructor recommends at the completion of the second to last module."

"Where are you going to apply? Any ideas?"

She shook her head. "Not really. Anywhere I can, I guess."

Within a couple of minutes, they arrived and signed in at the main desk. The smell that assaulted Charlotte as she walked through the main doors into the residence never got better. Once she arrived in the atrium, where the fresh hibiscus flowers hung and the warm aroma of apple pie was fresh, Charlotte could breathe easier.

They followed the corridor to the lounge, and looked around the amazing space. A few elderly residents sat at the tables with family or friends; however, there was no sign of Champ or Mrs. Kennedy.

"Do you see them, Joe?"

"No, not at all." He pointed to one of the staff members. "I'm going to go ask."

Charlotte stood where she was, and watched as Joe walked over to talk to the Sister. She noticed his expression change from concern to sadness. Suddenly, her stomach tightened. Unable to remove her eyes from the silent conversation, she followed him and tried to read his lips until he returned.

"She's going to go and let Mrs. Kennedy know we're here. She'll bring her over to the couch over there."

"But that's not everything, is it, Joe?"

He held her hand, and motioned over to the couch. "Come on."

"Tell me."

"Not here." He sat down and patted the space beside him.

Charlotte braced herself for bad news. *Oh please don't let it be what I think it is.*

"Mrs. Kennedy had a rough morning, but she's okay. As for Champ, well…"

She swallowed hard and squeezed his hand, watching Joe fight with his emotions.

"Champ had a stroke last night. The big one. He died very early this morning."

Charlotte covered her mouth to stop the sound threatening to fall out. She knew when they signed up to be weekly visitors as part of the Youth-Elderly Connection Program, death was always a possibility, but she'd never prepared for it.

Mrs. Kennedy and Champ had become family, in a way. At least to Charlotte, who had no real family aside from Joe. She saw them more than her aunt and cousin.

Joe's eyes were glassy, but the tears never fell. His brows furrowed, but not from anger. His hands clenched around the container holding the bouquet.

"Joe, I'm so sorry."

He bit his lip to stop the trembling. "Thanks, Charlotte."

She held back her own tears and wiped them away as she noticed the Sister escorting Mrs. Kennedy towards them. Faking a smile, she exclaimed, "Happy Birthday!"

The octogenarian smiled. "Thank you, deary." She sat across from Joe and Charlotte.

"These are for you," Joe said as he placed the flowers on the small table beside the elderly lady.

"Thank you. They're lovely." Mrs. Kennedy regarded him carefully. "Who are you?"

"I'm Joe, ma'am."

"Do I know you?" She touched a thin, arthritic finger to her forehead. Her grey brows winkled in deep thought.

"Yes."

"I wish I could remember. Are you family? You look like I should know you."

He shook his head. "Friend."

"Why can't I remember you?" Her voice cracked in distress as she tapped her head. Lowering her gaze, she stared into the bouquet, and tugged on a pretty blue flower. "When did you start growing irises, Elizabeth?"

Charlotte sighed. It troubled her when Mrs. Kennedy referred to her as Elizabeth. Charlotte had spoken with the nurse, who explained the only person Mrs. Kennedy remembered was Elizabeth. She no longer recalled her family, or friends, just this garden growing Elizabeth. And for whatever reason, Charlotte reminded her of the phantom lady. "This is my first batch," she lied.

"They're beautiful." She leaned in and inhaled the fragrant aroma. "They smell good. Makes me remember that day we planted the roses."

Charlotte's face lit up. "Tell me about it." The nurse told her once to encourage all memories as it helped to keep the neural pathways open.

Mrs. Kennedy frowned, and placed her hands into her lap. "Well. It was spring, I think. Or was it winter? No it was spring. Elizabeth, did we plant the roses in the spring?"

"I don't remember."

Irritation flooded across the sun kissed and wrinkled face. "Well, if you can't remember, how am I supposed too?"

Alzheimer's a bitch. Charlotte leaned back into the sofa. "I'm sorry, Mrs. Kennedy."

"Who's Mrs. Kennedy?"

"You are."

"I am? I don't remember getting married. I'm too young." She looked down at her hand and shock registered across in her dark eyes. "I can't be old. It's impossible." Her speech was a whisper as she thought out loud. "I have a wedding ring." Her voice faded. "Who did I marry?"

Joe had been sitting there, silent in his own thoughts, however, he noticed the spiral Mrs. Kennedy was in. It never ended well, and he knew it was time to call in reinforcements. "I'll be right back," he said to Charlotte, as he rose up and went hunting for a nurse.

He returned with a nurse immediately, who took Mrs. Kennedy by the hand.

"Wait," Charlotte exclaimed to the nurse. She looked at the elderly lady, who was shaking her head and twisting her hands together. She seemed to have aged years before her eyes. "Can I give her a hug?" she asked the nurse. With confirmation in the form of a nod, Charlotte then asked, "Mrs. Kennedy, may I hug you?"

She opened her frail, bony arms and welcomed Charlotte into them.

She felt the elderly lady melt against her, and loved it. Breaking it off only when Mrs. Kennedy pulled back, she placed a kiss on her weathered cheek. "Take care, Mrs. Kennedy. We'll see you soon."

"Goodbye, Elizabeth," she said as the nurse led her away.

"It's Charlotte," she whispered under her breath.

Joe tugged on her hand. "Let's go. It's been a hard visit." He draped his arm across the top of Charlotte's shoulders.

They stopped at the front door and laced up their runners.

"Let's do the ten-mile run back home," suggested Charlotte as she jumped on the spot just outside Caritas Covenant.

"No way. I don't think I could do the ten. How about the six?"

"Fine, wimp. We'll do six. Race you to the half-way point." Charlotte sprinted down the block, thoughts racing as fast as her feet pounded the sidewalk. Getting into her groove, she easily made it to the designated marker within twenty minutes. She did some jumping jacks while waiting for Joe to arrive. She saw him round the corner and laughed. "Did you get lost?"

Panting, Joe stopped beside her. "Geez you're fast!"

She smiled. "When my mind is racing it's easier to go fast."

"I need to rest."

"Seriously? It's been three miles." She jumped around him. "You okay?"

He sat on the nearby bench. "Do you ever think about death?"

Yeah, almost daily as a child, but not quite as often now. "Occasionally." Slumping, she studied his face. "You're really upset about Champ, aren't you?" His lack of response confirmed her question. "Is he the first person you've known to die?"

"No. My grandparents died when I was little, but I never knew them. When dad died, I really didn't care. But Champ... I saw him almost every week."

"I know." She patted his thigh as she sat down. "It's hard." She looked at his face. His jaw trembled, and his eyes glazed over.

"Do you think he suffered?" His warm voice broke as he buried his head on his hands.

She swallowed, hard. "Honestly? I think he was suffering before. I hope at least that the last one was quick and painless. I believe that he's at peace now." She wiped away his stream of tears. "He's probably up there right now, chasing some lady around, eating cookies, and kicking everyone's ass in crib. He never let anyone win."

With that, Joe smiled a bit. "You're right. He never lost a game of crib, that's for sure!" His tears ran and stained a wet path on his cheek. "I hope it never happens to me."

"Death?"

"No, the pain and suffering part. When I go, I want it to be quick."

She shuddered. "Really? No advanced warning?"

"None."

"Oh." Sadly she leaned her head on his shoulder. "Well, don't die anytime soon. Okay?"

"I'll do my best."

"I couldn't imagine my world without you in it."

"Nor could I you, Charlotte." Like the big brother he was, he kissed her forehead. "But don't you worry, I'm not going anywhere anytime soon."

"Good. Because that scares me almost more than anything else."

They sat there awhile, and watched as people strolled by. In the distance, they heard the shrieks of children's laughter coming from the park. She stared at her shadow and watched as it faded with the rolling clouds. "Storm's coming."

He checked out the darkening sky. "Indeed." His watch beeped, signalling the turn of the hour.

"Let's go slowpoke. I need to be at work for four."

Chapter Seventeen
✿✿✿

Any time Charlotte and Andrew spent together, they spent studying. Andrew was always so busy studying and trying to maintain his 4.0 GPA that Charlotte was way ahead of where a normal paced student would be. She figured that the way she was pouring effort into her studies, she'd be applying for her practicum by the end of June for sure, if not earlier.

Most young couples went out on dates, went to the movies, and made sweet love to each other. All. The. Time. Her relationship with Andrew had none of that. If they weren't studying, then they were working. On her off days, when Andrew was working, Charlotte either sat with him in the projection room, or she hung out at JT's Pizzeria, smoking more than she should, and volunteering to help Joe with the paperwork, or help dispatch orders. She started to feel like she didn't have much of a life.

Charlotte's frustration with her relationship with Andrew, or lack of one, grew like a bad weed. How could they call each other boyfriend and girlfriend, when their time together wasn't really being together? She missed him and craved his company, so she made do to study in the projection room, with minimal lighting. Anything to just be near him. Putting her foot down, she demanded that they do something outside of studying at SEARCH. He agreed. It had been too long since they'd spent any time together outside of work.

Under the guise of having him study at The Fortress on Valentine's Day, she told him to follow her home after work.

Since it was a Friday night, Joe was at JT Pizzeria, so the place was all theirs. They both knew it would be after two am before he arrived back home.

Andrew dropped his backpack by the kitchen table, as Charlotte cleared away the newspaper spread all over it. Joe had been reading an article under the "Food" section, and had a recipe circled in red.

"There, a space cleared for you." Charlotte smiled after wiping down the table. "You set up your stuff." With a sultry pout on her lips, she unbuttoned her top to reveal a powder-blue lacy bra.

"Thanks," he smiled, following her fingers with his eyes as she undid another button. "But maybe tonight I'll take off from studying. It is Valentine's after all." He winked his blue-greens and closed the gap between them. "You were right; I needed to get away from the monotony of SEARCH."

Charlotte beamed in return. "But you have mid-terms in a couple of weeks. I'll just stand over here and watch you study. I'll try not to distract you." She winked as she released another button from its hole.

"Oh, you are a temptation, Cat. How could I study seeing you standing there, wearing this?" He hooked a finger under the blue strap of her bra. "One night won't hurt me. I promise." He crossed his heart with his finger. He smiled, wrapped his arms around her, and gave her a lingering, passionate fuelled kiss.

Charlotte gasped for air. "Wow," she said after catching her breath. "I've missed that." She reached behind her back for his hand, grabbed it, and led him through the kitchen, down the hall and into her room. She turned on the lava lamp, allowing the diffuse orange sunset-like glow to light the space.

She stood up and spun into his arms. Planting kisses along his neck, she tugged up his shirt, freeing it from his pants. He remained rooted to the floor. "I can't, Cat. I have no protection," he sounded deflated.

Smiling, she let go of his hand, walked into her ensuite and returned with a couple of condoms in her palm. Andrew's face lit up. "Just in case you ever wanted to spend the night."

"Like New Year's eve?"

"I'd hoped, but it's okay." She sat on the edge of her bed and released the remaining buttons on her shirt, all the while staring up at him.

"We're a unique couple, aren't we?" Andrew pulled his shirt off over his head, and tossed it onto the floor. His chest, muscled yet sleek, begged to have hands run up and down it.

Charlotte stood up and tipped her head back, allowing her coppery waves to sweep along her back as she pressed her lace covered breasts against his bare chest. "Yes we are." She caressed his pecs with a flicker of her tongue.

He groaned. "How long has it been since we've been together like this?" He leaned down and kissed along the top edge of her cup, hearing her moan deep within. The bronzed tips of his hair tickled her chin, and the five o'clock shadow electrified her sensitive skin as it caressed her chest.

"Too long," Charlotte gasped between breaths.

He didn't hear her reply as he breathed slowly into her ear, "I need you." His hands slid around her sides, caressing the small of her back, feeling her tense, and then release as she allowed his hand to slowly inch his way into the back of her pants. Then he traveled his hands slowly up her back, and he placed his hands around Charlotte's face and kissed her velvety lips. "I've missed this."

"I know," she panted, "we've been busy." She felt on fire, and she liked it.

He pressed his lips onto hers, but then pulled back, hesitating. "I don't want to scare you, again."

"You won't." She pushed against him. "I want this so much." She tangled her hands in his hair, holding him to her as she kissed him, feeling his soft lips part in hesitancy and anticipation. "It's been so long," she moaned with pleasure as his soft hands slipped lower.

"Sorry, I need to make more time for you." He kissed her. "For this." He nuzzled her again and pulled back, gazing into her eyes. "You've been patiently waiting for me at the end of each shift."

"Well, I just need to see you. I don't want to be the one who's responsible for a drop in your marks, so I don't press it."

Andrew held her tight and paused. "I'm sorry. Please don't think you'd be responsible for that."

"I don't want to be a distraction."

Like a feather in the breeze, he touched her cheek. "You are a most welcome distraction. You should distract me like this more often." He brushed her lips with his thumb.

She wouldn't stop talking, even though her body yearned for more touch. "I keep wondering if things will be better when we're not nose deep in textbooks." A soft touch along her spine. "I'm looking forward to a summer of no studying, just playing." She trembled with ecstasy as he stroked a finger over her breast. "A couple more months will be worth it for a summer of just you and me." She put her arm around his neck, kissed his collarbone and trailed kisses down to his navel.

He stopped her heading south and pulled her up. "I'm sorry again," he started, "I guess I forgot to tell you."

She straightened, feeling the mood falter. "Tell me what?"

He sighed and in his accented voice said, "Jon and I are going to Russia for the summer. We'll be gone for nine weeks."

"Nine weeks!"

"Sorry, it slipped my mind." He leaned forward to kiss her, hoping to pick up from where they just left off; his body begging hard for her.

"No," she stammered out putting some distance between them. "How could you have forgotten to tell me?"

"I don't know. Seems crazy to forget something like that, I know. Dad's paying half our fare, and mom paid the other half. It was our Christmas present from them."

Charlotte sat down on the end of the bed, and smoothed out the messiness. *I know you haven't seen him since last Christmas.* "When are you leaving?" she asked sadly as she traced a line on her bedspread.

"We leave at the end of June and come back just before the end of August."

She looked up at him, and with a surrendering voice stated, "So you'll be gone for your twenty-first birthday."

"Yeah, but I'll be here for yours." He smiled, hoping to break the sudden tension in the room with a soothing tone and a warm touch to her arms with his hands.

She pushed his hands away and retorted, "Great, so I have this part-time boyfriend, who'll be completely absent over the summer, and then will be deep into his final year when he gets back. What a great relationship."

Andrew looked at her. "Couples spend time apart all the time. Wars. Husbands that travel..."

"That's not a very good defense, Drew. We're neither of those things. We're not married, and you're not travelling nine weeks for business. Nor are you going to fight in any wars."

"I know." He slumped down beside her and put his hand on her leg. "Just trying to make this easier."

"I'm going to miss you so much, more than I already do now, and I can see you NOW. I'll be very lonely without you."

"I feel like all I'm doing is apologizing tonight, Cat. I'm sorry, again." He looked at her, long and hard. He stared into the eyes that threatened to explode with tears. He didn't know what to say that would stop that dam from bursting. "Cat? Maybe we should..." he started, but he didn't want to finish, he already saw the look that flashed across Charlotte's face as she figured out what he was going to say.

"Don't!" She spoke in a pleading voice, "Please don't go there. You told *me* not to go there a few months back, remember?"

Andrew hung his head. "Cat, please I'm not the best boyfriend in the world."

"No, please don't," she whispered.

"I've been ignoring you for far too long. I've put my studies ahead of our relationship, and I'm sorry. I haven't been there for you."

The threatening tears gave in and spilled over. "You have been, Drew. Remember? Just before New Years and every other time before that?"

"But only when you really needed me."

"I really need you all the time. I just don't tell you," she whispered.

He wiped a tear from her cheeks. "It seems when I'm not rescuing you, that we're not really together."

"That's not true, Drew." She shook her head.

"Think about it, Cat. We're great together when I'm rescuing you. You and I do *that* very well together."

She couldn't deny that he put everything aside when she was truly in need of rescuing. She nodded.

"I can't always be your hero."

"Oh God, you'll always be my hero." That changed his frown into a half-smile. "Always."

He kissed her, and only probed with further intensity, when he felt her respond.

"Why do you do that?" she broke out, breathless, from their embrace to ask.

"Do what?"

"You hesitate, waiting almost." He picked at a tendril of her wavy copper hair with his fingers. "Oh my gosh!" she exclaimed in near silence, realization dawning on her face when he didn't immediately answer. "You think I'm damaged goods. That you need to be gentle so as to not scare me."

Andrew didn't meet her intense gaze.

"You can't possibly break me more than I already am."

"You need to stop talking about yourself like that."

"Then you need to stop treating me like a child."

"Cat, I don't want to be the one who scares you or makes you feel... I did it once."

"Haven't I told you that I trust you? That I feel safe with you. Do you think I keep those things around, because I hope we're not intimate?" She glanced at the condoms that lay still sealed on the bedside table.

Andrew sighed. "Again, Cat, I'm sorry." He didn't move.

She reached for his face, placed it in between her hands, and then went in for a kiss. Urgent and wistful. Through her tears, she cried out, "I love you, Drew, so much more than I ever thought was possible."

He responded in kind, "I love you too, Cat. Always have." He kissed her back and wrapped his arms around her.

"What do we do?"

"Beyond tonight? I think we both know where that's heading," he said and his eyes betrayed the silent sadness he was trying to hide.

Charlotte lay down on the bed and got under the covers. She curled into a ball. Andrew lifted the covers, slid in behind her and held her tight.

"Let's not worry anymore about tomorrow and beyond." He kissed her nearly naked shoulder. "Do you want me to go?"

Charlotte rolled over to face him. "No, I never want you to go, and that's the problem." She searched his face, and gazed into his hurting blue-green eyes. "I want you to make sweet love with me."

He clutched at her back and pulled her close, sealing the gap between them in a second. "I'm going to make love to you like it's our last night on Earth."

"Excellent." As she kissed him, she felt a fire re-ignite from deep within. It warmed her up from the inside out, and within no time at all, the blankets were kicked onto the floor.

B reathless and sweaty, their love-making finished and their hearts temporarily satisfied, Andrew spread out and quickly fell asleep. Charlotte, however, lay in bed, wide-awake. After listening to his light snores, she got up, put on her nightshirt and a housecoat, and ventured into the kitchen to have a light snack. Quietly she sliced up some cheese and placed a few crackers on to a plate. Then she heard a key in the lock, and the door chimed.

She poked her head into the foyer. "Hey, Joe."

He jumped. "Charlotte. You scared me. I didn't expect to see you up at this time of the night."

Charlotte glanced at the clock over the stove. It was after two. "Yeah, well I couldn't sleep."

Joe hung up his coat on the coat rack. He pointed to the strange jacket.

"Drew's," she whispered.

"Oh?" Joe's face lit up with a huge smile, and he followed Charlotte into the kitchen.

Best to get it over with and tell him. She grabbed the small plate of sliced cheese and crackers and walked into the living room. "We're breaking up."

Joe accompanied her, his mischievous smile replaced by a frown. "You're breaking up?"

"Yeah. At least I think that's where it's going."

Joe studied her, and sat down on the couch beside her, stealing a cracker in the process.

"You don't seem super upset about it."

"I know, right?" She took a bite. "I was earlier, but it makes sense. We hadn't been intimate in along while, not since before Christmas really." Joe almost choked on his cracker. "And lately, it seems like we're just hanging on. Schoolwork's a priority... for both of us, maybe more so him, understandably. We just don't seem to have much time for each other." She passed another cracker to Joe. "Unless, he's rescuing me, as he said."

Joe scratched his head. "Well, you did have a nasty year of needing that."

"I know, but now that I'm not, and I'm more, stable, shall we say, it just seems that the passion isn't as strong. No scratch that – the passion's there, it's just never taken advantage of." She had a slice of cheese and continuing on saying, "I've never met his mom, and he's never met my aunt. Aside from our friends, he doesn't know anyone I know. We don't go out like we used to." She was rambling, and she knew it, but it was the drowsiness talking. Her shoulders fell. "Maybe Drew was never 'the one'."

Joe said nothing for a moment. "Well, I don't know what to say to that. I'd hoped that he was your one."

"I think I did too. I don't know. " She leaned back against the couch.

"Love has blinded you, my dear."

Charlotte screwed up her face.

"You want something so bad, that you have tunnel vision. You're not seeing the big picture."

"Oh, I'm seeing it alright. I want him, heart, body, and soul. But it's not the same in return. Someone else I've pushed away."

"I don't think you've pushed him away."

"Really? He's known since Christmas that he was going to Russia for nine weeks, but only got around to mentioning it to me today."

"Ouch."

"I know. Isn't that weird for a boyfriend/girlfriend relationship?"

"So his timing's off, big deal."

"It is a big deal, Joe. He's known for what, six weeks that he's leaving?"

"Geez, you're both so young. So he didn't tell you. He would've eventually. You would've noticed when he was gone." He smirked, and she smacked him on the arm. "Maybe this time frame isn't for you? Maybe ten, fifteen or twenty years from now, it will be the perfect time for your relationship. You both need to grow up a little. Mature a lot more so you can stop being so short-sighted."

"Great, so I'm supposed to hang on for that long." Her laughter had an edge to it.

"Yeah." Joe laughed while shaking his head no. "You *are* right for each other, and you really do complement each other, but maybe now is not the right time for forever." He patted her leg.

"So in the meantime?"

"You live. Isn't that what I told you on New Year's Eve? Just live and love right now. It's too early to decide on forever." He stole another cracker off her plate.

"Great. So I'll just live a lonely life until that perfect moment, years down the road, finally comes around."

Joe scowled at her. "You won't be lonely. I promise. At the very least, you'll always have me. Besides, you'll probably be living with me forever anyways." He laughed and Charlotte giggled too loud for that time of night. "We'll be all old like, sitting in this living room, wondering where the years went, and why we're still single. I'll still be managing at JT's Pizzeria; you'll be selling tickets to the latest science event. It's quite the life, isn't it?" Their overtired laughter interrupted as Joe looked over Charlotte's shoulder, towards the hallway. "Andrew," Joe stopped laughing to greet him. "Cracker?" He laughed again.

"Hi. Did I miss something?" Andrew looked at the two people laughing on the couch, his magazine perfect hair smooshed on one side from sleeping.

Charlotte stopped her giggles and spoke up, "No, we were just talking about how I would likely still be living here for the next twenty years, selling tickets to the next big science event."

Andrew failed to see the humour in that. "Okay."

Charlotte looked up at Andrew. "I told Joe that we were breaking up."

"Oh." Andrew looked with caution at Joe. "Sorry, Joe."

Joe shook his head, the laughter dead. "Hey, it's between you two. You know what's best for your relationship." Then he added in a mocking tone, "She's allowed to stay with me for twenty years, but then she's out on her own." He laughed. "Not one day further." He stood up. "I'm going to make Charlotte a snack, since I've eaten most of her's. Want anything, Andrew?"

"No, thank you." He flopped down beside Charlotte. "You're okay with this?"

She looked at him. "At first, when you fell asleep, I wasn't. Then I started thinking about it. Well, actually, I've been thinking about it for quite some time, and it just makes sense. So now? Yeah, I'm okay. I can live with this decision, for now." Andrew looked like he was going to say something, but she stopped him. "Don't apologize. Please. I don't think I can take another apology, especially since a relationship is two-sided."

He nodded and leaned back. He opened his arm, and Charlotte took that invitation and snuggled into him. She pulled a blanket over her legs.

"Are we still going to be friends?" she asked, desperate to know.

"Yes, I promise."

She snuggled in deeper, "Good. *That* I couldn't live without." She listened to his heart beating. "I still love you."

"And I love you too."

"I know you do." She closed her eyes.

Joe walked back into the room with a plate full of cheese and crackers and a paternal smile crossed his face as he looked upon the pair. "Help yourself," he said putting it down on the coffee table. Both Andrew and Charlotte shook their heads no. "Well, more for me then. Want to watch a laser disc?"

"Sure," Andrew said, not wanting to move Charlotte. He was enjoying this snuggle time and figured it was probably his last with her. He needed to savour it and make it last.

Joe popped in a laser disc, *Wallace and Gromit* and sat back on the couch. Before the opening credits started, Charlotte's hold on Andrew relaxed, and he knew that she had fallen asleep.

Andrew whispered to Joe. "You hate me, don't you?"

"You're kidding, right?" His green eyes pierced through Andrew's.

"No."

Joe snickered. "Au contraire, mon ami, I love what you've done for her."

Andrew blushed a bit.

"Charlotte's a survivor. It's her nature and all she knows how to do. Her spirit gets broken, but she finds a way to mend it, slowly and usually alone, but she moves on. You. You are the one, the only one I've noticed, that's great at mending what's broken in her heart. You've changed her in a way I've never been able to. She's made so much headway since you've come into her life."

"How so?"

"Think about it, amico. I mean *really* think about it. With everything that's gone over in the past year, what do you think?" Joe munched on a cracker sandwiched between some cheese.

Andrew thought about it, hard. When he first laid eyes on Charlotte, she was reserved, secretive even, about her life. She never shared any personal tidbits about her life and kept to herself. Then she did start coming out of her shell, albeit slowly. Until that bastard Chad messed her up. However, as he reflected on that, he did think she came out of that faster than he would've thought was possible. She started to depend on him, and trust him. She was cautious still, even though they weren't a couple. She confided in him about Lucy, and her dependence on him grew. She'd always trusted in him, and he never let her down. Andrew's face lit up with the realization of what Joe was explaining.

"There you go. You see what I mean?"

"Is our breakup going to set her back?" He kissed the top of Charlotte's head.

"I hope not. She'll handle this, but she'll still be your friend. She'll need that. And you'll still be hers. Right?"

Andrew smiled. "Like you two."

"Yep. I love her so much and would do anything for her, and she'd do the same. But we're not meant to be together. Our relationship, our friendship, was a lifesaver, originally of necessity. I can't stress enough how I needed to protect her from Lucy, and how, even though we tried, it wasn't going to be anything romantic. Maybe it will be the same for you."

"Great, now I'm depressed." Andrew mumbled.

Joe carried on, "I was so excited when she talked of you. I knew, deep down, you were going to do something wonderful in her life. And you have thus far. Maybe a few years down the road, who knows? When school isn't such a focus, and you've both matured a little more, maybe then?"

"Maybe then what?"

"Maybe that'll be the moment you're both looking for now, but not finding. Like I told Charlotte, you both have tunnel vision and an attitude of instant gratification. Once you look at the big picture, and see the beauty of the whole thing, then things will click. But you both need to agree on what you are needing the other for. She's not a toy to be played with, and she needs to realize that you are infallible."

The sounds from the movie were the only sounds as the two men looked at each other.

Joe snickered, breaking the silence. "And maybe I'm blowing smoke up your ass too!"

"Maybe." Andrew's laughter had an edge to it. "But maybe not." His tone suggested he was now considering what Joe had said.

"Time will tell. For now, do what you need to do. Go to Russia, and live your life."

"Like that saying, 'If you love someone, set them free. If they come back, they're yours and if not, then it wasn't meant to be'…"

"Yeah, something like that." His smile was tired but genuine.

"Was it hard for you two?"

"To break up?"

"To be together."

"Never, but I was friends with her long before. She hung out at my house. It was always safe there for her. Then something sparked, or changed between us. She was hanging out in the kitchen, watching me work on making a meal of some sort, and it happened. It didn't last long though. I think it was the age difference between us. But she felt safe with me, and I knew it. She always had. In her own way, she depended on me, on David, and my mom. She doesn't depend on anyone, she's too afraid of getting hurt. So I protected that, and never gave her a reason doubt me." Joe leaned against the back of the couch and continued on with his monologue. "I'm okay with being like her big brother. It was easy to tell her that we were better friends, because she knew it too. I think she just needed to experiment and see what would happen. But we were never in love. And that's what's different between you and I. She's given her heart and soul to you."

"I know."

"Let me ask you something."

"Okay."

"Do you love her?"

"Yeah, I do, and she knows it too."

"Are you in love with her, or just the idea of being in love with her?"

Andrew sat in silence, staring out into neverland.

"I don't want you to actually answer that. I do, however, want you to seriously think about it."

He reflected through his spoken thoughts. "You've given me lots to think about, Joe."

"Good. Because I like you and consider you a good friend. Otherwise I wouldn't tell you anything." His wink was warm and put Andrew at ease.

"Thanks for the chat, Joe."

"Anytime, my friend. My door is always open."

"Thanks. I'm going to take her to bed." Andrew slid out from under his sleeping beauty.

"Need a hand?"

Andrew lifted her up into his arms as if she were a piece of paper. "Got it. Have a good sleep, Joe."

"Oh you too!" He winked again as Andrew carried Charlotte out of the living room.

Andrew rolled his eyes as he walked away.

Chapter Eighteen
✿✿✿

They pulled into the staff parking stall. Andrew put the car into park. "You ready?" he asked. Charlotte shook her head, closing her eyes against the oncoming tension headache. "Give me a minute." She rubbed her temples.

He reached for and held her hand. "Are you nervous?"

"Yes." Her insides were shaking, and she was thankful that she'd eaten a few hours earlier. Her stomach was in knots.

"Charlotte, it's not a big deal. Paul just wants to discuss your practicum with you."

She let go of the breath she'd been holding. "I know. But he has connections. He knows, through his in-school science setups, which is a good school and who'd be more willing to accept me for those eight weeks."

"So? That's a good thing isn't it?"

"Yes, of course. But what if I screw up and say the wrong things and he decides not to help me anymore?"

"Charlotte," he began, noticing the tension in her eyes, "you'll be fine. You've almost completed your modules. This is the next step." He gave her hand a squeeze. "When were you thinking of starting, if he makes the right connections?"

"Whenever… it's April 5th already. I doubt I could get anything for May, so it's more likely September, but I'd need to let Russell or Norah know as soon as it's confirmed, if it gets

confirmed, so I don't get any day shifts during the week."
Charlotte rambled on.

Andrew smiled. "Yeah, then we can work the same shifts."

She looked at him. "We do for the most part anyways." Since
their breakup in February, they'd managed to work more shifts
together. Their weekend shifts had a little more upheaval, but the
weekday evening shifts, they arrived together. Andrew would
swing by after school, have a snack with Charlotte and they would
head to work for the 4pm shift. Then Andrew would drive her
home, and every Friday night he'd spend the night. She was
constantly in shock over how much better their relationship was
since the boyfriend/girlfriend titles fell to the wayside. He was
over more, their sex life was regular (and awesome), and they
were both happier.

The bronze-haired male tapped his watch. "It's nearly four and
Paul wanted to chat with you before he leaves at 4:30. Come on."

Sighing, Charlotte exited the car. She glanced around, and
came to focus on the gorgeous man in front of her. He was so
handsome, the afternoon sun dancing off his hair, the golden
stubble on his face, his eyes studying her. He looked so grown up
in that moment, and every once in a while, she felt like a grown
up too. Right now, was one of those moments. *I'm about to
discuss my future, and get what the world views as a "real job".*
She couldn't be more apprehensive.

"You coming, beautiful?" He extended his hand to her.

She held on to that soft hand, running her thumb up and down
the length of his.

"You'll be fine, I promise."

She leaned into him. "Thanks." They stopped walking the short
distance from the staff parking to the administration doors.

"Good luck, Cat."

"Thought I'd be fine?" She joked, paling a little.

"You will be."

He bent down and gave her a tender kiss. On the lips. It never
failed to make her weak in the knees. Breathlessly, she smiled.

"See you after work. If you get a chance, call up."

"Deal." She blew him a kiss.

"Love you, Cat!"

"Ditto, Drew." She turned and headed in the direction of Paul's
office.

Hours later, after a super busy Friday night, Andrew finished up before Charlotte. He sat in the GM's office, in the manager's chair as Norah finished counting the float.

"So, Paul was pleased?" he asked.

"Yeah, I guess. He said he'll put in a few calls early next week and see. Figures I'd be better with the younger crowd, so he'll call elementary school connections first. It wasn't as nerve wracking as I expected."

"Good."

"He also wants me to think about being a summer camp leader."

"Really? Paul didn't mention anything to me about that." Norah piped up, looking at Charlotte as she placed the last of the money into the safe.

Charlotte nodded. "Because I haven't said yes, yet." She looked over to Andrew who shrugged his shoulders.

"Well, let me know. We'd need to replace you for the summer if you accept." Norah closed and locked the safe. If she sounded upset, her smile betrayed that.

"I know." She stood up, stretching and arching her back. "Alrighty, let's go home, Drew."

They left the building, fingers interlaced, pressed together and Andrew drove them to the Fortress. He grabbed his overnight bag from his trunk and followed Charlotte up to her apartment. She turned off the alarm, and reset it for just the door, and then the young lovers headed down to her room.

"Friday nights are my favourite," Charlotte said as she slipped out of her now standard issue blue denim uniform top. She threw it into her hamper.

Andrew bent down, and pulling her close, kissed her tenderly, but with increasing passion, on her lips. "Mine too." He brushed his fingers down the length of her cheeks, trailing down her neck and slipped them over her shoulders. He unhooked her emerald-green bra and allowed it to slide down her silky arms.

She wrapped her fingers in his hair, holding him to her and moaned in delight as she felt her chest free. "I love you, Drew."

"Love you too."

Their fingers tangled together, and their hearts raced. Neither spoke, only emitting sounds of gasps and groans. This time together was not a time for lengthy discussions, but for carnal knowledge and a deep connection.

With a healthy flush in her cheeks, she placed her messed up head on his shoulder, and sighed heavily. "Oh, Drew, that was wonderful."

He kissed her forehead, after moving away some sweaty coppery strands. "Agreed."

"I love you."

"I know you do."

"I could do this forever." In saying that sentence, she felt him tense. He always did when she mentioned it.

"Cat?"

"I know." She pouted. "We don't discuss it. But in all definition, we are a couple Drew."

"Cat, please don't go there. Let's enjoy this." He twisted his body away from her.

She sighed. He was giving her what she asked, time with him, for them to be together. She was thankful that he did that, and it meant a lot to her, so why did she want more? "Do you ever think about the future?"

"You know I do. Kind of have to, with the school work and all."

"I mean beyond that."

"Cat, stop."

"What?"

"Let's not fight tonight."

"I'm not fighting, I'm asking. It doesn't have to be about us."

He lamented as she snuggled onto his shoulder. "Yes, I think about the future."

"What about?"

"Working hard enough so that mom doesn't have to. She's done so much for Jon and me and sacrificed much more. I feel like I should pay her back, figuratively, so she can relax in her age and live lots."

"That's very noble."

"It's not noble, Cat. It's just how things are done in my family. Especially with dad half way around the world." His voice was terse. "This conversation is over. Okay?"

She flipped over onto her side of the bed. "Goodnight, Andrew." She felt him roll away from her, and once she heard the sound of his breathing become slow and regular, she allowed her tears to flow.

A few weeks later, Andrew surprised Charlotte when he showed up unannounced at the Fortress. She opened the door, and he burst through, a huge grin on his face. Without warning, he reached forward and kissed her. After catching her breath, she asked, "What brings you by, Drew, it's not Friday." She stepped back, happy but surprised.

"I know it's not Friday, silly." He winked at her. "I wrote my last exam today."

"That's great." She gestured for him to come in. "Joe's just making lunch, care to join us?"

"Oh no, sorry. I didn't mean to interrupt."

"It's not a problem, Andrew," called Joe from the kitchen. "There'll be lots of food, although it won't be ready for some time."

Andrew followed his copper-haired beauty into the kitchen. "Hey, Joe."

"Hey, Drew. Congrats on finishing up the year."

"Thanks." He turned to Charlotte. "You working tonight?"

"No."

"Me neither. I want to celebrate. Let's go and do something." He looked at her expecting her to say yes. Or something.

She had no words. Finally, Joe nudged her encouragingly to speak. "Ah, sure. Yes." She looked over to Joe, who was smiling.

"Great! What should we do?"

She walked over to the screaming kettle and poured a cup of hot water. "Tea?" she asked him.

"Sure."

She poured another mug full and added a tea bag to it. She walked over to the couch and sat down.

"You haven't said much, Cat. What should we do? You've always wanted a real date, so tell me." He stood beside the couch, and was bouncing with excitement, until he sat down beside Charlotte.

She laughed, sort of. "Well, give me a moment. It's been a while since I've planned a date." She looked at him. He was giddy, and bursting with relief. He looked exuberant with joy, with his face relaxed and his blue-green eyes sparkling like gemstones. All that lay ahead were a few easy weeks at SEARCH and then off to Russia for nine weeks.

He urged her on, "Anything you want."

"Anything eh?" she smiled. "Give me a few more minutes." She sat there thinking. "Well, I've always wanted to get a tattoo, and there's that new Brendan Fraser film I'd like to see."

"Is it a chick flick?"

"Yep." She smirked.

"Okay, let's go see it. But you owe me." He wrapped his arm around her.

She giggled. "There's hope for you yet, Drew." She winked at him.

"What type of tattoo do you want? This is something you've never mentioned."

"I don't know. Something small, obviously, as I'm a wuss when it comes to needles. Maybe something that symbolizes us."

"Like a magnet?" Joe chimed in, "because you two are such polar opposites sometimes."

Charlotte turned to look at Joe, then got up and walked into the kitchen. "You're brilliant, Joe."

"I know that, but about what specifically?" The tall lad wore a face-splitting smile. His apron declared that one should "Kiss the Cook."

"About the magnets. We are very polar. On occasion."

"Yeah, so... it was a joke, Charlotte." Joe shook his head, and continued puttering around in the kitchen.

"No. I think my tattoo should have something to do with that."

"Gee thanks, Cat." Andrew rolled his eyes. "No picture of a heart with my name inscribed in it?"

She walked over to Andrew. "Umm. No. Maybe an expression or something."

The phone rang.

"Can you grab it, Charlotte. My hands are full," Joe asked as he grated some cheese.

"Sure," she pounced over to the phone in the living room. "Hello? ... Oh hi Miranda... Serious?... Wow, thank you so much.... I'm very excited. Yes, see you on Monday." She clicked the phone off and looked at both men, who were staring very intently at her. "I'm doing my practicum at Rutherford." She started jumping up and down.

Joe wiped his hands and gave her a big hug. "That's great news, Charlotte." He let her go as Andrew jumped over to her.

He gave her a congratulatory kiss. She kissed him back even harder, then wrapped her arms around his waist as he cupped her face in his hands.

"Get a room, you two." Joe kidded from the kitchen, after watching the displays of affection. "In fact, just head down the hall. Lunch will be another forty-five minutes at least."

Andrew and Charlotte looked at each other.

"Oh right, it's not Friday," Joe howled with laughter from the kitchen.

"Now, about that tattoo…" Charlotte mumbled.

Her left wrist was still stinging, and presumably healing, a few days later when she walked through the front doors of Rutherford School. She tried to cover it up with a long sleeve shirt, but the material rubbed against the wound, so she tugged up her sleeves a bit. Charlotte tucked her wild, wavy copper hair into the neatest ponytail she could manage, and slipped into a pair of black dress pants, a silk tank top and a black jersey button up. She hoped she would fit in.

She checked in at the office, and immediately the teacher with whom she would be working appeared. The woman named Miranda had black hair, olive skin, and wore impressive heels that had to be over 4" high. It made her the same height as Charlotte.

"Hi, I'm Miranda Toner." Like an old friend, she embraced Charlotte, which she wasn't expecting. "It'll be so nice to have someone pitching in and helping me out. What great luck." She waved her hand in the air. "Come. I'll give you the quick tour, and then we'll head down and get started."

Charlotte spent the day, and then the remainder of the week, working in Miranda's grade two class. Being called Miss Cooper was incredible, and she loved the energy the kids had, but they wore her down. Combined with the full time volunteer position at the school, she had also worked three evening shifts. She was flat-out exhausted by Friday..

She finished her shift and hung out in the GM's office on Friday night, waiting for Andrew, who would come by and drop off his key shortly. A weary Charlotte followed him out to the parking lot.

"See you at the Fortress?" she asked as she walked past his car, stumbling to her own.

"Are you kidding? You're in no shape to drive. I'll take you home and tomorrow your car will already be here." He stood there, watching as she easily conceded defeat, and walked back to his car. "There you go." They hopped into the alabaster-white Fiero. "First week was tough eh?"

She attempted a smile, but couldn't. Part of Andrew's appeal was that she never had to fake anything, so she allowed herself to feel devoid of energy. "Yes and no. It's different than working here. There are so many of them to attend to, chase after, and help. It's just go go go! But it's really great. I enjoy it. Miranda's pretty cool, and the kids love her."

After parking in the visitor parking at the Fortress, the young couple headed up to the apartment. Charlotte de-armed the place, and they headed to her room.

She stepped into her bathroom and emerged a few minutes later in jammie bottoms and a soft t-shirt. She tried to strike a sexy pose, but Andrew just laughed.

"Oh, Cat, we're not going to do this. Not tonight. Maybe in the morning when you've slept a bit." He walked over to her and tipped up her chin. He planted a sweet, soft kiss on her lips.

"But it's Friday."

"And you're physically exhausted. It's okay."

"But there are only six weeks until you leave. I need to make the most of them."

He reached for her hand. "Come on, let's go watch a movie or something. We can cuddle on the couch."

She padded barefoot behind him to the oversized couches, and climbed into one, while Andrew selected a movie.

"Does Star Wars work for you?"

"Always."

Andrew loaded the first disc into the player and sat back on the couch with Cat's head on his lap. While the movie played, Andrew combed his fingers through Charlotte's soft hair. He stroked her shoulder until she fell asleep. Andrew must have been tired too, because he fell asleep before the disc needed flipping, and woke up to Joe turning off the TV.

"Hey." Andrew blinked awake, and focused on Joe.

"Sorry, did I wake you?" Joe asked while placing the remote back on the coffee table.

His sleepy eyes betrayed him. "Nah, just resting my eyes."

Joe smiled a knowing grin.

"What time is it?" Andrew asked, stretching as much as he could.

"Two thirty."

"Wow. I should move Charlotte to bed."

"I'll get her." Joe bent down, and picked her up.

She mumbled incoherently as he took her down the hall, and placed her in her king sized bed. He kissed her forehead after he covered her up.

Andrew was right behind him. "Thanks Joe. See you in the morning."

Joe patted him on the shoulder, and waved as he exited the room. "Night."

He could hear Joe arming the Fortress as he undressed and slipped under the blankets. He was back asleep within minutes.

Chapter Nineteen
✿✿✿

A few weeks later, Andrew surprised Charlotte by showing up on Monday at Rutherford School. After being called down to the office, Charlotte smiled a megawatt smile when she saw the love-of-her-life-but-not-her-boyfriend standing tall in the office. He looked good, as always. As she approached him, he smelled good too.

"Hey, beautiful!" he said as soon as he turned and saw her.

"Hey, yourself." She hugged and kissed him. "Come down to my room. We're just finishing up and you can meet Miranda."

They walked hand in hand through the building, which felt like, to Andrew at least, as if they were going in circles. Finally, after passing a bunch of children's artwork, they arrived at the Grade 2 room.

Charlotte entered the classroom and made introductions. "Miranda, this is my friend Andrew. Andrew, Miranda."

Miranda smiled from her desk and stood up. She was the same height as Charlotte, despite the 4" heels. "Ah, Andrew, I've heard a lot about you. It's a pleasure."

"As I've heard about you." Andrew's eyes were crystal clear, making the blue-green colour especially bright today.

"Charlotte and I were just finishing up," dark-haired Miranda said as she passed Charlotte a stack of papers. "If you could put these through the photocopier and leave them in my mailbox, I'd appreciate it."

"Will do."

"Oh, before I forget, I have a pair of tickets to see Clay Walker this week. Would you two like them?" She flipped through her desk drawer.

Charlotte looked at Andrew, who was drawing a blank. "Who's Clay Walker?" he asked.

Miranda laughed as she looked up at Andrew. "A country singer."

"Oh, well, then, I'll pass."

Charlotte looked apologetic. "He doesn't like country music."

"Fair enough. It's not for everyone." She resumed her searching. "My fiancé, Gabe, and I are going. If you still want to come, I'm sure I could find someone else for the other ticket."

Andrew looked at Charlotte, who looked as though she were asking permission. "As long as it's not a Friday night. Only three Friday's left." He winked as he whispered to her.

Miranda was still glancing down, but overheard and responded, "It's this Thursday night."

"Then yeah, I'd love to go. Thanks."

"Great. We can work out the details later. See you tomorrow, Charlotte. It was nice to meet you Andrew." She stood up and started wiping down the chalkboards.

"That will be so much fun. I love Clay Walker." Charlotte was giddy.

With affection in his voice, Andrew joked, "You don't get out much do you?"

She punched him playfully as they stopped in the office to finish her work.

A carnal appetite kept the young lovers from much conversation that Friday night, so Charlotte and Andrew sat together with warm mugs of steaming coffee at the island, as Joe prepped breakfast. He awoke early that morning and was making the trio a breakfast.

"How was the concert?" Andrew asked.

"It was good."

"Who ended up going with the other ticket?"

"Well, there was Miranda and her fiancé Gabe, who works in insurance. He's very nice. Their wedding's this summer.

Anyways, they brought Gabe's older brother, Jack. He's a lawyer."

Joe laughed. "A lawyer? Really. Was he an asshole?" Charlotte shot him a dark look. "Most lawyers are assholes."

Andrew nodded in agreement.

"Well, he wasn't. He seemed nice. A little aggressive, but nice."

Andrew turned on his stool, and Joe stopped mixing. Both stared hard at Charlotte.

"Okay, aggressive is the wrong word. How about contentious? I don't know the right word..." She looked from Joe to Andrew and back.

"Explain." Joe demanded in his big brother like voice.

"Well, I met Miranda and Gabe at school, and we stopped by Jack's apartment to pick him up. He was nice, very friendly, and he wears a cowboy hat. He's tall, but not as tall as you, Joe." She smiled. "So we get to the concert, and we're singing along and everything's great. He insisted I have a beer, to which I firmly told him no. He put his arm around me, which I politely took off." She noticed Joe and Andrew tense up. "But that was it. I think he was just being friendly."

"That's it?" Joe searched her eyes. "That's it, she says."

"We went to the after party dance, and we danced until Miranda said it was time to go. He's a good dancer, a very strong leader. I've never had someone take such control on the dance floor before." Again, she saw her men tense. "But it's all good. Gabe and Miranda dropped him off. He bid us a good night, and then they dropped me off. Nothing happened. I'm just not used to such a strong personality." She shifted in her seat, trying to get comfortable.

Joe went back to chopping and mixing, but Andrew continued to stare at her.

Charlotte looked into Andrew's emotion filled eyes. "What?"

"I don't like him."

"Just like that? You haven't even met him."

"Any guy that tries to force himself on someone, I don't like."

"He wasn't forcing himself on me, Drew. And why would you care anyways? It's not like we're officially a couple or anything."

Joe mumbled as he turned his back, "And here we go again."

"Why do I care? Because I do. I love you, Cat, and I don't want to see you hurt."

"It's not like I'm going out with him, An-Drew."

"That's a relief," he said.

"He didn't even ask for my number."

"And would you have given it, if he did?"

"No. I don't work that way."

"Did he try to kiss you?"

"Of course not."

"Good."

Charlotte sighed and hung her head. "Andrew. You are my man. Get it? I'm committed to you, heart, body, and soul. I wish I meant more to you than just a play thing."

Joe placed his long fingered hands on the counter before them. "Okay, Andrew, Charlotte, let's take it down a notch before this gets out of hand, and somebody," he looked directly at Charlotte, "says something they're bound to regret later. Okay?" He handed each a pepper. "Chop these please, and take care not to damage yourselves."

Charlotte glared at Andrew.

"We have two weeks left. Please, let's not fight about our relationship," Andrew pleaded in a hushed voice, searching Charlotte's face. "Besides, you know that's not how I think of you." He cocked an eyebrow at her. "Let's enjoy our last couple weeks together." He put the knife down on the counter and gave her hand a little squeeze. "Okay?"

She stared into his eyes. They held so much emotion, a longing maybe? A desire to not fight over the same topic. Something. *What is it with guys and not wanting a relationship, but having no issue with a friends with benefits thing? It's clear to me that if I did go out with Jack, it would bother him. So why doesn't he think of me as a girlfriend?* Forcing a smile, she said, "Okay. No more fighting about us, or a lack of us, or whatever it is you want to call it."

"Charlotte." Joe's stern tone shook her. "Be nice."

Andrew's last night with Charlotte came too fast. They were sitting on the balcony, enjoying a summer sunset, and Charlotte a post-coital smoke, enjoying the last Friday evening together.

Andrew lounged in the deck chair and tousled his bronze hair, which seemed to dance in the setting sun. "Can you promise me something, Cat?"

She took a long drag on her cigarette and blew it away. "I can try."

"Can you give up that nasty habit altogether when I'm gone?" She laughed with gusto. "I guess I could. I have nine weeks." Then her smile faded as she turned back to watch the sun go to bed.

"Doesn't it mess with your asthma?"

"Surprisingly, no. Maybe all the inhaled smoke helps keep my lungs dry." She snorted and then stopped, lowering her head. A loud sigh followed.

"Yeah, I'm going to miss you too. Going to miss us, and going to miss this." He reached out his hand to Charlotte.

She extinguished her smoke, pulled out a mint from the pocket of her jeans, and popped it into her mouth. "What will I do without you for nine weeks? That's sixty-three days of not talking to you on a daily basis. At least nine times of not making love with you and feeling safe in your arms. I don't want this night to end." She looked at the setting sun and watched as the horizon pulled it lower. "When the sun comes back up, you'll already be gone." She looked at him, "I'm really trying not to be selfish when I say all that, as I know it will be good for you to see your dad again. It's been far too long. And I know that the change of scenery and a complete break from this place will really be good for you." She rambled.

"I know you feel that way, and you're not being selfish. A part of me, a huge part of me, is really going to ache without you." He gave her hand a little squeeze. "What about Miranda? You could hang out with her.'

"She's getting married in a couple of weeks."

"Right." They watched together as the oranges and reds changed to purples and navy blues, and some of the brighter stars started appearing. In the quiet of darkness, Andrew stood up. "Just a sec." He entered the living room, turned on some music, and stepped back out on the balcony. "Dance with me."

"Here?"

He reached for her hands. "Here."

She stood up and held his hand, as he placed the other firmly on the small of her back. "You'll have a great summer, you know."

"But I'm going to miss you."

"You'll be so busy with the summer camps, you won't even have a chance to miss me."

She leaned against his shoulder, and held firmly to his hand. They swayed in time to the music, never missing a beat. "It's so easy to be with you," she sighed. "You're like an extension of my body. We just fit perfectly together."

He said nothing in response, but twirled her around on the large penthouse deck, avoiding the two deck chairs and tower heater, now tucked into the corner. He held her close, kissing the top of her head.

"Nine weeks is a long time."

"It won't be that bad." They danced together, silently, in perfect unison, for a couple more ballads. He kissed her as the last song ended. "It's time for me to go, Cat."

She grasped on to Andrew, feeling his arms wrap her around him, until he released her. "Just promise me you'll write. You have that email address of mine, right?" Joe and Charlotte had recently jointly purchased a home computer, and enjoyed learning about the Internet, something so foreign to them both.

"Yes, already packed in my bag."

"I'll check it every day."

He stroked her cheek with the barest of touch, "I'll try to be sure there's something for you to read – I don't know what the Internet will be like over there or what kind of access dad has. Our emailing is minimal at best, but for you, I'll try." His finger ran a trail down her cheek, over her neck, and paused at her collarbone where he planted a bittersweet kiss.

"Then write me letters, if it's too hard to email." She begged, holding back the tears, her hands a vice grip on his arms.

He kissed her hard on the lips, leaving nothing to the imagination, and lingered longer than he should have. "I will. Cat, I need to go." He grabbed his bag and started walking away. He paused at the door, and gave her a hard hug, and another sensual kiss that left them both breathless and wanting more. "I love you, Cat. See you soon, okay?"

"I love you too, Drew." The tears started falling.

Andrew let go, and walked through the Fortress door, closing it behind him.

Charlotte leaned her head against the door, unable to move away. She wasn't sure where Joe emerged from, but she was glad he was suddenly there. He wrapped his long arms around her, and let her finish expelling her tears. Afterwards he made her a cup of tea, and together they snuggled up on the couch, and fell asleep.

C harlotte sent Andrew an email a couple of days later.

To: Andrew Wagner
From: Charlotte Cooper
Monday July 1, 1996 12:42
Subject: Missing you
It's Monday. How was your flight? You left your hoodie here, but maybe you did that on purpose? Love smelling it, makes me feel safe. Start my first week of camp tomorrow. Excited. Am I doing this right? Love and miss you.
Cat.

S he checked her email program every day until four days later, after work, she had a message in her inbox. Eagerly, she clicked and read.

To: Cat Cooper
From: Andrew Wagner
Thursday July 4, 1996 18:59
Subject: Re: Missing you
Hello Beautiful. Flight was good but long. Glad you found my hoodie. Yes, you are doing the email correctly.
Farming is harder than I remember. Dad has us up at sunrise and we work until sundown most days. I think of you every morning when I see the orange of the morning, and again when the sun sets. Pop helps out too, where he can, and his little girlfriend runs the ranch house. Thank goodness, because I'm too tired to cook after working in the fields. How was your first week with the camps?
Love and miss you too.
Drew.

Charlotte smiled like a giddy little girl who ate too much sugar, and hit reply.

To: Andrew Wagner
From: Charlotte Cooper
Friday July 5, 1996 19:15
Subject: Re: Re: Missing you
Yay, glad you are there safe and sound. Sounds like your dad is going to make you work hard all summer. Time will fly quickly for you I imagine.
Camp was good. Loved it. Looking forward to the new batch of kids on Monday. Weekend off so I'm heading over to help Joe out with some paperwork. It will give me something to do. Miranda called and is mailing me a copy of her review on my performance at school. She says it's all good. She also called and asked if I would come to her wedding on July 20. No way I can persuade you to come home for that weekend, is there?
Hugs and kisses,
Cat

She diligently checked her email every day in hopes of seeing a response. *I have no life apparently, because all I do is work and wait for an email that never comes. I wonder what he's doing, and I wonder if he thinks of me too.*

It was almost two weeks before Charlotte saw a reply.

To: Cat Cooper
From: Andrew Wagner
Friday July 19, 1996 05:42
Subject: Re: Re: Re: Missing you
Hello Beautiful.
Having a lot of fun. It's great being here – getting into a rhythm with the farm. Heading to the beach tomorrow for the day. Dad says we've earned it. Its good seeing Jon work so hard.
Won't be able to come to the wedding with you. Sorry. But you knew that already by now.
I miss our Friday nights, and our Saturday morning snuggles. Not the same waking up without you.
Got to run, Dad is calling.

Drew.

Charlotte swallowed hard. It was true that Friday nights weren't the same. She volunteered to help Joe out with whatever needed to be done, as long as it was away from the customers. Usually, she helped dispatch delivery orders or assisted with ordering supplies. Whatever she did, she wasn't home on a Friday night feeling sorry for herself. Sometimes, although she'd promised Andrew she'd stop, she sat with Joe and had a smoke or two. She hit reply, and paused, wondering what to tell him.

To: Andrew Wagner
From: Charlotte Cooper
Saturday July 20 1996 10:36
Subject: Re: Re: Re: Re: Missing you
Hey Drew. Glad to hear the farming is becoming routine. Are you going to give up your degree and become a farmer now? Enjoying the fresh air and sunshine? How far is the beach from you?
I'm going to Miranda's wedding today. Joe was going to come as my date but Chelsea told him that they were going to talk tonight. I think things are really rocky between them right now. So I'm going alone. I won't know anybody.
I miss you. So much.
Love, Cat.

She hit send, and then went to get dressed for the wedding. She wasn't excited about going and hanging out with perfect strangers. She knew three people who would be attending, the bride, the groom, and Jack.

More days passed without a word from Andrew, and she grew restless waiting. She did receive a postcard of a sunset from him, so that took the sting out of the lack of emails, although it was postmarked for July 4th. She wondered what his country looked like, what the farm was like, and what he looked like. Probably all tanned and sun kissed skin, his bronze hair naturally bleached lighter from the sun.

Joe sat at the computer late on Wednesday evening when he called out for Charlotte. "You have an email from Andrew." He rose up from the chair at the computer desk. "It's all yours. I'm going to bed."

She patted his shoulder and gave him a hug. He'd been so desolate, since he and Chelsea broke up. She'd offered to cry with him, or make him tea, but he refused her constant offers. He said he just needed to be alone. It was hard to see him like this, mopey and quiet, but she respected his need to do what he needed to do. After watching him walk away, she turned to the computer and opened her email.

To: Cat Cooper
From: Andrew Wagner
Thursday August 1, 1996 06:03
Subject: One Month to Go
So how was the wedding? Did you party all night?
Yes I am enjoying the fresh air. It's a different environment. The beach is nearby, about an hour's drive away. It's a great way to unwind.
Jon's got himself a little girlfriend. When I say little, I mean little. They're cute together. She's all of 5 feet tall! Reminds me of Miranda. Which in turn makes me think of you. I miss you.
How are Joe and Chelsea? Been thinking about them, and hope everything worked out.
One month to go. Booked my return trip home for Friday Aug 30. I'll spend Saturday with Mom and then I hope to see you on Sunday? Class starts on the third. So that should answer your question about me taking up farming.
Love you,
Drew.

Charlotte replied quickly, hoping he was still on after calculating the time zone difference.

To: Andrew Wagner
From: Charlotte Cooper
Wednesday July 30, 1996 20:20
Subject: Re: One Month to Go

Jon has a girlfriend? Too cute.

Joe is miserable! Chelsea broke up with him the night of the wedding. Since then he's trying all sorts of new recipes. Think I've gained 100 pounds sampling everything but he's really good and the things he's coming up with! Oh my! Trying to persuade him to open his own restaurant but he says he's not ready for that yet.

Got my review – Miranda loved me. There's a spot opening up and she highly suggested I apply for it, so I did.

Wedding was good – Jack was the best man and it suited him well. He has a kind of take-charge personality. I danced a lot. With Jack. Doesn't dance like you do though but he's good... I keep thinking of that night on the balcony. Often.

My heart aches for you. A month still seems like a long way away.

Missing you tremendously.

Cat

A ndrew didn't reply immediately as Charlotte hoped. The days whizzed by though. Charlotte filled her day teaching her campers in the day camps and after that, hung out at JT's Pizzeria, lounging in the office with Joe, or if they were both home together, sampling Joe's creations.

Concerned that she hadn't heard from Andrew in nearly two weeks, she sent him a quick email.

To: Andrew Wagner
From: Charlotte Cooper
Tuesday August 13, 1996 20:07
Subject: Hello?
Hey Drew. Haven't heard from you in two weeks. Hope everything is okay?
Miss you.
Cat

A quick ping signalled a reply. Charlotte's face lit up.

To: Cat Cooper
From: Andrew Wagner

Wednesday August 14, 1996 06:10
Subject: Re: Hello?
Beautiful,
Been very busy. Let me re-read your last email and get back to you. Give me 10?
Drew.

She was excited to hear, or read from him. She got up and made herself a cup of tea while waiting for his reply. In addition, she managed to file her nails and write up a quick to do list for the next day. Eventually, through sheer will, the tell tale ping sound arrived.

To: Cat Cooper
From: Andrew Wagner
Wednesday August 14, 1996 06:35
Subject: Home soon…

Hey Charlotte,
Sorry to hear about Joe. I hope he's healing his heart better since the last email.
Even if you have somehow managed to gain 100lbs since I saw you last, you would still be breathtaking and beautiful. I'm glad you are around to help him and keep him in line. I miss his company, and his fantastic breakfasts. Tell him I say hi.
Jon and his girlfriend broke up too. It was good while it lasted but he's working hard again.
So you danced all night with Jack? I still don't like him. Have you gone on a date with him?
Heard anything back from the school after sending in your application? I've got my fingers crossed for you.
I'll be on here for a bit yet. Got to send an email to Mom. If you're still there, email me back.
Drew.

To: Andrew Wagner
From: Charlotte Cooper
Tuesday, August 13 20:43
Subject: Re: Home Soon…
No haven't heard back from the school.

No haven't had a date with Jack. Never asked for my number, not that it matters. I'm waiting for you Drew.
Remember? I love YOU.
Cat.
P.S. What's with calling me Charlotte?

To: Cat Cooper
From: Andrew Wagner
Wednesday, August 14 07:02
Subject: Re: Re: Home Soon…
Glad there is no date with Jack. Too bad about the school. I'm sure you'll hear something soon.
Sorry, it's how I've been talking about you. When I tell people how much I love my Cat, they look at me weird. It was easier to talk about you as Charlotte.
I know you love me. I love you too. Saw the most amazing sunset the other night, and thought of you. Looking forward to coming home. Have another couple of beach days ahead, and soon I'll be homeward bound.
Drew

To: Andrew Wagner
From: Charlotte Cooper
Sunday, August 25, 1996 20:15
Subject: Happy Birthday
Happy Birthday Drew.
Hope you receive this before starting your day.
Just wanted you to know that I am thinking of you. Like always. One week until I can see your handsome face again. I'm counting down the days and hours. I'll get home on Sunday around 4:30. Did you want to sleepover that night? We both work at 4 on Monday, I checked the schedule, so I hope you'll consider my offer.
I'm back to being a cashier this week in the evenings, as I got hired at the school, and will be there all week getting a classroom set up. Not sure what class I'll be with, but I'm very excited.
Love you. See you soon.
Cat

Chapter Twenty
✿✿✿

On Saturday, Charlotte cashed out her float with Russell. Over the summer, Russell enjoyed his new rank in seniority, becoming a General Manager and bossing everyone around. He stood over Charlotte watching her count the cash, making her redo it if *he* miscounted. She was just eager to get out of there. She knew Andrew was back in town, and really wanted to give him a quick phone call when she got home, just to hear his voice.

She had counted her float, three times, when a knock came at the door.

Russell sauntered over and yanked open the door. Someone passed something in. "Give this to Charlotte please. It's a special delivery." Russell walked over to Charlotte and dumped the tote bag on the counter. "For you."

"Who's it from?"

"Colin? He gave it to me to give to you. Jeez, Charlotte, I don't know everything." He rolled his eyes as he stared at her.

She signed over her float to Russell and grabbed the non-descript package. Apprehensively, she then opened the plastic bag. Looking in, she saw a variety of wrapped packages, and some cans of pop. Her face was a puzzle of questions. A note sat on top of it all. Curiously, she unfolded the note. It read:

Bring the bag into the park,
Look for the blanket before its dark.
And then you look and then you'll see,
It's exactly where you'll find me.

With her smile stretching from ear to ear, she grabbed the bag and her purse and left the GM's office in a rush. She ignored Russell's questioning taunts, and was at a full run by the time she exited the main doors. She circled the building, searching for the blanket, and continued to run along the paths in the park. She felt like she'd run miles on the hard concrete paths, until, south of the building she spotted a red blanket, lying tucked just back off the paths, nestled in between a small grove of pine trees. She had just stepped off the path, when she spotted him. She ran at full speed and leaped into his waiting arms.

"Andrew!" She cried his name out repeatedly, as she kissed him all over his cheeks and lips.

He kissed her back and then broke it off by setting her down on her feet. "You are so beautiful. How I've missed your face." He studied her as he held her hands and lifted them outwards. "Where's this 100lbs you put on?" He smirked. "It seems like you've actually lost weight."

She ran her hands over his arms, noticing how taut and sinew they were. *Working a farm for a few weeks had paid off. Hubba-hubba.* He was much more muscled than before. He looked fantastic in his black t-shirt and cargo pants; they brought out the golden colour of his skin. "I've missed you too. Seems like you've been working hard."

"You've no idea." His accent was much stronger, almost as if the past nine weeks he'd only spoken in his native tongue. He gestured for her to sit on the checkered blanket. "Thought this would be a great way to say hello."

She kicked off her sandals and placed the plastic bag in the middle after kissing him again. "Oh, Drew, this is so romantic." The faintest hint of scarlet stained her smile. She couldn't stop staring at him.

"You okay?"

"Oh yeah!" Her smile split her face in half. "Just thinking how good you look. Really. You are much darker, so very tanned. It makes your eyes really stand out." She reached out to caress his face and tousle his hair. "Your hair is considerably lighter, and much longer than I've ever noticed." She stroked his cheek, feeling the day old stubble she'd missed.

He grabbed her hand and kissed the top of it. "Come on, let's eat. I'm hungry for Canadian food." He reached into the plastic bag, pulling out a wrapped sub and passed the sandwich to her.

Charlotte laughed. "You think this is Canadian?"

"Haven't had one since before I left." He tore open his wrapper and took a man sized bite. "Mmmm."

She watched him moan through his messy sub and inquired about the farm, the work he did, and his Russian family. After listening to him speak briefly about it, she asked, "Are you excited about going back to school on Tuesday?" She sat close to him, stretched out her legs and wrapped them over his.

"I'm really not terribly excited about going. It's a tough year ahead. Eight short months to get everything done, and I get to start applying for jobs in the new year." He sighed, "A lot to do. I was thinking I might go and get my MBA as well. Start that in May, when I get my degree, but it's not a definite."

"More schooling? I thought you'd be finished."

"I would. This'd just enhance everything. Then I can own my own business."

"Can't you do that now?"

"I could. Or I'll be able to, but this'll just make me a better boss, have better skills."

"Oh," she said with a depressing edge to her voice. She was looking forward to spending countless school free hours with him. Hoping to distract him, she asked, "What's your work schedule going to be like?"

"If I'm lucky, and if Tony okays it, one shift during the week, and one on the weekend. I don't think I can do much more than that." He paused, and looked at Charlotte, his eyes twinkling with longing. "Tell me about your summer. How were the camps?"

Charlotte's smile was again face splitting. She felt as if she'd smiled more in the last few minutes than she had all summer. "Oh, Drew, it was so fantastic. I loved it. Teaching the little ones about astronomy was so much fun. I can't believe I was paid to do that."

Andrew relaxed while listening to Charlotte go on and on about some of her campers, while he finished his sub. "Awesome! I'm so glad. It was hard to tell exactly how much fun via the emails. How was your first week at school?" He lay down on the blanket, but propped himself up on one elbow.

"It was good. Miranda introduced me to all the new staff, and showed me the rooms I'll be working in."

"Rooms?" he picked up, "What grade?"

"A couple actually. I'll spend Monday, Wednesday, and Friday mornings in grade six, teaching the science unit. The teacher there is super nice and always finds science boring, so she asked me if I wanted to teach it. Plus, the grade six's study... wait for it... ASTRONOMY!" Charlotte couldn't stop smiling; she was lit up from within. "It will be a small class, so far about twenty students, so it'll be super manageable. Then Tuesday and Thursday mornings, I'll be working with Miranda and her grade twos."

"What are you doing in your afternoons?"

"I don't know yet. But I'll be back here in the evenings." She lay beside him, and put her head on his rock hard abs. "What about you?"

"Full days at school. No time to relax, but that's okay. I've been preparing for this, and everything is paid up. No tuition fees hanging over me so I'll graduate debt free." He twisted a wavy, coppery strand of Charlotte's around his finger.

"That's fantastic."

"Yeah, I'm super happy about that. So is mom. One less thing for her to worry about."

"How's Jon doing?"

"Well, he's starting business management next week. He's heavily in debt – spent all his saved up money partying in Russia."

"He spent it all? Your mom must be pissed."

"She had some money saved up for him, but not enough to get him through the year. He's got to apply for student loans, and his high school marks weren't great, but if he works hard, he could apply for scholarships for next semester."

"Wow."

"I know."

They lay in silence for a bit. Andrew continued to stroke Charlotte's hair, letting the wavy strands fall across his chest. "So what are you doing for your twenty-first birthday?"

"Drew, that's a ways away."

"Not so far. It's like what, five weeks? Twenty-one is a big deal."

"It's just another day." She turned and peered at him. "What did you do for your twenty-first? You never got back to me." She pulled his hand away from her hair and wrapped her fingers around his palm, noticing how his once soft hands were rough with calluses.

He smiled as a fond memory surfaced. "Jon and I, we spent the night in Krasnodar. Across the street from our hotel was a great little bar. It was so fantastic. Ah, we had such a great time. Danced all night long with this krasivaya dama," he said in Russian, "named Oksana. She was hot."

Pangs of apprehension beat through Charlotte. "Did you sleep with her?" she asked without thinking, through gritted teeth. Hostility beat it's way through her veins.

He chuckled. "Yeah, but it meant nothing. Really. Just sex. Pure and simple. There was no love shared." He looked honestly into her eyes. He paused, feeling his hand glide between her fingers. "Didn't you, you know, over the summer?"

She sat up, releasing his hand, and glared hard at him. "No and who would I have done that with? I'm committed to you. Obviously more than you're committed to me."

"Oh." He pulled her back down against him and ran his hand along her arm. "Well, we haven't been a couple for a really long time, Cat."

"How do you see us then?" she asked, hoping this question would yield some truth.

"You and I - we're just friends with benefits. Excellent benefits."

She sighed and watched the first few stars start to appear in the twilight. "I don't know about that anymore." She continued to look up at the sky, mentally recognizing a few constellations, and then turned her head towards him. "Drew, can I ask you something?" she hesitated.

"Of course, Cat. You should know that."

She took a deep breath. "Do you love me?"

"You know I do."

"No, I mean really love me? Like I'm all you think about. The first person you think of in the morning, and the last before bed."

There were a few sharp breaths, and a long pause in the conversation. "Cat, I do love you. I'd do anything for you. I thought about you all the time back home. Why do you think I'm here today to see you, and not tomorrow?"

"What about Oksana?"

"History."

"Really? You sowed your wild oats and all that with her?"

"Cat, she was something I did spontaneously. Didn't you do anything spontaneous over the summer?"

"No," she said. *But I'm about to.* She half smiled and continued to play with his hands, then released one, and watched as he ran a hand through his brighter bronze hair. Her stomach tightened, and her mouth went dry. "Well...I've been thinking..." She paused, and looked him in the eyes. She couldn't get her mouth to work.

"What? Tell me." His blue-greens softened as he looked at her. The longing in them was over-powering. It was as if this was the first time he'd ever seen her. "Geez, you're so beautiful in the twilight. Truly breathtaking. Your eyes seem to have a real golden look about them, and your lips... wow. I've missed seeing you like this." He pulled her towards him to kiss her, to feel her soft lips against his. He could feel a slight tremble as her lips parted to anticipate him.

She put her hand on him and pushed away. She took another deep breath, and settled back on his lower abs. "You flatter me, Drew, really, but let me say my thought..." Another long pause and she closed her eyes. "What if there's no one else for us?" Another gulp of air, a swallowing of pride. "What if it's only you and me?"

Drew tensed beneath her, and after the passing of a dozen heartbeats said, "I think I'm following you, but I want to hear it directly from you, just so I'm not mistaken."

She crunched herself up into a sitting position, and placed her hand above his heart. It beat against her palm as it sped with her hesitation. "I need to ask you something, Drew." She felt him tighten, and the heart pumped faster still. "Do you see us together in your future?"

He looked up at the stars, avoiding her eyes and not responding for many breaths. "I don't know how to say this without you getting upset. Because no matter how I answer, you won't be happy."

She braced herself, anticipating the worst. "I want the truth. It hurts less than being led astray."

"Okay, the truth." He stared into her eyes, held her hand, and gave it a quick kiss. "I love you. Pure and simple. I would do anything for you, and you know that. I see us together, but like this. Lovers, friends."

She couldn't stop her mouth from speaking, "Like a married couple?" She paused, letting the words sink in. "Because that's what we're like." He was very quiet. "What if we got married, Drew, to each other?" The tension built and started to enclose them, trapping them in a forest of oncoming hurt. "I've been thinking about it all summer long. We're so awesome together, and even when we said we wouldn't be boyfriend and girlfriend, we were still acting like it. With the sleepovers, and the hanging out. All of it. What if we're just meant to be together? For always?" She straightened out and turned to face him head on.

"I think you have a warped view of what marriage is." Drew propped himself up on his elbow. "Are you proposing, Cat?" His face was devoid of any emotion.

"Yes... Well, no, not really. I'm just proposing that we think about marrying each other. A few years down the road."

"Cat, I don't think that's a good idea." He looked her squarely in the face. "We're too young, with our lives still ahead of us."

"You didn't think it a bad idea last year, when I was pregnant." She hung her head, her hair falling like a curtain against her cheeks, hoping it would shield the hurt.

Drew slumped back down and looked up into the twinkling nightfall. "That was different. The circumstances were different."

"I see." Her voice lowered into a half whisper. "So when it was convenient, it was okay. Now, not so much. I understand."

Drew pulled her down beside him and wrapped his strong arms around her, holding her tight to him. "I do love you. Maybe like a married couple, I don't know. Please don't take my lack of a 'yes' to mean that my love for you is gone or has changed in any way. I think we just need to wait. Explore our options."

"Explore our options, Drew? Like Oksana?"

Andrew growled. "That's not what I meant."

"Then please explain it better, because I'm confused. Really confused."

"Don't you think that's moving the relationship too fast? Us getting married?" He looked into her eyes and felt sad as he took in her somber expression.

"Geez, Drew, I'm not saying we get married tomorrow."

"But still, it's too fast. We don't even live together!"

"Too fast? I guess from your 'I'm not your boyfriend' perspective it can seem like it's moving too fast, but in reality, I don't think so. We're together. Ask anyone – our relationship is very boyfriend/girlfriend, regardless of what you think. We're together, couple like."

Andrew shook his head, trying to figure out his next few words. "We can still be together, like we were before I went home." A pause. "Marriage at our age doesn't work out well."

"How would you know?"

"My parents were married at our age, and look how well that went. Joe's parents split up when he was little." Braced for a look, he carried on, "And look at your parents. That *really* didn't work."

"My dad didn't even know about me, so that blows your theory."

"Actually it verifies my theory. Young people do stupid things. I don't want to do something stupid."

"Because marrying me would be stupid?"

"Argg… Charlotte, you are reading too much into this." Anger in his voice made it rise higher. Taking a couple of deep breaths after running his fingers through his messy hair, he steadied himself. "Look, if I decide to marry you, or anyone for that matter, I want to make sure that it will last a lifetime. Too many people enter it so lightly. So let's just enjoy what we have now, and see if it evolves into something more serious."

Charlotte rubbed the mark of her tattoo on her left wrist, as if hoping to will the words into truth. "I don't know that I can continue to do that, Drew." She looked up from the tattoo, and into his clouded blue-greens. "I love you so much, but if there isn't a future for us, a definitive one, then I don't think I can be that friend for you. I can't just be someone you sleep with without there being more to it than that." She swallowed and stammered out, "I know it sounds rotten and extremely selfish, but if I can't have you for a relationship, a boyfriend-girlfriend-committed one, then I think I shouldn't, no scratch that, then I CAN'T give you anymore of me, because my heart can't take it anymore. I've waited patiently for you, as I love you so much and want to be with you forever, but if you're not ready to be with me in that capacity, then I think its best we go our separate ways. Make it a clean break. Completely. No more friends with benefits. I want the whole package."

"Cat, are you freaking kidding me?" His fists tightened, in response to his anger. His eyes blazed, and he jumped up onto his knees.

"Think about it, Drew. I waited all summer for you to come home, and I saw no one else. Didn't even think about anyone else. And you? You banged some chick on your birthday. Maybe there were others that you're not telling me?" She took a quick breath, "You don't see us as anything more than friends, and yet I do. A complete reversal of where we were almost a year ago, where you wanted more, and I held back. But I've fallen for you so hard. You. Are. My. Everything." Her voice rose in pitch. "Now I know that that reflection is not the same. I want you permanently in my future."

Andrew pulled Charlotte closer, keeping her from running away, his hands holding onto the tops of her arms. "Charlotte, please. You're overreacting. You don't know what you really want. Let's talk about it. Don't say... please don't say..." He was on the brink of tears.

"Am I? Am I really? I know what I want. I want you. Forever. I don't think that's overreacting!" She tugged out against his strong hold. "I've tried to talk to you about this so many times, but it keeps boiling down to this, Drew." The well of tears in her eyes pushed against their hold and with her next breath, the dam broke. She cried out in the saddest voice, "I have to give up on us, even though I love you, and my heart will never be the same." She extracted herself suddenly from his slackened hold, and gathered up the garbage. She stood up, waiting for him to speak. "Say something, Andrew. Say anything. I'm about to give up on you and walk away."

Andrew felt as if he'd just been punched in the gut. Time slowed, as if the earth had stopped rotating. He couldn't believe his ears. His brain raced to form a coherent sentence, or even a word, or a syllable, but nothing made sense, nothing smart was able to pour forth from his dry mouth. He watched her rise up off her knees, and surveyed the lovely little way she collected up the garbage. He saw the river of tears streaming down her flushed cheeks, colouring them with streaks of shiny despair. His body was numb, and he couldn't make his hands move to reach out for her.

Having him not react, unleashed a new wave of hot stinging rejection. "Goodbye, Andrew Wagner. I'll love you forever." Then she turned and walked away, trying to carry herself with grace, although her insides were crumbling and a painful hurt flowed through her veins.

It was then that the earth started spinning again, time quickly un-paused, and he watched her leave, never turning back.

Chapter Twenty-One
✿✿✿

Cutting Andrew completely out from her life was one of the hardest things Charlotte had ever done. Everywhere she went, there was a memory. When she opened up her modules to pull out some notes of ideas to bring to her first week with the school kids, there was a note that Andrew had doodled while they'd been studying together. Her bedroom contained constant reminders, things that helped her get through the summer - photos of them, his hoodie he'd left behind, a toothbrush he kept in her bathroom, an opened package of condoms. Worse were the memories that showed up when she slept, of sweet tender kisses, dances and laughter; the happier days.

She knew she had to make a clean break, but wasn't sure where to begin. She packed up his things into a white box. She added all the sweet little notes he'd written, every photo of the two of them, his toothbrush, the hoodie, a few dance mix CDs, and anything else that she saw that reminded her of him. On top of it all she added the condoms, having no further use for them. She wrapped the box with a red velvet ribbon. She planned to give it to him on Saturday when she saw him at work. There was no way to escape that. She needed the shift, and couldn't up and quit. Maybe she'd tuck the projection room key into the ribbon. She laughed through her pain at that thought, and then cried some more.

Thankfully, or unthankfully, depending on how and when she looked it, the week at school went by fast. It kept her mind devoid of thoughts and memories of Andrew. When she woke on Saturday morning, however, she felt unprepared for her day. She didn't know if he was working a day or an evening shift, but she was on the one to nine, so either way, she'd pass him by. He hadn't called her all week, and deep down in her heart, it hurt. A lot. Although she'd been the one to end it, she'd secretly hoped he would at least try to contact her, and get her to change her mind.

She rolled out of bed, and sauntered down the hall to the kitchen to make herself a pot of Folgers. She stared at the dripping coffee, willing it to brew faster, when she caught sight of Joe out of the corner of her eye.

"Morning," he announced, padding into the kitchen in shorts and a faded hypercolour t-shirt that Charlotte had ruined when she washed it accidentally in hot water, instead of cold. His mop of golden hair was messy, like he'd rolled out of bed a minute ago.

"Morning," she said as she leaned on the counter, studying the way the dark liquid fell into the pot.

"You made coffee. Can I make you breakfast?" He started pulling out a skillet, and various items from the fridge.

"Sure."

Joe started chopping up some vegetables. "No word from him?"

She shook her head, and interrupted the brewing java to pour a mug's worth. She put the pot back and continued to watch it brew.

"Sorry."

"Whatever," she wept and brushed away a stray fallen tear. Changing the topic she asked, "What are you making?"

"Frittata. I like the way it sounds." Joe continued his prep not looking in Charlotte's direction. "What's on your schedule today?"

"Work at one. You?"

"Don't know yet. I'm in at four, so I'll probably kick back and play some N64."

"Sounds fun." She pulled out a couple of plates, and proceeded to set the table. The coffee finally stopped brewing, so she poured Joe a cup and set it at his place. The friends sat in silence as they dined on the frittatas. "This is very tasty, Joe."

"Thanks." He put his fork down, having finished. "I wanted to make sure your day got off to a solid start." He looked at her, concern etched across his furrowed brow.

She wiped some more tears away. "I can't believe it's over, like really over. He should be sitting here with us."

Joe sighed, picking his words carefully, "As much as I wanted you two to make it work, I think you did the right thing by ending it completely, instead of being strung along."

"Then why does it hurt so much?"

He passed her a napkin. "Because it does. Love hurts. I'm sorry."

She gathered the dishes, and put them into the dishwasher. "Thanks. I'm going to my room now." She was half way down the hall, when he called out to her.

"Charlotte?"

"Yeah, Joe?" She turned around, folding her arms across her chest.

"It will get easier. Today will be hard, but next week will be better. And so on. I promise."

"Okay, if you say so." She spun back around and went into her room. She flopped on her bed, and cried until it was time for her to get ready for work.

She showered, and applied a little makeup, thinking that if she wore mascara, she'd have to hold herself together, and not cry, or else risk the runny mascara look. She said goodbye to Joe, and was standing at the elevator, waiting, when she remembered the box of Andrew's stuff. Quickly she retrieved the ribboned box, and headed in for work, hoping against hope, that this would be a good day.

S he checked the schedule when she got in, and noticed Andrew had the evening shift. Dang, she'd have to watch out extra hard for him at their shift change, at dinnertime, and when she cashed out. *So much for a good day.*

Charlotte added the projection room key to the red velvet ribboned box, preparing it for his arrival. She placed the box beside her till. At 3:45, she spotted him. He looked good, with a new haircut, but the stubble had turned into a beard, and it aged him. His bronze tips seemed as if they'd seen some extra sun. He meandered up to her till. She said nothing, and passed him the box. Puzzled, he looked at it, but said nothing either, having noticed that the key was on top. Trying not to care, but unable to stop herself, she watched from under her eyelashes as he grabbed the box and walked over to the elevator, never turning around. She let out the breath she didn't remember holding. *One down, two to go.*

Shortly thereafter, Gregory descended from the elevator and in a voice louder than was necessary snickered, "Way to ruin his night, Charlotte." He laughed heartily as he walked over to chat with Russell, who stood at the entrance to the GM's office. Gregory said something to Russell, who looked over at Charlotte and laughed.

Charlotte flushed in anger, which turned her ears bright red, but she tried to focus on the line up of customers in front of her, instead of the snickers coming from her right.

At 5:45, and thankful for a couple of customers, Charlotte noticed Andrew step out of the elevator. She tried not to stare, but was overcome with curiosity. He looked a little worse for wear. His eyes didn't shine the way they usually did, and instead seemed hooded and dark. His backpack slung low over his shoulder, and his hand deep in the pocket of his jeans. He slumped right past the desk, blatantly ignoring Charlotte and the other cashier, and headed down the hall to the café. She sighed with relief, until she felt Russell's nefarious presence behind her.

He'd snuck up quietly, and stood there with his hands on his hips, and smugness on his indignant little face. "You can take your supper break now," he said in a demanding voice.

"Now?"

"Yep. See you at 6:15, and not a minute past!" He shook a short stubby finger in her direction, like a parent scolding a child.

"Can I eat in the office today?"

"No you may not. That's not what the office is for." He liked to assert his position of power over the staff, most especially Charlotte.

"Can I eat back here?" she asked timidly.

"No. Go eat in the café, Charlotte." He shooed her away, leaving the few customers in line to wait for the cashier beside him, as he'd obviously rather taunt Charlotte than help out.

She grabbed her purse and privately cursed at Russell while walking down the hall. She saw him, sitting there, with his bag on the table and the box, no longer neatly wrapped in the red velvet ribbon. *Drew.* The ribbon looked sloppy, as if tied in a great rush. *I'm sorry.* She made the briefest eye contact with him before ordering a slice of pizza and a tea. Feeling her hands shake, she paid for her meal, and headed out of the café, passing the desk where Russell sat with a smug look on his face, and out the main doors.

She turned left towards the administration area, and stood by the door. Suddenly, she felt ill, and very cold. She hadn't brought a jacket with her. She threw the uneaten pizza into the garbage. Setting her tea down on the cold, hard cement, she rummaged through her purse until she found a pack of smokes buried in the bottom. Sighing with relief, she opened and ignited a smoke, enjoying the cool feeling of the menthol entering her lungs. She heard the approaching footsteps, but refused to turn in the direction of the sound.

His calm, soothing, heavily accented voice called out to her, "Cat?"

Steadfast in her determination to not cave to him, she turned even further away, taking a long, punishing drag from her smoke.

"Cat, we need to talk."

She refused to look at him, but her heart couldn't ignore the pleading in his voice. *He's here. Now. Talk to him.* Beating it's command, it begged her to turn and face Andrew, but her mind, strong with conviction, argued the case for staying exactly like she was.

"Look, I'm giving the box back. The pictures, the little notes, the mementoes, and the hoodie. Everything. Those are all yours. I want you to have them, that's why I gave them to you in the first place."

She heard him step closer, so she took another long punishing drag. *I know how much you hate me smoking, so for the time you stand there, I'll pretend to be a chimney. As much as I want to look as you, I just can't.*

"You can either take the box, or I can leave it at the front desk where I'm sure Russell will go through it before you return."

At that, she spun around, her heart shrinking, and saw the outstretched hands with the box cradled between them. Cigarette firmly ensconced between her fingers, she reached out, wordlessly, and took the box. Accidently, her hands grazed his and she felt that simmering flame ignite. He did look worse for wear. The dark shadows under his eyes were huge, his skin looked sallow and faded.

He nodded at her, and took a step closer. Her heart skipped a beat, as he bent down towards her ear, and whispering in his accented voice proclaimed, "You are my most greatest love, Cat. I'll love you always. Read the note." A soft stubbly kiss grazed her cheek, then he turned and shuffled back into the building. Charlotte fought the tears, staring up at the sky, trying to get gravity to pull them back into their ducts. Extinguishing her cigarette, she grabbed her tea and headed back into the building. She stopped briefly in the washroom to freshen up, to wipe away some of the smeared mascara and to pinch some colour into her paled cheeks. She tucked the box under her desk, beneath her purse and finished her shift in near silence to the staff around her.

After work, Charlotte headed home, and once inside her room, she found a spot at the far back top part of her closet.

I don't want to see this box. I don't want to read the note. I don't want to know why you rejected me, and then act like it's not a big deal. I never want to see it again. She shoved the box back in as far as she could, and then with amazing accuracy, threw a t-shirt over the top to hide it. Falling back onto her bed, she cried herself to sleep.

The next few weeks were equally difficult. The school days went by fast, and she started to get her footing with the students and staff. She was glad she had applied herself last year and finished her course ahead of schedule. She was happy working at the school, away from the place that filled her heart with misery, longing, and heartache.

Working at SEARCH became her purgatory. She was clearly miserable there, and Russell enjoyed exploiting her unhappiness. He constantly taunted her, especially whenever Andrew was around. Russell's partner in crime, Gregory, was also a willing participant in their sick game. Together, they'd make some snide remark, and then point and laugh. Russell was so un-professional; she wondered hourly how senior level staff had promoted him. All he did was make her shift unbearable, and she was sure, by proxy, that it wasn't enjoyable for Andrew either. Russell would make Andrew wait until Charlotte had finished with a customer, so she could give him the key to the projection room, claiming that Charlotte was responsible for signing them in and out. Russell made her take her supper breaks whenever he noticed Andrew taking his. It was as though he enjoyed seeing the pain on Charlotte's face. There were few people that Charlotte truly hated in life, but Russell was on that list.

Somehow, she trudged through her weekly visits to purgatory and at Miranda's insistence, they went out to the bar to celebrate her twenty-first birthday, the Friday before her actual birthday. She certainly didn't feel like celebrating. Miranda had invited Jack to join them, and by dancing all night, Charlotte found her missing smile, at least temporarily. She even managed to laugh a little, despite her still shattered heart.

Jack and Charlotte had a great rhythm on the dance floor. He was a very strong leader, and Charlotte insisted on sitting to rest for a couple of songs as her feet were sore from dancing in her heels. So he took them off her feet, and had her dance in bare feet. It felt oddly weird, and yet, somehow right. They danced all night, until last call. At that point, she decided to go home. Jack walked out the door with her, and escorted her to her car.

"I hope you had a good birthday?" he asked sweetly, wiping away some trails of sweat that poured out once he lifted his cowboy hat.

"It definitely improved."

Jack smiled. "I wanted to get your number. After the wedding." He looked directly at her, no hint of shyness or awkwardness in his stance.

"I'm sure Miranda would've given it to you."

"Maybe, but I'd rather have gotten it from you." He leaned against her car.

She looked at him hard. Was this tall man, with dark brown hair and dark eyes, in the beige cowboy hat, really asking for her number? She stood there motionless, not knowing what to do.

"So, can I get your number?" He tipped closer towards her, his smile perking up on the left side.

She reached into her car, and searched for a piece of paper and a pen. She scribbled her number on it and gave it to him.

He tucked the ripped paper into his jean pocket. "Thanks. I'll call you. Soon." He tipped the brim of his hat and started walking away.

"Wait!" she yelled out to his turned back. "Jack, there's something you need to know first."

He turned on his heels and stepped back closer to her, shadowing her from the light she'd parked underneath. In a voice that contradicted his unanticipated nervous stature, he calmly responded, "Yes?"

She let out a low breath into the cool air of early Saturday morning. "I'm just getting out of a long relationship that ended thirty-five days ago. He was the love of my life, and every day has been a version of hell since we split. I'm not ready for something new. I just thought you should know that." By her sudden confession, Charlotte managed to shock herself.

He looked down at her and asked, "Did you leave him or did he leave you?"

"Does it matter?"

"A little. My chances are better if you were the one who did the dumping." He thrust his hands into his pockets.

She stared down at the ground. *I knew I had to be the one to walk away, but it wasn't really my choice. I couldn't allow myself to be dragged anymore through the relationship, or lack of one really, that would lead nowhere. I knew I had to be the one to end it. But it wasn't what I really wanted.* She looked up into Jack's face. "It's complicated."

"Okay…" The cowboy hat clad man paused and after further closing the distance between them inquired, "Let me ask you something." He stared through her exterior and right into her soul. "Tonight, when we were dancing and spinning around, were you thinking of him?"

Charlotte wracked her brain, and thought long and hard. *Surely, I had, hadn't I?* Until she mentioned to Jack just now, Andrew hadn't been in the forefront of her thoughts. *Weird.* She stared towards the exterior of the bar, focusing on the flashing neon sign, and then looked up at the tall man standing patiently before her. "No."

"Well then, guess there's no problem. I'll just keep you dancing." He winked and smiled as he stepped back, allowing the streetlight to flood her face. "Talk to you soon." With that, he turned and walked across the parking lot to his big pickup truck.

Shaking her coppery head, she got into her car and headed home. She pulled into her underground parking stall at the same time as Joe did.

"Happy Birthday, Charlotte!" he exclaimed when he saw her. "It's now officially your birthday."

"Yes, it is. I'm now legal in all countries." She laughed as they took the elevator up to their apartment. Removing her shoes, she gasped at how dirty her bare feet were. After asking Joe to grab a pair of socks to wear down the hall, she gave him a quick kiss on the cheek and went to shower. The bottoms of her feet were black and sticky from dancing barefoot, at a bar, and hard to scrub clean. However, after a cleansing shower, and for the first time in nearly five weeks, she didn't cry herself to sleep.

Charlotte slept in until almost eleven, and after getting ready for work, joined Joe in the kitchen. She could smell that he had a lunch cooking.

"For the birthday girl must have her favourite." He smiled as he passed her a plate of spaghetti with Bolognese sauce, and fresh garlic bread.

"Joe, this is delightful."

He smiled. "Thanks."

"The spaghetti tastes amazing!"

"Hand made – none of that store bought stuff. It's really easy to make too." Joe's hair was slicked back, making it darker than usual. He nodded towards the counter. "I also packed you up a supper. Now you won't have to go to the cafeteria to order, and you don't have to heat it up, so you can eat wherever."

"Joe, you're too sweet."

"I know." He winked at her. "Doing what I can to make your day special. Why don't you come by after work today? We'll go out for a bit when you get there."

She shook her head. "You're the manager. You can't leave."

"Not for the night, but I'm sure I could for an hour. You won't be there until nearly 10, so it's not so busy. Meadow should be working today too. I'm sure she'd love to see you."

"Okay. Just for an hour." She smiled at him.

Joe finished eating, and Charlotte wrapped up her unfinished plate. She helped him clean up and headed into work.

She parked her car and saw the white alabaster Fiero parked a few stalls down from her. *Well, at least he'll be gone by four, and I can enjoy supper in peace.* With blinders on, she walked in through the front doors, and headed straight to the GM's office.

Knocking on the door, Russell let her in. *Damn. So much for a Happy Birthday.* However, she knew he was only on until five. After that, anyone would be an improvement. She signed in, grabbed her float, after Russell told her there was a package at the desk for her, and left the office. She stopped dead in her tracks when she saw a helium balloon bouquet on her chair. The balloons all read "Happy Birthday". She put her float into the drawer, reached for the card, and opened it. She instantly recognized the handwriting.

Happy birthday Cat.
I'll love you always.

The letter wasn't signed, but that didn't mean she didn't know whom it was from. No one else on earth called her Cat. She sighed, and put the balloon bouquet as far away from the computer as she could. She hated drawing attention to herself. She worked through the hour, even enduring a key drop off from Andrew. She spoke her first words to him in five weeks when she thanked him for the balloons.

"I finally got you talking to me, and all it took was a few balloons." He smiled at her, and with that sweet expression, jump-started her heart again. Strolling behind the desk, a swagger in his step, he stood there looking charming and endearing. His blue-green eyes sparkled at her. He looked trim and dapper standing there in his black top tucked into his beige pants. "Would it be too much to give you a hug? I know you're still mad at me."

She sighed, "I'm not mad at you." *Anymore. Anger is not what I feel. Raging disappointment is more like it. Disappointed that I let myself fall for you. Disappointed that I let you in. Rejected, because you let me walk away. Sad, because I wasn't enough for you. Hurt because I love you so very much.*

"So can I give you a hug?" He stepped forward, an easy grin on his face.

The phone at her desk rang. Her co-worker grabbed it.

Her hand went out to stop him. *I can't. I need to stay strong.* "Not now."

He stepped back, still smiling. "Fair enough. I got you speaking to me at least." He winked those devilishly admirable blue-greens at her. "I wanted to ask why you didn't…"

"Charlotte," Colin interrupted, "phone's for you. Line 2."

She picked up line 2. "Hello, Charlotte speaking... oh hi... thank you... no that's fine... umm... not much I think... sure that'd be okay... could I meet you there instead?... yes, seven works just fine... okay, see you then, Jack... bye." She hung up the phone and met Andrew's curious gaze.

"Jack? As in Miranda's Jack?" He raised his eyebrow.

"One in the same." Without missing a beat, she added without smiling, "We're going out for dinner on Wednesday."

He took a step back and clasped his hands together. He was still smiling, but only just. "That's great."

"What did you want to ask me?"

"Nothing." He nodded towards the front of the desk. "You have customers, Cat."

She turned around and helped Colin deal with the line-up. She watched as Andrew walked passed them, shoulders hunched, and out the doors. No goodbyes, no see-you-laters, he just left.

Chapter Twenty-Two
✿✿✿

Charlotte met the tall and handsome Jack at Milestones for dinner. She showed up on time, and noticed that the dark eyed gentleman, wearing his cowboy hat, was already there.

"Hi, Jack."

"Good evening, Miss Charlotte. Glad you made it." They walked in side by side, and Jack requested them a table.

The server escorted them to the back of the restaurant and once seated, Jack said, "I was a little surprised that when I asked for your number, you gave me your work number. Why's that?" He leaned across the table, and spoke in his best prosecutor voice.

Charlotte, completely surprised by his direct question, responded with, "Well, umm… it's a safety thing. I don't really know you and the first number I thought of was my work number."

He studied her, weighing her response. "Okay, I think I can understand that."

Charlotte sighed internally with relief.

The waiter came over, and Jack ordered a hi-ball, Charlotte an iced tea.

"Now, every time we've met, you've never ordered alcohol. Why is that?" He took off his cowboy hat and hung it from the attached coat hook on the side of their spacious booth.

What's with the direct questions, Jack? "Gives me nasty side effects," she said as she closed her eyes against a memory

"It does that."

"No, I mean, I'm really affected by it. Almost like an allergy to it." She sounded defensive.

"Umm... I see." He picked up the menu and started looking through it. "Can I be honest with you?"

"Honesty is the best policy."

He smirked and spoke, "I have to admit that the other night, when you told me you were just coming out of a relationship, I was a little put off. But I appreciate you being honest with me. Therefore, I'm going to be honest with you. I, too, came out of a bad relationship. About a year ago. Took me a long time before I was ready to see anyone else. I honestly didn't think I'd find someone, until Miranda started talking about this lady at her work and how lovely she was." He winked a brown eye at her, "Then I met you at the concert, and spent part of a wedding with you, and figured, hey, maybe this lady's different. Maybe she's going to be something special in my life. I really enjoyed dancing with you last Friday night."

Charlotte gulped down half her iced tea, staring and scrutinizing the man sitting across from her. "I really don't know how to respond to that, Jack."

"You don't need to. I just wanted you to know."

"But you don't even know me."

"But I'd like to."

She continued to look at him, noticing the way he didn't take his eyes off her, and the steady way he held his menu. She felt her hands shaking, from intimidation perhaps?

"Look, I don't want to scare you. I'll respect any pace you need to set, in the event of there even being a relationship to pace. Assuming we even make it through dinner without me completely sticking my foot in my mouth."

She couldn't help herself, a small giggle escaped from her lips.

"Whew! Thought I was a goner." He smiled back, his smile somewhat lopsided yet very endearing.

The tension gone, they ordered their dinners and immediately resumed their conversation.

"So Jack, Miranda tells me you're in law. What do you practice?" She folded her hands together.

"Well right now, I'm part of a giant law firm downtown, earning my keep, working on my LL.M; my master of law degree, if you will. I should be done within a year. I'm specializing in family law. I've only been practicing for a little over eighteen months, but a few of my buddies and I, we're wanting to open our own private practice. That's our five to ten year plan. In the meantime, we want to live and enjoy life. Travel a bit, get married, kids for some of us."

Charlotte sat back against the booth, listening to him and how planned out everything was for him. "You? Do you want kids?"

"Already have a daughter. Her name's Justice."

How fitting.

"She just turned two in August." He looked at her and added, "I can see the wheels turning. Yes, the relationship ended when Justice was less than a year-old. Leah and I weren't getting along. We were on separate paths, if you will. I see Justice on Tuesday and Thursday evenings and the odd weekend. It's better for her to have stability with her mother. But one kid's my limit, although my mom wants lots of grandchildren, since I come from a large family of five boys."

She clarified, "Five boys? Wow. Your mom must be a saint."

He laughed a deep throaty laugh. "Not a saint, no."

"Have you lived in Edmonton all your life?"

"Only since I was a child. My brother, Gabe, was born in Quebec City before we moved here."

"You're French?"

"Mais oui!" He smirked. "French was my native tongue."

"Wow, cool. I don't know much French. Took it through high school, but that was about it. Barely passed."

"Having two languages has helped my career immensely."

"I can only imagine."

Their food served hot, they continued to make small talk over little bites.

"Tell me something personal about yourself that I wouldn't already have heard. Miranda's such a gossip." He pushed his plate away, and pitched forward on the table, locking his fingers together.

Shocked, she quietly piped up, "I don't share personal information."

"Ever?" He studied the closed book sitting in front him.

Charlotte was unsure, but thought he looked incensed. "Not really. My best friend Joe knows all there is to know about me, and... the other guy." Her expression deteriorated at the thought of Andrew.

Jack let out a whistle. "In your whole life, only two people really know you? What a shame."

"Well, Joe's brother, David, knows a bit, and their mom, but yeah. And that's enough for me. For now." Her demeanour remained resolute.

Jack attempted a smile. "I can't imagine living like that. How does anyone know how to make you happy if you can't share things like your favourite colour? Or favourite game? Favourite song?"

Charlotte couldn't help but giggle. "Well that, sure. I thought you wanted to know something personal."

"That *is* something personal, as it's different to each person. It helps me know you a little better, and that's what makes it personal." He winked and his smile stretched from his lips up to his eyes.

"Okay, what do you want to know?"

"Hmm," he sat back and rubbed his chin thoughtfully. "Favourite colour?"

"Orange."

"Favourite TV show."

"ER."

"Really? Medical dramas, very interesting. No law dramas at all? Favourite meal?"

"My best friend Joe makes the best homemade, from scratch, spaghetti and meatballs, with the yummiest homemade garlic bread."

"Nice! Got more than a one word answer with that." He paused again. "Favourite day of the week?"

Charlotte dropped her smile. *It used to be Friday nights and Saturday mornings. But what is it now?* She suddenly felt very sad and lonely. Her head drooped.

"What? What did I say?" Jack scrambled, looking more than a little surprised that asking that particular question wiped the conversation clear off the table. He ran his hand through the dark, short strands of his hair.

She shook her head and tucked the wayward strand of hair behind her ears.

Gathering his thoughts he stated, "Okay, that was clearly some sort of trigger. My apologies." He stared at her through the uncomfortable silence, noticing the subtle way she pulled back into herself. "Well, I see we've come to the end of our meal. Shall we go?" He reached for his cowboy hat.

Charlotte blinked away the raining memories and extended her hand. "I'm okay." She took a deep breath. "Like I told you before, I'd just come out of a long relationship. Friday nights and Saturday mornings were my favourite days of the week. Because of him. After we broke up, I had no more favourite days." She lowered her head again.

"Because you weren't with him?"

She looked up, focusing on his brooding, yet comforting gaze. "Yeah."

"I see. Well, then, if we we're going to make this relationship work, at a pace that'd work for you, then I'd need to find a different day to make your favourite." He looked delighted as he put his hat on. "Thank you for sharing something personal with me." He stood up from the booth, and offered his hand.

She accepted it, but once out of the booth, pulled her hand out of his grasp. He paid for dinner and walked her over to her car.

"Thanks for meeting me, Charlotte."

"Thanks for asking me. I had a good time."

"Good. I'm glad. Maybe Wednesdays will be a good day for you." Sporting a wink, he stepped closer to give her a hug.

Charlotte stepped away. *I just can't, Jack. It's too soon. I'm not ready for any kind of physical contact. I wish you could understand.*

Jack stood on the spot and whispered, "He really did a number on you, didn't he?"

"Only when he broke my heart. He was my everything. It's hard to get over that."

He thrust his hands into his jeans. "I imagine it would be. But I can be persistent, and patient." He searched her eyes. "Can I have another date with you on Saturday?"

What? Seriously? She was outwardly shocked. "I work Saturday nights. How about Sunday night?"

"Fair enough. I'll call you tomorrow at SEARCH, since I don't have your home number, and we can work out the details."

"Perfect. Thank you, Jack." She opened her car door. "Have a good night."

"You too."

As Christmas approached, Jack and Charlotte started slowly dating twice a week, usually Sunday and Wednesday evenings. Dating Jack was a unique form of difficult for Charlotte. She was still not sharing anything deeply personal, rarely held his hand, and had only kissed him, quickly, a handful of times. She was thankful that he lived up to his end, being patient with her.

It was the first Saturday in December when Andrew and Charlotte finally had a conversation with more than a few short words. Ironically, Russell was responsible for bringing them back together. He was heading up a focus group, for SEARCH, and needed people from every department to participate. Because the Board of Directors backed it, participation was mandatory. As coincidence played, both Charlotte and Andrew had their names randomly selected to participate.

They met up in the Astronomy Room for a couple of hours that evening after work. Charlotte noticed how Andrew conveniently placed himself at her table. There were four other tables present, and she had half a mind to move. She felt uncomfortable being in such close proximity to him, but at the same time, she couldn't move. She was torn between wanting to punch him in the chest, and pull him close to inhale his natural scent. He kept looking at her, opening his mouth as if he wanted to say something, but held back. Every time she glanced in his direction, which was more often than she wanted to admit, his blue-greens were on her. The focus group wasn't particularly interesting for Charlotte, but she paid attention, answered all the questions, and was very eager to leave.

"Hey, just wait," Andrew said, putting his hand on hers after Russell dismissed them.

She looked down at his hand and could feel the magnetism pulling her back towards him. Her blood pumped to the beat of a heart that beat faster than it had in a long time. She felt torn between wanting to yank her hand away, and holding on to it. *Damn, his hand feel soft again*. In the end, she left her hand laying flat on the table, with his on top. She felt like a drug addict as she sat beside him, wanting to feel more.

He said nothing until everyone had left the room. Once the last person was inside the elevator and the doors sealed shut, he unwillingly let go of her hand. "So, how have you been, Cat?"

"Stop, Andrew." She put her hand out in front of her, and her metaphoric foot down, as she stood up.

"What? Can't a friend ask how another is doing?"

"We're no longer friends, Drew. I thought that was clear."

"No," he started, "you decided that we weren't going to be friends with benefits. You never said anything about not being friends at all."

She looked down and rubbed at a spot on the floor with her shoe. Feeling secure in getting it clean, she connected with his gaze. "Fine. How's Oksana?"

He looked taken aback by her direct question and composed himself before answering. "I told you she meant nothing. She doesn't have my email, or know that I live here and not there. She truly meant nothing to me." He sat on the end of the table, putting his feet on the chair. "It's been hard for me, Cat, to not be with you. I miss us. We had something special."

"You're right. We *had* something, and *you* chose to throw it away," she reminded as the anger boiled beneath the slip of her tongue.

"I didn't throw it away. You didn't give me a chance to explain. You up and ran away, Charlotte." He shook his head.

"There was no running involved."

"Fine, you walked away." He leaned his elbows on his legs. "I died a little that night."

She settled down in a nearby chair, at a different table. "Why are you telling me this? You think it's been easy for me? I DID die that night!" Her voice grew in strength.

"It doesn't appear so."

"Well, appearances can be deceiving," she spat out. "Drew, you slept with someone else and then rejected me!"

"I never rejected you. I just didn't say yes at that moment." Andrew sighed. "I didn't want it to be like this."

"Like how?"

"Us fighting."

"Well, it's all we're good at with each other."

"No, it's not. We have a lot of great memories."

"Our last few months together were littered with fights, Drew."

"Half full, half empty. I remember many great nights of unbridled passion, and many mornings of pure joy. Once you accepted the friends with benefits title, things between us improved." He let it hang in the air between them, as he slipped off the table and approached her. He watched Charlotte's face progress from anger to sadness.

"But…"

He placed his finger over her lips. "Stop. Before you say something you'll regret." Hoping to lighten the mood and change the topic, he inquired, "Did you hear about Russell?"

She raised an eyebrow. "No."

"Colin reported him to Norah. He told Norah all about you, well us, and how Russell was making your work life a living hell."

Charlotte let a smile sneak out. "So that's why he's working on the admin side."

"That would be why."

"I must remember to give Colin my gratitude." She looked at Andrew warmly. *Oh God, how can he stand there and look so beautiful? How can he have this power over me?*

"So how have you been?" he asked again, feeling that the conversation was now getting off to a better start.

She contemplated for a breath or two. "Good. I've been good. What about you?"

"Aside from missing you, I'm okay. School is good. Finals start on the tenth. I'm spending Christmas with mom, Jon, and his girlfriend of the month. You know, the usual." He jumped off the table, landing closer to her than she expected. "What about you? What are your plans for Christmas?"

"I'm having Christmas dinner with Jack's family." She watched him nearly choke on his own spit.

"Really? I had no idea you were that serious."

"Me either, really. But he asked if I'd join them, and I said yes. I'd love to meet his family. Joe's going to Calgary with his mom and David, so it's perfect. I won't be alone."

"Wow." He ran his fingers through his hair, and then re-crafted a few haphazard pieces. "So what's he like?"

She thought for a moment. "Studious, like you, but different. He's working on his Master of Law degree in his spare time. He studies and gets decent grades, but he doesn't push for the highest marks. He's already working for a law firm and puts in about fourty hours a week, but he has a good balance of play, and work, and study." It wasn't meant as a shot at Andrew, but it certainly came out that way. She noticed how he pulled back as if she'd cracked a whip. *I'm not apologizing. If the truth hurts, so be it.* She carried on, "He comes from a big family. He has four other brothers."

"That's a few."

"Yeah, I can't imagine what that would've been like growing up." She drifted off to a childhood memory, and then shook it off. "Anyways, I guess Jack's parents are eager to meet me." *You never invited me to your mom's house for dinner, at any time, let alone meet any of your family.* She looked into Andrew's somber eyes. "But he's really nice. It's like he knows my boundaries, and he doesn't push them."

"Yeah, well, your wall is hard to miss."

She said nothing, but continued to stare at him, her mouth twitching slightly.

"What?"

"Really?"

"Cat, you're not as invisible as you think. People notice, especially around here. Your body language speaks volumes." He watched her slump a bit. "It's not a bad thing, Cat." He reached out for her.

"No?"

"Oh, Cat, not at all." He leaned closer and whispered, "As a friend, I'm going to ask. As a friend, you don't need to answer." Charlotte hesitated, but gravitated closer. "Are you drinking around him?"

She straightened back up. "Not that it's any of your business, but no," she said firmly. "And we haven't gone *there*. Yet," she added as if it would be happening tomorrow.

Andrew sighed. "Good. Good."

"What?" she asked to his Cheshire cat grin.

"Oh, nothing," he continued to smirk, assuming, hoping, that the relationship had yet to be consummated. "So, does he hang out at The Fortress?"

"Umm... NO!" she pronounced it so forcefully, that it even caught her off guard. Collecting herself, she explained, "He doesn't like the fact that I live with a boy."

"You told him that?"

"Yeah, but I also told him he had to deal with it." Smugness filled her face. "He also doesn't have much love for you."

"This should be interesting," he said, "why?"

"Because you're you. The one that…" she couldn't bear to say the words aloud. *The one who still holds my heart.* "Anyways, I told him that his timing in my life really sucked, as I was getting over a very loving relationship." She looked deeply at him. "And that my heart wasn't a toy. One false move and it was over. There would be no second chances."

He cleared his throat. "And you wonder why he walks on eggshells around you."

She chuckled a bit. "Well, I didn't really wonder, but thanks for pointing it out." She grabbed at her bag she'd placed on the table and in doing so, a book fell out.

"*French for Dummies*, Cat?" He picked it up and leafed through it.

"What? His whole family speaks French, and I need to brush up on mine." She seized the book from him and shoved it back into her bag. "I'd rather not spend an evening having everything translated to me."

"You never got a *Russian for Dummies*." He sounded hurt.

"Well, I've never met any of your family. That opportunity was never presented to me."

He rocked back on his feet, his ego bruised. He asked slowly and cautiously, "So they only speak French?"

"No, but I want to impress them."

"Cat, they'd be foolish to not be impressed by you. Look at you, look at how wonderful you are."

She felt her cheeks pink up. "Stop, okay? Just stop trying to butter me up."

"I'm not trying to, Cat. I'm just telling you like it is." He stepped closer to her, and lifted up her chin, ever so slightly. "Can't we be friends?"

He was so close. Her body tingled under the delicate touch of his fingertips. Her heart acknowledged the effect by speeding up and furthering the spread of colour on her cheeks. In a barely audible whisper, she exclaimed, "Sure. Friends."

He responded to her answer by slowly bending down and placing a quick peck on her left cheek.

The brushing of his lips against her burning cheeks added to her racing pulse, and weakened her stance. *I can never last against you when you kiss me, even if it's only on my cheek.*

"Thank you," he breathed into her ear, "for being my friend." He broke the connection, and stepped back, admiring his flame red Cat. "Always so beautiful."

She caught her breath and wobbling slightly, leaned against the table. She steadied herself, and said to him, "I need to get going."

"Can I walk you out?" He tried to predict her answer, and as always, she threw him a curveball.

"You'd better."

He gawked at her.

She winked.

They both smiled, and embraced for a quick, friendly hug. The connection between them no longer unbroken and they both knew it. Together they exited the building and walked fantastically close together, huddled together for warmth, rekindling and renewing. While waiting for their cars to warm up, the pair stood together wrapped in each other, warming up and breathing life into the missed friendship.

Charlotte spent Christmas evening with Jack's family. They all treated her nicely, except for Jack's mom, who kept giving her the stink-eye. It seemed everything Charlotte said, was something that irked her, causing her to raise her eyebrows with suspicion. Jack's brothers were all warm and accepting of her, especially Gabe who eagerly took open shots at Jack, doing the brother thing and making him look small around his girlfriend. Charlotte hung out mainly with Miranda, and the two girls bonded together. After Christmas eve dinner, she joined the entire Noellette family in walking through the freshly fallen snow to the nearby church and celebrating with Christmas Mass.

Charlotte was uncomfortable in the church, and it showed as she twitched in her seat and wrestled with her inner demons. She felt uncomfortable in the house of the Lord, as she believed there was no higher power, and if there was, He did a terrible job protecting her when she was young. Jack and his family showed her off to so many people, complete strangers, that it unnerved Charlotte, especially when Mr. Noellette announced her as the newest addition to their family.

Everything was so brand new, and way beyond her comfort zone. She felt out of place, and continuously teetered on the edge of creepy and uncomfortable.

Jack too, seemed different. He constantly had his arms around her, and was always kissing her, almost as if he was marking his territory. He wasn't like that when they were alone, and gracefully accepted the boundaries she enforced, keeping the public displays of affection to a bare minimum. But around his family, he threw caution to the wind. It angered Charlotte, and she brought it up on his way to drop her off, once they'd said goodbye to his family.

She buckled herself into the passenger seat of his huge pick-up truck. "What was that all about, Jack?" She had her arms crossed, and anger flashed in her eyes.

"What was *what* all about, Charlotte?"

"The way your family, and you, kept telling everyone that I was a member of this family. We're not married, not even engaged!" She stared hard at him. "And the way you were pawing me. You had your hands all over me." She threw eye daggers at him, her body quivering with waves of anger.

"What? I was just showing you off."

"By putting your hands all over me? I don't do PDAs. You know that!"

"I thought with the Christmas spirit, that maybe you'd change your mind."

"I didn't. It made me very uncomfortable, Jack. VERY uncomfortable."

He drove in silence for a bit. "I'm going to be honest with you."

Charlotte braced herself. She wasn't sure why she suddenly needed to prepare for a battle. She stiffened up, and noticed that Jack was also doing the same.

"I'm a man, and I have needs. I agreed to go slowly with you while your heart was mending, but it's been, what, four months now since you broke up with him."

One hundred and sixteen days, but who's counting?

He quickly looked at her, his dark brown eyes boring into hers. "We've been dating for nearly three months. I would think by this point in our relationship that I should be able to kiss you in public without you having a freak out about it." He turned his gaze back to the road.

Her eyes widened, and she slumped back in her seat. She had no response, no recourse to this. *Of course, he's right. He should be able to hold my hand and kiss me once in awhile, so why does it feel so awkward?* She said nothing, looking at him through the sides of her eyes. He kept his focus straight ahead.

"Can you concede that much to me? I promise my hands aren't laced with poison." A smile leaked out of his lips.

She sighed. "I suppose I can do that. I owe you at least that."

"Thank you." He reached for her hand that she held firmly on her lap, and lifted it to his lips. He kissed the top of her hand. "See, no burning sensation," he said it in a light-hearted way that made Charlotte grin. "I know you've been damaged, but I will try my best to heal you and make you forget your heart was ever broken. If you'd give me that chance."

She hated that word "damaged" as it implied to her more than Jack could ever understand. She knew he was right though. If she wanted to be in this relationship, she needed to give him something. Isn't that what the arguments with Andrew were usually about? She'd make it her new year's resolution to give more to him and to be a better girlfriend.

Chapter Twenty-Three
✿✿✿

The New Year's Eve party at Joe's was a mild success. Everyone ate and drank, but the atmosphere was meek. It was a completely different mood than last year's joyous event. It was as if everyone was waiting for the ball to drop so the party would end, and they could go to sleep, or go home. The conversations weren't flowing, and Joe refused to bring out Twister. He mentioned to Charlotte that it wasn't a Twister crowd.

There was no Meadow and Brad. They'd parted ways just before Christmas, and Meadow was hibernating at her parent's place. Chelsea was missing, and Joe had replaced her, begrudgingly, with Carla, a new little girlfriend, but their chemistry seemed to be one of convenience. Charlotte suspected it was a fling, because he didn't seem half as happy with her as he had with Chelsea.

Andrew was also missing, Charlotte noted with surprising pain. However, Jack was there. It was the first time he was in The Fortress, but he wasn't happy about it. Everyone seemed off. It was a depressing end to the year.

The New Year's ball dropping ceremony in New York was re-broadcast in their time zone, and the four guests in attendance watched as the ball dropped, and the New Year rang in. Jack and Charlotte kissed. Joe and Carla kissed, quickly. Carla and Jack gave each other a peck on the cheek, and Joe and Charlotte embraced for a long hug, and pecks on the cheek. Joe gave

Charlotte back to Jack, who stood there with an impatient look on his face.

He reached out and grabbed hold of Charlotte, kissing her eagerly and with more passion than she'd anticipated. Reminding herself that she'd try to give him more, she capitulated. He responded to her surrender with an unparalleled yearning and pushed harder into her barely parted lips.

She sensed his amorous affection, feeling it against her hips. She could feel his tongue forcing and searching her out. She tried to be willing and compliant by kissing him back, and she forced herself to enjoy the experience. However, images of Andrew kept popping into her head like an unwelcome guest. She fought hard to push them away.

Jack caressed her neck with kisses and moved up to her ear where he whispered, "Let's go to your room." He backed her against the wall.

She pulled away and pushed back with her hands. "No, let's not." She stared at him, and looked up into his dark brown eyes, trying to figure out what emotion was there. Anger? Disappointment? Hot rage? Rejection? Maybe all of it in a quick flicker of a second. "I think it's time for you to leave." She stood there and folded her arms across her chest, her eyes getting slightly misty.

"What? Really?" He looked at her face, running his finger down her cheek. "I'm sorry. You responded, so I thought it was okay." He seemed genuinely concerned.

She continued to stare at him in a very defensive pose. The last time she'd had someone in her room was Andrew, and for now, that'd be the way it would stay. She couldn't be with anyone else, in that room, with the ghost of that relationship still hiding in there. Her devil on her shoulder argued with her.

Is Andrew here?
No.
Is Jack here?
Yes.
You enjoy sex?
Yes.
Do you enjoy being with Jack?
Of course.
Then it's time to let go, and go get it on.

But it feels too soon. I don't feel ready to take that step.

She tried reasoning with herself, but felt like she was losing her mind. Instead of the mental argument, she held Jack's hand, and tried to quiet the tears that felt forthcoming. She led him to the couch and sat down. Stunned, Jack sat beside her. Charlotte looked over at Joe, who was helping Carla into her coat. She watched as Carla exited and Joe walked over to her.

He tapped her shoulder gently, bent down and gave her a quick kiss on the cheek. "Goodnight, Charlotte. Don't stay up too late." He turned to Jack and shook his hand. "It was nice to finally meet you, Jack. Take good care of her."

"I will if she'll let me," he said with tenderness as Joe waved and headed down the hall to his bedroom.

Charlotte heard the door click shut and leaned back against the couch, exhaling.

Jack shifted in his seat. "Charlotte, I need to ask you something."

She turned her weary head, and looked at him. He looked very somber.

"Should we continue to go out?"

She blinked rapidly, searched his face, and then combed through her mind. Sitting beside her was a wonderful man. Jack was exceptionally patient with her, more than someone should be. He was easy to look at, with his rich brown hair, and eyes that matched. An impeccable dresser, he had a great sense of style. He was polite, and a gentleman. Most of the time, he made her forget about Andrew, especially when he made her laugh. He always included her with his family, and took her out to places; to the movies, dancing, and several fine restaurants. He balanced everything in his life, and made her a priority, something Andrew could never seem to do. He was everything she wanted, so why was she not listening with her heart? While her logical mind said "Go, go, go!" her angelic heart held her back.

His eyes drooped, and his shoulders slumped. "I take it by your lack of an answer that we should break up."

"Jack, I'm thinking about all the great things about you, and it boils down to me. You're a great guy."

"Here it comes."

She sighed. "But I wonder, deep down, if I'm still not ready. We started going out so quickly after I... well, after we... when the relationship ended."

He picked up her hand and rubbed the top of it. "I know your heart has a history, a deep, very personal, and very broken history that you try very hard to protect. I'm trying to help that by being someone better for you. Showing you that love doesn't have to hurt. I don't know what happened between you and Andrew, and I honestly, I *don't* want to know, except maybe to know what he did so right that you carry that relationship still in your heart. But it's over right? You're not still secretly going out with him?"

She shook her head no.

"I promise to be gentle. To be the man you need, the real man you deserve. To dance away your cares and make you smile. 'Cuz when you do, it lights up a room. I love seeing it, and I feel even better when I know I'm the one that put it there. Plus, my family adores you."

"Your mom sure doesn't," Charlotte added.

"She'll get used to it. She was like that with Miranda too." He continued rubbing her hand, pleading his case, "If you can tell me what you're afraid of, I can try to help avoid it."

Seriously, why am I not falling in love with this man? He's so honest and genuine. She rubbed her thumb over his hand. "I'm afraid of getting hurt, again." With that confession, her heart suddenly felt like a piece had its first stitch in healing.

"So am I, but I'm not so guarded."

"I have to be. It's all I know."

"Then let me help you find a new way. Open your heart to me, Charlotte. I can give you everything you need. If you'll let me."

She blinked rapidly, causing her eyes to blur. "But I can't let you in."

"With time, you will," he said soothingly.

"It's scary in there. My heart's an ocean of deep dark secrets and broken promises."

"Then we'll sail it together." He wiped away a fallen tear with a gentle flick of his finger. "Okay?"

She smiled wearily through a couple of tears. "Okay."

He delicately lifted her chin, and placed a tender kiss on her soft lips. Then he broke it off and gazed into her eyes. "No more tears," he said adding, "I promise to be more... understanding

about everything. I know when I broke up wi~~th~~ _H.M. Shander._
I certainly wasn't ready for anything until I he
year later."

"Then why are you so persistent with me? I
how hard it is."

"Because, there's something about you that
Perhaps it's your mysteriousness, or maybe it's
But I know if I'm not persistent, then someone ·
up, and I'll have missed my chance to find out."
closer to her. "So, I can ride out the storm with y
calmer waters, if you will. I want to help you hea
and I'd like to be the guy you fall for."

For the first time that evening, she felt a smile tug .
heartstrings. "Thank you, Jack, for saying that. It's been .
months since it happened, but it still feels so fresh. Some day
so hard to deal with."

"Can I be honest?"

"Always."

"Maybe working with Andrew isn't the best thing. I think
that's a reason you're having a hard time moving past this. You're
still seeing the man who destroyed your heart, on what, a near
daily basis?" He glanced around the apartment. "He's everywhere
_I_ look. Your work, your home. He was such an important part of
your being. No wonder you're having a hard time getting over
him. I'm sure there are many memories lingering in your
bedroom, and that's why I'm not allowed in there." He stole a
look down the hall. "It's difficult to move on when the ghosts of
relationship past haunt you. So, I strongly suggest you give up
working at SEARCH."

Charlotte nodded. Everything he said made sense, perfect
sense. "But I'm only a point five at school. I need the hours at
SEARCH to help pay my bills. I can't leave." Although she knew
that wasn't entirely true. Joe never charged her rent, but she did
buy groceries, and helped pay for the utilities, in addition to their
extensive movie collection and other fun extras.

"Can't? Or won't?"

Both. Her face soured with that thought and another tear fell.

"It's just something to think about, Charlotte. It's my job to
find solutions to problems, and this problem has a pretty easy fix.
Cut him out of your life."

ce.

minutes. Her logical mind spat out.

to hear her inner voice as he added an afterthought,
y. No emails. No phone calls. No hanging out. No
gether." Her mouth dropped open, and as quickly, he
er under chin, helping her close it. "See what I mean?"
wisted her hands in her lap.

arlotte, I hate making ultimatums. It makes a person choose
sser of two evils, so I won't give you one. However, I don't
t to be one either. You need to decide - a solid future with me
a future by yourself. There aren't many men who would tag
long the way I've been."

She sat there resigned, staring at Jack, who laid it all out on the table. *The way you've described it, there isn't really any choice, is there?* It didn't take long to answer his non-ultimatum. "You're right, Jack. I promise to try a future with you."

"Thank you." He beamed as he stood up, pulling her up with him, "I'll try my best to make it worth your effort. No more tears." He soothed away the dampness under her eyes. "But more dancing. Let's always have the dancing." He grabbed the remote and with ease, turned on the CD player. Selecting a country album, he placed it into the drive and pressed play. He clutched at her hand, placing the other firmly on her back, and started moving with her in time to the music. They danced together, bodies touching until the early morning hours.

Jack left Charlotte with a smile on her face, and another stitch in her heart. He kissed her again, and then bid her a good night, telling her, "Thanks for the evening and the heart to heart. I promise you, things will get better, and I'll make the time fly."

Chapter Twenty-Four
✿✿✿

In the six short weeks since New Year's, a lot changed and improved with Jack. With each small step in their relationship, he showered her with gifts, whether it was a huge bouquet of flowers delivered to her at school, and sometimes at SEARCH, or another romantic token of his affection. He liked taking her to the best restaurants, and they frequented events that the firm he worked for sponsored or got tickets to. He made her feel like a princess and treated her like one too. They laughed a lot together, and somehow, they always found time for dancing.

Joe was in the kitchen, fretting about which meal to make for his new girlfriend of the month, Vanessa, who was vegan. He was stumped trying to find a recipe that didn't include dairy, meat, or eggs, and he was panicked.

The phone rang and flustered, he snapped a terse "Hello?" He cradled the phone on his shoulder.

"It's Jack, is Charlie there?"

Joe visibly relaxed and resumed flipping through his collection of cookbooks. "No, she's in the shower. What's up?"

"I need to ask you something."

"Go ahead."

"I want Charlie's hand in marriage."

"You what?" He dropped the cookbooks on the counter.

"I'm going to propose."

"No, I got that. Wow! Don't you think it's a little soon? I mean you've only been together a few short months."

"I'd like your blessing."

Joe sighed, "I know you'd like that…" He peered down the hallway, looking for Charlotte. "Jack, honestly, this is something I need to discuss with her. Although I'm flattered you would ask me for her hand, even though I'm younger than you, I can't say yes, yet."

No response from Jack.

"I gather from your silence this was the answer you'd hoped for." He paused and then added, "Let me talk to her, and then I'll call you. If she's completely happy in this relationship, then I'll give you my blessing."

"Thanks."

"When were you planning on asking her?"

"Tonight."

"Geez, not a lot of time to discuss it, but I'll try to talk to her before you pick her up, deal?"

"See you in an hour."

"An hour? Okay, bye." Joe hung up the phone and strode down the hall. He rapped on the bedroom door before he entered.

"Joe!" Charlotte screamed as he marched into the room.

He covered his eyes when he saw a glimpse of pale flesh coming from the open door to her ensuite. "Are you decent?"

In haste, she wrapped her tiny frame in her pink bathrobe. "I am now."

"Good enough. Listen, we need to talk." His face was serious, his brown eyes much darker, his lips pulled tight.

"I'm getting ready for a date. Can't it wait?"

He shook his head.

"Wow, what's the urgency?"

He plunked himself down on her bed, patting the space beside him.

"Is everything okay?" She studied the deep frown line across his forehead.

"Charlotte, I need to ask you something."

"Yeah, anything." *His look tells me I'd better sit down.*

"About Jack." He noticed how she pulled back a bit, and looked away from his eyes. "He's pretty serious about you, you know?"

"Yeah, I know."

"And he's going to take things a step further. A huge step." He sighed deeply. "Charlotte, he's asked for your hand in marriage…"

Surprise crossed her face. "He's going to propose?" She fell back against the bed, her damp hair landing across her face.

"Yeah. What do you think about that?"

She sat up and then started to pace about her room. She made three complete circuits from her ensuite to her closet and back. "I think it's quick. Very quick."

"I agree. You've only been together for what? Four months?"

"Officially? Something like that. We've only really been serious, in my opinion, since New Year's Eve." She paced back over to her closet, and stared at the hanging dresses. Picking out Jack's favourite, the full-length blue striped one, she hung it on the back of the door.

"So… what are you going to do?"

"I don't know."

"Charlotte, I need to know," he inhaled and exhaled, "do you really love him?"

She turned around. "Yes. Yes I do."

"Can you see him in your forever future?"

Tension hung in the air for a breath. "I'm not sure. Maybe? Forever seems like, well, forever. It's hard to imagine."

"But you had no issues with forever with…"

"Don't! Please, don't." Her heartbeat nearly doubled its usual speed.

"Are you over…?"

Lowering her head and voice, she said, "He doesn't want me, okay? He never came back and fought for me."

"And if he did?" Joe studied the contemptuous look on Charlotte's bare face. He knew that look, and knew it well. "Charlotte, Jack's going to ask you to marry him, to spend forever with him. If you have any reservations at all about it, don't say yes."

Her lips trembled. "It wouldn't be like we'd be getting married tomorrow, right? People plan weddings years into the future."

"I don't know. Something tells me this won't be a long engagement."

Charlotte's stomach did a flip, and then tightened. She let out a long sigh. "Jack loves me, and wants me. He's given me everything I've ever wanted. His family has accepted and welcomed me. He cares for me, and goes out of his way to make me happy. Since I've been with Jack, I've never had to cry myself to sleep."

"To be fair to…" He momentarily stopped when that look crossed her face again. "You really didn't cry yourself to sleep over him *until* he was gone."

"Why? Why are you saying this?" With hands on her hips, she started to bite her lip.

"Because you need to look deep in your heart and know which decision is right for *you*." Standing up, he crossed the short distance to her. "You're not the type of person to change your mind, even when it means saying no to something when you've already said yes. You're too loyal that way." He kissed the top of her forehead. "Whatever decision you make tonight, make sure it's the right one. For you."

"And what is the right one?"

"Only you'll really know."

"You're sure he's going to ask tonight?"

"It's Valentine's Day. The most romantic day of the year. Of course he's asking tonight." Smiling, he headed for the door.

"Where are you going?"

"I need to think about whether I'm going to give Jack my blessing or not. He wants to know when he picks you up."

"What are you going to tell him?"

He turned and looked at the woman standing before him. She looked so young and innocent, hardly old enough to be married in his opinion. "A couple of things just popped into my mind that I need to ask."

"Fire away."

"Does he know about your past?"

She stepped towards her bathroom. "He says he doesn't want to know. Whatever happened is over and done with, and nothing will ever change it. He told me if I can't let go, I'll never move on."

"Wow. That's… umm… deep." He pinched the bridge of his nose. "Last question." He stared long and hard, knowing the answer would be more than a verbal response. "How many days since you and Andrew split up?"

"167." She started to look towards the floor, when Joe lifted her chin up with a finger.

"Thank you. For your honesty."

"I love him, Joe."

"I know you do."

It was the day after Valentine's Day and Charlotte was chatting with Norah in the GM's office. She showed off the new sparkly piece of jewellery on her left hand.

"He proposed? WOW!" Norah exclaimed. "How exciting!" She gave a hug to the newly engaged Charlotte.

"So, Norah," she started and then deliberated over her next words, "with the engagement, came a promise to Jack. I'm giving my two weeks' notice."

Norah gasped, "Really?"

Charlotte nodded and fiddled with her wrapped ponytail. Jack always complained that she needed to look more like a refined lady, rather than her usual "hair down rumpled look", but the pony tail pulled harshly on a couple strands of hair and was giving her a mild headache. "It just makes the best sense for Jack and I. It's too hard for him to have me here where I am constantly around him."

"Andrew?"

"Yes."

She sat in her chair. "Is that the best decision for you?"

Charlotte shifted uncomfortably. She didn't want to leave, but understood Jack's side of the discussion. There'd always be a history between her and Andrew, and it was hard on Jack to see that. He insisted that the best way to move on from Andrew was to cut all ties and associations with Andrew. Charlotte just wasn't sure how to tell Andrew that. She nodded slowly in response to Norah's question.

"Wow, well, we hate to lose you." She stood up, and passed the float over to Charlotte. They opened the door and started walking to the cashier's desk. "Promise you'll keep in touch and tell us the wedding date?"

Before Charlotte could respond, Colin, one of Charlotte's co-workers, spun around smiling having overhead Norah talking. "You're getting married?"

Charlotte smiled and nodded. With that, the gift shop cashiers then came over to congratulate her.

"Can we see the ring?" someone asked, and Charlotte turned around to show off her beautiful, sparkly, engagement ring.

She was just lifting her left hand up when she saw Andrew approach the cashier's desk.

"You're marrying him?" his voice high pitched. He stared at her, hurt flashing in his eyes, and a hint of betrayal in his voice.

The small crowd thinned, quickly. Charlotte was speechless. *This wasn't the way I wanted him to find out.*

In a voice that was hardly a whisper, he blurted out, "I didn't think it was *that* serious." He shook his head, grabbed the key off the desk, and stormed over to the elevator. He punched the "up" button so hard that Charlotte heard it crack from the desk. He stomped in and didn't turn around as she watched it rise up to the third floor. She felt very small, and a stitched piece of her heart snapped open recalling that look of hurt on his face.

She put her float away and logged in. *This is exactly why Jack doesn't want you working here anymore.* Her leaving would not only benefit her and Jack, but also had positive repercussions for Andrew too. It wasn't fair to him to have Charlotte around.

She finished her shift and put her coat on. In a move she didn't think through, she grabbed the spare projection room key, and ran to the elevator before she could change her mind. She needed to talk to him. Badly. Desperately. She stepped into the elevator and felt her heart slide into her feet as she ascended. With careful footing on her suddenly weak legs, she carried herself over to the projection room door and put the key into the lock, turning slowly. She quickly opened and shut the door, trying to minimize the light flowing into the darkened room.

Andrew was already standing at the base of the metal stairs before her eyes had fully adjusted to the shadowy space. "What do you want?" he snapped at her.

"I came to talk to you."

"Why?"

"I wanted to tell you personally. I didn't want you to find out this way."

"Too late."

"I know. I'm sorry." She twisted the ring on her finger. She wasn't used to the weight of it. Her eyes adjusted to the low lighting and she saw him nod towards the ring.

"When did that happen?" He wasn't going to waste words apparently.

"Last night."

"Valentine's Day. How typical," he said under his breath. "Obviously you said yes."

"That much is apparent."

"Why?"

"Because he asked."

"That's the reason? Not because you love him, or anything else like that, but because he asked?" He sounded very mad as he threw his hands into the air.

She folded her arms across her chest. "I do love him."

"But that wasn't your immediate answer."

"It's complicated."

"What is?"

"Things."

"Are you in love with him?"

"Yeah, I think so." She stared at him as he stormed away from her and towards the wall of glass.

He stomped back over to her and stepped within her personal boundaries as he slowly uttered in her ear, "Cat, you've been in love before. Surely you know the difference."

His warm breath fired up a deep longing in her heart. His soothing, yet unyielding accented voice made her hands tremble and legs feel even weaker. His lips were close enough to her cheeks that she was sure he felt the sudden heat beneath. She had no vocal response for him, and he knew it too.

In a voice that seemed to belong to someone else, she mouthed, "I'm marrying Jack. April twelfth."

"April of this year?" His voice was one of disbelief and utter shock.

"Yes."

"Talk about fast tracking it."

"I have no family, Drew. It should be easy to put together. At least that's what Mrs. Noellette said. Eight weeks is lots of time. Especially since it's not going to be über fancy or large." She looked deeply into his eyes. The hurt was still there, and she knew that she was responsible for it. "I'd love it if you attended." She put her left hand to his chest, and felt the muscles beneath the shirt he was wearing. In a soft voice, she said, "Tell me you'll come."

"You want *me* to attend *your* wedding! Your wedding to another man? Fuck off! The only wedding of yours I want to attend is the one where I'm the groom!" He recoiled from his own vitriol and with a sorrowful look, begged of her, "Cat, please tell me you're not making a huge mistake." He tucked that wayward strand of copper hair that escaped her ponytail, his fingers brushing the tips of her ears.

She struggled to catch her breath. "It's not a mistake."

"People don't get married at twenty-one!" He shook his bronzed hair, but still hadn't stepped back. "Unless they're pregnant." His blue-greens suddenly got huge with that possibility as they scanned down and settled on her tummy.

Charlotte's eyes got even bigger. "ANDREW!" she yelled out. The air escaped from her lungs, punched out of her with his shocking words. "Is that what you think? I'm only worth being married to if I'm carrying a baby?" She tipped her head to the side. "Answer me!"

"You're too young, Charlotte."

"Really. Still sticking with that statement are you?"

He shrugged his shoulders and walked over to the desk. He picked up his books and slammed them into his backpack. "He's not right for you."

"Trying to tell me that I'm better off without him? To be alone?"

"No!" He spun around and looked at her. "Not alone."

"Then what?" she asked in a loud voice. She examined his deflated stance. His head hung, his shoulders slopped inwards. She softened her voice and said, "I gave my two weeks' notice today." She hung her head too as she said it.

He said nothing, and again walked away from her to the bank of windows. "Why?"

She lifted her head, and watched him stare out the giant windows into the theatre below. There was a long, awkward gap of time between the pair. With concern, she marched over to him and bellowed, "Because of situations like this. It's too hard on you and I to be like this. I can see that."

"Did he ask you to leave here?" Turning on his heels, he faced her, wanting to see her reaction. "The truth."

"Yes, but it makes sense." Her voice quivered with the truth, and she wrapped her arms around herself. The reels spun by beside her and had thinned before either said a word. Then Charlotte spoke up. "Well, I'm going to go now. Thanks for the conversation." She headed for the metal stairs.

Andrew in hot pursuit of her. "Cat, wait."

"What?" She stopped in her tracks and turned around to face him.

He stood there with an expression on his face that was unreadable to her.

"What, Drew?" she stammered out loud.

"I don't know, but I'm thinking. Give me a minute. I don't want you to leave, okay? I feel like if you leave now I'll never see you again." He sounded desperate, and sad. Very sad.

She relaxed her tense state and held herself back from wanting to reach out to him. Looking at him, she saw the longing in his eyes, and noticed how hard he was fighting to reach out to her. With a glance down, she saw his hands straining against the edges of his pockets. She twisted the ring on her finger again.

He spoke clearly, weighing his words. "You are rushing into this, for reasons I wish I knew."

"I'm not rushing into this, Drew."

"Cat, you've know this guy for what, six months? You've been dating him for four months. Who proposes that quickly? Better yet, who accepts that quickly? Someone who's rushing into things." He hesitated, and a look of understanding and judgment crossed his face. He spit out, "Is this because I turned you down? Are you suddenly so desperate to be married, that the first guy who proposes, you accept?"

She had no answer for him, at least nothing that zipped out of her mouth. She loved Jack, and she knew he loved her, even though she never really shared much about herself. He seemed okay with that. They had lots in common, and loved to go dancing together. They laughed and never fought. She could see a future with him, maybe some kids if he gave in, a house. Accepting his proposal was a way to tell him that she was coming around, and that there was hope. He waited for her, and by him setting the date, she knew she had limited time to clear her closets of the ghosts.

She had been too quiet for too long, and taken too long to respond to his question.

"What are you thinking, Cat?"

Words swirled in her head, but she whispered, "Nothing."

Andrew shook his head. "You know you're making a mistake, don't you?"

"It's not like that. You don't even know him."

"Do you?"

"I know enough, and marriage is learning about each other. You grow together."

"That sounds like something out of a Hallmark card." Andrew stared at her. "That's not the Cat I know. Does he know about you, Cat? Like *really* know you?"

Her brow furrowed, and her eyes tightened. Her heart raced and sweat started forming at the base of her neck.

"If he doesn't know you the way I know you, then he can't possibly love you the way I do." He stood there, waiting for her to say something. When the silence became too much, he hit below the belt. "Do you trust him enough to share with him about Lucy?"

Her heart nearly stopped. *How dare you!*

"What about Chad? Does he know about that?"

She blanched, and hated knowing that he was hitting a nerve.

"Does he know about the baby?" Even in the limited light, he saw her pale further, and grasp the hard metal railing beside her. "He doesn't, does he?" He watched as she buckled, her knuckles turning white from the grip she exerted on the metal. In a quick breath, it looked like she was trying to reassemble herself. "How can you give yourself to someone in marriage and not tell him of that? Afraid he'll run?" He breathed hard and fast. "Don't you get it, Cat? I. Never. Ran." His face sincere and loving. "You never had to hide anything from me. You were safe with me. You trusted me to keep your secrets safe."

"Stop it!" she yelled. "Stop making me feel this way!" She clutched at her chest feeling it beat hard against her breasts. With each breath, her chest walls tightened further, threatening to do her in.

"And what way is that?" He stepped closer to her. Close enough to hear her ragged breathing. For a moment, he worried he'd pushed her too hard. "You don't trust him, do you?"

With a gulp of air, she breathed, "I trust that I've firmly closed the door on those chapters of my life, Drew. I'm willing to make new ones. I'm *trying* to move on." Her voice was stronger than she appeared, and her appearance was deeply rattled.

He crossed his arms and paused in thought. "And that includes my chapter?" Walking in circles at the base of the stairs, he glanced over. "Cat, I need to know. Why did you stand me up?"

"Huh?" She looked at him quizzically.

"I waited all night for you."

She looked hard at him. "Drew, I don't have the slightest idea of what you're talking about!"

"I know. You never read the note did you?"

Confusion abound in her mind, she tried recalling what he referred to. "What note?"

"You gave me a box full of our stuff. I gave it back to you, and told you to read the note." He watched as that memory surfaced and crossed her face.

She gripped harder onto the railing. "I never read it." She shook her head and lowered her voice, curiosity hinted in her tone. "What did it say?"

"It's too late."

Exasperated, Charlotte threw her hands in the air. "Then why the hell did you bother mentioning it?" She turned back to the metal stairs and took a step up, ascending towards the door.

"Cat!" he yelled, "Please. Wait!" He sounded desperate. "Do you really want to know what I wrote?"

She turned to face him and stood on the first stair, so she could be on eye level with him. "Please, tell me." Her heart pounded with morbid curiosity. Her eyes wildly searched his face for a hint.

He took a deep gulp of air. "I said yes."

Yes? She rolled the word over repeatedly in her mind. She started to put the pieces together, when he answered her unsaid question. Feeling faint, she sat on the metal grate, and fought to control the absolute upside down tornado of emotions swirling in her body.

"I didn't give you an answer that day in the park. I couldn't make my body move. Couldn't form any words. You stood up and told me you'd given up on me. How could you give up on me? How could you leave?" A crack in his voice. "I died that day. I went home, and thought over everything you said, and everything you didn't say. I tossed it over in my head, and I talked to my mom about it."

You talked to your mom? About us? Shock crossed Charlotte's face, and her heart raced hearing everything Andrew vocalized.

"She cracked me upside the head, swore at me in Russian and told me that I was a fool. To let you slip away. I couldn't disagree." He shook his head. "Then I saw you the following Saturday. You looked how I felt – miserable. Seeing everything in the box, it hurt me really bad, but it made me get my act together. So I penned you the note. I said yes. Did you hear me? I said yes! I didn't want to let you go."

Charlotte stood there, motionless, blankness registering on her face. She couldn't believe her ears. *Why didn't I read the note? Damn foolish, stubborn pride.*

"I've never stopped loving you, Cat. Never."

Trying to form some words, she stumbled out some verbal diarrhea, "But why… you could've… why didn't you…you should've said…" Huge regretful tears formed in her eyes.

Kneeling on the ground before her, he carried on. "You started dating Jack, so I let it go. I didn't think it was so serious. I thought it was some kind of rebound thing. Then in the astronomy room, I felt that you hadn't really given up on me. I could hear in your heart that you still hoped for us. So I waited. I thought you'd end it with Jack."

"I nearly did," she breathed out.

"Then you met his family, and everything was running downhill so fast. I didn't have time to think. And now you've accepted his hand in marriage." Unshed tears now filled Andrew's blue-green eyes. "I should've fought hard for you, and if you marry him, I'll forever regret having not tried."

She wanted to hold him, and wrap herself into his arms and never let go. If this were happening before Jack's proposal, it wouldn't be hard to break up with him. Now? She'd already told Jack yes. How could she recant? She didn't want to be responsible for breaking his heart. It'd be easier to leave Jack if he were the one who broke it off, but she knew that would never happen. She'd fallen in love with his family, something she'd wanted her whole life.

"Don't forget, ever, that I love you. Always. Forever," he cried as he said it. "Please, stay with me. Here. Now. I said YES. Please, don't leave me again, Cat."

She couldn't move a muscle. Her legs were like cement, holding her to the ground. She could hear the anguish, and feel the heartache in his voice. Every cell in her body told her to jump into his arms, to stop their hearts from breaking completely. However, she couldn't shift a limb, or even open her mouth and say something, anything. *Dammit, why did you have to write the note? Why didn't you corner me and tell me face to face, before I started dating Jack?* In her mind, she suddenly was very angry with Andrew. He was being selfish. *You let me go! You let me walk away and now that I've given my hand to someone else, you suddenly want me back. Where the hell were you months ago?*

Then her thoughts turned to Jack. *So patient, he waited and rode out the storms with me.* He had helped her in so many ways, helped her to move on and see that there could be a life without Andrew, and it would still be good, pleasant, and happy. *Jack makes me happy. He has plans for our life. A house together as soon as we're married. Many trips – he wants to show me the world. And he doesn't make me cry.* He could give her almost everything she wanted. She stood up, and took an ascending step, one foot closer to the door. Except Andrew. She would have to crush that tie, permanently. End it. No more friendship. No working with him. No conversation with him. Cut him out completely. Forever. *Forever?*

She stepped back down and looked at Andrew. Big mistake. Searching his face, she saw his look –deeply wounded and desperately lost. Again, the urge to run to him was overwhelming. She wanted to jump into those strong arms, finally meet his family, and be an important part of his life. Finally. *How could I be with you for so long and NOT have met your family. Isn't that weird? Were you ashamed of me? Would I embarrass you somehow?* She couldn't think of a reasonable answer to why she'd never met Jon or Mrs. Wagner. Just like that, anger flared again. She took a step back up and heard him moan in pain.

She glanced up and saw that she was only three steps from the top. Her future balanced precariously on either staying in the room or walking out of it forever. She looked down at the metal grates below her. She didn't like being in this position again. The one to make the decision. *Why do you force me to make the choices? Jack never does. He always tells me what's best. There are no options, no "go ahead and chose while I wait". And dammit, he's usually right.* With a heavy heart, she stepped up another step.

"Cat, please," Andrew cried out, "please don't leave." He wiped his tears with the back of his hand. "What do I need to say to make you stay?"

He stood at the base of the stairs. She could jump from here into his arms, and into an uncertain future, a happy one, but still fraught with insecurities. *I don't know where I stand with you. Ever. You want me around when it's convenient to you. I don't think I could spend a lifetime waiting for that. Even though I love you so much.*

On the other hand, she could sprint up the remaining metal stairs to a guaranteed future. She did love Jack. She knew she did. She didn't want to cause him grief, especially unwarranted. He deserved better. Nevertheless, she didn't want to break what sounded like was barely left of Andrew's heart.

Either way, there would be hurt and suffering, on both sides. She couldn't look down, where she knew Andrew stood, watching her make the toughest decision of her life. What was it that she wanted? She wanted Andrew and every cell in her body wanted him, but could she wait? How many years would she have to wait to be a priority for him? She wanted to be ahead of his studies and a part of his family the way she was with Jack's. What happened if she waited for Andrew, and he changed his mind? Then she'd be no further ahead than where she was now. Where, if she opened the door, there was a life waiting for her, all planned out, a husband, a future and a family.

Tears streaming down her face, she stared at the challenge before her. A certainty ahead, the unknown standing at the base of the stairs, waiting to hold her. She wondered if she could just teleport out of there, and never have to make the decision. *A few months ago, even two days ago, this would've been an easy decision, but now, with a ring? Dammit.* She had enough uncertainty in her life – she needed stability. In that moment of clarity, she grabbed what was left of her breaking heart, and shattered it completely.

With shaking hands, and rivers of hot tears, she sprinted up the stairs before she could change her mind. She heard his anguished cry as she opened the door and fell through. The solid thud of it slamming, sounded behind her. Suddenly she couldn't move. Her feet stopped responding to the demands of her brain. She felt so detached; mind separated from heart. She collapsed against the door and slid down. Her body convulsed from the hard cries escaping her body. Her knees pulled up, her head between them. Her copper hair fell over a shoulder. She soaked her knees with her tears of indecision.

Twenty minutes later, the door opened behind her, and Andrew stepped over her. She didn't want to look up and see his face. She held tighter to her knees. He asked her something incoherent, his voice devoid of emotion as he mumbled. She heard him lift the receiver on the phone above her head and punch in some numbers.

In between his sobs he said, "Hi… I need to speak to Joe please. It's an emergency… Hey, it's Andrew… Charlotte's had an incident at work here, and can't drive herself home… Long story… physically, no… I can't… even longer story… thanks… I'll meet you at the front door, and bring you up… thanks Joe." He hung up the phone. Standing there, he watched her body shake, as stinging tears fell down his cheeks. After a few minutes, he took the elevator down, and saw Norah locking up the main doors.

"Just wait…" he called out, feeling his heart beat outside of his body as he ran to her.

"Have a good night, Andrew." Norah said, holding open the door for him, having not seen his expression. When he didn't move forward, she turned to him and a horrified look crossed her face.

Andrew wiped away his tears of heartache. "I'm waiting for Charlotte's roommate to come and pick her up. She's outside the projection room. I told him I'd let him in." He wished he felt as composed as he thought he sounded.

Norah searched Andrew's face and put her hand on his shoulder. "Are you okay?"

Andrew's eyes were red and slightly swollen. "Nope. Not at all." He wiped away a tear, and tried to focus on her. She was very blurry. Suddenly everything in his life was blurry. He started to sob and was thankful the building had closed, and nobody other than Norah was here.

"Charlotte?"

"She made her choice," he articulated in cracked whimpers, "and it wasn't me." His voice broke further, as the sobs controlled his body. "Here's Joe." He wiped his face.

Joe slammed his Mercedes into park and ran to the main door. The tall Joe, with deep concern scratched into his face assessed Andrew. "If you're this bad... Where is she?"

Andrew's eye gazed upwards.

Joe raced over to the elevator and punched the "up" button. It chimed as it opened. He stepped in and Andrew haunted close behind. Neither said anything further, and Norah let the door close, sealing the two together for a short spell. Joe looked down at Andrew. He was a walking devastation. Joe knew Andrew found out about the engagement.

Andrew mumbled, "I love her, Joe. I love her. But it's not enough."

Joe wanted to give him a hug. He really liked Andrew, and Joe's heart broke for him as he was pretty sure Andrew didn't have any heart left to break.

The elevator doors opened, and in a quick second, Joe saw Charlotte curled up on the floor. Joe rushed forward. Andrew stood motionless in the elevator, no longer looking forward, but down at the gap between the elevator and the third floor.

In one swift movement, Joe lifted Charlotte off the floor, and into his scrawny arms. He carried her over to the waiting elevator, and as the doors closed, Charlotte's body heaved and a horrible sound escaped her mouth. Joe looked at Andrew, who wasn't looking at either of them, but whose face had gone as white as a ghost hearing that deathly horrible soul crushing sound. The elevator chimed "M" and opened to Norah still standing there. She gasped loudly, and Andrew solemnly shook his head, tears escaping with every second that ticked by. Without a word from anyone, they all walked to the main doors. Norah raced ahead and opened them.

Joe carried what was left of Charlotte over to his waiting car. Leaning against the car as he opened the door, he put her inside. He buckled her lifeless form in, and went to his side. He searched the area for any signs of Andrew, but he was nowhere around. Joe drove home in dead silence. She didn't need words right now.

Once at the Fortress, he supported her as they walked to the couch. She lay down and pulled herself into the fetal position. Covering her up, he kissed her forehead, and lifted up the handset on the nearby phone while rubbing her legs. He dialled the number programmed into the speed dial.

"Hello Jack?... it's Joe, Charlotte's roommate... "

Epilogue
✿✿✿

"You ready?" Joe asked the bride.

Charlotte fiddled with the last few buttons on the back. "I can't finish." She looked at him with a desperate pleading in her eyes.

Joe sauntered behind his best friend and finished sealing up the bodice of her dress. "All done."

"I would never have picked out this dress. Not in a million years." She laughed and pulled up on the top of her sweetheart neckline. Her lack of a bust contributed to the top part of the dress not staying up high enough. "Can it go any tighter?"

"No, it can't. You maybe wouldn't have picked this out, but Mrs. Noellette did a damn fine job picking it out for you." He spun her around. "You look beautiful in it, Charlotte." He planted a soft kiss on her cheek and re-adjusted his tux.

"I feel like a clown, I've never wore so much makeup in my life. And I think it'll take hours to undo my hair."

Miranda had insisted that Charlotte get her hair and makeup done, and escorted her to a nice little salon. Charlotte spent the whole morning being treated like a princess, with a facial before the priming and primping began. It was new to her but she enjoyed herself immensely. However, after the salon visit she felt like she didn't resemble herself. Instead, she looked like a model fresh off the pages of Blushing Bride. Her hair pulled up and off her face, allowed it to be polished and yet natural looking. The soft coppery waves pinned back, yet dangled down her back. They even managed to control that wayward strand of hair. A wisp of bangs brought out the shape of her face, framing her eyes perfectly. The makeup artist drew attention to the hazel-green eye colour and the soft pink pout of her lips. A dusting of blush highlighted the apples of her cheeks.

Joe passed her the wedding bouquet – a fragrant display of champagne coloured roses. "For you."

"Thanks." She fluffed her dress once more, and nervously twirled the engagement ring now hanging on her right hand.

Joe stepped out and surveyed the small crowd inside the church. He came back with his report. "Looks like everyone's here. The first five or six rows are filled."

"Mostly of Jack's family and friends."

"Mom's out there."

"Really?" Charlotte's eyes lit up.

"Yeah, of course she is. She wouldn't miss this. David's here too." He patted down his pockets, as if searching for something.

"Well I figured he'd come. And that about sums up my friends."

"No, I think I saw a few of your SEARCH friends."

Charlotte looked up with hope as she peered into Joe's eyes. "Is he here?"

"No," Joe said solemnly, while shaking his head, "I didn't see him."

"Didn't expect to, but I hoped. I mailed him an invitation." She blinked away her sadness.

The last time Charlotte saw Andrew, was the day she walked out on him. In the two weeks of her remaining shifts, they never passed each other, fate keeping them apart. It saddened Charlotte, but she understood it was all for the best.

When she left SEARCH, she had a mere six weeks to prepare for the wedding. Mrs. Noellette and Miranda took over every little detail, with a little input from Jack, and even less from Charlotte. The ladies booked a time slot at the church, and selected the location for photos and the supper, and what to eat at the supper. All Charlotte had to do was show up and smile. Miranda and Jack's mom took care of every other detail, which she thought was very strange. Miranda was chosen as her Maid of Honour, and Meadow her bridesmaid. Charlotte would have preferred it the other way around, but Mrs. Noellette insisted that this is the way it's done, especially with all the time Miranda invested in pulling together the event. The one thing Charlotte insisted upon, and no one refused, was her choice of Joe for the man to walk her down the aisle. After all, he was the only family she had, and in many ways was her father and big brother.

Charlotte had six weeks to pack up her room at the Fortress and move in with Jack. They bought a little house in Beaumont, and their possession date was the day before their return from their two-week honeymoon in Barbados. Mr. Noellette promised to ensure that everything was good on possession day, and the moving crew would move Jack's possessions into their new home before they returned. Charlotte didn't have much to move; she'd given most of her stuff away when she moved in with Joe. All her clothes and personal effects, aside from a suitcase of stuff, were stored in the Noellette's garage until moving day. Their house was also only a few blocks away from his parents, and Gabe and Miranda's.

So much would change from her wedding day onwards. She'd be living in a French speaking community, her visits with Joe reduced from near daily, to maybe once a week, and her name would be changing.

Miranda broke Charlotte's reverie when she knocked on the door, and poked her head in. "They're ready to begin, are you?"

Charlotte looked up at Joe and then back to Miranda, nodding her head. "Ready to give me away?"

Joe pushed the lump in his throat down. "Never." He took a deep breath. "I'm not giving you away, either. Just for the record." She wrapped her right hand through Joe's left, and the pair of them walked out the door and into the worship centre.

Andrew stood in the far corner of the church, tucked under a shadowed arch. He snuck in, at the last possible minute, hoping no one saw him. He didn't understand what the driving force was behind his presence, on her wedding day. Morbid curiosity, maybe? To see if she would actually go through with marrying Jack? He'd dressed all in black, a symbol of death, and indeed a huge part of him ceased to exist after that night in February when she chose Jack over him.

The traditional wedding music sounded from the pipe organ, and the main doors to the nave trumpeted wide. Meadow stepped out first, decked out in a satin royal purple ball gown, attached to the tuxedoed arm of a tall groomsman, who bore a little resemblance to Jack. Then Miranda stepped out wearing her four-inch heels that matched the shade of her gown. She clung to the arm of the groomsman, whom he guessed was her husband Gabe the way she looked at him. Andrew followed them up to the front with his blue-greens.

While holding his breath, he waited until he could see her. An angelic vision in pure white lace and silk, she breezed through the doors, Joe on her right side. An iridescent veil covered her perfect face, but he could see the hint of a shy smile playing on her lips as she looked up the aisle to her future.

Andrew hugged the shadow and followed as *his* Charlotte, his perfect, beautiful Cat, strolled up to the front, in time to *Pachelbel's Canon*. Joe lifted her veil and planted a kiss on each of her cheeks. Andrew watched as Joe shook hands with Jack, who beamed like an idiot, and placed Charlotte's right hand into Jack's expectant one. He noted that as Joe stepped back towards the pew, he wiped his eyes before he sat down in the first pew. His presence was noted when Joe looked around, and suddenly focused in his direction as he stood under the arch at the back of the church. Joe gave him a wink and weak smile.

Andrew sat down in the furthest pew from the front, and watched with disbelief as Charlotte recited her vows to honour and obey, for better or worse. Her voice carried like a melody, clear for all to hear, strong and unwavering. He couldn't bear to look up, when five minutes later, the preacher declared them man and wife. Feeling his heart suffer irreparable damage, he stole back into the shadows as the newlyweds sauntered down the aisle. Charlotte looked happy. Truly happy. They headed out to the front steps, with the congregation following behind. He joined the expulsion of wedding goers, and when he breathed in the fresh air, he stole another quick glance at Charlotte, who looked breathtaking and radiant. He pushed away from the line of well-wishers, and headed to his car.

"Andrew, wait!" A familiar voice called out from behind.

He turned and looked up sadly to Joe's face. "Hey, Joe."

"I'm glad you came." Breathless from running to catch up, Joe patted Andrew's shoulder.

"I'm not. She really did it." He hung his head, and rolled his shoulders inward.

"She did, and," he added in a serious tone, "she seems happy."

"Good," he spat out, and then regretted it. Truth was, he was happy for her, he just wished it was *him* she was with, and not Jack. He enjoyed seeing her lit up from within. It had been too long.

"Are you going to come and see her?"

He looked past Joe to the receiving line on the church steps a few paces back. The wedding party lined up at the top of the stairs, shaking hands with the wedding guests. "I don't think that's a wise idea, Joe."

"She asked about you before the wedding started." Joe looked down on Andrew. "It would be closure. For you both. Neither of you got to say goodbye." He reached out and gently, like a big brother, gave Andrew's shoulders a squeeze.

He continued to look past Joe, and in a divine separation of the crowds, he saw his angel. Through her hazel-greens, she looked right at him, fixated on the person who dressed all in black and to whom Joe was talking with. Andrew looked up at Joe, reflecting on his words. "Closure eh? Okay, let's go and say goodbye."

Joe patted him on the back, as he turned around and walked with Andrew towards the receiving line. He was the last in line as the others gathered in small groups or headed back to their vehicles.

Andrew patiently waited his turn. Then he shook the hand of the unsuspecting groomsman who didn't realize this was the person who was in love with Charlotte. Nico beamed with pride, as he introduced himself as Jack's baby brother. Meadow on the other hand, looked at Andrew with confusion. Moving on, he shook hands with Gabe, and then with Miranda, who glared at him with contempt and suspicion, her eyes narrowing to tiny slits. Trying his best to ignore the glares, and with a courage coming from deep within his soul, he moved on and shook Jack's hand, offering his sincerest congratulations. Jack smiled wilfully, but never removed his brown-eyed glare as Andrew stepped to the left and turned his full attention to the bride.

"Cat, you look beautiful. More than that, but I can't think of the right word for it." He leaned forward a bit, and Jack's forceful hand on Andrew's chest halted him on the spot.

Charlotte looked taken aback, switching her focus between her past and present. "Jack, it's okay."

"It's not," Jack stammered out. "It's our wedding day," he said through gritted teeth and a half smile.

Andrew twisted to face Jack, man to man. "I came to say goodbye."

"Goodbye?" Charlotte whispered as she leaned closer.

Jack looked skeptical, but removed his hand from Andrew's chest as the wedding party, mainly Gabe and Nico, gathered closer.

Gabe asked Jack, "Everything okay here?"

"Yes, this is Andrew." He continued to glare at Andrew.

"Oh," Gabe said, taking in the bronze haired Russian standing in front of his new sister-in-law.

Charlotte turned to Jack and asked in a sweet voice, "Can I have five minutes please?"

Jack looked at Gabe, and then down to his bride. "Three."

Taking opportunity by the hand, she led Andrew down a few steps to the sidewalk, away from the open ears of her husband and brothers-in-law. "You're saying goodbye?"

"Yes. After my finals, I'm leaving for Russia."

"How long will you be gone?"

"I don't know. Months. Years. I haven't figured it all out yet. I need to rethink my life, Cat."

Her voice laced with curiosity and sadness combined, she asked, "How will I be able to keep in touch with you?"

"Considering you haven't since you left SEARCH, I'd wager that it's not that big a concern for you. Remember, you're supposed to sever all ties with me." Andrew's eye flashed with anger, followed by disappointment.

Charlotte looked longing into Andrew's eyes and reached out a hand to briefly touch his. "So it's over."

"That's what you chose." His chest deflated with the punch of his words.

She hung her head sadly, and whispered, "I know, but I truly didn't think it'd be forever."

With a gentle lift from his fingertip, he raised her chin and looked into her beautiful green, gold, and brown-flecked eyes. "Nothing either of us says or does will make this easier or better. Okay?"

"Okay," she whispered.

"It's your wedding day, and you look truly beautiful. Now, go back to your husband before he finds a way to sue me for going over our three minute limit."

"Okay."

Andrew leaned in, despite the angry glares from Jack, Gabe, and Nico, and hugged Charlotte tight. "I will always love you."

"And I, you."

"Good bye, Cat." His voice hitched ever so slightly.

"Goodbye." Her voice broke.

He stepped away, but not before giving her a quick peck on her cheek. He turned and strode away from the ominous glances from the wedding party and without looking back, crossed the street and got into his vehicle, leaving his life with Cat behind.

To be continued in…

Ask Me Again

Acknowledgements
✿✿✿

I would like to thank, first and foremost, my family.

To my husband, Mike, who would spend evenings beside me listening to the typing of the keys as I spent endless hours of finishing off a thought that would last well into the middle of the night, and required copious amounts of caffeine the following morning. Thank you for listening to me drone on and on about it.

To my handsome boys, Shane & Alexander - I want you to know that you are never too old to reach for your dreams. You always make me smile and I'm super proud of you. Remain true to yourselves and always be amazing, unless you can be Batman, then always be Batman. ☺

For NaNoWriMo (National Novel Writing Month). The 50,000 words written in the month of November 2013 was inspirational for getting this project off the ground, and fulfilling a lifetime dream of mine. I'm proud to say I was a 2012, 2013 & 2014 winner.

For my friends, beta testers and critiquers (Sonja, Leah, Maggi, Jennifer, Allie, Lianne, Emma, Dawn, and Anya) who beta-tested my manuscript, highlighting what they liked and didn't, and pointed out the obvious, so I could improve. Your advice was more than I could wish for and I'm blessed to call you my friends.

To my editor Kim – thank you for all your edits and corrections, and for putting up with my endless emails and questions. You rock. If I ever visit Hawaii, we're having coffee.

To my cover creator Brett – thank you for your beautiful work. You're a trooper to deal with my endless emails, and confusing questions.

In the words of Stephen Hawking - *"Remember to look up at the stars and not down at your feet. Try to make sense of what you see and wonder about what makes the universe exist. Be curious. And however difficult life may seem, there is always something you can do and succeed at. It matters that you don't just give up."*

Keep reading for a preview of

Ask Me Again

the much-anticipated sequel to
Run Away Charlotte

❀ ❀ ❀ *Chapter One* ❀ ❀ ❀

Thirteen Years Later…
Sunday, September 12

When she said *I do* she never imagined this was what her life would be like.

Sure, she played the part of a doting wife: smiling politely, laughing at the right moments, and never, ever ruffling her husband's feathers. No, she made that mistake once – she wouldn't be making it again. She dressed for and acted the part, playing it well. On the outside, she was happy: happy for her husband and for all that he'd accomplished.

But she wasn't happy. Not even close.

It was a quiet ride back to the suburbs following another one of Jack's company events. Leaning her head against the passenger side window, she was overwhelmed with exhaustion. It had been four hours of acting tirelessly as Jack's picture-perfect wife at another one of his company's meet and greets. Glancing at the dashboard clock, she saw that it was just after ten as the Noellette's rounded the turn that would take them home.

As they passed by the other, smaller houses, she noted more than half the neighbours were home, with the odd windows sprinkling light over the garages. Their huge house, tucked away on a quiet cul-de-sac, stared down at them with empty dark windows. Jack drove their Escalade onto the driveway, the front porch momentarily caught in the spotlight. She exited the truck and marched up the long pebble driveway. One of the tiny solar lights along the edging leading to the house had burned out. *Better get that fixed in the morning.*

Charlotte clicked her heels past her black Mercedes, to the garage door. Looking forward to a good night's sleep after the exhausting dog and pony show of Jack's work party, she entered the house and kicked off her shoes with a sigh. The sigh turned into a squeal when her toes hit the water-laden floor in the mudroom.

What in fresh hell?

Curiosity getting the better of her, she splashed into the kitchen to see where the water had started spreading from. In the background, Jack cursed.

"What the hell?" Jack sloshed behind her, soaking the back of her bare legs, water hitting the bottom of her dress. He brushed his way past Charlotte into the kitchen, snapping on the lights as he went. "There's water everywhere!"

She watched in apprehension for Jack's reaction as he glanced around for the source of the issue.

"The dishwasher," he said dropping to the floor and nearly ripping the cabinet door off its hinge as he tried to locate the shut off valve. "Damn."

Stunned, Charlotte stood in the inch of water. She rubbed her face in exasperation. Everywhere she looked, the lights reflected back at them, rippling in the moving water above their hardwood floors. The water was all over the kitchen floor and had seeped into the dining room. As she looked towards the living room at the back of the house, the darkened line of wetness advanced towards the back wall, soaking most of the living room carpets as well.

With the water shut off, the problem now looked her hard in the face. *Where am I supposed to start soaking up the water? How am I going to take care of this?* Glancing over at Jack, who had thrown his cell phone onto the counter, she wrung her hands together and sloshed back and forth on her heels. Pinching the bridge of her nose she opened her mouth to speak but Jack spoke first.

"Gabe's on his way over," Jack said, looking as confused and helpless as Charlotte. For just that small second, Charlotte didn't feel alone. For that second, he looked like the old Jack—the one she fell in love with. The one she'd agreed to marry. The one who'd swept her off her feet, and promised her the world. But the moment was over as fast as it started. Face hardening, Jack splashed past Charlotte once more. "I'm going to check the basement."

She stood there silently looking around, mentally assessing the damage and wondering what would have caused the dishwasher to malfunction. All over their floor. "I don't even know where to begin. Why did this happen?" she muttered. A knock came from the window beside the front door, startling Charlotte.

"Hey, Gabe," she said glancing at her brother-in-law as he stepped into the foyer. As things were within the Noellette family, everyone knocked once and then entered their family's house. It was the way things were. No one waited to be welcomed in – they were always welcome. "That was fast. Did you run?" She forced herself to smile. Gabe lived on the street behind them, close enough that taking a path between their houses would often be quicker than driving.

All the Noellettes lived near each other. It had the potential to drive Charlotte crazy, but in some ways, many ways really, she was glad. At least her step-daughter, Justice, grew up knowing her family and had roots, unlike herself, with no family to speak of – except an aunt she no longer talked with. But it irritated her on occasion as well. Privacy was hard to come by. Secrets were difficult to hide. Anything that happened, the family knew about within minutes. She was positive the rest of the family already knew they'd had a flood.

Gabe's endearing laugh made Charlotte relax a little. "Drove actually. What happened?"

"Dishwasher broke while we were out wining and dining some VIPs." She turned to walk through the pond that was once her kitchen, to the back stairs that lead to the basement to see the extent of the damage for herself. She didn't make it all the way to the back of the house when Jack appeared at the stairs.

"Basement's wet, and the ceiling looks drenched," he said to Charlotte, and went over to Gabe. Jack ran his hand through his thick dark hair. It was thinning on top, but he mentioned once to Charlotte he still liked the fact that he could still run his fingers through it. "Come on, Gabe. I'll show you the basement."

Gabe patted Charlotte on the shoulder when he went by. The two men walked to the back of the house and disappeared downstairs.

She retrieved the mop and bucket, and starting in the foyer wiped it pointlessly across the floor. The mop head soaked the second it hit the floor. *This is going to take all night.* Her shoulders ached already.

The men surfaced after a few minutes.

Gabe said shaking his head, "There's a lot of water damage down there. The ceiling's wrecked. The carpets will need replacing, maybe the bottom portion of the walls too. The legs on all the furniture, including Justice's bedroom furniture, could be damaged too."

"When can you get the ball rolling?" Jack demanded.

Gabe owned Noellette Insurance and had access to the best repair crews. If anyone knew how to deal with this mess, it was him. "I've already contacted the best man for the job. I have an emergency team already on their way to help suck up the water and even start removing the wet crap tonight. Then we can assess at that point, how to move forward." Gabe looked over at Charlotte. "It will be fine. The guy I've contacted is outstanding. I promise you, Charlotte, you won't be disappointed."

Jack stood alongside his brother. "I don't care who he is, as long as everything will be taking care of."

"I assure you both, it will be." Gabe had a goofy smile on his face as he winked at Charlotte.

She shook her head, puzzled by his expression. "Is there a lot of damage in Justice's room?" Worried how her sixteen year-old stepdaughter would react. Charlotte was glad it was her other Mother's week.

As if Jack could read the emotions on Charlotte's face, he said, "It's a good thing that she hangs up her stuff. The damage seems minimal. As long as the ceiling doesn't collapse, it should be fine."

Justice's room sat underneath the foyer, rather than the kitchen where the water was deeper. Charlotte could only hope that the water wouldn't leak through the ceiling, and into her bedroom.

"Do you have a shop vac, Jack?" asked Gabe.

Jack shook his head.

"Okay, I'm going to run home and get mine. See if we can suck up most of the water tonight. I'll be right back."

She walked Gabe to the door and watched as he disappeared around the front of the house. Charlotte closed the door and surprised to see Jack right behind her, jumped out of her skin. "You scared me." She tried to laugh, although she was sure neither of them was in a laughing mood. "I guess I should start cleaning up?"

He stood over her, brows furled and creases forming around his tightly drawn eyes. Although a half foot taller, the way he bore down on her, it made the distance feel much greater, making her feel even smaller than she already felt. "You can try. That mop isn't going to soak up much." He turned and disappeared into the basement again.

"I know." She hung her head as she splashed back to the kitchen. The more she looked around, the worse she felt. Her heart started pounding and her stomach flipped. *Not here, not now.* She paced slowly around the island, sliding her feet through the water rather than stepping through it. Ironically, it was rhythmic and oddly soothing, and the cool water lapping against her ankles grounded her. *Slow down heart. Breathe lungs. This is not the time to panic.* "It will all be fine. In the end," she muttered as she lifted herself onto the island, and closed her eyes. Pushing down the intense feeling of nausea, she managed to get herself under control quickly. This time.

She listened for any sounds to distract her mind. Jack's cursing over the wet carpets in the basement floated to the main floor. It was distant, but it forced her to really focus. Then her ears went to the front door, where a knock beat against it, and the door unlatched.

Gabe.

"You okay?" Gabe asked as he stopped in the foyer with the shop vac.

She nodded unenthusiastically and inhaled a huge breath of air. The panic attack had subsided, but her stomach was still in knots. Sliding off the island, she retrieved the mop once again.

"Hey, we'll use this." He rolled the shop vac over, plugged it in and started it up. The reservoir filled rapidly, requiring Gabe to stop and dump it into the sink constantly.

Charlotte liked Gabe. He was the only one of Jack's brothers that treated her with respect. Maybe it helped that his wife, Miranda, was one of Charlotte's closest friends. Gabe never called her 'Charlie'; a name Charlotte despised, and he genuinely seemed to care about her. Like Charlotte, they had no children, but always treated Justice like their own.

Moving the dining room chairs out of the way, Gabe accidentally knocked against the table. A giant bouquet of flowers teetered and then fell, the glass vase smashing against the oak table. "Oops," he mouthed in mock horror as he looked at Charlotte carefully, turning off the vacuum. "It's okay, it's only stuff, Charlotte. It can all be fixed or replaced."

"I know," she said, tears threatening. "I just wonder if I did something."

"Because you can control the dishwasher?" He patted her shoulder but quickly dropped it when Jack came bounding up the stairs into the living room. "Hey, Jack."

Jack looked into the dining room and noticed the flowers spewed across the table. "Did you break the vase, Charlie?"

"The table got…"

Before she finished answering, Gabe spoke up. "No it was me. I banged into the table."

"Klutz." Jack smiled at him.

Sure, if I had done it, you'd be angry. But not with your brother.

"I have a two man crew on their way over now to help soak up the water. Tomorrow, first thing in the morning, my contact with Second Call Restoration will come here to assess everything," he told Jack, but then winked at Charlotte. "Could you watch for them? I can't hear anything over the sound of this vacuum."

After looking at Jack for approval, she nodded. With her soaked feet she headed first to the bathroom, quickly stripping off the pantyhose, then walked barefoot to the front door. The noise from the running vacuum as it gurgled up water was hard on her ears, even standing out on the porch. Thankfully, it stopped every couple of minutes when she assumed it was being dumped.

While waiting, and staring into the dark of the night, her phone vibrated with an incoming text.

Can you call me?

Smiling, she dialed. "Hey, Joe." Joe Harrison was her best friend, and had been since she was twelve. He became her adopted family when her mother died from a drug overdose, and the Harrison's took her in until family was located.

"You're up?"

"Obviously." She rolled her eyes and a slight smile ebbed at the edge of her lips. "What's up?"

"Can I come over? I won't be long, just want to talk to you in person."

She shifted on her feet. It was late for Joe to want to come over, but judging by the sound of his voice, it was about something serious. "Of course you can. See you in a little bit."

She clicked off her phone and was startled a bit when she noticed Jack standing there. "Geezus, Jack." It bothered her when he showed up unannounced and quiet like a mouse as if he was trying to catch her off guard. It made her jump every time.

"Who was that?"

"Joe. He sounded really upset. He's on his way over."

Jack rolled his dark eyes and turned back in the house. "Probably fired another cook."

Charlotte followed him into the kitchen. "No, I don't think so. He didn't sound upset like that. It was different."

He paused, and then shook his head. "Well, you would know."

"Yes, I would. He's my best friend." Jack understood, from the limited bit Charlotte had shared of her life before Jack, that Joe was the only family she had. He never begrudged her hanging out with him.

"I know." Jack opened the fridge, and rummaged through the contents pulling out two bottles of beer. "This is the last of the beer."

"I'll pick up more tomorrow."

He twisted off the caps and threw them on the counter after nodding. "There's more water than we thought. But at least we're pulling out as much as we can." He shrugged.

"What a mess." She glanced around. For the first time since arriving home, she noticed he was no longer wearing his leather coat. She bit her lip as she glanced around for it. Where had he set it down? If she didn't find it, she might forget to hang it back up. And if it wasn't where he could grab it the next time he wanted to wear it, he would blame her. Again. Her stomach knotted at the thought. She also felt selfish because her feet were cold and wet but her comfort wasn't important at the moment, other tasks beckoned her. Sighing, she asked, "What do you think happened?"

"Water line break or something. I don't know, Charlie, I'm not a plumber." Jack walked up to her and paused, as if he was going to say something else but changed his mind when the vacuum Gabe operated stopped.

Thankful for the break in tension, Charlotte stepped back. She was even more grateful when the doorbell rang and she could walk away. Opening the door, two big, burly men with bulging biceps held bright orange vacuums and stood on her front porch. "Come on in." She led them to the kitchen where Jack still stood expectantly, and he led them further into the house.

Charlotte excused herself and stepped outside to catch her breath. She sat on the two-seater porch swing Jack had installed for her on her twenty-ninth birthday, back in the days when things seemed better -- happier. The air was fresh with the smell of the blossoming lilies and hydrangeas she had planted in the brick garden edging along the front patio. It was a calming fragrance, and coupled with the soothing motion of the swing, it relaxed her.

A flash of lights from the driveway blinded her temporarily. She sighed with relief as Joe ambled up the walkway, past the waterfall structure and up the front steps. "Hey."

The tall and lanky Joe stood before her, a helpless look on his face. Defying his Italian heritage, he had a head full of blond, wavy hair, which usually hung in his expressive green eyes. "Hey, Charlotte."

"Sit down." She patted the seat beside her and watched as Joe folded his six foot two frame into the swing. Studying his face intently, Charlotte knew she wasn't wrong about her hunch. Her best friend struggled with something.

"Mom's back in the hospital. Her liver's failing, much faster than they expected."

Charlotte's hand covered her mouth and stifled a gasp. "But what about a transplant? Can't they bump her up on the list?" Claire Harrison's liver disease had been diagnosed only recently. As excellent as she was in caring for others, she'd neglected her own health.

"I think they will, but without a donor..."

"Oh... geez. I'm sorry, Joe." *My Madre, my poor Madre, I thought we still had more time. Months yet.* Swallowing down a morsel of grief, she asked, "When are you heading down?"

"Tonight. Chelsea and Hannah are staying home for now -- at least until I talk to the doctors and see how bad it truly is." He looked around the front porch and then back towards Charlotte. His head jerked toward the driveway. "What's with the vehicles? You having a party, and chose not to invite me?"

"Yeah, and that's why I'm sitting out here, alone." She forced a weak smile. "The dishwasher broke." She stood and brushed at the wrinkles in her dress. "Come see for yourself. Keep your shoes on."

Joe followed Charlotte into the house. The sounds of three vacuums running in the basement filled her ears. However, she was surprised to see that most of the water on the main floor was already gone. She needed to distract herself from her thoughts of Madre, and the noise of the vacuums just weren't enough, so she paced around the kitchen island.

Joe's mom was like a mother to Charlotte. In fact, for a short time in Charlotte's life, she was. Growing up, Charlotte was not comfortable calling her Mrs. Harrison, and definitely not mom, so together they agreed on the name Madre, which is Italian for mother.

"Oh, hey, Jack," Joe said as Jack came into the kitchen. "Sorry about the flood."

"Thanks." Jack walked over to Charlotte. "We're going to move the furniture into the garage, so the vehicles will need to be moved."

Charlotte nodded as Jack dug out his keys and passed them to her.

"You hanging around?" Jack asked the taller man.

"No. Heading to Calgary right now."

"Kind of late, isn't it?" Jack asked.

Joe thrust his hands deep into the pockets of his jeans. "Mom's liver is failing and it's best if I get down there ASAP."

A look of genuine concern crossed Jack's face. "Sorry to hear that. She'll be okay?"

"For now I guess, but I'll know more when I get there."

"Well, I hope you get some good news."

"Me too."

Jack kissed Charlotte on the cheek. "We're going to start bringing up furniture now. The vehicles, please."

That signalled the end of the conversation. *Yes, bringing up the couches is far more important than talking to Joe about his dying mom. My mom.* She looked at her friend, who understood the command.

"I can help, Charlotte, but then I need to go. I just wanted to tell you in person." Joe walked to the door that led into the garage.

She tossed him her keys from a drawer marked 'C' for Charlotte. They pulled out the vehicles, manoeuvring around Gabe's Mustang and the cleanup crew's van, trying to park everything on the driveway, and yet still making sure the other vehicles were accessible. Gabe and Jack appeared with the first of many pieces of furniture, the other two helpers behind them with a coffee table.

At the end of the long driveway Joe asked in a voice soft enough for only Charlotte to hear, "Everything okay?" He searched her eyes for the truth.

"Yeah." She bit her lip.

"You know what I mean, right? I heard his tone."

Folding her arms across her chest, she said, "We had a flood. Of course he's going to be terse."

He sighed. "I knew better than to ask. Knew you'd defend him." He shook his head and brushed a wavy curl out of his eye.

"Update me about Madre when you get there. Give her all my love."

"Indeed, I will." Reaching down, he gave her a hug and his big brotherly type kiss on the forehead. "Let me know what happens tomorrow with Second Call. I expect all details." He gave her a quick wink.

"Why did you just wink at me?"

"Details, Charlotte. I'll want all of them."

"I'm sure it won't be that exciting. Insurance and repairs – fascinating stuff," she said sarcastically as he opened the door to his brand new Mercedes. "Drive safe, my friend." She waved as he drove away, thinking about the odd way he winked at her. *Wait a minute, I never mentioned anything about Second Call. How does he know what clean up company we're using?* Letting a long breath release, Charlotte headed back into the house.

Yawning, Charlotte rolled over and turned off her alarm. Seven came too early, especially since it was after two before they got all the basement furniture stacked into the garage, and nearly three when the main floor furniture was added to it. Wanting to steal nine more precious minutes, she instantly fell back asleep. The ringing of her phone jostled her back.

"Hello?" she answered groggily, pushing her wavy red hair out of her eyes, and focusing on the numbers on the clock.

"Charlie, you weren't sleeping, were you?" Jack scoffed.

"No, Jack. Just hadn't got out of bed yet." She cleared her throat. "What's up?" Sitting up slowly, she adjusted her twisted sleep shirt and wiped the drool from the side of her mouth.

"According to Gabe, the Project Manager is supposed to come out right away to start ripping out the carpet, including the hardwood and drywall. You'll need to call the school and get a sub. You're not going in today. Maybe not the rest of the week, either."

"The week?" She fell back on the bed. *Miranda won't be happy having someone else take my spot. It ruins her mojo having to explain her daily routine to someone else. At least I know what to do and when to do it.* Charlotte had been Miranda's aide ever since she completed her diploma, and they were in sync with each other, anticipating the other's needs before either verbalized it.

"We'll know more once the PM comes in. Our adjustor will also be out sometime today, but I've asked her to wait until I can be there. I have court at nine, but should be done by lunch. Text me only if you need me."

"Okay." Her eyes stung from a lack of sleep. "When is the wet carpet person coming again?"

"He's the Project Manager, Charlie. I imagine he'll be there soon. So get up and get dressed. I gotta go."

She hung up, and rolled over, heavy with exhaustion. Charlotte called in and left a message with the administration about her impending absence and then fired off a quick text telling her sister-in-law Miranda that she wasn't coming in. It was highly likely she already knew that, as Gabe would've told her. After pushing herself into a cold shower, she stepped out of the bathroom fresh and clean, and having applied a minimal amount of makeup, she grabbed her phone.

A few incoming texts from Joe assured her that his mom was doing as well as could be expected and would be released when home care was set up. He was making those arrangements with his brother David filling in the gaps. Madre had only a few weeks left on earth and they'd been told to prepare for end of life. Another text from Miranda confirmed that she assumed Charlotte would be missing work, and had already called up a replacement for the week. Frustrated over the news of Madre, and the ease of being replaced, Charlotte headed down into the dank and damp smelling main floor of the house.

With no table to sit at and have her breakfast, she ate leaning over the sink, careful to not spill on herself. She washed her dishes in the bathroom sink since the water was turned off to the island and tided up as best as she could. Her phone rang and caller ID indicated an unknown number. *Seriously, it's eight am. What telemarketer calls this early?* "Hello?" she snapped.

"Mrs. Noellette?"

"Yes?" The voice wasn't familiar.

"Hi, it's Jess from Second Call. I'm calling to confirm that the owner will be out to your house within the next thirty minutes."

The owner? How many strings did Gabe pull to have the owner come out personally? She put the phone against her other ear. "Yeah, that's fine. Thanks." She ended the call and pocketed it. Running barefoot downstairs with a flashlight, as Jack shut off the power to the basement as a precaution, she assessed the damage with her own eyes. The carpets were damp against her naked feet, and the air tasted of thick humidity. The wet plaster and dankness of the dark basement made Charlotte cover her nose.

She peeked into Justice's empty bedroom wondering what her step-daughter would think when she came home to this. *No doubt she'll be pissed off that her privacy's been invaded, but what else could we have done? We had to move her belongings upstairs, which she won't be thrilled about either. She was more than happy to move to more private quarters down here, than be down the hall from us.* Thankfully, Justice's floor remained mostly dry, and was only marginally wet at the entrance to her room, but the ceiling above looked dark and ominous. "What a mess," Charlotte said placing her hand on her hip.

She walked back out into the now empty family room and stared around blankly. "No one got hurt, things can be replaced," she repeated to herself, "it's just a huge inconvenience."

The doorbell rang and Charlotte sprinted up the stairs to the front door. She gasped when she pulled open the wide door and the blue-green eyes of a man who once held her heart stared back at her.

"Hello, Cat." He grinned from ear to ear.

"Andrew!"

About the Author
✿✿✿

H.M. Shander has been writing since the misfit age of fourteen, as a way to tackle her active imagination. Growing up, and learning life lessons the hard way, have reinforced the importance of writing as a way to unwind, heal, and process life's challenges. She knows and speaks four languages (two exceptionally well); English, French, some American Sign Language, and Sarcasm, some of which serve her well within her variety of real world jobs as Mother, Birth Doula, Teacher, Librarian, and Sales Consultant. Despite how busy her life can be, there is always time to watch the sun rise, try to catch a rainbow, wish on stars, and listen to the robins sing.

She loves Edmonton, a Big City with a Small Town feel. When not working, or writing, and the kids are in bed, you can find her curled up beside her husband with a good book and a cup of tea.

She can be reached at hmshander@gmail.com and would love to read your comments about *Run Away Charlotte.*

Made in the USA
Charleston, SC
09 June 2016